THE

FRONTIE

PART 2: ROGUE CASTES

EPISODE 15

INTO THE SERPENT'S LAIR

RYK BROWN

The Frontiers Saga Part 2: Rogue Castes
Episode #15: Into the Serpent's Lair

CHAPTER ONE

Penta Mogan stared out of his office window at the vast emptiness. He had spent so much of his life in space, years passing in minutes. Wives long dead. Children grown with adult offspring of their own. So often, he had returned to his homeworld only to find himself younger than his own children.

And then there was his shipboard family. His wife, Terya, and his daughter, Nori. They had aged only days during his return to Nor-Patri, while he had aged months. It was difficult to understand for those who led their lives on the surface of a single world, but time was indeed relative.

It was an inescapable fact for interstellar civilizations; at least it had been, until the people of Earth had invented the jump drive. Now, instead of two groups of observers, those in motion and those at rest, there was a third. Those who circumvented relativity. While the warrior castes saw the jump drive as the ultimate weapon that would give them the ability to rule the galaxy, the leadership castes saw it as an affront to their isolationist beliefs.

Although Penta understood their fears, he could not comprehend their reluctance. The Jung had spent centuries conquering the nearby galaxy, capturing foreign technology and making it their own. The empire had been built on this edict. Nor-Patri, the crown jewel of the empire, would not exist had the Jung not taken control of it nearly a millennia ago.

But the wars had taken their toll on the empire, especially over the last decade. The warrior castes' failure to secure the Sol sector by conquering the birthplace of humanity had only served to feed the isolationist movement back on the Jung home world. Nor-Patri, nor any of the Jung core worlds, had seen war in centuries; not since the Day of Blood, when the Dusahn caste tried to seize control. To the citizens of the original empire, war was something that happened elsewhere. Therefore, it had been easy for the pacifists to rise up and gain support. Nor-Patri was a peaceful, orderly world. A planet-wide city with near-zero crime or aggression. For centuries, it had been a shining example of what the Jung Empire was trying to bring to all human-inhabited worlds. But after centuries of peace, the empire no longer tolerated the violence that had begotten that tranquility.

All of that changed when Zhu-Anok was destroyed. Billions died, while billions more found their lives all but destroyed. The lives of every person on Nor-Patri were forever changed by that event, even more so than on the Day of Blood. Their call for the Tonba-Hon-Venar had come swiftly and without opposition. Pacifists, isolationists, and warriors alike had been unified with one goal: the destruction of Earth.

And then came Nathan Scott's surrender. Suddenly, the people had been given a scapegoat upon which to hang their hatred and need for vengeance. Suddenly, they need not sacrifice what was left of their empire for the sake of revenge. Suddenly, they had been given a path to peace without further sacrifice. Their anger had given way to hope.

The door slid open, and Admiral Korahk entered his leader's office. "Good morning, my Lord." When the dom of his caste did not respond, he asked, "Something troubles you?"

"Have you ever wondered what your life would have been, had you lived it out on the surface?"

"Boring and short, I would imagine."

His subordinate's quick response surprised him. "Our lives are no longer than others," he said as he slowly turned to face the admiral. "Relativity aside."

"Relativity is for scientists and philosophers," the admiral said dismissively as he took a seat across the desk from his leader. "Were you able to convince Terya to leave?"

"What do you think?"

"Yes, I was unable to get my wife to take our family to safety, either," the admiral admitted. "Something about 'we are a warrior family,' and all that."

"Well, it is unlikely that the Sol Alliance can take out all three battle platforms," Dom Jung-Mogan stated. "Perhaps their loyalty will be rewarded."

"And then neither of us will ever hear the end of it," the admiral joked.

"Of this I am certain," Penta agreed.

"The Ton-Orso is still having problems," the admiral reported, returning to the reason for his visit. "We've had to slow the battle group further to avoid losing their cloak."

"How much of a delay will that cause?"

"We're still going to arrive two days ahead of schedule."

"As long as we beat Dom Kirton's forces," Penta replied. "I could not live with that koratoch getting the glory of the Tonba-Hon-Venar all to himself."

Admiral Korahk nodded but said nothing.

"You have a question?" Dom Jung-Mogan wondered.

"Are we still to destroy Earth?"

"You thought otherwise?"

"No, but on more than one occasion, you have expressed sadness over the waste of such a resource."

Penta sighed. "The idea of destroying the one world that is perfectly suited to support our species does seem wrong. I have made no secret of that belief. But I also understand the symbolism of its destruction to our own people. Bacca might not have been of pure blood, but he was a very capable leader. His failure showed that the people of Earth cannot be molded into a proper Jung world. Destruction is the only option."

"Then why don't I believe you when you say it?" the admiral asked.

"Because I wish we could effectively wipe all her people from existence and claim the world for ourselves...intact," Penta replied with a sigh. "Alas, complete destruction, quickly delivered, without mercy, is the only chance we have to survive."

"Is it not the responsibility of the warrior castes to die for the empire?" the admiral questioned.

"It is the responsibility of the warrior castes to ensure the survival of the empire," Penta corrected. "We are the last of the great battle platforms, but we are more. We are also the arks of the empire. Once we destroy the Earth, it will trigger an all-out assault by their jump-missile ships. Few of our people will survive, if any. These three ships may be all that is left to rebuild the empire."

"Then why not just let Dom Kirton sacrifice his forces for the Tonba-Hon-Venar?"

"Believe me, I've considered it," Penta admitted. "Especially when the problems began developing on the Ton-Orso. Unfortunately, my pride is stronger than my sense of survival."

Admiral Korahk smiled. "The curse of a true warrior."

Dom Jung-Mogan sighed in resignation. "Three weeks then?"

"Three weeks, and the Jung-Mogan caste will take its place in Jung history."

Penta turned slowly back to face the blackness outside once again. "Assuming there is anyone left to write it."

* * *

Cameron looked at Nathan, dumbfounded. "You said that? 'I'm going to end you?'"

"I'm so proud," Jessica chuckled from the far end of the conference table.

"Do you really believe that was a good negotiating tactic?" Cameron wondered.

"You had to be there," Nathan defended.

"You realize you're forcing him to lash out," she opined.

"I gave him a choice," Nathan argued.

"Give up or die," Jessica chuckled.

"If he is smart, he will lay low for some time," Nathan stated.

"Build up his forces," Lieutenant Commander Shinoda added. "That would be the smart play."

"We need to turn the people of Takara against him," General Telles said.

"How do we do that?" Vladimir wondered.

"By cutting off trade with other systems," Nathan explained.

"Takara doesn't need to trade with other systems to survive," Lieutenant Commander Shinoda insisted. "They've got all the resources they need in their own system."

"But they don't have everything they want," Nathan pointed out. "The Takarans are accustomed to having access to a wide variety of goods from all over the Pentaurus sector. For more than a century, they have wanted for nothing. The one thing the Dusahn did correctly when they took over was to make certain they did not disturb that balance. Instead, they took wealth away from the noble classes and spread it amongst the commoners."

"After taking a generous cut for themselves," General Telles added.

"Of course," Nathan agreed. "The point is, if we cut off all trade between the Dusahn and the rest of the sector, we'll be creating unrest among their population."

"There will be shortages at first," Lieutenant Commander Shinoda stated. "Many of their products are imported. Dollag, which everyone associates with Takaran society, actually comes from Palee. I think like ninety percent of it is imported."

"They will adapt," Cameron warned.

"But it will take time," General Telles replied. "It takes three years to raise a dollag steer to slaughter age. And they do not reproduce quickly."

"Takara is a meat-heavy society," Lieutenant Commander Shinoda added.

"That's one of the things I like about it," Jessica commented.

"That's one of the things I don't like about it," Cameron added.

"Any shortage created by a trade embargo will eventually be countered by their own internal production," General Telles stated.

"But in the meantime, the general population will be unhappy and blame the Dusahn," Jessica opined.

"More likely, the Dusahn will convince their subjects that we are to blame," General Telles stated.

"You think that's why he requested that we meet?" Nathan asked.

"I believe he expected you to refuse an offer of peace," the general explained, "in order to set us up as the villain in the eyes of Takara."

"And possibly in the eyes of many of the Pentaurus worlds," Lieutenant Commander Shinoda added, "all of which stand to lose considerable revenue."

"Which is why we must link the Pentaurus worlds up with the rest of the alliance worlds. Trade with those worlds will offset the loss of trade with the Dusahn," Nathan explained.

"That will only work for so long," Cameron stated. "What's your plan to end him?"

"My plans haven't changed," Nathan assured her. "I still plan to challenge him to personal combat for rule of his caste."

"Assuming the Jung don't kill you the moment you arrive," Cameron reminded him.

"They are facing their own destruction," Nathan told her. "If I can offer them a way to survive, I'm pretty sure they'll take it."

"The warrior castes won't," Jessica stated.

"That's why we're going straight to Nor-Patri, to speak with the kor-dom himself," Nathan explained.

"I still think you're taking a huge gamble," Jessica told him.

"With which?" Nathan asked. "The Jung or fighting Griogair?"

"Take your pick," she replied.

"The Jung cannot be trusted," General Telles stated plainly. "You of all people know this."

"Trust can only exist with proper motivation," Nathan replied. "All I have to do is find it, and then keep it in play."

"I'm not convinced that's even possible," Cameron stated.

"Look, neither side wants to back down, and neither side wants to be destroyed," Nathan explained. "A change in leadership of the Sol Alliance is the only way that one side can back away from the fight without appearing weak. We have the tools we need to make that happen. Even better, if we do it right, we can bring down Galiardi legally."

"Are you certain there isn't an alternate motive for wanting to take Galiardi down?" Cameron challenged.

"This isn't about revenge," Nathan assured her. "In fact, I doubt we'll ever find enough evidence to convict him in the death of my father and sisters."

"Can you live with that?" Cameron asked, point-blank.

"If all of this finally comes to an end? Yes, I believe I can."

"I wouldn't be able to," Jessica stated.

Nathan turned to Vladimir, wanting to move the briefing along. "How's the ship?"

"I've checked over all the repairs completed while we were away," Vladimir replied. "They seem to be in order."

"Then the ship is ready to go?"

"As ready as she's going to be," Cameron said. "She's taken a beating the last few months."

Nathan looked at Vladimir.

"She's ready."

"Then I'd like to take her to SilTek and have them put in additional jump energy banks," Nathan announced. "Enough to double our one-minute jump range."

"You want to jump two thousand light years?" Vladimir wondered, a bit surprised.

"I want to be able to move the Aurora to any point within this alliance and be able to return immediately, should the need arise," Nathan explained. "That includes the Sol sector."

"We'll have to find room for them," Vladimir warned. "A lot of room."

"Use the starboard forward flight deck," Nathan instructed.

"Where will we put our fighters?" Cameron asked, somewhat surprised by his suggestion.

"We only have twenty fighters left," Nathan reminded her. "We can fit all of them into the main hangar bay, if necessary. Besides, for the foreseeable future, they're going to be defending Corinair along with the Nighthawks. The Aurora is pretty much a battleship now."

"Have you talked with Commander Verbeek about this?" Cameron wondered.

"Verbee is going to take command of one of the XKs," Nathan explained. "Sami will take his place as squadron leader."

"What about Kaplan?" Cameron wondered. "I was hoping we'd give her an XK command as well."

"And she'll get one," Nathan assured her. "But Verbeek's got more combat experience, and Kaplan's pretty much indispensable to the Mystic at the moment. Once we find a good XO to take her place there, we can move her."

"I'll have my people prep the bay for the conversion," Vladimir promised. "I take it you still want to keep the starboard catapults working for the jump missiles."

"Of course," Nathan replied. "Cameron, how is the comm-relay system going?"

"The network between the Pentaurus, Rogen, and Orswellan sectors is operational. It will be another week before we have the network to SilTek working."

"What about Casbon and the Akha?" Nathan wondered.

"That will be next," Cameron explained. "Another week or so. Meanwhile, we have a comm-drone jumping between Rogen command and the Casbon system once every hour, and both the Casbon and the Akha have a jump comm-drone they can use to call for help in an emergency."

"Good," Nathan replied. "I'd like a relay network set up to reach the Sol sector as well, with an end point near Tanna so that messages can go to either Sol or Nor-Patri."

"Technically, that's still disputed space," Cameron warned. "We'd be jumping a comm-drone through territory that the Jung still claim as their own."

"I'll take that chance," Nathan replied. "We can always move the relay point if necessary. But for now, I want to ensure I have reliable communications between the Voss and the rest of the alliance."

"I'll see to it," Cameron promised. "Any particular time frame in mind?"

"The sooner the better," Nathan replied. "The sooner we speak with the Jung, the sooner I'll have an idea which way we're going." Nathan looked around at the faces of his senior staff. "The end game is nearing, people. Things are likely to get a little crazy going forward."

"Crazier, you mean," Jessica noted.

"Crazier," Nathan agreed. "Just be ready to roll with the changes as we go. That's all I ask."

* * *

Lord Dusahn stormed out of the elevator and into the lobby, headed full steam toward his office on the other side.

"I take it things did not go well on Infernum," Commander Jexx commented as his leader passed.

"Twelve hours of travel only to be insulted by that child pretending to be a leader!"

"Then I suppose a cease-fire was not obtained," the commander stated, following his leader into his office.

Lord Dusahn spun around, glaring at the commander. "He threatened our empire! He threatened me!"

Commander Jexx chose not to comment further, fearing he might have already crossed the line.

"I want all our ships upgraded and ready for battle as soon as possible! And I want whatever world is providing them with their technology erased from existence!"

"These things will take time, my lord."

"We will strike out and harass their ships, their worlds..."

"My lord, that would not be advisable," Commander Jexx reminded his leader. "We are barely able to protect ourselves."

"The Chekta protocol protects us!"

"From complete invasion, perhaps," Commander Jexx pointed out, "but not from destruction of our warships."

"They must be reminded of whom they are dealing with!" Lord Dusahn continued. "I will not bow down to this..."

"I am not suggesting that you do, my lord," Commander Jexx interjected. "I am only asking that you be patient. We must play the long game. We must ensure continued trade with Pentaurus worlds, at least until we can replace those products with ones produced locally. We must ensure that our forces are adequate to discourage attacks against the empire. We must buy time. Time is the great equalizer. With it, we can rearm, resupply, and remake what we now have into something that will take us forward into the future. We must ensure the survival of the Dusahn Empire."

"You mean the dominance," Lord Dusahn corrected, glaring at the young officer.

"I mean survival, my lord," Commander Jexx reiterated. "Expansion and dominance can come later, once we have regained our former strength."

"And what do we do in the meantime?" Lord Dusahn questioned angrily. "Cower in our homes and pray that the Karuzari Alliance graces us with the right to exist?"

"Of course not, my lord," the commander promised. "But there are many things we can do that do not require direct conflict. We can sow the seeds of unrest throughout our enemy's allies. We can steal their technology. We can hire outsiders to destroy their resources, providing us with plausible deniability."

Lord Dusahn stepped forward, locking eyes with the commander. "That man threatened to end me. How can I not respond to that kind of challenge?"

"Responding is precisely what he wishes us to do," the commander explained. "For if we do, he will have the excuse he needs to attack. And if we lash out in force, he will have no choice to but to destroy us, Chekta be damned. That is what you would do, my lord. There is no reason to believe that he would not as well."

Lord Dusahn stood there a moment, fuming. "I will not allow Nathan Scott to dictate terms to the Dusahn Empire."

"No, you will not," the commander agreed. "You will ignore his threats, seeing them for the hollow words that they are. That is what a Dusahn leader does. That is what you have always done. That is why we follow you."

Lord Dusahn turned toward the window, staring out at the gardens below as workers toiled to return them to their former glory. "You will find me that world of theirs," he grumbled. "The one providing them with all of their advanced technology."

"Yes, my lord."

* * *

Fifteen men and women sat around the large, circular conference table, each of them well dressed in Corinairan business attire. Before them were dark, wood-grained nameplates engraved in gold leaf. The table was decorated with floral centerpieces, and attendants waited on all sides, ready to serve those in attendance.

Nathan and Deliza entered from a side door, guided to their seats by one of the attendants.

"Thank you for seeing us," Deliza stated confidently to the owners, as she and Nathan took their seats.

"We are honored by your presence," the man at the head of the table replied. "I am Ross Coulthard, primary shareholder in the Glendanon. Captain Gullen has spoken highly of you both, and of course, your noble actions are well known among the people of Corinair."

"Thank you," Deliza replied. "I assume everyone has had a chance to review the upgrades we have made to the Glendanon, as well as our proposal for her future use."

"I cannot speak for everyone but, as for myself, I have read your report with great interest," Mister Coulthard assured her.

"For the purposes of expediency, I'll assume that everyone has reviewed the document," Deliza began. "The Karuzari Alliance is proposing to increase the interior volume of the Glendanon's main cargo bay by sixty-seven percent and adding additional cargo pod racks along her forward ventral surface. In addition, her jump drive system will be converted to the 'bubble-field' system developed by the SilTek corporation, in order to allow her to accommodate smaller, non-jump-enabled cargo vessels docked onto her dorsal side. This will enable the Glendanon to act as both a cargo carrier and ferry platform."

"It is a fine plan, to be certain," Mister Coulthard agreed. "However, I suspect the concern of the shareholders will be how the Glendanon's operation will be financed."

"And how we are to make a profit," the woman across the table from Deliza and Nathan added.

Deliza glanced at the woman's nameplate, noticing the name. Iona McAllen. The name was familiar, but she couldn't quite place it.

"Just how long do you propose to charge only cost?"

"Cost plus ten percent," Deliza corrected.

"Cost plus ten percent hardly covers unexpected maintenance expenses," Iona pointed out.

"The initial lower rates are needed to make

interstellar trade affordable for all worlds within the alliance," Deliza explained.

"Why would we want to cultivate trade with worlds that have so little to offer?"

Deliza suddenly found herself disliking Miss McAllen.

"Most inhabited worlds are not as prosperous as Corinair," Nathan explained, interjecting himself into the debate. "However, that doesn't make them of lessor value as trading partners. If anything, low-cost access to interstellar travel and trade will cultivate growth, turning those worlds into sources of goods and culture that benefit all."

"You cannot know this to be true," Iona insisted.

"No, I cannot," Nathan admitted.

"Some of these worlds are isolated by choice," another shareholder stated. "Are we to subsidize those worlds as well?"

"A world choosing to isolate itself will probably not avail itself of our transportation network," Deliza told them.

"I believe that some of us may be missing the big picture," Mister Coulthard stated, wishing to steer the conversation in a more positive direction. "What is being proposed here is not just the upgrade of the Glendanon, but the establishment of an interstellar shipping conglomerate...perhaps the first of its kind."

"I don't know that I'd use the word conglomerate," Deliza protested.

"This operation will require ships, shuttles, traffic controllers, booking services, storage and holding facilities, customs facilities...all manner of supportive businesses," Mister Coulthard stated.

"Point taken," Deliza agreed. "However, such a network will take years, if not decades, to achieve."

"Or to become profitable," Miss McAllen added, once again reminding all in attendance of her concerns.

"The purpose of this alliance isn't profit," Nathan reminded her.

"Perhaps not, but it is the Glendanon's purpose," Miss McAllen asserted.

"The Glendanon's profit margins will grow in time," Deliza pointed out. "Based on our projections, the proposed rate increase over time, and the growth of demand as new worlds increase their trade with one another, the Glendanon should begin turning considerable profit within five to ten years."

"Ten years is a long time to wait for profit," Miss McAllen argued.

"How long did it take to build the Glendanon?" Nathan asked her.

"I wouldn't know," Iona admitted. "I bought into this syndicate after she was already in service."

"Five years," Mister Coulthard stated. "And this group had signed contracts from the Takarans before she was constructed."

"How are you going to pay for these upgrades?" Miss McAllen challenged. "Most of us have had our fortunes raided by the Dusahn. Assuming we can grow our businesses again, it will take us decades to be able to afford such upgrades."

"We can phase in the major upgrades as needed and as profits increase," Nathan suggested. "The Glendanon is already a massive vessel. It will probably take years for demand to exceed her capabilities."

"At which time we can reassess those upgrades and their costs," Mister Coulthard pointed out.

"Or we can charge full rates now, make profits

sooner rather than later, and weed out clients of lessor value," Miss McAllen countered.

Deliza noticed several shareholders nodding in agreement. "If you price the Glendanon's services so high that only the wealthier worlds can afford them, you are limiting your future market. Independent operators will quickly move to fill this void, and, over time, they will begin to steal your market share. At that point, you will be forced to lower prices in order to prevent further losses in market share. And as you all know, getting back lost market shares is far more difficult than keeping them to begin with."

"We don't know what the future holds," Miss McAllen argued. "The Dusahn are still a threat. Until that threat is removed, none of us can afford to pass up profits today for increased profits that might come tomorrow."

Again, Miss McAllen's words drew nods of support from around the room. The number of shareholders nodding their agreement was increasing with each point she made.

Deliza decided to change tactics. "Tell me, Miss McAllen, what would you propose for the Glendanon?"

"I think that's rather obvious," the woman replied, a snide tone tainting her words. "Return her to her original mission, charging current market rates. What better way to replenish the finances stolen from us?"

"To hell with the establishment of a peaceful alliance of worlds," Nathan commented, growing impatient.

"We all want peaceful interactions between worlds," Miss McAllen snapped back. "But please, explain to me why it is our responsibility to finance such efforts?"

Nathan glared at her. “The only thing necessary for the triumph of evil is for good men to do nothing,” he muttered.

“Pardon?”

Nathan bit his tongue for a moment before proceeding. “Why was it my responsibility to lead the fight against the Dusahn? Why was it my responsibility to liberate Corinair, a second time, thus creating this opportunity for you all to replenish your accounts? Why was it the responsibility of any of the men and women who gave their lives for this world and many others?”

“You, and those men and women, made personal choices,” Miss McAllen coldly stated. “We are here to do the same...to make personal choices. You may see me as a greedy woman, Captain Scott, but I am simply stating what everyone at this table is thinking.”

“Not everyone,” Mister Coulthard corrected, flashing a disapproving glance at Miss McAllen.

Deliza took a deep breath, letting it out slowly before continuing. “My report was clear and concise. There is no need to debate that which has already been clearly outlined in the document.”

“Then perhaps we should vote now,” Miss McAllen stated indignantly, sensing her pending victory.

“I said there was no need to debate that which was already clearly stated in my report,” Deliza corrected. “If you’ll indulge me a few more minutes, I’d like to point out what should have been obvious to you but apparently is not. And that is your world’s ‘right-to-use’ law.”

Miss McAllen dismissed her with a wave. “Our own government is in disarray. I doubt they could even come together to consider such a move.”

"But suppose they did," Deliza argued. "Suppose they were smart enough to realize that the fastest way to rebuild their civilization and their economy was to export to others in need. Suppose they decided that providing low-cost, interstellar cargo transportation was the best way to build positive trade relationships with all the worlds of the alliance. Suppose they had the foresight to see that invoking 'right-to-use' on the Glendanon was the fastest way to get those relationships established. How long do you think it would take for any of you to start receiving any profits from her operation?"

"'Right-to-use' requires payment to the owners of the claimed vessel," Miss McAllen asserted.

"After the emergency for which 'right-to-use' was invoked has passed," Deliza corrected. "How long do you think it will take to rebuild the Corinairan economy? How long will it take to replenish your financial accounts? Has the Corinairan economy fully recovered from her occupation by the Ta'Akar Empire? That liberation was seven years ago. Are you prepared to wait that long now?"

"A risk, perhaps, but one that is our right to take."

"Agreed," Deliza conceded. "However, I should also point out that, should you decide to return the Glendanon to her original tasking, at whatever rates and with whichever customers you choose to do business with, you will be faced with two new choices."

"And they would be?" Miss McAllen inquired.

"Whether to pay for the upgrades to the Glendanon that Ranni Corp. has paid for or allow us to remove those upgrades, returning your investment to its pre-Dusahn-invasion configuration." Deliza let a tiny smile escape as she added, "Do you really want your investment to be unarmed, unshielded, and only able to jump ten light years at a time? In an uncertain interstellar political environment?"

Miss McAllen glared at Deliza. "You have no legal right to demand payment for upgrades that this body did not authorize."

"Just as you have no legal right to demand that we leave those upgrades in place without compensation," Deliza retorted.

"I'm not certain a Corinairan court would agree with you," Miss McAllen countered, her confidence waning.

"Considering the disarray that your government is currently in, how long do you suppose that ruling would take? And of course, we would demand seizure of the asset in question until that ruling was delivered."

Miss McAllen had no response.

Mister Coulthard smiled at Deliza. "Perhaps now would be a good time to vote."

* * *

"That was amazing," Nathan complimented under his breath as they made their way down the corridor from the conference room. "I don't even know why I needed to be there. You had everything completely under control. I mean, you let them lead themselves into that trap."

"Your presence changed the tempo of the meeting," Deliza stated, smiling.

"How so?"

"If it had just been me, they would have seen a businesswoman looking to work the situation to her advantage. Your presence lent a different perspective: one of honor and purpose. It provided camouflage; a distraction if you will, allowing me to lead them to conclusions favorable to our cause."

"Remind me to never play poker with you," Nathan joked.

"A successful business negotiation requires that you know what your opponents want before the negotiation begins."

"How did you know?" Nathan wondered as they exited the building.

"Normally, considerable research is required. However, in this case, it was easy. For most of the shareholders, the Glendanon is the only asset the Dusahn were unable to take from them. Had they any other assets, they might have been willing to bet on higher profits over the short term."

"In other words, they can't afford to risk losing any amount of profit, even tiny amounts."

"Precisely," Deliza confirmed. "To be honest, had Iona not been there, the others would have voted in our favor from the start."

"Who was that woman?" Nathan wondered as they climbed into their waiting vehicle.

"I didn't recognize her at first," Deliza admitted. "One of her companies was once in a bidding war with Ranni Corp. They lost, of course, mostly due to her arrogance. I suspect she came into today's meeting with a chip on her shoulder. Just like last time, she let her emotions cloud her judgment. Not a good move in business negotiations."

"In any negotiations," Nathan agreed, remembering his brief encounter with Griogair Dusahn. "I should've brought you with me to Infernum."

Deliza smiled. "I probably would have gone off on the bastard as well," she admitted as the vehicle pulled out into traffic.

"Thanks."

"What are you planning to do?" she asked him.

Nathan sighed. "To be honest, I don't rightly know just yet."

* * *

Del stared at the Voss, his mouth agape as he took in the damage. Finally, he turned to Nathan and Dylan. "Did you even have your shields on?"

"We took a lot of fire," Dylan defended. "I mean, there were fighters and shuttles, and... and..." he looked at Nathan.

"Reapers."

"...Reapers all over the place. Jumping in and out, blasting us from all sides. They even had ground troops shooting at us."

"With what?" Del asked, pointing at the damaged aft cargo ramp.

"We had to drop the aft shields to let our people in," Dylan explained.

"How the hell did you manage that?" Del asked. "The shields aren't wired to drop individually."

"We had to get creative," Nathan explained. "Can you fix it?"

"Of course we can fix it," Del insisted. "But it may take a few days."

"You have two," Nathan replied.

Del gave him a cockeyed look. "We have to swap out your nacelles as well, you know."

"I'm going to want more gun turrets," Nathan added.

Del shot him a sidelong look. "And where might we locate them?"

"Outboard ends of the lateral access tunnels, on the sides of the nacelles, off the engineering compartments. One in the nose and a smaller one hanging from the back edge of the utility bay. Oh, and get that damned pressure shield working. We could've used that."

"Uh, it was working, Captain," Dylan told him. "It shared the same power circuit as the aft shield emitters. We lost the pressure shield when Marcus shot out the emitters."

Del looked at Marcus. "You shot out the emitters?" he asked. "On purpose?"

"It worked, didn't it?" Marcus replied.

Del's eyes rolled back.

"I don't suppose we could get stronger shields?" Nathan asked.

"Not without redesigning the nacelles to accommodate larger ZPEDs," Del replied.

"That would probably take a few extra days, wouldn't it," Nathan surmised.

"A few."

"I guess we'll have to wait on that," Nathan decided. "What about the P-Seventy-Twos?"

"What about them?" Del wondered, his brow furrowing in suspicion.

"Can we beef up their shields as well?"

"Same problem," Del replied. "Not enough room."

"Damn. I was hoping the new ones would have better shielding."

"New ones?" Del asked.

"Yeah, we lost the last two," Nathan explained.

Del was crestfallen. "The..."

"One survived, the other didn't," Nathan replied somberly.

Del's demeanor completely changed in that moment. "We'll get it done, Captain," he promised. "All of it."

"Thank you, Del," Nathan replied.

* * *

Nathan had said little since his arrival at Miri's home on SilTek. He'd visited with his niece and nephew, and he'd spoken with Neli and the Ghatazhak responsible for his family's security. However, he had offered no more than the usual small talk with his sister.

Miri watched as Nathan picked at his dinner. The two of them had waited to dine until the others had eaten, expecting private conversations about recent events. But none had been forthcoming. More than halfway through their meal, what little conversation had occurred had been about Miri's progress with her physical therapy.

Finally, Miri decided to press the issue. "When are you going to tell me what happened on Earth?"

"You already know what happened," Nathan replied.

"I know you lost Loki and Naralena, but that's all I know. Something else is bothering you."

"There are lots of things bothering me, Miri," Nathan insisted. "There are always a lot of things bothering me."

"Yes, and you usually can't shut up about them," she teased. "Now you've gone mute. What did you learn on your trip back to Earth?"

"What makes you think I learned anything?"

"Because I can read you like a book, little brother."

Nathan sighed.

"Now spill, or I'm going to make you finish the rest of this weird, mashed vegetable that Neli concocted."

"Since when did you resort to cruel and unusual punishment?"

"I've got a teenage boy and a pre-teen girl, remember?"

Nathan smiled for the first time since they had sat down to eat.

"Are things that bad back home?"

"Earth isn't my home," Nathan insisted. "It hasn't been for some time."

"You know what I mean."

"The entire planet is under martial law, and Galiardi refuses to hold an emergency election during a time of war. A war that he created."

"And the people are tolerating this?"

"They're split," Nathan explained. "Galiardi's got so much propaganda running that people have no idea what's true and what's not. Half of them want the Jung Empire wiped from existence; the other half want an immediate cease-fire. People are protesting all over the world. Many of those protests have turned violent, giving Galiardi an excuse to use deadly force against his own people. There is even an organized underground resistance attacking EDF assets."

"Well, maybe this resistance can bring Galiardi down?" Miri suggested.

"Not likely," Nathan replied. "Their numbers are too small, and they don't have the resources to mount a successful revolution. Even if they did, it would likely turn into a civil war."

Miri thought for a moment, picking at her own meal. "That's why you've been so quiet."

"Huh?"

"The right of succession," she told him. "You think that's the only way to avoid a civil war."

"I didn't say..."

"And you're worried that if you invoke the right, the fact that you're a clone will make matters even worse."

"It might," Nathan said.

"Yes, it might," she agreed. "But that's not why you're so quiet. You're afraid I'll want to invoke the right of succession myself."

"The people don't have to know that I'm a clone," Nathan stated. "Not that many of our own people are even aware of that fact."

"But you can't keep it a secret forever," she argued. "Sooner or later, the people will learn the truth."

"But if I call for an emergency vote..."

"That's a big gamble to be taking with an entire world, not to mention all the worlds that are allied with Earth."

"I don't see any other course of action."

"So you're just going to show up and demand to take over as president? A guy who was executed and buried seven years ago? How well do you think that's going to go over?" she asked.

"I imagine half the people will be willing to accept it," Nathan stated.

"Which makes the Earth no better off than before," she pointed out. "And of course, you'll still have Galiardi to deal with."

"Not if I arrest him."

"For what? Pop's assassination? You don't have any evidence. You said so yourself."

"For lying to the people about the Jung," Nathan argued. "For dragging them into an unjust war."

"Good luck with that one," she scoffed. "Like you said, half the people want to see the Jung obliterated. Part of me doesn't blame them."

Nathan looked crossly at his sister.

"I said part of me," she defended. After a sigh, she added, "It has to be me."

"What?"

"I have to invoke the right of succession. I am the oldest surviving kin, after all. I was also his personal assistant for seven years, so I'm quite familiar with how things work in Winnipeg."

"Miri, you're not ready."

"I'm never going to be ready, Nathan. Were you ready when you took over the Aurora? Were you ready when you assumed command of the fight against the Dusahn? How is this any different?"

"You have children."

"Which is precisely why I must do this," Miri argued. "How am I supposed to instill a sense of right and wrong, of duty and honor, in my children if I don't live up to those same ideals?"

"It's a miracle you even survived, Miri," Nathan reminded her.

"If so, then I'd like to think it was for a reason," she insisted. "Perhaps this is it?"

Nathan pushed his plate aside, leaning forward on the table, thinking.

"What?" his sister asked.

"I've often thought the exact same thing. Why was I revived? Why was I allowed to cheat death, if not for some grand purpose?"

"And what did you conclude?"

Nathan sighed again. "That my survival wasn't preordained. It was a gift given to me by others. Others who cared for me, and who believed that my continued existence might better humanity."

"Is that why you agreed to lead the fight against the Dusahn?"

Nathan chuckled. "No. Everything I just said was bullshit. I just did what felt right at the time."

"As I'm suggesting I do now."

"I guess it runs in the family," Nathan concluded, smiling at his sister.

"I guess so," she agreed. "Now, how about we go raid the refrigerator and find something good to eat?"

CHAPTER TWO

The jump flash subsided, and the violent shaking of his battered ship stopped. Unfortunately, his cockpit was filled with multiple alarms as critical-failure warning lights flashed all over his console. His fighter was coming apart, and there was nothing he could do to save it.

One light in particular caught his attention. 'Cabin Pressure' flashed bright red at the top center of his console. His cockpit was losing pressure, and he had only seconds to react.

The Earth loomed below. Everywhere else was the starry blackness of space. He was losing pressure and had only seconds to react. Attitude control thrusters fired intermittently, causing his ship to pitch, roll, and yaw unpredictably. He needed to get down into the atmosphere before it was too late, but his fighter wasn't cooperating.

For what seemed an eternity, he fought his flight controls, trying desperately to get his nose down. But every time it began to swing toward the planet, another thruster would fire, knocking his nose back toward space.

Finally, it swung down hard, and he shoved his throttle forward, lighting up his main engine again. His fighter lurched forward but then cut out, and another warning light came on. With any luck, it had been enough.

He closed his eyes and pressed the jump button, praying that it would work one last time.

* * *

"Did you see that?" the controller asked the person at the console next to him.

"See what?"

"I had a blip in low orbit, about halfway between Hawaii and Japan."

"I didn't see anything."

The controller pressed a button on his console, setting his display to jump back thirty seconds. "There it is again."

The other controller leaned over to see for himself. "Too small to be a ship. Too small to be a fighter, either. A comm-drone gone awry?"

"It pitched down and then disappeared."

"Probably figured out that it was in the wrong location and jumped out."

"It was headed toward the surface when it jumped," the first controller argued.

"Can't be a comm-drone then," the second controller decided, returning to his own console. "They don't operate in the atmosphere."

"Then what the hell was it?"

"Who cares? Just write it up and forward it to EDF. UFOs are their job, not ours."

* * *

His cockpit filled with blue-white light, and the ship shook violently, tumbling nose over tail wildly. As his fighter tossed about in the thick atmosphere, he caught glimpses of a vast ocean below...and land.

But he was losing altitude quickly, and his ship was out of control. He cut all power to his thrusters and propulsion systems, praying that his grav-lift systems still worked. His fighter had lousy aerodynamics, and controlled flight was nearly impossible without them. But at least his malfunctioning thrusters were no longer a problem.

Once again he spotted the land, and managed to turn his fighter toward it. He still had plenty of speed, more than enough to reach what appeared to be an island.

The status lights for his grav-lift system were flashing, cycling between red, yellow, and green, as if those systems couldn't decide whether or not they were functioning properly. He had trained for many different in-flight emergencies during his career as a pilot, but never anything like this. It almost would have been easier if everything had just stopped working. At least then he could glide in and possibly make a survivable crash landing.

But his broken fighter would not make it that easy. His grav-lift systems would not maintain repulsive power evenly, making it difficult for him to maintain level flight. Finally, he had no choice but to shut it down as well, betting that he had enough momentum to reach the island ahead. They had not anticipated ditching in the water, and his injuries would make it difficult for him to swim to shore.

Sparks popped from under his console, and smoke began filling his cockpit, making it difficult to see. He hacked and coughed, fumbling for the canopy jettison lever behind him. Why had they not included parachutes in these things?

His lungs burned from the acrid smoke, and his vision began to blur. Finally, his left hand felt a lever, and he pulled it with all the strength he had left. There was an explosion, and the cockpit filled with a rush of fresh air, sweeping the smoke away in the blink of an eye.

The wave of air struck him like a wall, nearly knocking him out. Had he not been securely strapped into his seat, he doubted he would still be in the cockpit. Squinting, he crouched down as best he could, trying to use the forward window to shield himself from the onrushing air. It was all he could do to see the trees as his fighter struck the top of them. Leaves and branches slapped at the fuselage of his doomed fighter, slapping him in the torso and face. Pain overcame him, and his fighter suddenly came to an abrupt halt, nearly breaking his shoulder straps and sending him flying.

He fell back in his seat, breathless. For a moment, he thought he had survived the crash, but then the entire ship fell straight down like a rock, slamming onto the ground below, causing everything to go black on impact.

* * *

Nathan sat across the table from Caitrin Bindi, quietly studying the document on the oversized data pads that Tekans seemed to favor.

“We will be setting up offices on Rakuen next month,” Caitrin stated, becoming uncomfortable with the long silence.

“You might want to hold off on that for now,” Nathan commented, his focus still on the data pad in his hands.

“Any particular reason?”

“The scope and area of this alliance may change radically in the future. If you want to be centrally located, Rakuen may not be the best choice.”

“Rakuen wasn’t chosen because of its central location,” Caitrin reminded him.

“Nevertheless, I’m not even certain it’s necessary to locate off of SilTek.”

“Except that SilTek does not wish the alliance headquarters to be located on SilTek.”

“This charter reads more like a business contract,” Nathan complained.

“That’s because it is a business contract.”

"When Ariana recommended our alliance be run as a business, I thought she was talking about budgets and stuff...you know, bottom line and all that."

"Good governments are run like good businesses," Caitrin insisted. "At least, the ones that last."

"I'm just not sure the business angle is going to go over so well."

"I believe what will sell the concept is the overall mission statement."

"To protect and serve; to promote the security and welfare; and to provide for the peaceful coexistence of all human civilizations. Sounds like what you'd see on the side of a law enforcement vehicle...except for that last part."

"I think it describes our purpose quite well," Caitrin argued.

"Except it's a bit broad."

"The responsibilities of the corporation are clearly outlined later in the document."

"As are the regulations governing the member worlds," Nathan countered. "That part has got to go."

"If all worlds are not operating by the same set of rules, our job will be far more difficult, thus profits will be greatly decreased."

"That's another thing," Nathan replied. "It shouldn't be about profits, it should be about results."

"A noble sentiment but impractical. Profits are needed for expansion, for research and development..."

"I understand all of that, but..."

"It's either a business, or it's a government organization run by committee."

"Can't it be both?" Nathan asked. "SilTek is."

“Applying SilTek’s corporate-government model on a galactic scale would be next to impossible,” Caitrin argued.

“Perhaps making it a non-profit would be better,” Nathan suggested.

“I’m afraid I don’t know much about the non-profit business model,” Caitrin admitted.

“From what little I remember from economics classes, it’s the same as the profit model, except that a board of directors approves the budget, sets the price of services, and decides what to do with the excess revenue.”

Caitrin shuddered. “Excess revenue?”

Nathan smiled. “What you would call profits.”

“And who would sit on this board of directors?”

“Representatives from each member world.”

Caitrin took a deep breath, letting it out slowly. “That might work in the beginning,” she admitted, “but as this alliance grows, the board will become so large that it would be impossible to reach a consensus on anything.”

Nathan thought for a moment. “You may have a point there,” he finally admitted.

“Which is why this alliance needs to be run as a corporation. One that is profitable.”

“I’m starting to see your point,” Nathan said. “However, member worlds must be free to run their worlds as they see fit, regardless of what other member worlds might think.”

“Again, this is going to cause problems. Different ideologies create conflict requiring compromise. Compromise results in neither party being completely happy.”

“That’s why it’s important that every world remain

its own sovereign state. The moment we try to govern them is the moment our alliance begins to fail."

"We must have some common ground as a starting point," Caitrin argued.

"Isn't freedom common ground?"

"For most, yes, but it's not enough."

"It has to be," Nathan insisted.

"Not everyone wants to be free, Nathan. Some prefer to be led. They prefer to be told what to do, in exchange for security."

Nathan leaned back in his chair, placing the data pad on the table. "That is freedom. Those people are free to live in a system that tells them what to do. There's nothing wrong with that. It only becomes wrong when people are forced to live in a way with which they do not agree. That is why every world must be free to govern their people as they see fit."

"Even if it is a brutal dictatorship?" Caitrin challenged.

"Even if it is a brutal dictatorship," Nathan agreed. "As long as their people are free to leave if they don't like living in that type of society."

"And what if a world decided they only wanted people with black hair and green eyes, and decided to abort all babies that didn't meet that criteria?"

"A bit extreme, don't you think?"

"Yet still a valid question," she insisted.

"I wouldn't agree with it, but if I expect others to respect my right to live my life as I choose, I have to respect theirs."

"That's going to put off a lot of worlds. They may not wish to associate with extremist worlds."

"Then they don't have to," Nathan defended. "No one will be forcing them to trade with those worlds, nor will they be forced to interact with those worlds. The most common factors among all failed civilizations throughout history are the belief that a utopian society can exist, and that the best way to achieve that utopia is to force people with vastly different beliefs to live together. All living creatures naturally prefer to associate with their own kind. The same is true with humans. Most of us are more comfortable among those with similar beliefs and ethics. The mistake leaders have made is thinking there is something wrong with this. Humanity is composed of thousands of cultures, each of them unique in their own way. All of them have at least some natural common ground, and generally that is where we can coexist. But just as you said, if you force a compromise, neither side is happy. We have to let people be who they want to be, even if we don't like it."

"Can we at least require that they not attack one another?"

Nathan smiled. "Sarcasm? Before lunch?"

* * *

The flatbed truck turned off the main, coastal highway onto one of the many dirt roads that led into the forest.

"Are you sure this is where it was?" the passenger asked the driver.

"I am certain."

"How far in do you think?"

"It cannot be far," the driver insisted. "When I first saw it, I thought it was going to hit the water."

"Last time you saw something, it was just a highway drone."

"Hey, that drone paid for the new muffler on this truck."

"Yes, a quieter truck has been such a blessing for

both our families," the passenger replied, a hint of sarcasm in his voice.

"What I saw was big enough to pay for a whole new truck," the driver insisted.

"There is nothing wrong with this truck," the passenger insisted, "other than the driver."

"There!" the driver announced, pointing to several broken treetops in the distance. "It went down beyond those trees!"

"There's probably nothing left of it."

"There is always something of value."

"If you mean something else to add to our junk pile, then yes."

The truck stopped suddenly, both men staring out the window in disbelief.

"My God," the passenger muttered, his eyes wide. He looked at his brother. "Udo, what have you found us?"

"I told you it was big, Kado," Udo said as he climbed out of the truck.

Kado also climbed out, cautiously following his brother toward the wreckage that lay before them. "What is it?"

"I am not certain," Udo admitted.

The object was narrow and about six or seven meters long, with two large engines on the back, just behind an open area, with something sticking up out of it. Just below the left engine, something had been torn off, and the front of the object was badly damaged.

"There's more wreckage over there," Kado stated, pointing to their left.

Udo looked to his left. "That looks like a wing." His eyes widened as he turned to look at Kado. "I think it's a spacecraft."

"It's too small to be a spacecraft."

Udo squinted, trying to make out the odd-looking object sticking out of a hole just forward of the craft's engine. His mouth dropped open, and he began running toward the wreckage.

"Udo! Wait!" Kado yelled, worried that his impetuous younger brother was running headlong into trouble.

"There's a person in it!" Udo yelled back as he ran. He reached the wreckage, climbing up onto the busted wing root to reach the unmoving occupant.

Kado followed, stopping short of the wreckage, watching his brother.

"I think he's alive!" Udo exclaimed.

Kado studied the unfamiliar markings on the side of the wreckage. "This is not an EDF ship," he decided. "Is it Jung?"

Udo looked around the cockpit, spotting familiar English lettering at various places around the cockpit, along with another language that looked similar. "I don't believe so."

"What are you doing?" Kado wondered.

"I'm taking off his helmet!"

"Are you sure that's a good idea? What if he can't breathe our air?"

Udo turned, casting a snide look at his brother. "He's human, not an alien, Kado! Now get up here and help me."

Kado reluctantly complied, knowing from experience that there would be no convincing his brother to do otherwise. "This is a bad idea."

"You think everything is a bad idea," Udo stated as he unbuckled the man's helmet and carefully removed it.

The unconscious pilot's head flopped back against the headrest, his hair matted with blood.

"He's bleeding," Udo said. "We have to get him out of here and take him back to the farm."

"Ayame will not like this," Kado warned. "Neither will Kamiko."

"I'll deal with Kamiko," Udo insisted. "Just don't tell Ayame, like usual."

"I am not afraid of telling my wife," Kado argued. "I just choose to avoid causing her undue stress."

"For yourself as well," Udo jabbed, unbuckling the shoulder straps securing the pilot in his seat.

"What about the wreckage?" Kado asked as he helped his brother pull the unconscious man out of the wreckage.

"Once we get him into the truck, we can use the hoist to lift the wreckage onto the cargo bed. But we must move quickly. I doubt we are the only ones who saw this thing come down."

* * *

The elder statesman stared at his uninvited guest, considering the man's suspicious offer. "A few months ago, your forces attacked this world, claiming it as your own. Now you offer us payment for that which you once took by force."

Lord Dusahn swallowed his pride, hard as it was to do. "The fortunes of my people have changed as of late."

"So I have heard," the elder statesman stated.

"I assure you, it is a temporary setback. Very temporary. Those who choose to voluntarily do business with us will be handsomely rewarded and will be granted favored status once the Dusahn Empire is restored to its previous state."

"And if we choose not to do business with you?"

Lord Dusahn thought a moment before replying, wanting to at least appear to be speaking carefully and respectfully. "I assure you, Chancellor, Volon will be much better off doing business with the Dusahn Empire."

"That sounds very much like a veiled threat."

"It is not a threat, just a fact," Lord Dusahn explained.

"Is this what you said to the Haven Syndicate as well?"

"The Haven Syndicate made threats against the Dusahn Empire. Threats that could not go unanswered."

The chancellor sighed. "I shall consider your offer, Lord Dusahn."

"I will send a cargo ship for the first load in six Volonese days," Lord Dusahn stated as he rose from his seat in the chancellor's office.

"I said I would consider your request," the chancellor reminded him.

Lord Dusahn smiled. "I am confident that you are wise enough to see the advantage of doing business with the Dusahn Empire, as well as the disadvantages of denying us that which we desire."

The chancellor said nothing more, watching as the Dusahn leader turned and exited the office. Once he was gone, the side door opened, and an aide entered.

"What are we to do?" he asked the Volonese leader.

"They are offering well above market value for the goods they require."

"And when they do return to their former status, then what?"

The chancellor looked at his subordinate. "Just

because I sit in this chair does not mean I have all the answers."

"Well, we cannot do nothing and just hope for the best."

"Of course not," the chancellor agreed. "We have a week to prepare. We shall do what we must to protect our people and our world."

"We cannot defeat them," his aide insisted.

"We may not need to," the chancellor argued. "We may only need to make dealing with us not worth the cost and effort to them."

"And how do we do that?" the aide wondered.

"I'm open to suggestions."

* * *

"Our latest intelligence shows the Jung are down to only a few dozen ships, most of them frigates or gunships," Commander Camaden reported.

"What about their battleships?" Admiral Galiardi wondered.

"We count only four, two of which are still too far away from Nor-Patri to be of any use in her defense."

"This proves what I've been saying all along," Commander Litano declared. "We can reduce the Jung Empire to rubble and suffer no loses of our own."

"I find that rather difficult to believe," Admiral Galiardi stated. "Are you certain there are no Jung ships currently within our borders?"

"We are still tracking sixty-plus ships along the border, but none inside Sol Alliance space. Two of them are battleships. But it would take at least a month for them to reach Earth. We should have no problem picking them off one by one before they reach us or any of our allies."

"Then it is time," Admiral Galiardi concluded.

"Gentlemen, I want a strike plan on my desk by the end of the week. One that first takes out those ships skirting our border. Then, and only then, will I authorize an all-out strike against the Jung Empire. I want to make damned sure we rid humanity of this threat, once and for all."

"Yes, sir," his advisers replied.

Another aide entered the room as the admiral's senior staff departed their daily briefing. "Admiral, I was looking through the daily reports from ATC, and I noticed an unidentified contact in low orbit over the Pacific about four hours ago."

"Probably just a sensor ghost or a meteorite," the admiral concluded, glancing at the report.

"It wasn't a ghost," his aide insisted. "And it changed course before it disappeared again."

Admiral Galiardi squinted, thinking. "Length of contact?"

"Twenty-three seconds."

"What was its new heading when it disappeared?"

"Its original heading was an ascent, as if it were on a departure course, then it pitched downward. Trajectory at the moment it disappeared would put it in the area of Hokkaido, one of the Japanese islands."

"A jump sub?" the admiral surmised.

"That was my first thought, except that its original trajectory made it appear to be a departure. It was my understanding that jump subs can't alter course in space."

"The original ones couldn't," the admiral agreed. "But who's to say it isn't possible. Send a search and recovery team to Hokkaido."

"But if it's a jump sub, it's probably already gone deep. The contact is four hours old."

"You could be right," the admiral agreed. "But

let's check anyway. The last thing we need right now is another incursion."

"Yes, sir."

Admiral Galiardi took a long deep breath, letting it out slowly and with great satisfaction. Destiny had handed him an opportunity, and he had taken it. All of the pieces were falling into place. Soon, he would be able to make good on the oath he'd sworn more than thirty years ago. The people of Earth, and by extension humanity itself, would finally be safe. More importantly, he would be in a position to keep it that way.

* * *

The flying cab settled in off the Voss's starboard side, kicking up dust as it set down.

"We have arrived at your destination, sir," the AI piloting system announced. "You may now safely exit the vehicle."

"Thank you," Nathan replied instinctively.

"Have a pleasant day."

"You too," Nathan replied, shaking his head and wondering why he had just said that. He walked toward the Voss, getting far enough away from the cab so that it could depart safely before stopping to take in the view of his upgraded ship.

"Good afternoon, Captain," Del greeted as he and Dylan approached.

"Good afternoon, gentlemen," Nathan greeted. "How are we looking?"

"She's ready to go," Dylan assured him.

"Port and starboard turrets have been installed, nose turret has been installed, and the tail gun in the utility bay is ready to go."

"Did you get the pressure shield working?"

Dylan chuckled. "That was the easiest thing we did."

"We also got the missile launch and recovery systems working, as well as the load selection system for the launch tubes."

"What about the shields?"

"All shields are now powered independently," Del assured him. "We had to run the additional power conduits along the outside of the hull due to time constraints, but they will be on the inside on the rest of the XKs."

"The new nacelles look different," Nathan commented.

"We added the additional jump energy cells to the dorsal side of the nacelles, then covered them up with cowlings to protect them. They're also wired independently, so if one of them is damaged, you don't lose the entire array."

"Good thinking," Nathan agreed.

"You now have a single-jump range of six hundred light years, and a one-minute jump range of twelve hundred, all with a four-hour recharge time."

"For both arrays?" Nathan asked.

"Thanks to the ZPEDs, yes," Del explained. "You can also stick to series jumps of ten light years each, with two-minute intervals between jumps. It would still take you four hours to get there, but you'd arrive with a full charge."

"It's always good to have options," Nathan said. "All other damage has been repaired?"

"Yes, sir," Del replied.

Nathan shook his head in disbelief. "How did you manage to get everything done in only two days?"

"Isn't that what you asked for?" Del wondered.

"Yes, but I figured something would have to wait," Nathan admitted.

"Well, we're still working on the swarm-tech for the Lightnings, so it'll be a few more days until we have new fighters ready for you."

"Still, your people really busted their humps."

"We didn't want you to lose anyone else because your ship wasn't up to snuff."

Nathan reached out and put his hand on Del's shoulder. "I appreciate that, Del."

"Besides, you'd be surprised how much you can get done when you don't sleep much."

Nathan nodded agreement. "That would explain why you both look so tired." He looked at Dylan, who looked as if he might fall over at any moment. "Perhaps you should let Josh fly us back."

"No argument there," Dylan agreed.

"Send everyone home for the day," Nathan told Del. "You all deserve it."

"Thanks, but we'll finish out the day," Del insisted. "We've still got a lot of XKs to convert."

"That we do, my friend." Nathan turned to Dylan. "Shall we?"

"Gladly," Dylan agreed, handing his wrench to Del.

* * *

The jump flash washed across the Voss's flight deck, fading away a second later. Before them was the familiar sight of Haven, orbiting its parent gas giant just beyond the ring of rocky debris that provided most of the desolate world's wealth.

"Nothing on comms," Josh commented as they approached.

"All channels," Nathan instructed.

"All channels, aye," Dylan replied as he tied

his captain's comm-set into the external comms array and set the system to broadcast on all known channels and media.

"Haven Control, this is Captain Scott on board the Karuzari Alliance ship Dalen Voss. We are requesting permission to land, to speak with your leaders." Nathan waited, exchanging glances with Jessica next to him, but they received no reply.

"I'm not even getting an auto-flight carrier," Josh added.

"Anything on the threat board?" Nathan asked.

"Sensors are clear," Dylan replied. "No ships in flight and none powered up on the surface. In fact, there seem to be very few ships still intact on the surface."

"I guess they were hit harder than our initial intelligence suggested," Jessica commented.

"Or a lot of them decided to bug out before the Dusahn come back to finish the job," Kit added.

"If the Dusahn meant to completely destroy them, they would have done so in the first place," Nathan surmised. "They wanted them to hurt just enough to be compliant, yet still be able to supply what they need."

"I thought Haven was a wasteland," Dylan said.

"It is," Josh replied.

"Haven is a wasteland, but Tikka's rings are full of rare elements, many of which cannot be found anywhere else in the entire sector," Nathan explained. "The fact that all those resources are locked up in small, collectible-sized chunks makes it far less expensive to mine, which makes the Haven Syndicate able to undersell competitors."

"Is that why we're here?" Dylan asked. "To make sure we have access to those resources?"

"More like to make sure the Dusahn don't," Jessica said.

"We invite everyone," Nathan corrected, "regardless of what they may or may not have to offer."

"Even if we don't like them?" Josh wondered.

"Especially if we don't like them," Nathan replied.

"Still nothing," Josh reported. "What do you want me to do?"

"Find a place to set down," Nathan instructed. "Preferably someplace near the syndicate headquarters."

Josh studied the sensor screen for a moment. "Not gonna be easy. There's a lot of debris down there."

"Do the best you can," Nathan instructed.

The Voss coasted smoothly above the rooftops of the surviving buildings, her grav-lift systems humming loudly. People in the streets scattered, fearing the unidentified, armed vessel. They too had heard rumors that the Dusahn had acquired makeshift warships from worlds outside the Pentaurus sector. For all they knew, this was one of them.

"Damn," Josh exclaimed as he peered out the port cockpit window. "Like gula bugs when you turn the lights on."

"They're afraid of us," Jessica stated.

"I suspect they're afraid of everyone right now," Nathan added.

"We should maintain a safe perimeter while we're skids-on-the-ground," Mori suggested.

"You and Jokay take ground watch," Jessica instructed.

"What about me?" Kit asked.

"You're coming with us."

"Let's keep the reactors hot and shields up," Nathan added as he turned to exit. "Subvert busted their asses patching us up. I'd prefer to get off this rock without a scratch."

"We'll keep the fires burnin'," Josh promised.

The aft cargo ramp hit the ground with a thud, kicking up dust. Immediately, two men carrying assault rifles jumped off either side of the ramp. They quickly moved into position, crouching behind the port and starboard aft gear struts, their weapons held ready as they scanned the area for threats.

"Clear to starboard," Mori reported over comm-sets.

"Clear to port," Jokay added.

"Drop aft shields," Nathan instructed. He peered out the back of the utility bay as the shimmering, transparent shield just past the foot of the ramp flickered slightly, then disappeared, leaving a ten-meter-wide gap.

"Aft shield is down," Dylan confirmed.

"Let's move out," Nathan ordered Kit and Jessica.

Marcus stepped up to the top of the ramp, watching as the other three headed down. "Damn, I didn't think Haven could get any uglier," he said, scanning the area. He spotted something in the distance, moving from right to left...something large. Its motion suddenly stopped, but then the object began growing in size. "Movement aft!" he warned over comms as he reached up for the newly installed tail gun with both hands.

"Looks like a vehicle headed our way," Mori announced.

Marcus twisted the release lever and pulled down hard, swinging the big, double-barreled cannon down from its storage position. The weapon made a loud click as it reached the bottom of its travel and locked into place. He grabbed it and swung it ninety degrees, so that its barrels were pointed aft out the door.

"Can you make it out?" Jessica asked over comms, as her group knelt down and raised their own weapons.

"Gimme a sec," Marcus grumbled as he powered up the weapon. The targeting screen between the control handles flickered to life, and he pressed the zoom button. "It's a vehicle!" he reported. "Open-cab cargo. Two in the cab and four in the back, all of them armed."

Nathan dialed in his scope, keeping his crosshairs on the distant target as it closed on them.

"Shall I raise the aft shields?" Dylan asked over comm-sets.

"Not yet," Nathan replied. "We may need to get back inside the shield perimeter in a hurry."

"Or we could move back a few meters and be inside the shields," Jessica suggested.

"Don't worry, Cap'n," Marcus told him over comm-sets. "I've got that fucker sighted and ranged. They so much as fart and I'll burn'em down."

"Nobody fires without my express orders," Nathan ordered firmly. "That includes you, old man," he added, glancing back at Marcus. "We didn't come here to start a fight."

The vehicle came to an abrupt stop twenty meters away from them, the men in the back jumping out to either side.

"I've got right," Mori stated over comm-sets.

"I've got left," Jokay followed.

"I've got center," Kit added.

"I'll just take out the whole fuckin' truck," Marcus declared.

"That's close enough!" Nathan yelled.

A man climbed out of the passenger seat, slung a weapon over his shoulder, and walked around to the front of the truck.

"I've got him," Jessica announced quietly.

"I've got the driver," Kit added.

"Easy," Nathan urged under his breath.

"Identify yourself and state your purpose!" the man now in front of the truck yelled confidently.

"Syndicate?" Jessica wondered.

"Probably a local group boss," Marcus sneered over comm-sets. "If the syndicate is down, the city would be swarming with shits trying to carve out a piece of what's left for themselves."

"My name is Nathan Scott!" Nathan yelled back. "We came to talk with the Haven Syndicate."

"That would be us!" the man replied.

Marcus's brow furrowed. Something wasn't right. He tapped a button on the side of his targeting display, changing to its maximum magnification. After making a minor adjustment in aim, he was able to put his crosshairs on the man in front of the truck. "Syndicate my ass."

"I know that guy," Marcus announced over comm-sets.

"Which one?" Jessica asked.

"The one doin' the yellin', and he sure as hell ain't with the syndicate."

"Are you sure?" Nathan asked.

"That asshole was on one of my crews," Marcus replied. "He got traded along with two other losers to another crew. If I remember correctly, we got an extra collector bin for the harvester out of the deal."

"Could he have been picked up by the syndicate after the Dusahn bombardment?" Nathan wondered.

"Syndicate don't like locals," Marcus insisted. "Actually, they fuckin' hate'em. No way they'd pick up a cocky piece of crap like him."

Nathan thought for a moment.

"What's our play?" Jessica asked.

"How do I know you're really with the Haven Syndicate?" Nathan yelled at the man. "And why are you pointing guns at us?"

"Same reason you're pointin' them at us!" the man replied. "Put down your weapons and come out with your hands held high, and we can talk all you want."

"You first!" Nathan yelled back.

"This is our world!" the man yelled. "We don't lay

down arms for no one. You wanna talk, come out and talk, but put your guns down, or we'll open fire, whether you come out or not!"

"That would be a mistake!" Nathan warned.

"I suppose we'll see!"

"Jesus," Nathan cursed to himself. "Why is it that men get so stupid when you gather them together and put guns in their hands?"

"It's a testosterone thing," Jessica replied, smiling. "Say the word, and we'll take them out. One shot for each target."

"Maybe two for Deeks," Kit joked, his weapon still trained on the driver.

"I heard that."

"What's it gonna be!" the man yelled. "We ain't got all day!"

"If you're going to be this inhospitable, we'd just as soon leave if it's alright with you!" Nathan replied.

"What?" Jessica asked.

"These fuckers ain't Syndicate, Cap'n," Marcus insisted.

"Better we don't take the chance," Nathan replied.

"Movement to starboard," Mori reported. "Six, maybe eight. Armed, moving to circle around us."

"Movement to port," Jokay added. "Count eight. Rifles and boomers. Thirty to forty meters, staying behind cover."

"Don't worry about them," Jessica instructed. "They can't get through our shields, at least not before we get back inside."

"Another contact to starboard," Mori reported. "Technical. Looks like a large gun mounted on a rover of some sort."

"They're going to try to get through our shields," Jessica warned.

"Dylan, get to the topside turret and get a lock on that gun to starboard," Nathan instructed over comm-sets.

Dylan looked at Josh. "Oh shit," he muttered as he jumped out of his seat and headed aft as fast as he could.

"I could hit'em with a thruster wash from the mains," Josh suggested.

"And light the whole place on fire?" Nathan scolded.

"Just tryin' to help."

"We need to fall back inside the shield perimeter," Kit said.

"As soon as we start moving, they'll open fire," Jessica replied. "Our only chance is to take all of them out now, all at once. Marcus, you take out the vehicle, including the driver and this asshole. The rest of us will take out the pukes on either side. Brill and Deeks to the outside targets, Kit inside left, and I take inside right."

"Wait!" Nathan ordered.

"There is no wait, Nathan," Jessica insisted. "We're about to get mowed down here."

Dylan scampered up the ladder, twisting his body around the underside of the control deck and sliding into the gunner's seat. "What do I do?" he asked as he powered up the weapon.

"When we start shooting, you take out that other truck," Jessica instructed.

"Got it," Dylan replied. He looked around outside his bubble, confused. "Which truck?"

Jessica squinted slightly, readying herself as the man she was targeting turned around to look behind him, shouting something to the others.

"Something's got them spooked," Kit announced, seeing the same behavior with his target.

"I see four of them!" Dylan reported over comm-sets. "One to my left...I mean...starboard, and four more aft, about two hundred meters out and closing!"

"Uh-oh."

Nathan looked at Jessica. "Uh-oh? Is that your tactical assessment? Uh-oh?"

"Target the one to starboard!" Jessica instructed. "The one to your left!"

"Oh this is not good," Dylan moaned as he swung his turret to the left. "This is sooo not good."

"Okay, I'm locked on the vehicle," Dylan reported nervously over comm-sets. "Should I fire?"

"Not yet," Nathan instructed.

"What the hell?" Kit said, as his target headed back toward their vehicle. "Are they leaving?"

Weapons fire suddenly erupted from the approaching vehicles. It was not aimed at the Voss, but at the men who were challenging it.

Bright yellow bolts of energy slammed into the back of the truck, tearing into the men firing back as they tried to get into the truck.

The man in front of the truck turned back around to face the Voss, raising his weapon to fire, but he never got a shot off. Three bright red bolts of plasma energy streaked over their heads, fired from Marcus's tail gun, slamming into the man, the truck, and its driver.

The truck exploded, flipping over onto one of the other men. Mori and Jokay opened fire at the same time, each of them firing a single shot to drop their targets. Kit fired as well, taking out his man with a double tap to the head, spinning him around before he fell in a smoldering heap.

Yellow-orange bolts of plasma slammed into the starboard shields directly in front of Dylan, causing the Voss's shields to flash brightly.

"Oh shit!" Dylan exclaimed. "Do I fire now?"

"Yes!" Jessica replied. "Fire!"

Dylan closed his eyes and pressed the fire button. His weapon screeched as bolts of energy leapt from its barrels, slamming into the doomed vehicle that had opened fire on them. The vehicle shot up in the air, then fell back to the ground, bouncing and flipping over as it became engulfed in flames.

Dylan opened his eyes. "Holy shit!" he exclaimed. "Did I do that?"

"Nice shootin', Tex!" Jessica congratulated over comm-sets.

Dylan glanced around as bolts of energy streaked about in all directions...all except toward the Voss. "What the hell is going on out there?"

"Swing aft and hold fire!" Jessica instructed.

"Got it!" Dylan replied, swinging his turret back to the right again.

"Cease fire!" Jessica instructed the others. Seconds later, the firefight ended.

"Whoever that is, they're still coming," Kit warned.

"Another gang?" Nathan suggested.

"Could be," Jessica agreed.

"It ain't a gang," Marcus assured them over comm-sets. "Well, it is, but it isn't."

"Could you be a little more cryptic?" Nathan wondered.

"It's the syndicate," Marcus explained.

"Well it's about fucking time," Jessica declared, standing up and lowering her weapon.

* * *

Nathan and Jessica were ushered into Jenno Motto's office by four heavily armed guards.

"The infamous Na-Tan," the man behind the desk exclaimed. "The young captain who refused to die, even when executed. Have you come to witness the results of your handiwork?"

"And you are?" Nathan wondered.

"Jenno Motto, head of what's left of the Haven Syndicate."

"And you blame me for this?"

"I suppose that would be unfair, as I imagine you believed you were doing the honorable thing at the time."

"That means a lot," Nathan replied, "coming from someone who enslaves people in order to increase profits."

"I enslave no one," Jenno stated, obviously

unbothered by the familiar accusation. "The act of acquiring debt with only themselves as collateral is what enslaves those who end up here. I am merely purchasing those debts and giving them a chance to repay their debts."

"By working and living in brutal conditions for decades," Jessica remarked.

Jenno pointed at her. "You are not the first to disapprove."

"Color me shocked."

"He is correct," Nathan told Jessica. "I'm sure most of these people ended up here due to their own poor choices."

Jessica looked shocked. "Some of our best people came from here," she reminded him.

"For which you technically still owe me compensation," Jenno pointed out. "However, I am willing to ignore that fact for the time being."

"How gracious of you," Jessica snarled.

"Easy," Nathan told her.

"I suppose you've come to offer us the protection of your grand alliance," Jenno surmised.

"Something like that," Nathan confirmed.

"Haven has survived four empires," Jenno told them. "It will survive the Dusahn."

"Survive?" Jessica challenged. "Is that what you call what's going on outside?"

"Our harvesters were unharmed. Our processing facilities were unharmed. We are still able to function."

"And how many workers did you lose?" Nathan inquired.

"More than we would have liked," Jenno admitted. "However, there will always be others. The debtor's prisons are full of people who would rather labor away on Haven than rot in a damp cell eating crap."

"You have something other than molo to eat here?" Jessica snapped.

Jenno smiled. "An acquired taste."

"Protection is not the only thing we have to offer," Nathan explained, trying to push past Jessica's distractions. "We are setting up trade and communication routes. We're even setting up a dedicated ferry ship that can move cargo as well as smaller, interplanetary cargo ships, to any point along the network. You could expand your markets, and your new customers would not have to worry about logistics."

"So now you are trying to put independent cargo carriers out of business?"

"No, we're simply trying to help improve the economies of our member worlds," Nathan argued. "To give them access to new markets they might not otherwise have, as well as to products they might not even know about."

"We have all the customers we need," Jenno said. "More customers means more production, which means more workers, which means more logistical support for those workers, which means more complications...you get the idea. Quite frankly, Haven is barely able to support our current population."

"You'd be able to import what you needed to support a larger population from other worlds," Nathan countered.

"We already do, but only the essentials. Again, we like to keep things simple."

"That's fine for you and your people," Jessica interrupted, "but I wonder what the workers would say?"

Jenno looked at Jessica, then back at Nathan. "This is precisely why we have no interest in becoming part of an alliance. Too many rules."

"We have no intention on telling you how to run your world," Nathan assured him. "Only that you do not prevent your people from leaving if they don't like the way you run it."

"I doubt any of our workers like it," Jenno laughed.

"You know what I mean, Mister Motto."

"I do, but again, I must pass. However, I do wish you the best of luck in defeating the Dusahn. From what I hear, you're going to need it."

Nathan sighed as he rose from his seat. "Thank you for your time, Mister Motto. Should you change your mind, I can be reached through the Corinari."

"Yes, I heard that they had been reactivated," Jenno commented as he rose. "My men will see you safely back to your ship. The streets of Haven are not safe these days."

* * *

"That guy is a fucking idiot," Jessica declared as they exited the Haven Syndicate's headquarters. "The Dusahn will force them to do business with them, or they'll finish them off for good and just set up their own mining operation."

"We've got eyes on the Dusahn around the clock," Nathan reminded her. "If they jump a ship to Haven, we'll be there to intervene before they get a shot off."

"You're going to protect that asshole?" Jessica wondered, surprised by his statement. "After he told us to get lost?"

"He didn't tell us to get lost," Nathan insisted. "He just said he wasn't interested. We can't force membership on people."

"We also can't provide protection to people who aren't willing to be part of our alliance."

"If we come back, it won't be to protect Haven, but to prevent the Dusahn from leaving their own system. We can't let them interact with anyone, member or not. Now if someone else decides to attack Haven, they're on their own. And yes, I hope they get what they deserve."

"The people stuck on this rock don't deserve it."

Nathan sighed as they climbed into the vehicle with the escorts. "In a way, they do."

"What?" Again Jessica was surprised.

"Jenno was right when he said that most of these people are here because of their own poor decisions."

"Not all of them. You know, once they work off their debt, they have to work years more just to earn passage home. Many of them never leave. They either continue working for shit wages, or they open their own business, or farm, or whatever, and scratch out a meager existence. Do those people deserve to be unprotected?"

The vehicle sped off down the dusty road, weaving around the rubble that still littered the streets.

"I do see your point, Jessica," Nathan replied. "But we can't protect everyone. Furthermore, we can't force the government of a world to join, just like we can't dictate how our members govern their worlds."

Jessica looked at all the miserable people going about the task of rebuilding their devastated little city. "How can we turn our backs on these people?"

"If you allow yourself to feel the pain of all those who suffer in this galaxy, you will forever be in pain yourself."

Jessica turned and looked at Nathan.

"Jerson Bussard," Nathan added. "A twenty-first century French philosopher who led a revolution in his country."

"Was he successful?"

"Nope. Failed and executed," Nathan said as their vehicle bounced down the road.

"Maybe you should quote someone who wasn't executed."

"What he was trying to say is that in order to help many people, you must first accept that you cannot help everyone," Nathan explained. "We can help these people by eventually defeating the Dusahn, but we cannot do more for them than their leaders are willing to accept."

"Even if their leader is full of shit?"

"Not everyone is going to want to join our alliance," Nathan replied. "Most will have the same suspicions as Jenno: that we're going to try to tell them how to run their world."

"But we're not planning on doing so, right?"

"Right. But many alliances have claimed as much in the beginning. We are going to have to prove ourselves to people like Jenno."

"So you think he'll join later."

"No, I don't. Haven is unique because of their ring system. They can get by just fine the way they are. They'll never become anything more than a dusty shithole, but they'll be profitable, and that's all Jenno cares about. That's probably all that the people who work for him care about as well."

Jessica shook her head. "I still say Jenno's an asshole."

* * *

Udo came in to change the bandages on the pilot they had rescued. For two days, he and Kado had managed to keep the man hidden from their families by stashing him in the storage loft of their barn.

Just as they had on the first day, the man's wounds seemed to be healing remarkably well. Some of the lacerations had been all the way to the bone, yet he had bled very little, and the bones Udo could see before were now hardly visible, since the wounds had nearly closed.

After finishing, Udo opened the window to allow some fresh air into the dusty room. As he swung open the shutters, the pilot moaned. Udo spun around, his eyes wide. The man moved. Not much, but he moved.

Udo rushed to the pilot's side as the wounded man's head rolled to one side, then came back toward Udo. Finally, the pilot opened his eyes. Only a tiny bit at first, since the bright morning sunlight was more than he was ready for.

The pilot struggled to focus on the man standing before him, groaning again as the multitude of pains in his body registered in his brain.

"Lie still," Udo urged. "You were badly injured, but you are safe." Udo grabbed the bottle of water on the side table and opened it, offering it to the pilot. "Are you thirsty?"

The pilot reached out, carefully taking the bottle. He examined Udo a moment, then took a sip. "Where am I?"

"On our farm."

"You live here?" the pilot asked.

"Not here. This is a barn. But I live less than one hundred meters way."

The pilot looked around as best he could. "This is a barn?"

"It is a storage room in the loft," Udo explained.

"I apologize, but we had to hide you from our wives. They would not understand."

"We?"

"My brother Kado and I found you. I saw your ship fly past overhead and crash in the hills."

The pilot laid back, closing his eyes. "You should not have rescued me. They will be searching for me."

"They already have," Udo assured him. "But they did not find you."

"They have sensors..."

"Their sensors are confused by the cows below you," Udo explained.

"Cows?"

"Yes, cows. You know...mooo?"

"I'm not familiar with them."

"Then you cannot be from this world," Udo declared, wide-eyed.

"I'm not."

"I knew it!" Udo exclaimed, only partially to himself. "Where are you from? How did you get here? Why are you here? What kind of ship were you flying? How is it you can heal so quickly? Do you have nanites inside of you? My brother thinks you are Jung. I told him you are not. Are you Jung?"

The pilot closed his eyes again. "I am not Jung."

"Then who are you?" Udo wondered. After a moment, he said, "My apologies. You must be hungry."

"I could eat."

"I will be back shortly with food," Udo promised, turning to exit. He suddenly stopped and turned back to the wounded pilot. "I am Udo. Udo Kitakawa. What are you called?"

"Loki," the pilot replied. "Loki Sheehan."

CHAPTER THREE

Their jump flash faded in the blink of an eye. Before them, the familiar sight of Palee lay in the distance, the planet growing larger in their window with each passing second.

"Ah, Palee," Josh stated affectionately, sighing. "I've had my face slapped and my ass kicked many a time on that world." He turned to Dylan to his right, adding, "I've gotten lucky a few times, too."

"Gotten lucky?" Dylan wondered, unfamiliar with the euphemism.

Josh shook his head. "So young."

"What's that mean?"

"Just raise Palee Control on..."

A threat alert sounded.

"What the..."

"We're being targeted," Dylan said, studying the threat display.

"By Palee?" Josh exclaimed in disbelief, reaching for the shield controls on the center pedestal.

"What are you doing?"

"Raising shields," Josh replied. "Cap'n," he called over comm-sets. "We're being painted."

"Painted?"

Josh shook his head again as he increased the Voss's speed and prepared to maneuver. "I should write a guide to Earth euphemisms for newbs."

"Newbs?"

"Who's painting us?" Nathan asked as he made his way forward from the back of the command deck.

"Only got one ship on the board," Josh reported. "An old dunner barge."

"Palee doesn't have any defenses," Jessica insisted, entering on Nathan's heels.

"Pretty sure that barge doesn't either," Josh insisted.

"The targeting beam is coming from the planet," Dylan reported.

"Should I activate weapons?" Josh suggested.

"Not yet," Nathan insisted.

"Something just launched from the surface," Dylan reported. Accelerating quick... It's a missile!"

"What the..." Jessica started to say.

"I've got an escape jump dialed in, Cap'n."

"Did anyone hail them?" Nathan wondered.

"We transmitted a handshake signal the moment we came out of the jump," Josh replied.

"Did they answer?"

"Yeah! With a missile!" Dylan exclaimed. "Ninety seconds to impact!"

"Well, it's not a jump missile, or it would already be here."

"Second launch!" Dylan announced, his voice sounding more tense.

"Those missiles are slow as fuck," Josh stated.

"Can you evade?" Nathan asked.

"Can I evade," Josh replied. "What do you think?" he added as he turned toward the incoming missile.

"Not toward the planet, Josh," Nathan scolded.

"I was going to jump past them, get down low..."

"And scare the crap out of them?"

"Why not? They're scaring the crap out of Dylan, here," Josh retorted.

"They're not scaring me," Dylan insisted.

"Why the hell are they attacking us?" Jessica asked.

"We're in an unfamiliar ship, and they've probably

heard that the Dusahn have acquired additional ships."

"They think we're the Dusahn," Jessica surmised. "Shoot first, ask questions later. I'm starting to like them."

"Sixty seconds to the first missile impact," Dylan warned.

Nathan reached up for the overhead control panel between Josh and Dylan, activating the communications array and selecting all channels and frequencies. "Palee Control, this is Nathan Scott on the Karuzari ship Dalen Voss. We have no hostile intentions. Please break off your attack."

"Forty-five seconds," Dylan updated. "Are we going to do anything?"

"Drop shields," Nathan instructed.

"What?" Dylan exclaimed.

"Don't worry," Josh told Dylan as he reached for the shield controls. "I can jump us out of the way before the first one hits."

"And if they are jump missiles?" Dylan challenged.

"Then we're truly fucked," Josh replied. "Shields are down, Cap'n."

"I know what that word means," Dylan said. "Especially since you use it so often."

"Yeah, I thought you were trying to cut back on the foul language," Jessica said.

"Life is more fun with it," Josh replied.

"But you're setting a bad example for the children," Jessica teased.

"Seriously?" Dylan complained.

"Palee Control, we have lowered shields, and our weapons are offline," Nathan announced over comms. "Please abort your attack. We are here to help you defend yourselves. We can't do that very well if you blow us out of the sky."

"Sky?" Dylan wondered.

"I really gotta write that guide," Josh mumbled.

The threat board beeped another warning.

"The first missile just disarmed its warhead," Dylan reported. "It's changing course...away from us."

"And the second missile?" Nathan asked.

"Same," Dylan replied, breathing a sigh of relief. "It looks like they're turning around and heading back to the planet. Why would they do that?"

"Palee was once protected by the Palean Militia," Nathan explained. "It was basically just a branch of the Takaran defense force assigned to protect their ally. Their planetary defense missiles were designed to return to orbit if aborted, to make them easier to recover."

"Why not just jump out and recover them?" Dylan wondered.

"That was before jump drives," Josh stated.

"They probably reactivated them after the Dusahn attacked Haven," Jessica surmised. "A bold move, since the Dusahn never formally returned control of Palee back to the Paleans."

"Dalen Voss, this is Palee Defense Command. Do not activate shields or weapons, or you will be fired upon. Does your ship have remote auto-flight?"

"That's a good question," Nathan stated. "Does it?" he asked Dylan.

"That depends. What is remote auto-flight?"

"That would be a no," Nathan surmised. "Palee Defense Command, this is Nathan Scott of the Voss. Our ship does not have remote auto-flight; however, we are familiar with standard approach procedures for your world. If you will provide us with an approach clearance, we will follow it to the letter."

"Stand by."

"I'm picking up two more contacts," Dylan reported, his voice getting tense again.

Nathan looked at the threat display. "Too large to be missiles, and the trajectory is all wrong. Probably interceptors."

"To intercept us?" Dylan asked nervously.

"Probably to escort us down," Jessica stated.

"Relax, Dylan, they're just putting up a show of force, just in case."

"In case of what?" Dylan exclaimed. "Don't they know we're the good guys?"

"Times are tense in the Pentaurus sector," Nathan told him. "Nobody knows who to trust."

"Clearance data is coming through now, Cap'n," Josh reported.

"Where are they sending us?" Nathan asked.

"Porten Field, outside of Landis."

"A bit remote," Nathan decided.

"They're being real careful," Jessica stated. "They must be spooked."

"I guess we'll find out," Nathan said. "Take us in, Josh."

* * *

After a thorough inspection of their ship and a twenty-minute ride in an old surface shuttle that clearly had Palean military insignias recently slapped onto its sides, Nathan and Jessica finally found themselves in the Palean prime minister's office.

"I apologize for firing upon your vessel," Prime Minister Torman stated. "Its configuration was unfamiliar, and we have heard rumors that..."

"Apologies are unnecessary, Minister," Nathan assured him. "These are difficult times for us all."

"You are the last people we would fire upon," the prime minister insisted. "The report on the inspection of your vessel was forwarded to me during your incoming flight. It contains technologies we have never seen, the most curious of which is that it does not seem to utilize lift thrusters, or even ducted fans. How is it able to get off the ground?"

"It uses an array of anti-gravity emitters," Nathan explained. "We call it a grav-lift system. We are incorporating this technology into all of our smaller spacecraft."

"Your ship was not originally a warship."

"No, it was a light cargo ship that we adapted for our use. We are in the process of adapting eleven more."

"To use against the Dusahn?" the prime minister surmised. "They hardly seem large enough for such a task."

"They may be small, but they pack quite a punch," Nathan assured him. "However, combat is not their primary mission. We are also hoping to use them to grow our alliance."

"You are planning to build larger ships, then?"

"In time, perhaps. For now, these should suffice."

"And this alliance?" the prime minister wondered. "It will provide protection for its members?"

"Not just protection, but communication and logistical support."

"I assume there will be a cost associated with these services."

"Only to cover the operating expenses," Nathan assured him. "We seek no profit, only peace and security for all."

"And you came here to invite us?"

"I did."

The prime minister took a breath, pretending to consider the proposal. "On behalf of the people of Palee, I accept your invitation."

"Don't you want to know the terms, first?" Jessica suggested.

"Considering the circumstances, I doubt that your terms are less acceptable than those offered by the Dusahn, which we have rejected."

"A brave move," Jessica commented, "considering what happened to Haven."

"In all honesty, we rejected their offer before they attacked Haven," the prime minister admitted. "Since then, we have been scrambling to reactivate what little hardware we had left from the time when the Takarans were our allies. Unfortunately, it is woefully inadequate, as you have already seen."

"A formal charter is being developed," Nathan promised. "Meanwhile, we will set up a comm-relay station in your system. This will allow you to maintain communications with our alliance and to call for help if the Dusahn should return."

"And how quickly can you respond, should we be under attack?" the prime minister wondered.

"A few minutes at the most," Nathan assured him. "But if the Dusahn return, do not wait for them to attack before calling for help."

The prime minister smiled. "I most certainly shall not."

* * *

Marcus stood waiting at the top of the ramp as Nathan and Jessica climbed out of the shuttle and headed toward the Voss.

"That didn't take long," Josh commented as he came up behind Marcus and spotted them.

"'No' don't take long," Marcus grumbled.

"Then why are they smiling?" Josh wondered.

"We thought you'd be gone longer," Marcus said as Nathan and Jessica headed up the ramp toward them.

"It took about three minutes for Torman to say yes," Nathan replied.

"If the rest of them are this easy, we'll have the entire sector signed up in a few days," Jessica stated.

"Except for Haven," Marcus reminded her.

"Screw Haven," Jessica replied.

"Finally, something we agree on," Marcus chuckled.

"Where to, Cap'n?" Josh asked.

"No reason to let grass grow under our feet," Nathan said. "Let's see if Paradar will be as amicable."

Josh laughed. "I'll add that one to my guidebook," he decided, turning to head for the flight deck.

Marcus noticed two men unloading some crates from the shuttle to bring to the Voss. "What's that?" he asked Nathan.

"Dollag steaks," Nathan replied. "The prime minister's idea of a thank-you gift."

"Perhaps I was wrong about this world," Marcus decided.

"Wrong about what?" Jessica asked.

"Marcus thought Palee was a shithole," Nathan explained.

"Marcus thinks every world's a shithole," Jessica commented, patting the old man on the shoulder as she passed.

"She's right," Marcus admitted. "I do."

* * *

"Then you fight against the Earth?" Udo asked Loki, as he fed him another spoonful of food.

"I fight for the Earth," Loki corrected. "I fight for all people."

"How can you fight for all, if you fight any one group?"

"It's complicated," Loki told him, leaning back against the wall.

"Would you like more?"

"Not now, thank you."

Udo set the bowl down, picking up the bottle of water. "Water?"

"Later, perhaps."

After thinking a moment, Udo continued. "These Dusahn you speak of, they were once Jung?"

"Yes, long ago. They were exiled from the Jung. I don't know all the details, but apparently they wandered the galaxy for centuries, looking for worlds to conquer that would provide what they needed to build their own empire."

Udo sighed, looking down.

"Did I say something wrong?" Loki wondered.

"Men who seek more than they need often find themselves with more than they desire."

Loki looked confused. "I must have taken a blow to the head, because I don't understand that."

"It is an old adage among my people. It speaks to the evils of want. My people believe that happiness is a state of mind and not a state of possession. True happiness only comes when one stops searching for it."

"Okay."

Udo smiled. "I realize our ways are probably different than yours."

"Not as different as you might think," Loki assured him.

"You are from a place further than I can even comprehend," Udo said. "How can we not be different?"

"Do you have a family?" Loki asked.

"I do. A wife and two daughters."

"I have a daughter as well," Loki told him.

"Then why are you here, instead of caring for your daughter?" Udo wondered.

"Others care for her so that I may fight for her and for them," Loki explained. "And for you."

"By others, you mean your wife?"

"My wife was killed by the Dusahn," Loki told him.

"I am sorry." Udo thought for a moment. "Then that is why you fight?"

"Yes and no. I fight because it is the right thing to do. I fight because if we do not, people like the Dusahn, or the Jung, or the Ta'Akar, or even your Admiral Galiardi, will oppress those who cannot fight."

"But do not all such people believe they are doing what's best for their people?"

"Believing you are doing what's best for all does not automatically make it so," Loki explained.

"But someone must decide what's best for us. We are of too many differing beliefs and opinions to coexist without some sort of rule," Udo insisted.

"I'm not saying that we don't need leaders, but those leaders should not be thrust upon us against our will."

"Then you fight against tyranny," Udo concluded.

"I fight to preserve freedom."

"There are many levels of freedom," Udo insisted. "Some more important than others."

Loki closed his eyes, a slight smile on his face. "You and my leader should talk."

"Then you do follow someone."

"Yes."

"Who do you follow?"

Loki's smile broadened. "You wouldn't believe me if I told you."

* * *

"What the hell?" Marcus exclaimed, spotting Nathan and Jessica walking across the tarmac of the Paradar spaceport. "You haven't even been gone an hour."

"I guess it's easy to sell something everyone needs," Jessica bragged.

"I expect we'll get similar responses from all the worlds closest to Takara," Nathan explained.

"Where to next?" Marcus wondered.

"We're heading back to the Aurora for now," Nathan replied. "We'll visit Ursoot and Volon the day after tomorrow, once we return from SilTek."

"Why not just knock them off the list today?" Marcus questioned.

"Other responsibilities," Nathan told him as he passed. "Button her up."

"You got it."

"If it's going to be this easy, maybe you should send someone else to sign up these worlds," Jessica suggested as they exited the Voss's utility bay.

"At this stage, the Aurora and my face are what sell this alliance."

"No modesty at all, huh?" Jessica commented.

"Isn't that why you recruited me?" Nathan challenged.

"Nah, I just missed giving you a hard time," Jessica teased.

"You had Telles."

"Nowhere near as much fun, trust me," Jessica told him. "What other responsibilities?"

"Meetings, captain stuff, oh and don't forget the hand-to-hand combat training," Nathan replied.

"You're not still thinking about fighting Griogair, are you?"

"Not if I don't have to," Nathan admitted. "However, it would be best if I was prepared."

"And you think a few hours of training a couple times a week is going to do it?" she teased. "So naive."

Nathan paused, watching her pass into the common room before her. "Do you ever tire of insulting me?"

"Never!" she called back to him.

* * *

Loki woke to the sound of someone coming up the stairs but was surprised when it was not Udo who appeared once the door opened.

The man said nothing, crossing the room and setting a bowl of food on the table next to Loki's bed before going to the far side of the room and taking a seat near the window.

"Where is Udo?" Loki asked, sliding himself back to sit up against the wall.

"Eat," the man instructed.

Loki picked up the bowl. "You must be Kado," he stated. "Your brother has spoken of you." Loki took a scoop of food and put it in his mouth. "My name is Loki."

"I do not care what your name is," Kado snapped. "You will stop telling lies to my brother."

"Okay," Loki replied, perplexed.

The man rose and left the room without another word, locking the door from the outside.

Suddenly, Loki felt far from safe.

* * *

Nathan and Jessica descended the Voss's ramp, followed by Dylan, Josh, and Marcus.

"Welcome back, Captain," Del greeted.

"What do you have for us?" Nathan asked, shaking Del's hand.

"Two new P-Seventy-Twos, complete with swarm-tech loads. Not only that, but the AIs have been upgraded as promised."

"Outstanding," Nathan congratulated. "What about the vehicle we asked for?"

"Over there," Del replied, pointing to a six-wheeled, open-cockpit vehicle parked nearby.

"You're kidding," Marcus grumbled.

"That thing's ancient!" Dylan exclaimed. "Does it even run?"

"We had to do a few upgrades and repairs, but she works fine. I know she's not much to look at, but you said you wanted a wheeled vehicle. I'm afraid we didn't have much to choose from on SilTek."

"Why can't we have a flying car?" Josh wondered.

"Better to keep it simple," Nathan insisted. "Besides, I wanted something that wouldn't attract attention."

"Oh, we're gonna get attention," Marcus insisted. "We're gonna get laughed at."

"I don't know," Nathan disagreed, moving to take a closer look. "A coat of paint, some new trim, maybe a roof. It might work out just fine."

"She's got her own mini-fusion reactor and a battery backup, so you can roll out while the reactor is still spinning up. Because of that reactor, she's got pretty much unlimited range."

"Nice," Jessica agreed. "Maybe it will work."

"That thing is uglier than the Seiiki's rover," Josh commented.

"You'll need this," Del said, tossing a small object to Nathan.

"What is it?"

"A remote. Press that button, and the vehicle will come to you."

"What's the red button for?"

"Shields," Del replied, smiling.

"You put shields on a rover?" Marcus said in disbelief. "I might like this thing after all."

"This is the frosting on top," Nathan told Del, holding up the remote. "Well done."

"Thank you, sir."

Nathan looked out at the row of four XKs. "Those ours?"

"Yes, sir," Del replied. "We've managed to set up a bit of a production line. The next XK should be ready in about a week. The third one about a week after that."

"How the heck did you manage to get things moving so quickly?" Nathan wondered.

"Word got out," Del explained. "People just started showing up."

Nathan looked concerned. "How much is this going to cost us?"

"Uh, they're volunteers," Del explained. "Most of them aren't even old enough to have a job."

"Well, just make sure they don't fall behind on their homework," Nathan joked.

"Homework?" Del wondered.

"Another one for the guide," Josh decided.

Del looked at Dylan, confused.

"Long story," Dylan told him.

Del shook it off, turning back to Nathan. "I don't suppose you've picked out names for the other XKs yet, have you?"

"Not all of them," Nathan admitted. "But I know what we're going to call the next one."

* * *

Nathan sat quietly as he studied the document on his data pad. Despite his objections during their previous meeting, the second draft seemed even longer and more complex than the first. "I thought you were going to simplify this document?"

"I did," Caitrin insisted.

"I'm not seeing it."

"Well, for starters, I rewrote much of it so that it's more a statement of the basic tenants of this alliance, rather than the actual rules that will govern it."

"I thought you were the one insisting that we need rules," Nathan questioned.

"We do, and there will be," she insisted as she poured herself another glass of juice. "You sure you don't want to try this?"

"I'm good," Nathan replied, continuing his examination of the document with a scowl on his face.

"What's wrong?"

Nathan sighed. "It's not that there's anything wrong with the document. I mean, I agree with the tenets, but it just feels like we're trying to push our own beliefs onto others."

"You're misinterpreting the words," Caitrin insisted. "The document clearly states that we will not interfere with the rights of member states to self-govern."

"Provided certain conditions are adhered to," Nathan countered.

"If we can't agree on basic things like human rights, equality, fair trade, freedom of speech, rights of ownership, due process for the peaceful resolution of disputes...how are we going to operate? What common ground are we going to build upon?"

Nathan paused, collecting his thoughts a moment. "I've been thinking about this a lot lately, and the only thing I can come up with that is universally accepted is freedom. But I'm not talking about individual freedoms as much as I'm talking about collective freedoms. You see, throughout history, humans have not been free to move into whatever community best fits their beliefs. Distance, finances, national boundaries; all of these made relocation difficult, often impossible. We have been forced to live among those of differing beliefs, even if we didn't wish to, thus requiring a myriad of compromises for the good of the community. This is why utopia is unachievable for the whole but possible for the few. Unfortunately, this too requires at least one compromise. In order to be free, we must allow others to be free as well, even if we find their ways unacceptable."

"Yet you are still setting forth some rules," Caitrin said.

"Yes, but only for the sake of working together for a common purpose, that purpose being the security of all member states."

"States being?"

"Any organized collective seeking to join our alliance. A nation, a world, a system, a collection of systems, or any combination thereof."

"And if there is more than one collective on the same world?"

"Those who want to join can do so," Nathan replied. "Those who do not, will not."

"How do you provide protection to one nation on a world but not others?"

"It is problematic, I admit. However, I doubt that particular situation will be very common. Most of the worlds I have visited have small populations, usually located in the same general area. Those who are global generally have either a global government or at least a structure to provide diplomatic relations between nation-states. But again, these are matters that can be debated later by the members and added to the charter in the form of amendments."

"Wouldn't it be better to be prepared for as many eventualities as possible from the start?" Caitrin suggested.

"The more rules we have, the more reasons prospective members will have to fear joining. Haven has already rejected the idea, without even knowing what the rules would be, and they were just recently attacked by the Dusahn. If we're going to grow this alliance quickly, we need to make it as simple and uncomplicated as possible. Plus, the more that the members are involved in the evolution of the governing document, the happier they will all be. Ideally, we would love to invite representatives from every inhabited world to provide input, member or not, but that isn't feasible."

Caitrin shook her head in dismay. "What you are proposing is going to be very complicated."

"We're talking about connecting all the lost colonies of Earth, Caitrin," Nathan replied. "Complicated is the only thing it can be. That's why we have to start with as few rules as possible and create the other rules as they become necessary."

Caitrin sighed. "Well, we're going to at least need a document that binds the founding members until a formal charter can be developed. This will need to include funding to get us through to ratification."

"Agreed."

"So again, you want us to stick to the rule of fives," she surmised.

"Five rights, five rules, five requirements, and five protections...for both the members and the alliance," Nathan confirmed. "That's all we need to get started."

Caitrin sighed again, picking up her glass of juice. "I may need a raise before long."

* * *

Nathan made his way through the Aurora's main lower deck, on his way to the Ghatazhak's makeshift training room.

"Nathan!" Vladimir called from behind, jogging to catch up. "When did you get back?"

"A couple of hours ago," Nathan replied as they continued down the corridor together.

"Is the Voss completed?"

"Fully," Nathan replied. "Three more turrets added and two new P-Seventy-Twos with swarm tech."

"Very nice. What about her range?"

"Sol in two jumps with a single four-hour layover," Nathan replied. "And get this; they've set up a sort of production line. They should be able to put out an upgraded XK every week; ten days max."

"That is very good news," Vladimir agreed. "But not as good as my news."

Nathan looked at him with suspicion. "Do I want to know?"

"The Aurora now has a two-thousand-light-year, one-minute jump range," Vladimir boasted. "And she will still have plenty of jump energy left for combat."

"Now that is good news," Nathan agreed. "Well done."

"It would have taken twice as long without the SilTek engineering droids," Vladimir admitted. "Can we keep a handful aboard, just in case?"

"I'll see what I can work out."

"Want to get lunch?" Vladimir asked.

"I can't," Nathan replied. "I have to go get my ass kicked."

"Can I watch?" Vladimir wondered.

"No thanks," Nathan insisted. "It's embarrassing enough as it is."

"They are Ghatazhak, Nathan. They can kick everyone's ass."

"Don't you have something to fix?" Nathan wondered.

"Actually, no...for once."

"Perhaps you should take advantage of this rare moment and take a few hours off."

"I'm not sure I remember how," Vladimir replied.

"Maybe you can start by eating some of those dollag steaks we brought back from Palee," Nathan suggested. "There are about a dozen of them in the cold pantry in the captain's mess."

"That I can do," Vladimir assured him. "Good luck getting your ass kicked."

"Thanks," Nathan replied, turning to enter the Ghatazhak training room.

Once inside, Nathan found General Telles, Jessica, Sergeant Vasya, and Specialist Brill, all waiting for him.

"I'm not fighting all of you, am I?" Nathan wondered.

"Actually, you're not fighting anyone today," General Telles explained. "I believe we've humiliated you enough as of late. I thought it might be more productive to have you watch Vasya and Brill spar, and then we can teach you some of their moves, using Nash as your sparring partner."

"So I'm not getting my ass kicked today?"

"Not today," General Telles confirmed. "Unless that is what you prefer."

"No, no," Nathan was quick to reply. "Whatever you think is best," he added, stepping into place next to Jessica.

"You're such a wuss," she whispered, smiling.

"Yes, but I'll be a wuss who isn't sore tonight."

* * *

Loki had spent three days in the small storeroom in the barn loft, the last two of which he had been a prisoner, with the door locked from the outside. There was a window, but he was fairly high above the ground. In his current state, he wasn't certain that he could land without breaking something. Considering he had no nanite booster shots available, he felt it best to give the existing nanites currently circulating in his system more time to work.

He had not seen Udo since the evening of the first day, when they had talked at length. Since then, Kado had been the one to bring his meals. Other than the few words when they first met, Kado had said nothing.

Eventually, Loki was going to have to find a way to escape. He had no idea what the brothers had planned for him. At first, he feared they would turn him over to the EDF, which would seal his fate. However, had they planned on doing so, he would probably already be in EDF custody. They were keeping him alive for a reason; he just didn't know why. Had it just been Udo, Loki would feel far more comfortable. The man was incredibly curious and had seemed genuinely concerned for Loki's wellbeing. Kado, on the other hand, was a different story.

The best that Loki could hope for was that the brothers would remain undecided long enough for Loki to heal. The barn was old and appeared not to have been very well built to begin with. Loki was fairly certain that he could break out if he put his mind to it. He just needed to wait until he could safely put his body into it as well.

Loki heard the downstairs door close, followed by footfalls ascending the stairs. Kado was on his way, which concerned Loki. It was too early for his evening meal, which usually came well after sundown. The sun had not yet dipped behind the nearby mountains.

The worst flashed through Loki's mind. He listened more carefully, trying to discern the number of footfalls. Rhythmic; constant; definitely a single person. Yet there was something different about them. They were quicker, as if the person was more rushed than usual.

The footfalls stopped, and the door swung open, revealing Udo, a worried look on his face. "Oh thank goodness," Udo exclaimed, a sigh of relief washing over him. "I feared for your wellbeing."

"Why?" Loki wondered.

"Kado would not let me bring you food. He did not want me speaking with you."

"Yes, he told me as much."

"He is distrustful, suspicious of everyone and everything," Udo explained, moving to the window and carefully peeking out. "Has he been feeding you?"

"Yes, twice a day," Loki assured him.

"How do you feel?"

"Better but still weak."

"Are you well enough to travel?"

"To where?" Loki wondered, becoming concerned.

"There is a man I know in the city. He knows people. People with connections."

"Connections to what?" Loki asked.

"Not what," Udo corrected, "who." He looked out the window again, lowering his voice. "Insurgents."

"I don't know if I can walk very far," Loki warned. "Maybe in a few days..."

"No, no, no," Udo interrupted. "We must go now. There is no time."

"Why?" Loki wondered, becoming even more concerned.

"Kado wants to turn you and the wreckage of your ship over to the EDF," Udo explained.

"You recovered my ship?"

"Yes. We thought you were a downed satellite or a drone. We thought there might be some technology we could use or sell. We did not expect to find you."

"Why does Kado want to turn me over to the EDF?" Loki asked.

"He believes there will be a reward."

"That would be a huge mistake," Loki warned.

"That's what I said!" Udo exclaimed. "Wait, why do you think it would be a mistake?"

"I know things," Loki explained. "Things that Admiral Galiardi does not want the people of Earth to know."

"What kind of things?" Udo wondered.

"It's better that you do not know, trust me."

Udo thought for a moment. "I trust you," he decided. "But we must go, before Kado returns."

"Where is Kado?" Loki asked.

"He has taken his wife to visit her parents. He will return in a few hours."

"Maybe we can talk to him, convince him that..."

"You don't know Kado," Udo insisted. "It was all I could do to get him to wait until you were more fully recovered. But he fears that if we wait too long, the EDF will charge us with a crime."

"But won't Kado be angry when he gets home?"

Udo looked at him, a little embarrassed. "Is there any technology in your wreckage that is of value? Something we do not have on Earth?"

"Actually, there is," Loki admitted reluctantly.

"Then the insurgents will offer payment, and we will not run the risk of arrest for failing to contact the EDF from the start. Kado will be hard-pressed to argue if I am waving credit chips in front of his face."

Loki sat up, swinging his legs over the edge of the bed, wincing at the pain as he moved. He then stood up slowly and painfully. "Then I guess we'd better get going."

* * *

No one considered Lysan Proth a candidate to command a Dusahn warship, not even a small one. Like so many others who served the empire, only his father was of Dusahn blood. His mother had been Andonesian; thus, his features had always demonstrated that he was not of pure descent. In the Dusahn Empire, only those of pure bloodlines held command positions.

But that percentage had been shrinking for more than a century. While Dusahn ships were all commanded by pure-blooded Dusahn officers, there were many whose lineages were less than stellar commanding ground and support units. Few of them commanded actual combat units, but there were some. The fact was, Lord Dusahn did not fully trust those who were not pure of blood.

Many wondered if that would change after Lieutenant Jexx was suddenly thrust into the spotlight, becoming their leader's most trusted advisor and jumping to the rank of commander in the blink of an eye. Jexx's mother was from Truuna, and there were even fewer Truunian-Dusahn serving in uniform, let alone as officers. The Truunians were devout pacifists, which had made them easy prey for the empire. Only a few hundred of the male children with Truunian mothers wore the uniform of the empire, and nearly a third had deserted when the Dusahn abandoned Truuna. Because of this, those Truunian-Dusahn still serving were even more suspect. Pure-blooded officers believed that the Truunian-Dusahn who remained only did so because they had no means of returning to their home world. The bias against mixed-blood members of the empire had only grown worse.

Yet here he was, sitting in the captain's chair, commanding the newly christened Bor-Quarum, the first of the recently acquired gunships to have their upgrades completed and to be put into service for the Dusahn Empire.

Lysan's father would have been proud. His mother, not so much. Either way, Lysan didn't care. He was in command of a crew of twenty-six, all of whom were also of mixed blood. The fact that their commanding officer shared their stigma was a source of great pride to his crew, making them loyal to their commander before he had even proven himself.

Lysan had indeed been surprised when Commander Jexx himself had given Lysan the news of his command. Even more surprising had been his first assignment, the escort of a Dusahn freighter on its first trip to Volon since the world had been abandoned only months after annexation by the empire. A successful transaction and the safe return of the freighter would silence many pure-blooded nay-sayers still doubting Captain Proth's character and abilities. It would also open the door for other mixed-lineage officers still mired in positions of limited responsibility, where distinction was hopeless.

"Jump complete, Captain," the Bor-Quarum's helmsman reported.

"Position?" Captain Proth asked.

The sensor officer studied his displays a moment. "One million kilometers from Volon."

"Confirm course and speed."

"On course for orbital insertion. Insertion deceleration burn in five minutes."

Lysan turned his head slightly, calling to his second-in-command sitting at the tactical station to his right. "Assessment, Commander?"

"No contacts, no threats," the commander replied.

"Mister Ostro, send a comm-drone back to the Oro-Bowona. Let them know it is safe to join us."

"Message loaded; launching comm-drone," the communications officer confirmed.

"Comm-drone has jumped," Lieutenant Gartell reported from the sensor station.

"Hail the Volon Ministry," Lysan ordered.

"Aye, sir," Ensign Ostro acknowledged.

Lysan took a deep breath, preparing for his first official transmission as the captain of the Bor-Quarum.

"I have Chancellor Burland on comms," Ensign Ostro announced.

"Oro-Bowona has just jumped in behind us, Captain," the sensor officer reported.

Lysan pressed the comm-button on the small operations pedestal next to his command chair, activating his connection to the call. "This is Captain Proth of the Dusahn warship Bor-Quarum. We will be in orbit over Volon in four minutes. We look forward to a smooth and equitable transaction, paving the way for a peaceful relationship with your world."

"Nicely phrased," Commander Lobey stated, quietly enough so the Volonese chancellor would not hear.

"We welcome you to Volon, Captain," Chancellor Burland replied over comms. "We also wish for a peaceful relationship with your people. However, we cannot in good conscience provide support for the Dusahn Empire, no matter how lucrative they may be. We hope you understand."

Captain Proth felt his mood change, his father's genes kicking in. "I understand completely," he replied. "Unfortunately, I fear that you do not." He took a breath before continuing, hoping the words that followed would sound honest and considered. "Conflict can be easily avoided, Chancellor. All that is required of you is to choose to avoid it."

"The people of Volon are prepared to suffer the consequences of our decision," the chancellor assured him. "We hope that you are similarly prepared."

After another pause, Captain Proth replied, "I admire your conviction, sir. Good luck to you all."

Commander Lobey looked at his captain as his commanding officer ended the communication. "Good luck?"

"It seemed a reasonable response."

"I'm not sure Lord Dusahn would agree," the commander stated.

"He will agree with what comes next," Captain Proth assured his second-in-command. "Arm all weapons and prepare to attack. Primary targets will be infrastructure only. Hopefully they will change their minds before we are forced to destroy their entire society."

"Should we not notify command of their refusal?" Commander Lobey questioned.

"The Volonese are completely unarmed," Lysan explained, "and our standing orders are quite clear on the matter." Lysan took a deep breath. "This shall be the Bor-Quarum's first victory."

* * *

Loki sat in the corner of the dimly lit restaurant, picking at his meal while keeping his eye on Udo at the bar. It had taken half an hour for Udo to load Loki's wreckage back onto his truck, and another twenty minutes to reach town. If Udo was to get back home before his brother returned, he would need to leave as soon as possible.

Although the journey into town was not long, it had been a difficult one for Loki. The constant bouncing of the old truck had caused him great pain. He nearly lost consciousness more than once. But the time spent sitting and eating was helping. Loki was still weak, but the food was far better than what he had been eating the last few days.

A pleasant young woman came up to his table, adorned with an apron and carrying a small shot glass full of a light brown liquid. "An after-dinner drink, sir?" she offered.

"Uh..." Loki was unsure and looked toward Udo.

"Compliments of the house," she insisted.

"Okay," Loki replied.

The woman set the glass down on a napkin in front of him. "Shall I take your plate?"

"Yes, thank you."

The woman took his plate and departed, leaving him with his drink.

Loki raised the glass to his lips and paused. The smell was not what he expected; fruity and sweet. He took a sip, found it pleasing, then downed the rest in a single gulp.

In the distance, a man handed Udo a small object, nodding at him. Udo bowed his head politely, then headed back to rejoin Loki.

"Is everything alright?" Loki wondered.

"He has agreed to take you to meet with one of the insurgent cells. He has also paid us handsomely for the wreckage of your ship."

Loki looked disturbed.

"What is wrong?" Udo wondered.

"You are certain these insurgents are against Galiardi?"

"Quite certain," Udo assured him.

"I'm not sure giving them the wreckage was the right decision."

"Would it not be worse if it fell into the hands of the EDF?" Udo wondered.

"I suppose you're right," Loki admitted.

Udo sighed as the man he had been speaking with at the bar approached. "I'm afraid this is the end of our time together. I have enjoyed our conversations, and I hope you are able to find your way back to your daughter."

"Thank you for all your help, Udo," Loki replied. "And do not let your brother too heavily influence your outlook on life. That is yours, and yours alone."

Udo smiled. "Kado has less influence on me than he would like." Udo turned to introduce the man from the bar as he stepped up to their table. "Loki, this is Atushi. He will handle your transportation from this point."

"A pleasure," Loki greeted, bowing his head politely.

"Good luck to you, Loki," Udo said as he rose. He bowed politely, then turned and departed briskly.

Once Udo had exited, the waitress locked the front door and closed the curtains before disappearing into the kitchen.

"When do we leave?" Loki asked becoming uneasy.

"That depends," Atushi replied. "Do you feel sleepy?"

"Actually, I do," Loki admitted.

"Then soon," the man replied.

Loki suddenly felt dizzy, and his vision blurred. "Something is wrong."

"Just go to sleep," the man urged.

Loki's vision faded quickly to black, and he felt as if he were falling.

* * *

"This ship may not be much to look at, but it does have some teeth," Kit commented as he, Mori, and Jokay walked around the side of the Voss, examining the new gun turret installed on the outer edge of its port nacelle.

"How many guns did they add?" Jokay asked.

"Three," Mori replied. "Port, starboard, and one in the nose."

"How'd they put one in the nose?" Jokay wondered. "I thought there was a docking apparatus in there."

"They moved that to the port dorsal airlock."

"No dead zones in this ship's field of fire," Kit insisted.

"Ready to go, boys?" Jessica asked as she approached.

"Where are we headed?" Kit asked.

"Volon, then Ursoot," Jessica replied. "Both should be easy runs."

"Then why are we coming along?" Mori wondered.

"More guns, more hands," Jessica declared as she headed up the ramp. "Besides, we're going to stop off at a rogue asteroid group between Volon and Ursoot to test out the new guns."

"You mean they haven't been test-fired yet?" Jokay realized.

"Nope, we get the honor. Time to go to work," she added before disappearing into the Voss's utility bay.

"This should be fun," Kit groaned.

Jessica moved through the octagonal center compartment in the middle of the Voss's lateral corridor, then into the common room in between the port and starboard Lightning bays. "You get a working charter yet?" she asked Nathan, who was studying something on his data pad at the table in the center of the common area.

"Still in the works," Nathan replied. "But getting closer."

"Sooner or later we're going to need something for these people to sign."

"She'll get it pounded out in time," Nathan assured her. "It's not that complicated."

"Then why is it taking her so long?" Jessica wondered as she opened the fridge to get a bottle of water.

"Caitrin is still thinking like a businessperson."

"Maybe she wasn't the right person for the job," Jessica suggested, taking a long drink afterward.

"She'll get it trimmed down," Nathan assured her.

"Hey, when do we get to learn to fly the P-Seventy-Twos?" Kit asked as he and the others entered the common room.

"You guys want to fly?"

"We already know how to fly," Kit assured him.

"It was one of the new training requirements that Telles instituted back on Burgess," Jessica explained. "He was planning on building a full sim so we could keep up our skills, but then the Dusahn attacked."

"I guess there's no reason you can't," Nathan agreed. "If we're going to have a Ghatazhak squad on every XK, it would make sense to have backup pilots for both the Lightnings and the XKs. I'll see about getting VRs for them from Del."

"It would give us something to do during those boring diplomatic missions," Kit agreed.

"Cap'n?" Josh called over the overhead speaker.

Nathan instinctively tilted his head up. "Yes?"

"We're ready here."

"We're still waiting for Marcus and Vlad to finish recalibrating a few of the starboard emitters," Nathan replied. "Sit tight. They should be done in a few minutes."

"Got it," Josh acknowledged.

"That means we have time to check our gear," Kit decided.

"What gear?" Nathan wondered.

"Our mark two armor."

"You brought your battle armor?"

"Never leave home without it," Kit replied on their way out.

Nathan looked at Jessica. "What about you?"

"I don't have any yet," Jessica replied.

"Shouldn't you?" Nathan wondered. "I mean, you're the spec-ops lead on this ship, and those are your men."

"I doubt very seriously we're going to need it on this mission," Jessica replied. "Besides, I have my original mark one gear. And honestly, I prefer handheld weapons to built-in blasters. If they fail, you just pick up someone else's. There's usually plenty of them lying around."

"That's disturbing," Nathan decided. "Logical but disturbing. Why don't they feel the same way?"

"Boys and their toys," Jessica shrugged. "What you have to remember is that, at heart, the Ghatazhak are more like marines than spec-ops. They're more about rapid victory through intelligence and overwhelming force."

"Like a bull in a china shop?"

"More like a bull that can charge through a china shop only breaking the pieces they don't like. Spec-ops, while having similar training, use more of a gray man approach."

"Blending into the crowd," Nathan realized.

"That's right," Jessica replied, impressed.

"Hey, I had covert ops basics at the academy as well. Although I admit I don't remember much of it."

"But you remember gray man?"

"Only because the idea of not being noticed appealed to me at the time."

"Because of your family," Jessica surmised.

"Ironic, isn't it? I spent most of my life avoiding being a 'Scott'. Now it may be the only way to save Earth and possibly half the galaxy."

"You can't hide from who you are," Jessica stated.

Nathan looked at her. "Who am I?"

"You're exactly who you are supposed to be," she told him. "You're just like your father. You're the one who always does what he thinks is right. That's why you're a good leader. We can count on you not to follow your own interests at the expense of those who follow you. That quality is rare. It always has been."

"You know, there was a time when I found that attribute to be a curse."

"I remember," Jessica replied. "You were insufferable. I wanted to slap you most days."

"Well, thank you for not doing so."

"Don't mention it," she laughed. "But if you ever get that way again, I can't make any promises."

"I'll keep that in mind," Nathan promised.

CHAPTER FOUR

Nathan made his way through the short corridor connecting the Voss's common room to her command deck. "Time to go, gentlemen," he said as he crossed the length of the command deck toward the cockpit at its forward end.

"They all done?" Josh inquired from the pilot's seat.

"They're buttoning up now," Nathan assured him.

"Utility bay hatch is cycling closed," Dylan reported from the copilot's seat.

"Volon awaits," Nathan stated as he reached the cockpit area and took his usual position, leaning against the railing along the forward edge of the down ladder behind and between the pilots' seats.

"Port and starboard reactors are hot," Dylan reported as he and Josh turned back around to face their consoles.

"Flight Control, Voss," Josh called over comms. "Ready for departure."

"Voss, Flight. Clear to depart to port. Open vector. Safe flight."

"Voss, departing to port, open vector," Josh replied. He punched in their departure parameters and then activated the auto-flight systems.

Nathan's brows furrowed. "Did you just engage auto-flight?" he asked. "Without any fuss?"

"I'm trying to be more like Loki," Josh replied, a melancholy note in his voice.

Nathan remained silent, not sure how to respond.

"Don't worry," Josh assured him as the ship began to slowly rise. "It won't last."

"What won't last?" Jessica wondered, having just

come up the stair ladder behind Nathan from the deck below.

"Nothing," Nathan replied. "Your guys all ship-shape?"

"They're in the back, arguing over who gets which gun turret," Jessica replied.

"Clear of the pressure shields," Dylan reported.

Nathan continued gazing out the forward cockpit windows as the Aurora's aft propulsion section began to slide downward as the Voss climbed. Just as they reached the bottom edge of the windows, the Voss began her departure rotation, the stars moving from right to left.

Josh punched in a few more commands, setting their destination so the auto-flight AI could calculate their jump to Volon. "Destination set. Jump in two minutes."

The ship's main propulsion began to kick in. Although the Voss had inertial dampeners, like most ships, it allowed for a bit more of the sensation of flight to be felt by its occupants. Nathan found he actually preferred it that way, since it made the experience more like atmospheric flight. It made everything far more intuitive.

Nathan remembered the long summer days he had spent with his grandfather, learning to fly his aerobat. His grandfather had been a proponent of flying without instruments. Nathan's initial flight training with his grandfather had been with all the flight instruments covered from view. It was not until Nathan could safely fly without those instruments that his grandfather allowed him to fly with them. Nathan firmly believed that his natural flight instincts came from that initial training.

In spaceships, especially those with fully

buffering inertial dampening systems, the only way you knew what your ship was doing was with your flight dynamics displays. Fortunately, the Voss's dampeners were less powerful. As part of their ZPED upgrades, the SilTek engineers had offered to upgrade their dampeners to be fully buffering, but Nathan had declined. This decision baffled Dylan but had delighted Josh. The fact that Josh was such an instinctive pilot was probably why Nathan had so much trust in him.

"Want one?" Jessica asked.

Nathan glanced over at her, noticing the small purple fruit in her hand. "What is it?"

"Tolee. It's really popular on Corinair. I'm surprised you don't know about it, or should I say, that Connor didn't know about it."

"Marcus always steered me away from the cluster, for obvious reasons I suppose. Where'd you get them?" he wondered. "I don't remember seeing them in the mess."

"Cam has a private stash."

"Figures."

"Are you sure you don't want one? They're really good."

"Maybe later," Nathan replied, patting his stomach. "Big breakfast."

"Suit yourself," she said, taking a seat at the starboard auxiliary console just behind Dylan and throwing her feet up on the narrow desk in front of it.

"On course and speed for the jump," Dylan announced. "One minute, and we'll be approaching Volon."

Volon. Every time he heard the name, he couldn't help but think of Naralena, just as every time he saw Dylan sitting in the copilot's seat, he thought of Loki. Losing people under his command was tough. Losing friends was tougher. But Loki and Naralena had both been family. He felt their loss as deeply as those of his biological family. So much pain. So much loss. At times, it was overwhelming. His only defense seemed to be the knowledge that he was not alone in his suffering. Everyone had lost someone. It was a pain that bound them all together in their fight. The key was to prevent that pain from destroying all hope in one's soul.

"Twenty seconds," Dylan reported nonchalantly.

Nathan noticed a hatch indicator light on the overhead console. He reached up and touched the intercom panel above him. "Who's in the port nacelle?" he asked over the intercom. "We're about to jump."

"Eta ya," Vladimir replied over the intercom. "I need to monitor the jump field regulators during the jump, to make sure we calibrated them correctly."

"Wouldn't it be safer to do so from up here?" Nathan suggested.

"This compartment is completely shielded," Vladimir replied. "I will be fine."

"Five seconds," Dylan updated.

"Very well," Nathan replied, switching off the intercom.

"Jumping in five..."

Again Nathan was reminded of Loki, who had always counted off the last few seconds leading into a jump, much to the annoyance of Josh. Nathan wondered if Loki had done so out of a sense of procedure or just to irritate his friend.

"Four..."

"If we have time, I'd like to visit the bazaars on Volon," Jessica stated.

"Three..."

"Ania needs more clothes," she continued.

"Two..."

"That kid suddenly started growing like a weed."

"One..."

"That might be a nice diversion," Nathan admitted.

"Jumping."

The jump flash washed over the ship, spilling through the cockpit windows and illuminating the interior for a brief moment. Out of habit, all four of them closed their eyes, as the Voss had yet to be equipped with flash-dampening filters.

It was then that Nathan suddenly realized why Loki counted down the last few seconds before a jump. He probably continued the unnecessary practice just to annoy Josh. It was a constant game which the two of them played, one that Nathan found himself sorely missing.

"Jump complete," Dylan reported as the jump flash dissipated. "Volon, dead ah..."

"What is it?" Nathan wondered, alerted by Dylan's failure to complete his sentence. Nathan instinctively looked out the forward windows. Ahead was the planet Volon, growing closer each second. But there was something else: a small object. There was also a series of white flashes on the surface of the planet. "What the..."

"Someone is attacking Volon!" Dylan exclaimed.

Jessica dropped her tolee fruit onto the console desk, jumping back to her feet and moving closer to Nathan to get a better look.

"Who?" Nathan demanded.

Jessica quickly activated the intercom over

Nathan's head, switching it to ship-wide. "Battle stations!" she called over the intercom, her voice echoing through the ship's internal speakers.

"Battle stations!" Jessica called over the intercom speakers. "All hands to battle stations! This is not a drill!"

"What the..." Mori exclaimed, caught by surprise.

"Did we settle on who goes where?" Jokay wondered.

"I'm already in the port nacelle, so I'll take the port gun!" Vladimir announced over the intercom.

"I thought I was going to take the port gun," Mori said as he quickly put his gear down and headed for the exit with the others.

"Marcus takes starboard, Mori to dorsal, Jokay to ventral," Jessica instructed.

"What about me?" Kit asked back.

"You take the tail gun," Jessica instructed. "I'll take the nose. But suit up first, Kit. That pressure shield hasn't been tested under fire!"

"Looks like Kit drew the short straw!" Jokay laughed as he and Mori ran out through the forward hatch, headed for their respective gun turrets.

"Funny," Kit replied, stepping up to his mark two locker. He pressed the activation button on the front of the locker and turned around, placing his feet on the pad in front of the locker, shoulder-width apart, arms slightly spread. His mark two deployment system sensed that he was in position, and the doors swung open, retracting into the sides of the locker. The system began encapsulating him in the components of his armor, starting at his feet and working its way up, one section at a time.

"I've got a second contact," Dylan announced. "A cargo ship."

"Weapons?" Nathan asked.

"None," Dylan replied. "Not even shields. I'm running both contacts through the database now," Dylan reported.

"Whoever it is, they're painting us," Josh warned.

"Our shields are up, right?" Nathan asked.

"They snapped on the moment Jess called battle stations," Josh confirmed. "Dylan programmed the AI to raise shields automatically if it hears the words 'battle stations' or 'general quarters'."

"Good thinking, but you might want to check with me before you program the AI to do anything like that automatically," Nathan scolded.

"I thought it would save time and keep us safer," Dylan defended.

"Or send the wrong message to another ship," Nathan retorted.

"Sorry, sir," Dylan apologized. "I'll remove those lines of code."

"Better charge all weapons, just in case," Nathan stated.

"You're not worried about looking like you're sending the wrong message?" Josh joked.

"Just shut up and arm all weapons," Nathan chided.

Vladimir ducked under the outboard coolant

ducts, stepping over the stack of conduits running along the floor of the port nacelle's engineering compartment. On the other side was the hatch leading to the port gun turret. He slapped the door activation button on the wall, and the hatch slid open, revealing the clear turret canopy on the other side.

Stepping up to the entrance, he leaned in, immediately feeling the lack of gravity inside the cramped compartment. He reached over and grabbed the rail under the top edge of the canopy, leaning in further so that the artificial gravity created by the ship's deck plates would lose their pull on him, making his torso weightless. It was sort of a 'falling-over' motion to make the transition, only he didn't actually tip over. Instead, he used the rail to pull himself through the hatch and into the gunner's chair, twisting and contorting his large frame to wiggle into place.

"These things were not designed for larger men," Vladimir complained.

"I managed just fine," Marcus remarked over the intercom. "Starboard gun, ready."

"Dorsal gun, ready," Mori reported.

Vladimir finally managed to get into the seat, quickly fastening his restraints and activating his gun turret. "Port gun, ready!"

The ventral gun turret along the underside of the ship was even more difficult to get into, as it required the operator to turn completely upside down; a maneuver the cramped turret was not well suited for. Jokay had found that the easiest method was to do a handstand over the hatch with his feet along the vertical ladder, then pull his hands in and let the artificial gravity pull him through the opening, his momentum carrying him all the way into the turret bubble, his body already in proper orientation. From there, it was just a matter of sliding into the seat and strapping in.

"Ventral gun, ready," he reported as he charged his gun turret.

The last piece to go on was Kit's helmet. Once in place, the locker doors shut.

Kit's visor closed, sealing him up inside. The visor's internal displays lit up, situational and systems data appearing around its outer edges.

Kit stepped off the pad. He loved the sensation of movement in the mark two system. Unlike the assistive bodysuit of the mark one system, which was constantly squeezing at his body, the mark two system used servos and miniature hydraulics, along with weak anti-gravity emitters, to help the wearer move and give him additional strength. The mark one systems made him feel invincible, but the mark two made him feel like he could do anything.

Kit walked up to the left side of the rear cargo door, slapping the open button with his armored hand. The ship's AI sensed the presence of a vacuum outside and automatically activated the pressure shield over the perimeter of the hatch opening, its emitter glowing a pale blue.

Kit stepped back a few meters as the massive door began to fold down, and the pressure shield reached full power, shimmering a pale, nearly transparent blue. He walked backward several more steps, then reached up and grabbed the strap hanging from the large, double-barreled weapon that was stored up against the ceiling of the utility bay. He pulled down, dragging the weapon out of its folded-up position as the hatch continued to lower.

Once deployed, the weapon automatically activated and spun ninety degrees to face aft. At the same time, the overhead track lowered just enough to clear the top of the massive hatchway opening, then protruded outward two meters.

The ramp deployed to the point of being level with the interior deck, then stopped. Kit grabbed the weapon's handles and slid it aft, just far enough so that the business ends of the weapon's two barrels were protruding beyond the pressure shield.

Finally, Kit powered up the plasma generators of his weapon, lighting up the targeting display in the process. "Tail gun, ready."

"I am unable to identify the contact's origin," Lieutenant Gartell reported from the Bor-Quarum's sensor station.

"Armaments?" Captain Proth inquired.

"Multiple plasma turrets, missile tubes, plasma torpedo cannons, and point-defenses," the second officer reported from the tactical station.

"Shields?"

"They came on seconds after they jumped in," the sensor officer replied.

"Then they have detected us," Commander Lobey opined. "Shall I retarget some of our weapons from the surface to the new contact?"

"Not yet," Captain Proth instructed. "We do not know the identity of this vessel."

"They are heavily armed and are on an intercept course with shields raised," the commander reminded him. "That is all we need to know."

"Are we outgunned?" the captain asked.

"No, sir; we have the advantage, but not by much," the commander explained. "However, we do not know their shield strength, nor the range and capabilities of their missiles."

"Captain, the contact doesn't look like a warship," the sensor officer reported. "I think she's a converted cargo ship, like us."

"The Volonese may have contracted help from others," Commander Lobey suggested. "Perhaps from someone outside the Pentaurus sector; someone we are not aware of."

"That is a possibility," the captain agreed. "Are they still on an intercept course?"

"Yes, sir," the commander replied. "Best guess is that they will be in range and able to attack in approximately five minutes."

Captain Proth rose from his command chair, walking over to stand behind the sensor officer and look at the readings for himself. "Very suspicious, the timing of this unknown yet well-armed vessel."

"Captain, I recommend we establish a targeting lock on the unidentified vessel. If they do intend to attack, we need to be ready."

"Agreed," Captain Proth replied. "But do not turn any weapon toward the target, yet. If they are not here to interdict, then I do not wish to create another enemy of the Dusahn; not on our first engagement. We have more than enough enemies to deal with at the moment."

"Captain..." the commander began to object.

"You have your orders, Commander Lobey," the captain snapped.

"Yes, sir," the commander replied respectfully. "Targeting unidentified vessel."

"I'm not getting anything in the ship's database on the armed ship," Dylan reported. "However, the cargo ship appears to be an old Galean cargo ship." Dylan turned to look at his captain. "Who are the Galean?"

"Not who; what," Josh replied. "It's a company on Paradar that builds really crappy light freighters."

"Does that database include all the ships from the Aurora's database?" Nathan wondered.

"Yes, sir," Dylan confirmed. "I did the merge myself."

"Show me the scans of the armed ship," Jessica instructed.

"Putting them up on the overhead display," Dylan replied.

"What do you want me to do, Cap'n?" Josh wondered. "We're on an intercept course, and we're probably already in their weapons range."

"Are the two ships traveling together?" Nathan wondered.

"They're both on the same heading and relatively close together," Dylan informed him.

Jessica looked at the overhead display, studying the sensor readings. "Can you extrapolate a profile based on this?"

"Give me a second," Dylan replied.

"Hold course for now," Nathan instructed Josh.

"You got it."

The overhead display refreshed, and a line-drawing representing a profile view of the ship appeared.

"That's a Dusahn ship," Jessica realized.

"Are you sure?" Nathan asked.

"It's one of the six they picked up recently," Jessica replied. "I remember them from Shinoda's intel reports. Except they've been upgraded. He's probably escorting the Galean ship."

"What kind of upgrades?" Nathan wondered.

"Bigger guns and more of them," Jessica replied. "And these look like missile tubes; forward facing, like ours. You can bet they have Dusahn shields as well."

"She looks about the same size as us."

"A little bigger maybe, but I'd say we're a good match for her."

Nathan thought for a moment, then reached up to the comm-panel, pressing a few buttons. "Unidentified ship attacking the planet, this is the Karuzari Alliance ship Dalen Voss. Break off your attack immediately and power down all weapons, or we will be forced to open fire on your vessel. You have ten seconds to comply."

"They're not unidentified, Nathan. They're Dusahn," Jessica insisted.

"Better to play it safe for now."

A warning beep sounded from the center threat console, and a red light began flashing.

"We're being targeted," Josh reported.

"This is not good," Dylan added.

"I guess they don't plan on complying," Jessica commented.

"Go manual, Josh," Nathan instructed. "Be ready

for anything, and don't wait for me to give you orders if you think you need to go evasive."

"My pleasure," Josh replied, deactivating the auto-flight and taking the controls.

Nathan reached up and activated the intercom, setting it to open two-way throughout the ship. No matter where his crew was or what they were doing, they would all hear everything each of them said. "Two-way is on," he announced. "Everyone be ready." He then looked at Jessica. "Time to see how well this ship can fight."

"I'll be in the nose turret," Jessica replied, turning to depart.

Captain Proth did not look happy. His first mission as the captain of the Bor-Quarum should have been easy. Now he was not only bombarding a planet full of unarmed civilians, but he had a Karuzari warship bearing down on him. "Mister Ostro, instruct the Oro-Bowona to jump to a safe location, then update us with her new position. We shall call for her return once we have dealt with our uninvited guests."

"Yes, sir," the communications officer acknowledged.

"Captain, I must remind you that standing orders regarding armed contact with the Karuzari are to immediately notify command of the situation."

"If we do so, they will send the Nan-Sala, and we will be robbed of our victory," Captain Proth countered.

"If we fail?" the commander asked.

"Then we will not have to worry about violating our standing orders," the captain replied. "Prepare to attack with missiles," he added, "but continue our attack on Volon. We shall not give the Karuzari vessel the pleasure of saving even a single Volonese life."

Jessica slid down the stair ladder rails, landing gracefully on the lower deck and turning to head forward. Seconds later, she reached the forward airlock hatch and opened it. In its retracted position, the forward boarding ramp served as the floor of the airlock, allowing her to move through the airlock to the hatch of the newly installed gun turret in the Voss's nose.

Unlike the doors to the gun turrets on the sides of the nacelles, which had sliding doors, the nose turret had a manually operated hinged hatch, due to space limitations. She swung it open and stepped through, then closed the hatch behind her and locked it.

Jessica quickly took her seat and buckled her restraints. She activated her gun turret, then looked out beyond the canopy surrounding her. Unlike the other turrets, being at the bow of the ship meant she had no frame of reference around her.

Everywhere she looked was open space. The most she could see of the Voss were the very tips of her nacelles to either side, and only if she leaned as far over as her canopy allowed. At first, it was a bit overwhelming, reminding her of her EVA training a decade ago.

Jessica took a deep breath as she checked her weapon's targeting display.

"Missile launch!"

She only hoped the Voss's forward shields held.

If not, she wouldn't survive long. "Nose gun, ready," she reported over the intercom.

"Six inbound!" Dylan reported.

"How long to impact?" Nathan asked, knowing that Dylan was not trained in the task he was currently performing.

"Twenty seconds to impact!"

"Well at least they aren't jump missiles," Nathan said. "Activate point-defenses."

"Point-defenses have already activated," Dylan replied.

"Another change in our AI's programming?" Nathan asked.

"Yes, sir," Dylan replied sheepishly. "Sorry sir, I'll change that one back as well."

"No, that one I like."

"You gotta count them down as they're taken out," Josh scolded Dylan.

"Sorry,"

Josh glanced at the sensor display, then pulled the Voss's nose up sharply and jammed her throttles all the way forward.

Dylan's eyes opened wide as he was pushed back in his seat. "What are you doing?"

"It's called evasive action," Josh replied as he dialed up a micro-jump. "I'm going to jump over them and come out about two clicks."

"Ready the forward torpedo tubes," Nathan instructed.

"Jumping," Josh announced. As the jump flash washed over them, he yanked his throttles back and pulled back hard on the flight controls. As the ship pitched up, he rolled it over. "My pickle hot?"

"Your what?" Dylan asked.

"Jesus, kid!" Josh chastised as he reached for the weapons control panel on the far side of the center console.

"Let'em have it, Josh," Nathan ordered.

Josh came out of the maneuver, lined up perfectly on the Dusahn ship, flying backwards away from it. He jammed his throttles forward again, hoping to decrease the speed at which they were traveling away from their target as he held down the firing button on his flight controls.

Four red-orange balls of plasma streaked past either side of the cockpit, hurtling toward the enemy ship. A split second later, four more plasma torpedoes followed.

"They're firing on all turrets!" Dylan announced as bolts of glowing red energy slammed into the Voss's forward shields.

"Jesus!" Jessica exclaimed as the forward shields flashed bright red with each impact. Her tiny bubble filled with brilliant, red light and shook violently.

"Everything okay down there?" Nathan called over the intercom.

"I'm good!" Jessica replied. "This position just takes some getting used to! Feels like I'm all alone in a bubble with a gun and no damn control over where I'm going."

"Gunners are weapons free," Nathan instructed. "You get an angle, you fire!"

Vladimir swung his turret to face forward, lining his weapon up on the icon on his targeting screen. The icon flashed green, indicating that his weapon was locked on the target, and he pressed the firing trigger down and held it.

All four barrels opened fire. Left upper, right upper, left lower, right lower.

"Bozhe moi!"

The cycle repeated, his turret automatically adjusting its aim as the target drifted away from them. Seconds later, a blue-white flash washed over them, and the target was gone, and his weapon automatically stopped firing.

"Did you hit anything?" Marcus asked over the intercom.

"I have no idea," Vladimir admitted.

"Come port ninety, down fifteen relative," Nathan instructed. "Dylan, load a pair of shield busters, then queue up a pair of nukes. I want to end this quickly."

"Okay..." Dylan looked confused.

"What's wrong?" Nathan asked.

"What are shield busters? Do you mean shield-penetrating jump missiles?"

"Yes," Nathan replied, controlling his irritation. "Before you ask, 'nukes' means 'nuclear'."

"I know what 'nukes' means," Dylan defended. "Shield busters are loaded. Nukes will be next."

"Put a twenty-second jump delay on the shield busters," Nathan told him.

"Got it."

"That long enough for another ninety?" Nathan asked Josh.

"It is for me," Josh assured him.

"Jump delay is set, first two are ready for launch."

"Did you calculate the target's impact position based on last known course and speed?" Nathan asked.

"Uh..." Dylan glanced at his missile control console. "How do I do that?"

"Bottom left on the missile control panel," Josh told him. "The missile-targeting computer is tied into the sensors. Just select the target, and the computer will make the calculations automatically and update them at the moment of launch, so that the missiles come out of the jump as close to their target's calculated position as possible."

"Of course," Dylan said. "I should have known that."

"Ya think?" Josh chided.

"Be ready to jump us ahead three light minutes and then come to port again. I want us lined up on the target's port bow, a little below."

"Got it," Josh replied.

"Those missiles ready, Dylan?"

"Yes, sir," Dylan replied, breathing a sigh of relief.

"Josh, put our nose on the target's estimated position so we can launch. Jump to the next waypoint as soon as the missiles are away."

"No problem."

Nathan waited while Josh brought the ship's nose around.

"Lined up, Cap'n," Josh reported.

"Launch the first two missiles and reload," Nathan ordered.

Dylan swallowed hard, then pressed the missile

launch button. A mechanical zing reverberated through the ship as two missiles were flung forward through their launch tubes by their electromagnetic rails. Dylan glanced out his starboard window as the missile passed. “Oh my god,” he exclaimed.

“You’ve got twenty seconds to load the next two and give them targeting data,” Nathan reminded him as the Voss’s nose began to come back around to line up with its path of flight once again.

“Jumping to next waypoint,” Josh announced as the ship continued to yaw to port. The jump flash washed over them once again, just as Josh stopped the yaw maneuver. He jammed the throttles all the way forward again, and then initiated his next course change.

Again, Dylan was thrown back in his seat, unprepared for the sudden acceleration.

“How are those missiles, Dylan?” Nathan asked.

“Second two are loaded,” Dylan reported. He glanced at the targeting computer. “Targeting data is loaded.”

Nathan glanced at the clock on the overhead console. “Five seconds to spare. Not bad.”

Dylan felt a wave of relief come over him.

“Not bad?” Josh questioned.

“Mind your helm,” Nathan warned.

Josh rolled his eyes as he completed his turn. “On course for attack jump.”

“Launch the nukes and ready the plasma torpedo tubes,” Nathan instructed.

Again, Dylan pressed the missile launch button, forcing himself not to look out the window again. “Missiles away, forward tubes ready.”

“Stand by for attack jump,” Nathan instructed Josh.

Captain Proth paced nervously as his ship continued its bombardment of the planet below. An endless stream of scenarios ran through his head. Since he had learned of his pending new command, he had spent all his spare time studying the battles between the Dusahn and the Karuzari, especially those with the Aurora. What had always amazed him was Captain Scott's ability to be predictable, yet unpredictable. Time and time again, captains of Dusahn warships had assumed they had a strategic advantage, only to have that advantage taken away from them. In all the battles he had studied, there had been one commonality that stood out above all others.

Pride.

Pure-blooded Dusahn considered themselves superior in every way, especially those in command of warships. They often stood their ground, refusing to yield their position, even when doing so was the only survivable option. Those who did yield faced ridicule or even punishment upon their return. This pride was the Dusahn Empire's greatest weakness, and Lysan knew it. But to state this failing publicly would end his career and, quite possibly, his life.

Unpredictable. The word kept popping up in his mind.

Captain Proth stopped in his tracks, turning toward his helmsman. "Lieutenant Commander Callo, prepare a jump, and do so quickly. Five light minutes."

"Captain," Commander Lobey objected, "we will be forced to break off our attack on Volon."

"Volon can wait," the captain insisted.

"Jump is ready, sir," the helmsman announced.

"Missiles!" the commander warned.

"JUMP!" the captain ordered.

The Bor-Quarum shook violently, the first missile striking their shields and detonating as the jump flash washed over them.

"Jump complete!" the helmsman reported.

"Damage report!" the captain barked.

"Bow shields on the starboard side are down!" the systems officer reported. "Multiple hull breaches; deck two, sections five and six! Emergency doors on both sections have activated!"

"Shunt power to neighboring shields and expand coverage," the captain ordered. "Helm, come about and prepare to jump back. I want to be five kilometers from our previous position."

"Shunting power," the systems officer acknowledged.

"Coming about," the helmsman reported.

Captain Proth looked at his second-in-command. "All guns forward; load all missile tubes with nuclear warheads. They will be expecting us to still be in orbit. We will surprise them."

"Surely they have already jumped in and realized that their attack has failed," the commander insisted.

"They will linger long enough to scan the area in search of us," the captain replied. "But not for long. We will use their own tactics against them, but we must work quickly."

The jump flash faded, and once again Volon loomed large in the forward windows...only this time, there was no ship in orbit.

Nathan gazed out the window in disbelief. Vast swaths of smoke traced across the planet's atmosphere along the lines of the Dusahn ship's attack, obscuring the fires that were undoubtedly still burning below. "Find them," he instructed.

Dylan exchanged glances with Josh. "Scanning."

"Turn complete," the Bor-Quarum's helmsman reported. "Attack jump is ready."

"All guns are forward, all tubes loaded with nuclear warheads," Commander Lobey announced from the tactical station.

"Weapons free," Captain Proth instructed. "Fire at will."

"Weapons free, fire at will," the commander acknowledged.

"Helm, execute attack jump."

"Attack jump in five seconds," the helmsman replied.

"Are you seeing this?" Jessica asked over the intercom. "There have to be at least a hundred fires raging down there."

"Anything?" Nathan asked Dylan.

"Not nothing, but no warships. Just the jump missiles that missed."

"All four of them?"

"No, sir; only three," Dylan replied.

"So they've been hit," Josh surmised.

"If they were, it wasn't enough," Nathan surmised.

"How do you know?" Josh wondered.

"No debris."

"The debris could've been jumped with them," Josh suggested.

"That's possible," Nathan agreed.

"Do you think they left?" Dylan asked, hoping the engagement was over. "Maybe they decided it wasn't worth it."

"Unlikely," Nathan replied.

"The Dusahn rarely retreat," Jessica commented over the intercom.

"Especially when evenly matched," Nathan added. "Somehow, that ship's captain anticipated our missile attack and jumped out just in time."

"Then..."

"We need to get the hell out of here," Nathan decided, cutting Dylan off. "Josh?"

"Already on it," Josh assured him as he changed course away from the planet to get a clear jump line.

Six flashes of blue-white appeared to the left of the Voss as it turned away from the planet. Six missiles streaked from out of the flashes. Two of them were tracking ahead of the Voss, and one aft of the target. The other three, however, immediately struck the ship's port shields, their nuclear warheads detonating on impact in brilliant, white flashes of light.

Seconds later, another flash of light revealed the Dusahn warship that had launched them, all guns pointed forward and firing away.

Nathan picked himself up off the deck, having

been knocked off his feet by the detonations. "Jump us out of here!" he barked.

"Jump drive is offline!" Josh replied.

"Evasive!"

"Whattaya think I'm doin'!"

"All gunners! Sound off!" Nathan instructed.

"Nose gunner!" Jessica reported.

"Tail gunner!" Kit announced.

"Starboard gunner!" Marcus chimed in.

"Ventral gunner!" Jokay added.

There was a pause.

"Dorsal gunner!" Mori reported.

"Vlad!" Nathan called over the intercom. "Vlad! Sound off!"

Dylan quickly called up the weapons status display on his auxiliary view screen. "Port gun is offline! I'm not getting any telemetry from it!"

"Vlad!" Nathan repeated.

"I'm here!" Vladimir finally replied. "The detonations overloaded the port shields, dousing the port nacelle with radiation! The port gun is offline!"

Nathan felt relief washing over him, but it was short-lived. Energy weapons impacts slammed into his ship, violently rocking her. "Vlad! The jump drive isn't working!"

"I'm on it!" Vladimir assured him.

"Marcus!" Nathan called. "Help Vlad get the jump drive back online!"

"Son of a bitch!" Marcus exclaimed.

"Keep our stern to them, Josh," Nathan instructed. "Dylan, drop all forward shields and reduce midship shields to half power. Then divert all the extra energy to our aft shields."

"But half the ship will be unshielded!" Dylan protested.

"That's why we're showing them our ass!" Nathan replied as he moved to the starboard auxiliary station. "I'm calling for reinforcements."

"The target is taking evasive actions," Commander Lobey reported from the Bor-Quarum's tactical station.

"Target has dropped forward shields, and its midship shields are at fifty percent," the sensor officer added. "They are channeling all available energy to their aft shields."

"Why do they not simply jump away?" the captain wondered. "Is their jump drive damaged?"

"Unable to determine," the sensor officer admitted.

"Keep pounding them," Captain Proth instructed.

"I'm trying," the commander assured him. "But that ship's pilot is quite skilled."

"Lieutenant Callo, do not follow the target precisely," the captain instructed his helmsman. "You will only make it more difficult for our guns to track the target. Calculate the target's average course deviations and hold that as your heading."

Jokay kept his gun trained aft, firing only when the Dusahn warship following them momentarily slid into view.

"This would be a lot easier if you held this ship still for a few seconds."

"At least you're not taking all the fire!" Kit replied

as the aft shields outside the open utility bay door flashed bright red with each impact.

"A minute ago, you were complaining that you had nothing to shoot at!" Mori reminded him.

"Yeah, well, this little gun back here is for ground suppression fire, not shooting spaceships!" Kit exclaimed as he fired away at the constantly shifting target outside.

"Stop complaining," Jokay chuckled.

"You might want to consider using the stern tubes more often!"

"I'm trying," Dylan assured him.

"Damn it!" Nathan exclaimed. "They shot down the comm-drone!"

"How the hell did they do that?" Jessica exclaimed over the intercom.

"I don't think it was on purpose," Nathan replied as he prepared to launch a second comm-drone.

"Well launch another!" Jessica suggested.

"What do you think I'm doing?" Nathan replied.

"You can't launch one now," Josh warned. "We're too close to the planet."

"What?"

"They're not designed for this!" Josh explained as he continued jinking the ship about, to evade incoming fire as best he could. "They might not be able to break free of the planet's gravity!"

"Are you certain?"

"We've only got three more left! Do you really want to risk it?"

"Can you get us further away from the planet?" Nathan asked.

"Not quickly!" Josh replied. "Not without giving them a good shot at our unshielded areas, like where our asses are sittin' at the moment!"

"Our weapons are not having much effect on their shields," Commander Lobey reported. "Recommend we launch our attack drones. They may be able to outmaneuver the target and attack their unshielded areas."

"Those drones came with this ship," Captain Proth reminded his second-in-command. "They have never been tested in battle."

"I have studied their specifications," the commander replied. "I believe they will work."

Captain Proth hesitated, but only for a moment. "Launch the drones."

"I told you it wouldn't work," Vladimir said as he disconnected the damaged circuit board from the port jump drive's control rack.

"It would've worked fine if you'd beefed up the buffers going into this thing like I told you!" Marcus argued as he strung the new power cable across the port engineering bay.

"We needed the buffers for splitting up the shield grid!" Vladimir reminded him.

"Excuses," Marcus grumbled, walking back to the power distribution panel to start connecting the power line.

Vladimir pulled the damaged circuit board, tossing it aside and reaching for the spare lying on the deck next to him. "What are you doing?" he asked, noticing Marcus at the power distribution panel.

"I'm connecting a new power line to the buffers."

"Why?" Vladimir asked as he pushed the new circuit board into its slot.

"So that thing doesn't fry again! What the hell do ya' think?"

"But those are shield buffers!"

"A buffer is a buffer!" Marcus insisted. "It'll be fine!"

"The moment we jump, the shield section that buffer is serving will experience a fifty-percent dip in power! If we take a hit on that shield..."

"The dip will only be for a second," Marcus argued. "Two, at the most. What are the odds?!"

"What are the odds," Vladimir mumbled to himself. "With Nathan, not good!"

Four panels along the side of the Bor-Quarum slid open, revealing rows of small, hexagonal-shaped objects packed tightly together. One by one, the objects were ejected, their intervals and sequencing designed to allow all the drones to extend their maneuvering thruster arms to deploy immediately after release, all without interfering with the drones beside them.

Once deployed, the drones spread out, streaking away from the ship to either side, accelerating forward to catch up to the target vessel.

Kit stopped firing for a moment, spotting something unusual. Flashes of light, a whole swarm of them, spreading out and away from the Dusahn ship. At first, he thought it was debris; that one of their plasma blasts might have gotten through. It also could have been sparks from an overloaded shield emitter.

The thing was, they were not spreading out in any pattern. They were maneuvering.

"Oh shit," he muttered, aiming his gun toward the incoming objects. "We've got drones incoming!"

"Where?" Jokay asked over the intercom.

"They're spreading out from either side of the target and accelerating toward us!"

"They're spreading out wide!" Dylan reported, looking at the threat display. "They're going to come at us from all sides!"

"I'm targeting them with point-defenses," Nathan said as he entered commands at the auxiliary console.

"The drones are too fast!" Dylan replied. "Our guns will never be able to track them!"

Mori swung his gun turret around as fast as he could, trying to keep up with the drones as they passed. "They're too fast! The turret can't track them as they pass!"

"Just fire at the masses whenever you can!" Jessica suggested. "You might get lucky!"

"Marcus, are you busy?" Nathan asked over the intercom.

"Are you fucking kidding?"

"Get to the utility bay," Nathan instructed. "I need you to help Kit."

"Now?"

"Yes, now!"

"I'm pretty sure I can fire a gun all by myself, but thanks for thinking of me," Kit said.

"Stow your gun, Kit," Nathan instructed. "It'll be in the way."

"In the way of what?"

"The mines."

"We have mines?" Kit asked.

Dylan looked back over his shoulder. "We don't have mines..." He then looked over at Josh. "Do we?"

"About twenty of them passed right by us and are coming about!" Dylan reported over the intercom.

"I've got them," Jessica replied, adjusting her nose turret gun on the group to port.

"I'm redistributing power equally again to all shields," Nathan announced.

The tiny specks in the distance ahead seemed to stop moving. A few shifted slightly in one direction or another, and then became still again.

"Here they come, Jess," Nathan warned over the intercom.

"These things are impossible to hit!" Jokay exclaimed from the ventral gun turret.

"Not impossible!" Mori disagreed. "Just really fucking difficult!"

Jessica opened fire as the specks became hexagonal objects that began firing at her. "I fucking hate drones!"

Vladimir quickly connected the power cable that Marcus had run from the shield power buffers to the port jump field generator. Once finished, he reached up above the connection and pressed the actuator button, reopening the circuit. He looked to his left, eying the jump field generator control rack that he had been working on, expecting it to erupt in a shower of sparks, dooming the Voss to an emergency landing on Volon as their only chance of survival.

But no sparks came.

"Ha!" Vladimir burst out, practically laughing.

"Vlad!" Nathan called over the intercom. "I'm getting some wonky readings in the port shields."

"Ignore them!" Vladimir replied as he ran across the bay back to the port jump field generator control rack. "I'm rebooting the port jump field generator now! We should have jump capability restored in thirty seconds!"

"You need to work fast, Marcus," Nathan urged over the intercom.

"Work fast and nuclear warheads are two phrases that really don't belong together," Marcus grunted as he and Kit rolled the jump missile off the rack and onto the deck, where it landed with a thud. The two men looked at each other, wondering if they had not been gentle enough.

Marcus grinned. "Relax, kid. I'm sure they built these things to take a few bumps without detonating."

"I'm good," Kit assured him. "I'm just not used to working with nuclear ordnance."

"They didn't teach you about nukes in Ghatazhak

school?" Marcus joked as he removed the access plate from the side of the missile's forward section.

"They did," Kit replied, removing the panel from the opposite side. "We just never worked with live warheads. What about you?"

"Unfortunately not my first time."

After removing the access panel, Kit reached inside and began removing some nuts along the inner edge of the nose section.

"Whattaya doin'?" Marcus wondered.

"Detaching the nose from the vehicle body," Kit replied as he continued to work.

"Why?"

Kit looked at Marcus, puzzled. "We can't just push the whole damn missile out the back."

"Why not?"

"They'd ID it in a second, and their point-defenses would take it out."

"You think they're not going to spot a hunk of plutonium comin' at them?"

"Yeah, but it will take them a few extra seconds to realize it's a threat," Kit argued.

"You could be right," Marcus admitted, returning to his work.

The ship shook violently, nearly knocking Marcus over.

"Aft shields are down to forty percent!" Dylan exclaimed.

"Any time, Marcus," Nathan said over the intercom.

"Rewiring a nuclear detonator isn't like changin' a light panel, Cap'n."

"How the hell do you know how to do that anyway?" Kit wondered.

"Long story," Marcus replied as he worked.

"Another long story?" Kit smiled. "Can't wait to hear that one."

"The drones are forcing them to keep all their shields up," Commander Lobey announced triumphantly from the Bor-Quarum's tactical station. "Their aft shields are down to thirty-four percent."

Captain Proth could taste his first victory. His evasion of the Karuzari ship's attack had been inspired, and their disabling of the enemy's jump drive had been textbook. Even better, their relentless pounding of their aft shields was classic Dusahn. The battle at Volon would prove his value to the empire, as well as the value of others like him. "Move in closer to increase the impact energy of our weapons."

"It would be safer to remain at our current distance," the commander urged. "At the current rate of drain, their aft shields will be down in two minutes."

"I want that ship destroyed...now," the captain insisted. "Move closer."

"Aft shields are down to thirty-two percent!" Dylan exclaimed as the Voss was rocked by incoming weapons fire.

Josh glanced at the threat display as he continued to maneuver wildly. "That fucker is moving closer!"

"Good," Nathan replied. "Let him."

"Let him?" Dylan asked in disbelief.

"Let him," Nathan repeated.

"I feel obligated to point out that the closer they

get, the more quickly our shields are drained by their weapons."

"I'm aware of that," Nathan assured him.

"I'm also obligated to point out that we now have a working jump drive, and a clear jump line."

"Shut up, Dylan!" Josh scolded.

"I'm just saying..."

"Nobody asked you!" Josh replied, cutting him off.

Dylan took a breath, frustrated. "Aft shields at thirty percent," he reported. "They won't be able to withstand impacts at such close range once they fall below twenty-five percent."

Kit pulled on the missile body with all his might, using the additional strength that his combat armor gave him to separate the delivery vehicle from the forward warhead package.

Marcus closed the access panel on the side of the missile's warhead package, breathing a sigh of relief. "It's ready," he reported.

"How are we going to detonate it?" Nathan asked over the intercom.

"You don't have to," Marcus replied. "It'll detonate with the slightest exposure of energy."

"Then we shoot it?" Kit asked.

"No need," Marcus explained. "If they shoot it, it goes nuclear. If it touches their shields, it goes nuclear."

"Nice."

"All we have to do is toss it out the back," Marcus added.

"How do we do that?" Nathan asked.

"That's my job," Kit replied, stepping up to the warhead package.

"We'll have to drop the pressure shield first," Marcus warned. "It might trigger detonation as well."

"Then you'd better clear out of here," Kit suggested as the visor on his helmet dropped down and automatically sealed.

"Kit will toss it out the back!" Marcus reported over the intercom.

Another volley slammed into them, rocking the ship violently.

"Shields down to twenty-eight percent!" Dylan warned.

"We're going to have to time this right," Nathan decided. "Josh, prepare a one light-minute jump. We'll go on a five-count so that Kit can time his delivery."

"Got it," Josh replied.

"Whenever you're ready, Kit," Nathan called over the intercom.

"I'm ready, I'm ready!" Kit insisted.

"Jump is ready," Josh reported as the ship rocked again.

"Aft shields at twenty-six percent!" Dylan warned urgently.

"Let's do it," Nathan ordered.

Josh placed his finger over the jump button. "Jumping in five..."

"Jesus!" Jessica exclaimed over the intercom. "These damned drones are everywhere!"

"A group is passing under us!" Jokay warned.

The ship rocked as two more bolts of energy slammed into their aft shields.

"Four..."

"Aft shields are down to twenty-two percent!" Dylan exclaimed.

"We can't take another hit!" Dylan warned over the intercom.

Kit activated his mag boots, squatted down, and grabbed onto the handles on the warhead's stern mounting plate, bracing himself.

"Dropping pressure shield!" Marcus announced over the intercom.

The pale, blue pressure shield flickered, then disappeared, allowing the pressurized air inside the massive bay to be sucked out into space, taking anything that wasn't secured with it.

Using the additional strength of his combat armor, he lifted the heavy warhead to his waist, straightening his legs into a standing position.

"I can't believe I'm chucking rocks at a spaceship!" Kit yelled as he began to spin around in place.

"Three..."

Kit let go of the warhead flinging it out the opening at the back of the bay with all his might, praying that his aim was true.

"Two..."

"Warhead is away!" Kit reported as he ran toward the hatch controls on the left side of the door.

"One..."

Kit slapped the door close button, causing the massive utility bay ramp to begin rising toward its closed position.

"Jumping!"

"Target has jumped!" Commander Lobey reported from the Bor-Quarum's tactical station.

"Damn it!" the captain cursed. "We almost had her!"

"Unidentified object detected," the sensor officer reported. "Dead ahead; one kilometer and closing fast."

"What is it?" the captain inquired.

"Running full spectrum scans now."

"Debris?" the commander suggested.

"Did their aft shields fail before they jumped?" the captain wondered.

"It's possible that one of our drones did some damage," the commander opined.

"If it is debris, will our shields stop it?" the captain questioned.

"They should," the commander assured him.

"Radiological!" the sensor officer reported urgently. "It's a warhead!"

"Emergency jump!" the captain ordered as a brilliant, white flash appeared on their view screen, filling the entire bridge with the blinding light.

"You still with us, Kit?" Nathan called.

"Still here!" Kit replied over the intercom. "Rear door is closed."

"Nice job," Nathan replied. "Come about, Josh," he instructed. "If that nuke took out their shields, we're going to have to strike quickly before they jump out."

"Coming about," Josh acknowledged.

"Do we still have nukes in the tubes?" Nathan asked.

"Yes, sir," Dylan replied.

"Set them to jump the moment they clear the tubes."

"Setting missiles for snap jump," Dylan confirmed. "Range?"

"One hundred meters shy of whatever our range is at the time of launch," Nathan replied.

"At our current speed, that means they'll come out of their jump only a few meters from impact," Dylan warned. "They'll have no time to make final course adjustments."

"Which is why we're setting their detonators to proximity mode," Nathan explained.

"Aye sir," Dylan replied, fighting not to be overwhelmed by everything that was happening.

"Coming about now, Cap'n," Josh reported. "Where do you want to jump back in at?"

"Just astern of them," Nathan replied. "Flip us over and nose us down a few degrees. With any luck, that nuke took out their forward shields, and the missiles we're about to ram down their throats will bring the rest of them down as well. If so, we'll take out their main propulsion with our plasma torpedoes."

"Sounds fun!" Josh exclaimed, preparing for the maneuver.

"You people have strange ideas of what's fun," Dylan mumbled.

Sparks flew in all directions as consoles all around

the Bor-Quarum's bridge were overloaded by the sudden burst of radiation. A plethora of emergency alarms added to the chaos and screams of the bridge crew as they struggled to stay ahead of the damage.

"Report!" Captain Proth demanded as he climbed back to his feet.

"All forward shields are down!" Commander Lobey replied. "Midship and aft shield rings are down to twenty percent! Forward turrets are offline. Point-defenses are also down!"

"Engineering! Captain!"

"Main propulsion and maneuvering are still working," the chief engineer replied over the intercom. "Jump drive is also working, but the main reactor has automatically switched to safety mode, so whatever is in the energy banks is all the jump range we have until I can fix whatever is wrong with the reactor and get it back to full-power mode."

"Helm, report levels in our jump banks."

"Approximately three light years," the helmsman replied.

"Why so little?" the captain wondered.

"I am uncertain, Captain," the lieutenant commander admitted. "We had three times that before the attack started. We may have lost some of the charge due to that blast."

"Figure out if it's an instrumentation problem or a physical one," the captain instructed. "Three light years isn't enough to get home, let alone to complete our mission."

"Yes, Captain," the helmsman replied.

"Captain, we are in no condition to complete our mission," the commander argued. "We may not even be able to get home."

"Home?" the captain snapped, turning back to

face his second-in-command. "And what will await us should we return in disgrace?"

"Multiple contacts!" the sensor officer reported urgently. His expression suddenly changed. "It's the Nan-Sala! Gunships! Octos!"

"What?" the captain snapped. "How did..."

"The Oro-Bowona," Commander Lobey said. "Her captain must have informed command of the situation...per protocol."

Captain Proth's face was crestfallen. His dreams of proving himself, and all those like him, to the empire they served were gone. Crippled, unable to fight, unable to get home, and the enemy having escaped their grasp, his fate, and likely those of his crew, were sealed. Any whom were not executed faced the most menial of tasks for the rest of their days, along with the ridicule and disrespect of their peers. The situation could not have been worse.

Or so he thought.

"New contacts!" the sensor officer gasped. "MISSILES!"

The jump flash washed over the Voss's flight deck as the ship finished pitching over. The Dusahn warship slid into view, only a few hundred meters away.

The targeting computer beeped, indicating that the ship's forward torpedo tubes were lined up, and that the ship's AI had taken control of its attitude thrusters so that it remained that way.

"Firing!" Josh announced as he pressed the button to launch the first spread of plasma torpedoes.

Red-orange balls of plasma, two from each

side, streaked forward, slamming into the target's weakened shields. They flashed brightly, and tiny explosions of sparks appeared all over the aft side of its hull. The target's aft shields flickered, then disappeared.

"Their shields are down!" Dylan exclaimed with excitement.

The Voss shook violently, surprising them all. "What the..." Nathan began to say.

"Frigate!" Mori yelled over the intercom, the screech of his plasma cannons sounding in the background. "One twenty, twenty degrees up relative!"

Another volley slammed into them, rocking the ship and setting off more warning alarms.

"I've got gunships and octos below!" Jokay added.

"Drones are passing over the target, coming toward us!" Jessica warned over the intercom.

"Where they hell did they come from?" Nathan snapped.

"I don't know!" Dylan defended. "The contacts weren't there a second ago!"

"Well they're there now!" Nathan replied. "Josh, jump us the hell out of here!"

"I'm on it," Josh replied, quickly dialing up an escape jump and pressing the jump button.

Nothing happened.

"Josh..."

"I'm trying!" Josh insisted. "The jump status board shows ready, but nothing is happening!"

A terrible thought suddenly occurred to Nathan. I should have called for backup before we jumped back in.

CHAPTER FIVE

The intercom panel built into the desk in the captain's ready room beeped.

"Go ahead," Cameron answered.

"Captain, Intel," Lieutenant Commander Shinoda called. "Latest recon from Takara shows considerable movement. One frigate, at least four gunships, and about twenty octos have all gotten underway."

"Destination?"

"Unknown," the lieutenant commander replied. "Our recon drone jumped out before they did. Best I can say is that they were pulling away from Takara."

Cameron thought for a moment. "Do we have any spare drones available for tasking?"

"Negative. The one that just returned has to be recycled. I can have it ready to go in about thirty minutes if that helps."

"Never mind," she told him. "I'll retask one of the BARCAP teams."

"To where?"

"To where we hope they're not going." Cameron quickly changed channels. "Comms, Captain, get me Corinari Command, ASAP."

* * *

Talisha Sane glanced at her sensor display again. As expected, there were no contacts.

"I'm just saying that these patrols could be done by drones," her wingman continued. "I mean, we've only got twenty-eight Nighthawks left. Seems to me they should be saved for combat, not used for BARCAPs."

"You just want to spend more time with that waitress at Hodgers," Talisha teased.

"And there's something wrong with that?"

"Contact," Talisha's AI announced. "Comm-drone; squawking Corinari IFF codes."

"Looks like we've got an incoming message from command," Talisha commented.

"Probably that waitress," her wingman joked.

"No doubt." Talisha read the text message as it appeared on her screen, then shifted in her seat. "We've got an urgent retask," she announced.

"What now?" her wingman asked. "They want us to take over someone else's patrol area again?"

"Negative," Talisha replied. "They want us to recon the Volon system, ASAP."

"Now they have us doing the work of recon drones?" he complained. "Unbelievable!"

"Leta, plot a high-speed series jump to Volon and load."

"Distance to Volon is fourteen point five three light years from current position," Leta replied. "Suggest immediate course change to one five seven mark one four and accelerate at full power. First jump will be in two minutes. The series will require fifteen jumps. With ten second intervals, time to Volon will be two minutes and thirty seconds."

"Recalculate at max jump range," Talisha instructed her AI.

"Max-range jumps in series are not recommended," Leta warned.

"I'm aware," Talisha replied. "Calculate anyway."

"Five jumps, twelve second intervals. Time to Volon; one minute," Leta reported.

"Much better," Talisha agreed. "You ready?"

"Let's go take a look, boss," her wingman replied.

"Leta, take control and get us to Volon."

"Confirming max-range jumps?"

"Max-range jumps confirmed."

"Turning to new heading and executing jump series to Volon," Leta announced.

"Try to keep up," Talisha joked.

* * *

The Voss shook as the Dusahn frigate's guns pummeled their failing shields. Josh jinked the ship around, trying to evade the target locks of the enemy ship's main guns and popping off a few plasma torpedoes whenever their rear tubes lined up for a moment.

"We can't take many more hits from those big guns!" Dylan warned.

"I have an idea!" Josh exclaimed.

"Whatever it is, do it!" Nathan urged.

"You're not gonna like it!"

"If it keeps us from getting our asses blown off, I'll love it, I promise!"

"Hang on!" Josh exclaimed, pushing his flight controls forward.

The ship's nose dropped sharply, diving toward the planet below.

"What the hell are you doing?" Dylan yelled, his eyes wide.

"Frigates and gunships can't fly in atmo," Josh explained.

"Their fighters can!"

"Yeah, I got an idea for them as well," Josh snickered.

* * *

"Last jump, coming up," Talisha announced. "Shields up."

"We expecting trouble?" her wingman asked.

"The Voss is supposed to be here," she replied.

"We're doing recon on a system that already has an asset in place? Why not just send a comm-drone?"

"That's why we're raising shields," Talisha replied.

The jump flash washed over her ship, its brilliant, blue-white light subdued to manageable levels by the Sugali fighter's projection canopy.

"Multiple contacts," her AI reported.

"What have we got, Leta?" Talisha asked.

"One Dusahn frigate, four gunships, and one heavy gunship of unknown origin. The heavy gunship is badly damaged. There are also twenty octo-fighters diving toward the surface of Volon. There is considerable destruction to the surface civilization. It appears that the planet is under attack."

"Any sign of the Voss?"

"Negative. However, there is an unknown object that is also diving toward the planet, ahead of the octo-fighters. The plasma wake created by the object's interface with the planet's atmosphere is preventing our sensors from collecting any identifying information. I should point out, however, that the size of the object is similar to that of the Voss."

"Jump back to the Aurora and let them know what's going on here," Talisha instructed her wingman. "We need help and lots of it."

"What are you going to do?" he asked as he turned away.

"I'm going to see if that fireball is the Voss."

"Don't do anything I wouldn't do," her wingman told her, just before he jumped away.

* * *

The entire command deck of the Voss glowed bright yellow-orange, their ship engulfed in a brilliant trail of burning plasma.

"You know, this is draining the shields nearly

as much as weapons fire from those octos!" Dylan warned as the ship bounced and shook.

"So you want me to slow down and let them fire at us?" Josh asked, holding his dive.

"I didn't say that," Dylan defended.

"We'll be out of this soon enough," Nathan said. "But he is right, Josh. We are going to have to slow down."

"Why?"

"You said this ship isn't as maneuverable as the Seiiki, right?"

"Yeah, but that doesn't mean she can't handle what I'm about to do with her."

Nathan shook his head. "I don't even want to know." The plasma wake began to abate, the ship's rough ride subsiding with it. "Gunners, expect octos. Kit, you might want to get that back door open again."

"I'm on it," Kit replied over the intercom.

"Any chance we're going to be able to jump soon, Vlad?"

"I do not know yet," Vladimir replied.

"Not the answer I was looking for," Nathan retorted.

"Octos!" Mori reported from the dorsal turret. "Lots of them!"

"Twenty," Dylan updated, looking at the sensor display.

"Some of them are jumping!" Mori updated, the screech of his plasma cannons nearly drowning him out.

"At least the drones are gone," Jessica commented.

Four flashes of light appeared in the distance ahead and far below. "Four bandits ahead," she announced, taking aim and opening fire.

"Four more just jumped in to starboard," Mori warned. "Looks like they're splitting up to come at us from all sides."

Talisha dove through Volon's atmosphere at higher than normal speeds, protected from the heat of atmospheric interface by her shields.

"I have identified the unknown contact," Leta announced. "It is the Voss, as you suspected."

"Good thing I sent my wingman back for help," Talisha muttered.

"What are your intentions?" her AI inquired.

"I'm going to see if I can get a few of those octos off the Voss's back."

"Shall I target the Dusahn fighters with our point-defense cannons?" Leta asked.

"You have fire control," Talisha confirmed, knowing that her AI would not fire on human-occupied vessels without specific instructions from her human pilot. "If it's attacking the Voss, light them up."

"Understood," Leta replied.

Kit had redeployed the overhead mounted plasma cannon as soon as the ramp had come down far enough. Six Dusahn octos were already lighting up the Voss's aft shields, threatening to bring them down in short order.

Kit opened fire as the ramp continued to deploy,

his field of fire widening as the ramp descended down to level.

He paused fire for a moment, rolling the weapon further out onto the ramp to get an even wider angle. Once the weapon reached its maximum extension, Kit activated his mag boots, securing his feet firmly to the ramp to avoid falling. Though tethered to the ship, the last thing he wanted was to be flailing at the end of a tether while Josh was maneuvering wildly.

Again he opened fire, pounding the forward shields of the pursuing octos as their ship continued diving toward the surface.

Target icons littered his visor display, as well as the targeting screen on his cannon. But among all the dancing, red icons, one was different.

It was blue.

"We've got a friendly!" Kit yelled over the intercom.

Nathan leaned forward suddenly, looking toward the sensor screen. "What?"

"One fighter squawking Karuzari IFF codes!" Dylan exclaimed. "It's a Nighthawk!"

"Voss! Razor Three! On your six! Engaging octos! Try not to shoot me!"

"Three!" Nathan replied over comms. "Voss Actual! Is that you, Sane?"

"Yes, sir!" she replied eagerly.

"Please tell me you're not alone."

"Sorry, sir. I sent Six back for help."

"Four octos just broke off to take her on!" Dylan announced.

"Four octos are turning toward you!" Nathan warned.

"I see them," Talisha replied. "Suggest you jump ahead to get some range from those octos."

"If we could jump, we wouldn't be in this pickle," Nathan explained. "We'll go down low and find a way to line them up for you."

"Sounds good!" Talisha agreed. "I've got a full load of mini-jump missiles. I'll shake them up a bit."

"How'd you know?" Josh wondered.

"That you were going low?" Nathan replied. "You always go low, Josh. That's where you like to be."

"Yeah, you're right about that."

Dylan looked at Josh, concerned. "How low are we talking?"

* * *

Cameron paced back and forth across the Aurora's bridge. News of the departure of significant forces from Takara had given her plenty of cause for concern. She had people out there, people who might be at risk, but she could not act without further intelligence. She only hoped that information would come soon.

"Captain," Ensign Keller called from the communications console. "Corinari Command has scrambled a squadron of Gunyoki, just in case. They should be in orbit in one minute. They have been tasked to your command."

"Very well," Cameron replied, returning to her pacing.

"The tendency for Terrans to pace is most puzzling," her tactical officer stated.

Cameron stopped in her tracks, looking at the officer.

"My apologies if I overstepped my bounds, Captain," the officer offered. "I still have much to learn about your people."

"That's quite alright, Lieutenant," Cameron assured him. "Yuati, right?"

"Yes, Captain. Lieutenant Mio Yuati."

"You're from Rakuen, right?"

"I am," the lieutenant confirmed. "I am part of the officer exchange program that I believe you instituted."

"Of course."

"May I ask what it is about walking back and forth along the same route that helps calm Terrans?"

"It's just a way to burn off nervous energy, I suppose. A bad habit, really."

"People from Rakuen do not do this."

"Yes, I've noticed. Your people are very... controlled."

"It is something we are taught from birth," the lieutenant explained. "It does have its drawbacks, however."

"Such as?"

"Our range of emotions is very limited. When we do get angry, we tend to explode, as if releasing pressure that has been built up over a lifetime. It can be very unpleasant to witness."

"I imagine so," Cameron replied.

"It can also be very useful, if channeled properly."

"The problem is that most people have a hard time doing just that," Cameron stated.

"There are such people on Rakuen," the lieutenant agreed. "Perhaps not as many as on other worlds, but we have our share."

"Captain," Ensign Keller interrupted. "Flash traffic from Corinari Command. Volon is under attack by Dusahn forces. Razor Six reported a Dusahn frigate, gunships, and octos, as well as two unidentified ships, one of which is badly damaged. Razor Three stayed in the system to seek out the Voss."

"General quarters, Mister Keller," Cameron ordered, moving toward her command chair.

"General quarters, aye," the ensign acknowledged as the trim lighting around the Aurora's bridge changed to red and alarm klaxons began to sound.

"General quarters, general quarters," Naralena's recorded voice announced throughout the ship. Cameron had been unable to bring herself to change the recording now that she was gone. "All hands to battle stations."

"Connect me to the Gunyoki flight leader," Cameron instructed.

"One moment," the ensign replied. "Commander Hayashi in Tekka One is on comms, sir."

"Tekka Leader, Aurora Actual," Cameron called over comms. "Are you in orbit yet?"

"Aurora, Tekka Leader," Jenna replied. "We just jumped up and received the flash from command. We can be in the Volon system in three minutes."

"How fast can you put twenty-four Gunyoki on my flight decks?" Cameron asked.

"Twice as fast," Jenna replied. "On our way."

Cameron switched channels. "Flight, Captain. Twenty-four Gunyoki will be landing on our decks in the next minute and a half. Let me know once they are all down."

"Understood."

"Helm, the moment those Gunyoki are on board, we jump to Volon. Put us three light minutes out; that should provide us just enough old light to determine their orbit and speed. If they jumped directly from Takara, they'll be in an equatorial orbit. I'd like to surprise them if possible."

"Aye, sir," the helmsman acknowledged.

"Lieutenant Yuati, two shield busters and two nukes in the tubes if you please. I want that frigate destroyed on the first pass."

"Loading two shield busters and two nukes," the tactical officer replied.

"All hands report general quarters," Ensign Keller reported.

"Weapons and shields are charged and ready," Lieutenant Yuati announced. "Chief of the boat is in damage control."

"Flight reports Tekka squadron has jumped in and is setting down now. They should be on the deck in less than a minute."

"Course for Volon plotted, jump is loaded and ready," the navigator reported.

"Stand by to break orbit and jump to Volon," Cameron ordered.

* * *

Josh held his dive, despite the fact that the surface of Volon was growing closer at an alarming rate.

"Uh...Josh?" Dylan urged, his eyes growing wide. "Are you planning on leveling off soon?"

"Define...soon," Josh replied, a mischievous smile on his face.

Dylan noticed the devilish look on his pilot's face. "You worry me, you know that?"

"You wouldn't be the first," Josh replied. "You gonna find me a canyon or what?"

"Sorry." Dylan turned his attention back to the sensor display, setting it to terrain-following mode. Within seconds, he had a three-dimensional representation of the surface of Volon in the area toward which they were diving, or as Dylan thought of it, the impact zone.

He widened the scope, then widened it again and again until he saw something that looked promising. After tapping on the screen, the display zoomed back in on the area of interest, revealing a complex series of valleys and canyons along snaking river systems.

"I've got something," Dylan announced. "Not exactly a canyon, but a series of narrow valleys. It looks like they were carved out of the landscape by a complex river system."

"That'll do," Josh decided, glancing at the display himself to get a bearing and immediately adjusting their course toward it.

"Do you want a bearing?" Dylan asked.

"I've got it," Josh assured him.

"What do you want me to do?"

"Just don't let me fly into a dead end and slam us into a wall," Josh replied. When there was no response, he glanced at his copilot, who now appeared somewhat pale. "Relax, Dylan, I was kidding..."

Dylan relaxed a bit, although not much.

"...Sort of," Josh added.

"The four octo-fighters are maneuvering to get behind us," Talisha's AI warned.

"I'm aware of them, Leta," Talisha replied as she maneuvered into position to attack one of the octos currently attacking the Voss.

"I am targeting all four pursuers with point-defenses; however, they are unlikely to penetrate their defensive shields."

"Do it anyway," Talisha instructed as she armed

her internal missile bays. "We don't want them to think we're a boring dance partner."

"Firing all point-defenses," Leta reported.

Talisha glanced at the weapons status screen as all four point-defense cannon icons turned red, indicating they were engaged. She then turned her attention to her targeting screen, selecting all four of the targets directly in front of her. "Locked onto four," she reported as she moved her right thumb to the missile-launch button on the side of her flight control stick. "Launching missiles."

Talisha pressed the missile-launch button, holding it long enough to initiate the first missile launch before releasing it. As the first missile streaked forward from under her fighter, she repeated the process three more times.

"Four away!" she reported as the last missile cleared her nose and disappeared in a blue-white flash of light.

A blue-white flash of light appeared twenty meters behind the trailing octo-fighter, revealing a small missile, its engines still burning at full power. A second after it appeared, it struck the octo's aft shields and detonated.

Sparks erupted all over the octo, its shield emitters overloaded by the sudden influx of energy from the blast.

With another flash of light, three of the nearest fighters pitched up and jumped to safety before they too were struck.

The next two missiles, having lost their targets, were forced to shut down their drives and begin their fall to the surface, their warheads automatically disarming. The fourth missile had enough time to acquire an alternate target, guided by Talisha's AI, to which it was connected.

The missile adjusted its course, locking onto the new target, turning further to hold its lock as the newly targeted octo-fighter took evasive action, pitching down and rolling into a corkscrew dive.

The missile followed the fighter but failed to hold its lock when the fighter pulled out of its dive and jumped away.

Kit noticed the explosion of the first missile, as well as the shower of sparks it precipitated, and turned his weapon from the lead octo to the trailing one, continuing to fire. Within seconds, the bolts of plasma energy leaping from his barrels burned through the octo-fighter's armor plating and found one of its internal propellant tanks. The octo exploded, sending debris flying in all directions as the bulk of the wreckage began tumbling toward the surface.

"Nice shot!" Mori congratulated over the intercom.

"I guess this gun's not so bad after all," Kit decided.

"You got lucky," Jokay joked.

Realizing that her strategy was sound, Talisha quickly dialed up four more missiles, this time setting them to automatically launch in sequence.

"Aft shields down to fifty percent," her AI reported as the fighter rocked from the incoming weapons impacts. "Estimated time to aft shield failure is two minutes."

Talisha targeted two octos that had just come out of a jump to the right of the Voss, and then two of the four that were still on her six.

"Recommend evasive action to allow shields to regenerate," Leta continued.

"How long for full shield regen," Talisha asked.

"Forty-seven seconds."

"Too long," Talisha decided. "Voss! I'll peel'em, you cook'em!" she called over comms as she pressed the missile launch button again.

"Aft shields are taking a beating!" Dylan warned.

"Hang on!" Josh warned as he began to pull back on his flight controls.

The Voss's grav-lift systems screamed as they fought to keep the ship aloft.

All three of them stared out the front windows as their ship slowly began to level off, dropping into the narrow valley.

"Holy crap!" Dylan exclaimed, surprised that they hadn't slammed into the ground. "I can't believe you did that!"

"You ain't seen nothin' yet," Josh giggled.

Dylan looked back at Nathan. "Is he always like this?"

"Eyes on the terrain sensors," Nathan urged, breathing a sigh of relief as soon as Dylan turned away.

Two blue-white flashes of light to his left caught

Mori's attention as he fired away at the octos to stern. He quickly swung his gun turret to starboard as two more pure-white flashes announced the missile detonations. Both fighters diving toward the Voss's starboard side erupted in showers of sparks. Mori opened fire with all four barrels, immediately destroying one of the octos and damaging the other.

The crippled octo streaked overhead, black smoke and flames trailing from its side. Mori swung his gun around to pick the target up on the port side, but the damaged octo slammed into the mountainside, breaking apart. "A hell of a lot easier to cook once they're peeled!" Mori exclaimed with excitement.

"Talisha!" Nathan called over comms. "You need to shake the three on your tail and then come back!"

"I'm good!" Talisha assured him over comms. "Although I wouldn't mind if your gunners wanted to fire at the guys on my six!"

"DEAD END!" Dylan shouted, pointing out the front windows.

Josh glanced up, spotting the vertical face coming at them. In one smooth motion, he fired all his forward-facing docking and attitude thrusters to slow them down while jamming the grav-lift's power lever all the way to full.

The mountainside came at them quickly. In the blink of an eye, it filled all of the Voss's windows with its rocky view. Then the mountainside suddenly fell away.

Jokay stopped firing, bracing himself as the

mountaintop passed less than a meter over his head. Had his barrels not already been pointed along the hull, they would have been taken off. "A little warning next time!" he exclaimed as the threat of collision passed behind him.

Josh killed all forward-facing thrusters and pulled the grav-lift power lever back nearly as quickly as he had shoved it forward. The Voss responded sluggishly at first, then dropped down the backside of the mountain into the next valley beyond. "Sorry about that," he apologized to Jokay. "A little sooner next time, huh, kid?" he said to Dylan.

"Got it," Dylan replied, his eyes glued to the terrain display.

"Whoo-hoo!" Talisha exclaimed over comms.

Kit's eyes widened at the sight of two octos bouncing off the top of the mountain behind them, tumbling to their doom. "Holy crap! Nice move, Josh!" he exclaimed as he opened fire again.

"I wish I could say it was on purpose," Josh admitted over the intercom as the Voss began snaking through the next valley.

"Port gun is back online!" Dylan reported.

"I thought it was knocked out," Nathan replied.

"The radiation flash just caused a reboot of the gun's control systems," Dylan explained. "It's back up."

A thought struck Nathan, and he leaned forward

to look at the terrain display more closely. "Josh, turn right at the next fork, and go as low as possible."

"No problem," Josh assured him.

"Jess, move to Vlad's gun; port side...and hurry."

"On my way," Jessica replied.

"How long until the fork?" Nathan asked.

"One minute?" Dylan replied, uncertain.

Come on, Cam, Nathan thought.

The threat-alert indicator flashed, and its alarm sounded as Talisha unleased four more missiles on various octos ahead of her. She glanced at the threat display just as the new arrivals opened fire. "Uh-oh," she said as she pulled back hard on her flight control stick and jammed her main throttle to its stops.

"Three more octo-fighters have just jumped in," her AI reported. "There are now seven octos pursuing us."

"Yeah, I can count," Talisha replied. "Sorry guys, I gotta shake these buggers! I'll be right back!"

Jessica ran through the systems bay below the common area, through the center octagonal intersection, and headed down the corridor toward the port nacelle.

The ship rocked suddenly, swaying to one side and tossing her against the wall. Stumbling, she managed to keep going, stepping over conduits running across the floor at the end of the corridor as she ducked under the overhead ducting. She pressed the hatch controls, causing the inner hatch to slide open, then stepped into the airlock joining the port nacelle to the ship's main, central body. As soon as the inner hatch closed, the next hatch opened, and she headed into the port nacelle engineering compartment.

"Haven't you fixed that thing yet?" she yelled to Vladimir as she ran past.

"I'm trying!" Vladimir exclaimed. "Gospadee!"

"Can't you go faster?" Nathan suggested to Josh.

"Are you kidding?" Josh wondered, glancing back over his shoulder.

"Nope."

Josh chuckled. "No problem," he said as he eased his forward-motion throttles forward.

"Faster?" Dylan asked. "Are you sure that's a good idea?"

"No," Nathan admitted, "but it is an idea."

"I'm at the port gun," Jessica reported over the intercom.

"Port and starboard gunners, be ready to target the upper edges of the canyon walls, on my mark," Nathan called over the intercom. "Directly abeam of us. All other gunners continue firing at targets on our six!"

Talisha jinked her Sugali fighter from side to side, trying to avoid incoming fire as she rocketed skyward.

"Aft shields are down to eighteen percent," Talisha's AI warned. "I strongly recommend you execute an escape jump."

"You may be right," Talisha agreed as she pressed her jump button.

A subdued, blue-white flash filled her projection canopy and cockpit, and she suddenly found herself back in space, high above Volon. Again, her threat-warning indicator began flashing, only this time the threat was not from octos, but from gunships...four of them.

A series of energy blasts slammed into her starboard side, lighting up her shields. Several more followed aft, causing her back end to pitch wildly to port. More warning lights began turning red all over her console as additional alarms sounded.

"Aft shields have failed," Leta warned. "Starboard shields are at twenty percent. Port shields, thirty-seven percent..."

"I know, I know!" Talisha exclaimed, pressing her jump button again. Nothing happened.

"Jump drive is offline," Leta continued as the ship was struck several more times in rapid succession. "Four Dusahn gunships are closing from all sides. Main propulsion has failed. Reactor core destabilization alert. Imminent failure in thirty seconds. Initiating auto-rescue ejection sequence..."

"Not yet!" Talisha insisted. "I can still..."

All of her displays suddenly went dead, and her canopy projection system switched off, her canopy becoming transparent again. Along the sides of the outside of her cockpit, small doors opened, and the clamps holding her cockpit module released.

"Ejecting," Leta announced.

Eight Dusahn octo-fighters dropped in behind

the Voss, firing away as they closed. The Voss's guns returned fire, but the octo-fighters' forward shields kept the bolts of energy away.

Red bolts slammed into the Voss's aft shields at the rate of a dozen impacts per second, causing the weakening shield to glow constantly.

"Now!" Nathan called over the intercom speaker in Marcus's gun turret. "Blast the walls!"

Marcus spun his turret, tilting his controller to its maximum to bring the pairs of barrels on each side of him upward. He immediately opened fire, holding the triggers down tightly as his guns tore into the upper edge of the canyon walls passing by, blowing them apart and sending chunks of the mountainside flying inward behind them.

The incoming fire waned, then abruptly stopped, allowing the shields in front of Kit to stop glowing. Kit watched as the octos chasing them suddenly found themselves being pounded by rocks, some larger than the octos themselves.

The Voss shook as debris found the trailing edges of her nacelles, causing the deck below to pitch unpredictably. Despite the unsteady ride, Kit could not take his eyes off the sight before him as the Dusahn octo-fighters that had been on the verge of getting through their aft shields began falling from the sky, tumbling to the uneven terrain below. When the rocky shower ended, only two octos still pursued them, albeit from a greater distance than before.

"Now we're talking!" Kit exclaimed, taking aim and opening fire again.

"Oh my God!" Dylan exclaimed excitedly. "I can't believe that worked!"

"Sometimes you get lucky," Nathan stated, breathing a sigh of relief.

"Uh, guys?" Josh called, pointing at the sensor display.

Dylan looked at the display, his expression turning grim. "Razor Three is gone!"

"She jumped?" Nathan asked.

"No, I mean gone, as in destroyed!" Something else appeared on the sensor screen a moment later. "Wait! I'm getting a rescue transponder! She ejected!"

"Into space?" Josh wondered as he continued snaking through the winding canyon.

"The cockpits of Sugali fighters act as escape pods," Dylan explained. "Her AI probably sensed imminent destruction and automatically ejected her."

"It can do that?" Josh asked, surprised.

"The point is, she's still alive!"

Nathan reached for the comms panel. "Talisha! Come in! Talisha!"

Talisha was stunned by the sudden ejection and subsequent jump. As she shook off the effects, she looked around. Everything around her was shut down except for comms and life support, both of which were running on battery power.

"Talisha! Come in! Talisha!" Nathan called over comms.

"I'm here!" Talisha replied. "I'm good!" She looked around outside, not recognizing anything. Her cockpit was slowly tumbling, yawing to the right at about the same rate. All she could see outside were stars. "I have no idea where I'm at, but I'm okay for now."

Nathan breathed a sigh of relief, then looked down at the sensor screen on the center of the forward console. "Do we have her location?"

"She's in high orbit over Volon," Dylan reported. "Her ejection system must have been damaged as well. It's designed to jump her completely out of the combat area."

"Talisha, you're still in high orbit above Volon," Nathan called over comms.

"That can't be right."

"We're coming to get you," Nathan continued.

"You can't do that, Captain!" Talisha objected. "You have to hold out until help arrives! I'll be fine!"

"The hell she will," Josh disagreed. "She's already losing altitude. She doesn't have half the speed she needs to maintain a low orbit, let alone a high one."

"Talisha, can you survive reentry?" Nathan asked.

"I don't know," Talisha replied. "Everything is dead. All I've got are comms and life support."

"Then we're coming to get you."

"Captain..."

"I wasn't asking permission, Talisha," Nathan said, cutting her off. "Josh, let's go get her."

"You got it!" Josh replied, pulling back on his

flight control stick and pushing the throttles for his main engines forward.

The Voss pitched upward and accelerated sharply, pushing them back in their seats. Nathan held on tightly to the railing behind him to maintain his balance as they climbed.

"That's not how you're supposed..." Dylan sighed. "Never mind."

"Eyes open, people," Nathan warned his crew over the intercom. "We're going to rescue Talisha. Marcus, I'm going to need you back in the utility bay to help Kit with the rescue."

"Would you make up your mind?" Marcus complained as he unbuckled his restraints and clumsily maneuvered his oversized body out of the tiny gunner's chair.

"Stop whining," Nathan scolded jokingly.

"We need a bigger crew," Marcus grumbled as he made his way through the narrow hatch. "And a bigger ship!"

"You too, Jess," Nathan called.

"Me too what?"

"Go help Marcus and Kit with the rescue."

"What about my gun?" she asked as she unbuckled her restraints and slipped out of the gunner's chair.

"We'll have to make do with two guns for now," Nathan replied.

"Talk to me, Vlad," Nathan called over the intercom.

Vladimir stared at the shorted-out control boards before him, shaking his head. "I cannot fix this," he told Nathan. "Not without a new control board and four new power buffers."

"Can you reroute the energy in the jump cells to feed our shields?"

"That I can do," Vladimir replied, dropping the burnt control board.

"Can you extend our aft shield bubble a bit?"

Vladimir's brow furrowed. "How much is a bit?"

"We'll be in high orbit in twenty seconds," Dylan announced as the Voss rocketed out of Volon's atmosphere.

"How long until we reach Talisha?" Nathan asked.

"About thirty-five seconds," Dylan replied. "You're going to have to slow down, though, or we'll shoot right past her."

"Not my first rodeo, kid," Josh said as he adjusted his flight controls to intercept Talisha's escape pod.

"And that's another one for the guidebook," Dylan concluded, having no clue what Josh was talking about. "New contacts," he reported as the threat alarm beeped. "Four gunships just jumped in ahead of us. Looks like they're headed for her as well." Dylan looked over his shoulder at Nathan, uncertain. "Why would they do that?"

"Uh, because we're going there," Josh commented.

"They want to capture her," Nathan realized. "We need to hurry."

Vladimir pulled the power cable through the airlock connecting the Voss's port nacelle to the rest of the ship. Once back inside the main section, he pulled the cable just enough to reach the power junction box on the side wall of the corridor. After opening the panel's cover, he took the plug on the end of the cable and pushed it into the mating receptacle, giving it a twist to activate the connection. There was a loud pop, accompanied by a few sparks, causing Vladimir's hand to instantly go numb. "I hate this ship!" he exclaimed, shaking his tingling hand.

"The Voss is approaching," Talisha's AI reported.

"How long until we hit the atmosphere?"

"Eleven minutes and thirty-seven seconds. I would not worry, Talisha. There should be sufficient time for the Voss to effect rescue."

"Thanks for the pep talk," Talisha replied.

"We just got a huge surge in shield strength," Dylan announced.

"Vlad," Nathan called over the intercom. "Whatever you did, it worked."

"Why do you sound so surprised?" Vladimir wondered. "I can fix anything, remember?"

"You couldn't fix the jump drive," Nathan reminded him.

"Very funny," Vladimir replied. "For the record, I can fix it; I just can't fix it right now."

"All shields are back up to nearly full strength," Dylan added, shocked.

"Can you extend aft shields around Talisha's cockpit module?"

"I'm working on it," Vladimir assured him. "But the closer we are to her, the better. Extending our shields weakens them in the area of extension."

"You heard him," Nathan told Josh. "Get us in close."

"That was the plan," Josh replied. "Pitching over to fly ass-backwards."

"Can you just speak normally?" Dylan complained.

"What fun would that be?" Josh replied, initiating the maneuver.

Talisha peered out the left side of her canopy as her pod rolled over, spotting the Voss flying toward her, backwards.

Several flashes of light caught her eye. They were to the right of the Voss and at a far lower altitude, but before she could identify them, her rolling motion caused her to lose sight of them. "Leta, can you ID the contacts?"

"I am sorry, but I only have proximity sensors. I have no way to sense anything beyond a five-kilometer range."

"Voss," Talisha called over comms. "Jump flashes! I saw jump flashes below and downrange of you!"

Jessica entered the utility bay only moments after Marcus. She spotted the slowly tumbling cockpit rescue pod in the distance as it rose from below the ramp. The Voss stopped its pitching motion abruptly, continuing to close on the pod. "This is going to be fun," she commented, realizing the challenge before them. "Kit, you're the only one suited up. You're going to have to grab her and pull her in."

"You're kidding, right?" Kit could tell by the look on her face that she wasn't. "Let's do this," he declared, his visor dropping back down to seal up his helmet again.

"Three octo-fighters," Dylan announced. "They're on an intercept course."

"This may be a hot rescue," Nathan warned over comms. "Gunners, we have incoming octos. Below and down range."

"I don't have an angle," Mori reported.

"Josh, roll us ninety degrees so that both gunners can engage the incoming octos."

"Got it," Josh replied, initiating a slow roll.

"One hundred meters," Dylan reported. "Closing at three meters per second."

"You're going to need to slow down a lot more if you expect me to grab that thing," Kit warned over comms.

"Not until we get closer," Josh insisted as he ended the roll.

"Maybe we should start slowing now," Dylan suggested.

"Targets are in range," Jokay announced, the screech of his plasma cannons in the background.

"It'll take too long," Josh argued.

"He's right," Nathan agreed. "Approach fast, brake hard, grab quick."

"Sixty-five meters," Dylan updated. "I can't believe we're doing this."

"Just like catching rocks," Josh commented.

"How close do we have to be to extend shields around her, Vlad?" Nathan asked over the intercom.

"Twenty meters," Vladimir replied. "Any further and we might blow the emitters."

"Forty meters," Dylan updated. "We have to decelerate."

"I am, I am," Josh assured him, applying aft thrusters. The ship rocked and their shields flashed as the approaching octo-fighters opened fire. "That's not helping!"

Kit moved past the pale-blue shield that was keeping the Voss's utility bay properly pressurized, despite the aft end of the bay being open to space. "You might want to retract that gun," he warned Marcus as he moved out onto the ramp one step at a time, using his mag boots to keep him attached to the deck.

"Thirty meters," Dylan updated over the intercom. "Two meters per second closure."

Marcus grabbed the control handles on the back of the weapon, pulling the entire weapon back through the pressure shield and pressing the retract button on the side of the weapon's mounting bracket.

Kit kept his eyes on Talisha's tumbling cockpit rescue module as he braced himself at the center of the ramp. Suddenly, a blinding flash of blue-white light appeared just beyond the module, revealing a Dusahn gunship. The moment it appeared, its nearside gun turrets rotated and took aim on the aft end of the Voss. "Oh shit!"

Red bolts of energy slammed into the aft shields of the Voss, lighting them up in brilliant, red flashes.

Talisha instinctively ducked as red bolts of energy streaked past her on all sides, the interior of her cockpit bathed in red flashes as they passed.

Something struck the right side of her module, causing the entire unit to shift suddenly.

"What the..." Her entire cockpit unexpectedly shifted right, throwing her body against the left side. "What's happening?"

"A grappling system has attached itself to us," Leta reported. "We are now tethered to the Dusahn gunship."

"The gunship is moving away from us!" Dylan reported as the ship was rocked with incoming fire. "But so is the rescue module!"

"They've attached something to me!" Talisha reported. "They're pulling me in!"

"Josh! Move us in quickly!" Nathan ordered.

"This isn't going to work!" Josh warned. "We need to force that gunship to cut her loose!"

"Gunners!" Nathan called out over the intercom. "Pound that gunship!"

"Two more gunships jumped in!" Dylan reported over comms. "They're moving into position to attack!"

The ramp heaved under Kit's feet as the ship rocked from incoming fire.

"Shield strength is falling fast!" Dylan warned.

"I gotta break off!" Josh declared.

"Marcus!" Kit yelled. "Give me half gravity on the ramp!"

Marcus didn't ask any questions, just ran over to the control panel next to the forward hatch and activated the artificial gravity on the ramp, setting it at fifty percent normal gravity.

"Capsi, turn off mag boots and calculate range and rate of departure from the Voss of the rescue module. Update continuously and prepare a micro-jump."

"Calculating," his suit AI acknowledged. "Range, fifty meters and increasing at a rate of ten meters per second."

His feet now free, Kit ran back through the pressure shield into the utility bay, stopping around the middle of the bay.

"Departure rate increasing," his AI reported. "Twenty meters per second and climbing rapidly. Forty meters per second; fifty, sixty, one hundred, one fifty..."

"Josh!" Kit called over comms. "Line us up with Talisha and hold her steady for a few seconds!"

"Three hundred meters per second," his AI continued to report. "Range one point three kilometers and increasing rapidly."

"A few seconds is all you're gonna get!" Josh replied.

"What are you doing, Kit?" Jessica asked, already knowing the answer.

The ship rocked as more bolts struck their shields.

"Wish me luck," Kit replied.

"We're lined up!" Josh announced.

"Kit?" Nathan called over comms. "If you're about to do what I think you're about to do..."

Kit winked at Jessica, then charged out the back

through the pressure shield, covering the length of the ramp in a few seconds, finally jumping off the end into space. "Capsi! Track the target! Am I lined up?"

"Affirmative," his AI replied. "Range to target is three kilometers and climbing."

"Jump me to the target!" Kit ordered.

"Due to the target's speed, you will have one point five seconds to grab hold after coming out of the jump," his AI warned. "After that, the target will have accelerated beyond your reach."

"Just do it!" Kit instructed.

"Jumping in three……two……one……"

"Holy crap!" Marcus exclaimed over the intercom. "He fuckin' jumped!"

"What?" Nathan exclaimed in disbelief.

"Go Vasya, go!" Mori yelled in encouragement of his comrade.

"FINALLY!" Josh yelled. "Someone crazier than me!"

The ship rocked as more bolts of energy slammed into their shields.

"Shields are down to forty percent!" Dylan warned. "This is not good!"

"Go after her!" Nathan instructed.

"Go after who?" Josh wondered. "Oh, her," he added, realizing what Nathan meant. "I'm on it."

"Gunners! Stop that gunship!" Nathan ordered. "But check your aim! We don't want to hit Talisha!"

"Or Kit!" Jokay added.

Suddenly, Talisha's tumbling rescue pod was right in front of him. He reached out with both hands, barely managing to grab a piece of its exposed frame with one hand. He squeezed tight, feeling the strength of his built-in micro-exoskeleton clamping his fingers down tightly.

Kit felt as if his arm was about to be ripped from his shoulder, but he held on tight. Finally, he managed to get his other hand around and grab the frame, then pulled himself in close.

A helmeted man suddenly appeared to her left only centimeters beyond her canopy, startling Talisha.

"What's a nice girl like you doing all the way out here?" Kit joked, smiling at her.

"Are you insane!" Talisha exclaimed.

"Yes!" Kit replied. "Voss! I've got her!" The pod suddenly shifted sharply as the gunship began reeling them in. Kit nearly lost his grip, his body swinging free. "Sort of!"

"This is not going to work!" Mori warned over the intercom. "There's no way I can get a shot at that gunship unless you can get us on another angle!"

"I can barely keep them off our back!" Josh exclaimed.

The ship rocked violently, lurching to one side and nearly knocking Nathan off his feet. "You call that keeping them off our back?!" The ship rocked again as more incoming fire slammed into their shields.

"Shields down to thirty percent!" Dylan warned.

"Stay with that gunship, Josh!" Nathan ordered.

Kit managed to brace himself again, pulling his body back in tight to the side of Talisha's canopy. "They're pulling us in," he realized, moving carefully around the outside of the pod as it was reeled in closer and closer to the gunship that had captured it.

"What are you doing?" Talisha wondered.

"I'm going to cut the tether!" Kit explained.

"They'll just use another!" Talisha warned.

"Maybe! Maybe not!" Kit replied.

"That's a lot of maybes."

"They have to drop shields to reel them in, right?" Nathan asked.

Dylan looked back over his shoulder. "You're asking me?"

"Jess!" Nathan called. "Can you get a shot past Talisha and Kit with the tail gun?"

"It won't make a dent in their shields!" Jessica warned.

"Hopefully it won't have to!" Nathan replied.

"You can't do this!" Talisha insisted. "When we cross the shield barrier, you'll be killed!"

"They have to drop their shields to pull you in, right?" Kit surmised. When she didn't respond, he turned to look at her through the canopy. "Right?"

Talisha shrugged.

"Well I guess we're about to find out," Kit decided.

Jessica reached up and pulled the tail gun back down from its overhead storage position, allowing it to swing its barrels aft through the pressure shield once again. The targeting screen lit up and began searching for a target, just as a small blue-white flash of light appeared in the distance. "Shit!"

Dylan stared at the sensor display in disbelief. "They're gone," he finally announced.

"They've jumped," Jessica reported over the intercom.

The threat-warning light began flashing again, and the threat alarm sounded. "Incoming missiles! Six of them!"

"We can't outrun them," Josh warned.

"Our shields aren't going to hold!" Dylan added.

"Can you get us back down into the atmosphere?" Nathan asked. "There are only three or four octos left, right? We can probably defend against that."

"Believe me, I'm trying," Josh assured him as he began maneuvering like a madman.

"They've gotta be coming from the frigate," Nathan decided.

"Those missiles can't reach us down in the atmosphere, right?" Dylan asked.

"They can," Nathan replied, "and they will."

The jump flash subsided, and Kit opened his eyes and looked around. The Voss, the Dusahn octos and gunships attacking it, even the planet, were gone. "Okay, I wasn't expecting that."

Kit turned to face the gunship that was reeling them in, then jumped toward it, pushing off of Talisha's rescue module.

"What are you doing?" she yelled.

"Plan B!" Kit replied as he drifted toward the gunship. He reached out and grabbed the tether, gaining hold about halfway between the gunship and Talisha's rescue module.

Talisha's module swayed abruptly, being pulled by Kit's momentum. "You're insane!"

"No, I'm Kit," he replied. "Nice to meet you."

"Oh my God," she exclaimed. "Are all Ghatazhak this crazy?"

"Actually, I'm sort of a special case," Kit replied as he pulled himself along the tether toward the gunship.

"What are you going to do?"

"I'm cutting you free," Kit replied as he grabbed hold of the side of the gunship. He turned and pointed his wrist cannon toward the tether behind him and fired, severing the line.

"They'll just fire another one," Talisha told him.

"Not if I can help it."

"You should save yourself and let them take me."

"And where would I go?" Kit asked as he climbed inside the open bay on the underside of the gunship where the tether winch was located. With a push of his legs, he propelled himself across the bay, landing on the opposite side, next to the airlock hatch. A few taps on the control pad to the right of the hatch revealed that it was not locked. "Well that's just dumb."

"They're blocking us in," Josh warned as the Voss continued to shake violently with incoming weapons impacts.

"Shields are down to eighteen percent!" Dylan announced. "Missile impacts in forty seconds!"

"Why didn't they use jump missiles on us?" Josh wondered.

"They're afraid they'd take out friendlies," Nathan replied. "Dylan, find that frigate!"

"It's not on my screen!" Dylan replied.

"They must be firing from over the horizon, using targeting data from one of the octos," Nathan surmised.

The Voss suddenly lurched to port, struck hard on her starboard side.

"We've lost starboard shields!" Dylan reported. "Grav-lift failure in the starboard nacelle!"

"That means we can't land!" Josh realized.

"I guess we stand and fight then," Nathan decided. "Gunners! Target the incoming missiles!"

The outer hatch of the gunship's recovery bay airlock slid open, and Kit used the edge of the hatch to pull himself inside. Once he passed through the hatch, the artificial gravity inside the airlock pulled his feet to the deck, and he found himself standing upright again. He quickly turned around and activated the outer hatch, causing it to close, then turned back to face the inner hatch.

"Kit!" Talisha called as she watched the gunship pull away from her. "I can't see you! Kit!"

She watched in horror as the gunship began a slow turn to come about and reacquire her. As she suspected, they were not about to let her escape.

With the airlock now repressurized, the inner hatch slid open, revealing four armed Dusahn officers, all taking aim on Kit.

"Hello there!" Kit greeted, waving. "Can you direct me to your command deck?"

All four officers fired, their beams of energy ricocheting off Kit's personal shield, slamming into the walls, and luckily, into one of the Dusahn officers. "Well that was stupid," Kit said as he sprang into action.

"I got one!" Mori exclaimed over the intercom.

"That's three down!" Dylan reported.

"Keep our starboard side away from them, Josh!" Nathan barked.

"I'm trying!"

"Four down!" Dylan updated. "Ten seconds!"

"Got it!" Jokay yelled "I got that fucker!"

"Five down!" Dylan cried out.

"Brace for impact!" Nathan yelled.

Red-orange bolts of plasma streaked past them on all sides like a rain of fire. One of them struck the last missile a split second before it impacted their shields. Still, the explosion rocked the ship from side to side, tossing her crew about wildly.

"Sensors are offline!" Dylan reported.

"What the hell just..." Nathan began to say.

"Voss, Aurora!" a voice called over comms. "Hold course while we assist!"

"YES!" Nathan exclaimed.

"Gunyoki are away!" Ensign Keller reported from the Aurora's communications console.

"Lieutenant Yuati, disengage our attack on the octos and gunship," Cameron directed. "Let the Gunyoki deal with them."

"Aye, sir," the tactical officer replied.

"Multiple contacts!" Kaylah reported from the sensor station. "Eight missiles just came over the horizon. They're targeting the Voss."

"Helm, put us between those missiles and the Voss. Tactical, point-defenses!"

"Maneuvering into the missile path," the helmsman acknowledged.

"Engaging point-defenses," the tactical officer announced.

"Kaylah, launch a recon drone over the horizon to find the ship launching those missiles," Cameron ordered as the Aurora's point-defenses opened fire on the incoming missiles. "Lieutenant, put four missiles on the cats. Two busters and two nukes. I want that ship out of our space."

"Busters and nukes, aye," the tactical officer replied.

"The Aurora is acting as a shield against the incoming missiles!" Dylan reported excitedly. "There are Gunyoki all over the place!" he added, watching out the starboard window as the Gunyoki chased away the remaining octos and gunships.

"They're jumping away!" Mori exclaimed from the dorsal gun turret.

"I thought the Dusahn fought to the death," Dylan said.

"Not when they don't have much left to fight with," Nathan corrected, a wave of relief washing over him.

"Voss, Aurora Actual," Cameron called over comms.

Nathan reached up to the overhead comm-panel. "It's about time!"

"Sorry about the delay," Cameron replied. "I thought it prudent to bring some extra muscle to the party. Sensors show you've taken some damage yet again. Is everyone alright?"

"We've lost track of Kit," Nathan replied.

"Vasya?"

"Who else?" Nathan replied. "He was captured trying to rescue Talisha. A gunship nabbed them both and jumped away before we could get to them."

"I take it your jump drive is down," Cameron surmised. "I suggest you set down on our pressure deck to effect repairs while you take a Reaper down to complete your mission on Volon."

"What about Kit and Talisha?" Nathan asked. "I doubt that gunship jumped far, probably just enough to get away from us so that they could complete the capture."

"We'll start a search," Cameron promised. "If they're still in the system, we'll find them. Aurora Actual, out."

Nathan sighed, his head hanging down as the post-action fatigue began to hit. "Josh, do you think you can put us on deck safely?"

Josh let his head fall against the headrest. "I think I'll let the AI handle this one," he decided, turning to look at Dylan.

Talisha's eyes widened as the Dusahn gunship moved into position over her, much closer than before. As she had feared, another grappler slammed into the side of her rescue module, and the gunship began reeling her in again.

"Hey!" Kit called over comms. "What do you think we should name this thing?"

"Kit?"

"You want to name it Kit?"

"Where are you?"

"In the pilot's seat of this gunship," Kit replied. "The entire crew suddenly became unable to perform their duties......ever."

Talisha breathed a sigh of relief.

"I'll have you in the bay in a minute," Kit assured her.

"I take back everything bad I ever said about the Ghatazhak," Talisha told him.

"No need," Kit assured her, laughing. "It was probably true."

CHAPTER SIX

General Pellot stormed into SilTek Security's defense command center. Additional officers and technicians scrambled to their stations as alert klaxons sounded in the distance and threat condition lights flashed.

Upon entering, the general immediately looked to the collection of massive display screens along the front wall of the facility, noting that a single contact was the cause of the alert. "What have we got, Colonel?" the general asked.

"An unidentified ship appeared on our outer defense perimeter moments ago. Within seconds, it had jumped to the edge of our system."

"The Benicasi can't make repetitive jumps so quickly," the general said. "Ristani can, but we haven't seen them in a while."

"Intel shows the Ristani are currently involved in a dispute with the Sinato."

"Again?"

Another alarm sounded, interrupting their conversation.

"Target has jumped to high orbit!" one of the technicians reported urgently. "Automated defense systems have activated!"

"Batteries one four seven and one four eight have acquired and are launching intercepts!" the weapons officer reported.

"Target has jumped again!" the lead tracking officer announced.

"Where?" the general demanded.

"Far side. Target is coming about."

"Batteries five two four and five two five are launching intercepts!" the weapons officer reported.

"Who the hell is it?" the general wondered.

"Eight intercepts have jumped!" the weapons officer reported. "Target is engaging the intercepts!"

General Pellot watched the icons representing their intercept missiles disappear from the display as they neared the unidentified target. "Definitely not Benicasi," he said.

"Two impacts!"

The icon representing the unidentified contact remained on the screen.

"It must be shielded," the colonel decided.

"Six more intercepts have launched," the weapons officer announced.

"Target has jumped."

The general studied the other screens, finally finding the new location of the icon. "There!" he said, pointing.

"Target has jumped into the atmosphere!" the tracking officer announced.

"Defense batteries have locked on and are firing!" the weapons officer reported.

"Public alert sirens have been activated."

"Target is scanning the surface!" the senior sensor officer announced. "Wide beam, full spectrum, active!"

"All batteries are firing!"

"I want that target destroyed...NOW!" the general barked.

Suddenly, the icon disappeared.

The general glanced at all the screens again, expecting to see the icon but did not. "Did we get it?"

"Negative," the senior sensor officer replied.

"Target jumped again," the tracking officer added.

"To where?" the general wondered.

After several moments, the senior sensor officer reported, "No contacts, sir. Target appears to have departed our defense zone."

General Pellot did not look pleased. "How the hell did that ship evade our defenses?" He looked at the colonel. "Run all readings through all known databases, including the ones the Karuzari gave us. I want to know who the hell that was and why they were here."

* * *

Nathan entered the Aurora's bridge, sharing an appreciative nod with the Ghatazhak guard at the entrance when the guard did not announce his arrival.

"Welcome back," Cameron greeted, rising from the command chair. "I trust things went well on Volon?"

"They were a little preoccupied, what with all the damage they had to deal with," Nathan replied. "But they were interested."

"The fact that they were just pounded by the Dusahn probably had something to do with it," Jessica added as she entered the bridge.

"How's the Voss?" Nathan asked.

"Vlad and the SilTek engineering droids have been working nonstop since you landed. His last report an hour ago indicated that the damage was actually fairly light. He expects to have her back up to specs and ready for action in about fourteen hours."

"Gotta love those droids," Jessica commented.

"That's good news," Nathan stated, turning to head for his ready room. "You have the conn, Lieutenant," he ordered the tactical officer, indicating for Cameron to follow them.

Nathan and Jessica entered the room, with

Nathan heading for his desk while Jessica assumed her usual position sprawled out on the couch. Cameron entered a moment later, closing the hatch behind her.

"Something up?" Nathan asked, noticing that Cameron had closed the hatch.

"We received an urgent communication from SilTek Defense Command about an hour ago," Cameron began. "They were buzzed by a small ship of unknown origin a few hours ago."

"Buzzed?" Nathan wondered.

"It jumped through their defenses, only taking a few hits along the way, but apparently suffering no significant damage. It finally jumped into the atmosphere, flying over the city. It performed a full-spectrum scan before jumping away."

"It didn't attack?" Jessica asked.

"Never fired a shot."

"And they have no idea who sent it?" Nathan asked to confirm.

"They had no idea," Cameron replied.

"And we do?" Jessica surmised by her inflection.

"We still don't recognize the origin of the ship itself," explained as she handed her data pad to Nathan, "but Kaylah examined the characteristics of the target's sensor beams, and she believes they are very similar to Dusahn sensor technology."

"SilTek's too far away," Jessica argued. "It would take the Dusahn months to reach them."

"As far as we know, the Dusahn don't even know of SilTek's existence," Cameron stated. "However, they could have used their jump-trail tracking methods to follow one of our cargo ships back to SilTek. They could even have followed the Voss back to SilTek. Their gunships and octos do have series jump capability."

Nathan studied the data pad a moment. "I think this might be a Deca runner."

"A what?" Jessica asked.

"Deca is a small system on the outer edge of the Pentaurus sector," Nathan explained.

"I've never heard of it," Cameron said.

"That's not surprising," Nathan replied. "It's probably not called Deca in our star charts, and Deca doesn't allow any ships other than their own to enter the system."

"How do you know about them?" Jessica wondered.

"I saw a ship like this one on Lellandy once. Marcus is the one who told me about its origin at the time. They called them runners because they were used to run goods between Deca worlds."

"Worlds?" Jessica wondered.

"Deca has just a single gas giant, but it has dozens of moons orbiting it, four of which are hospitable, and six of which are colonized. They only began converting their ships to jump ships about a year ago. Story is that some idiot cargo captain tried convincing the Decans to let him haul some of their resources to other systems. But the Decans like to shoot first and ask questions later. They reverse-engineered the jump drive technology from the wreckage, and voila, they had access to a whole new group of potential clients for their resources."

"How did the Dusahn get hold of one of these runners?" Jessica wondered.

"Deca's not too far off the beaten path for them," Nathan replied.

"Then we're assuming that it was operated by the Dusahn," Jessica surmised.

"It would be the safest assumption at the moment," Cameron suggested.

"Have you informed SilTek about your suspicions?" Nathan asked Cameron.

"Not yet. Kaylah just gave me her report while you were landing. I figured I'd wait to speak with you about it first."

Nathan looked at the data pad again, sighing. "If this is the Dusahn, it changes things."

"How so?" Jessica wondered. "SilTek is outside of their reach, right?"

"An hour ago, I would have said they were outside of the Dusahn's recon range," Nathan replied.

"It took the Dusahn three days to reach the Rogen system," Jessica insisted. "A week to reach Orswella. SilTek is what, three times that distance?"

"How hard would it be to strap an antimatter warhead onto a runner?" Nathan pointed out.

"Great," Jessica stated. "Anything we can do to prevent that?"

"Short of toppling the Dusahn Empire?" Nathan replied.

"Maybe SilTek can beef up their defenses," Cameron suggested. "Come up with some new tech or something?"

"Other than a full planetary shield that can withstand an antimatter blast?" Nathan replied. "Doubtful."

"Surely they can come up with something," Jessica insisted.

"That was the whole point of that challenge," Nathan told her. "To demonstrate that their defenses could be defeated."

Jessica sighed, putting her feet up on Nathan's desk. "How much time do you think we have?"

"Assume for a moment that the Dusahn first started following our cargo ships three weeks ago," Nathan began, pushing Jessica's feet off his desk.

"Why three weeks?" Jessica wondered.

"That's when we liberated Corinair," Cameron explained. "After that, our ships were running back and forth between Corinair and SilTek on a regular basis."

"But they were using the evasion algorithm," Jessica pointed out.

"Which doesn't make it impossible to follow a jump trail..."

"It only makes it take longer," Nathan said, completing Cameron's sentence.

"Much longer," Cameron added. "And they had to be curious about where we were getting all our new technology from."

"It was only a matter of time before the Dusahn found SilTek."

"But why destroy it?" Jessica asked.

"Because they don't have the resources to conquer it," Cameron explained. "Denying us those resources is their best hope of survival."

Nathan thought for a moment, taking a deep breath and letting it out in a long sigh. "We can't wait," he decided. "We must go to the Jung and ask for help."

"Wouldn't it be better to simply take out all of the Dusahn's ships?" Jessica suggested.

"We could, but we'd have to take out every jump-capable ship they had," Cameron explained. "Warships, gunships, runners, shuttles, you name it."

"That would be nearly impossible," Nathan agreed.

"And they'd likely just retaliate by launching more jump missiles at Corinair," Cameron added.

"We can take out their surface-based jump missile launchers as well," Jessica argued.

"They'd just build more," Nathan replied. "And in secret. Hell, they could create jump missiles that could reach all the way to SilTek and deliver antimatter warheads that way. The only way to protect SilTek, and everyone else, is to defeat the Dusahn once and for all."

"But there's got to be a better way than asking the Jung for help," Cameron insisted.

"It's either that or provoke Griogair into blowing up his own empire," Nathan replied. "And I'm not ready to sacrifice billions, even if it means saving trillions more. Not if there's a better way."

"Even if that better way is to ally with an old enemy?" Cameron wondered.

"Believe me, it's not something I want to do," Nathan assured her.

"If you fight Griogair, he will kill you," Jessica reminded him.

"Which is also an outcome I'd like to avoid," Nathan replied. "The question is, how?"

"And you really think the Jung are the answer," Cameron repeated.

"I don't know," Nathan admitted. "But I intend to find out. After all, the Jung have just as much motivation to see the Dusahn defeated as anyone. Perhaps even more so."

"So when are we going?" Jessica asked.

"You said the Voss is supposed to be ready tomorrow?" Nathan asked Cameron.

"According to Vlad, sometime tomorrow morning."

"Then we'll leave tomorrow afternoon," Nathan

decided. "Meanwhile, we need to increase the frequency of our recon drone sorties to Takara and prevent them from leaving the system."

"Are you suggesting we operate a blockade?" Cameron wondered.

"I don't see much choice," Nathan replied. "Especially after their attack on Volon."

"That's going to be nearly impossible," Cameron insisted.

"Constant recons, coupled with constant patrols along all known shipping lanes in and out of the system, and regular recon of all potential destination worlds would be a good start," Nathan suggested.

"You're talking dozens of worlds," Cameron reminded him. "We don't have the resources to monitor that many destinations, let alone to interdict."

"Then start with our allies," Nathan suggested. "And keep the Aurora on quick-response readiness."

"It wouldn't hurt to keep some Gunyoki on board, as well," Jessica suggested.

"If a Dusahn ship gets past our blockade and shows up at one of our allies, the Aurora should be able to respond within a minute or two," Nathan stated.

"More than enough time for the Dusahn to hit them with a few nukes," Jessica pointed out, "or worse."

Nathan looked at Jessica. "You realize you're making my case for going to the Jung, right?"

"Believe me," Jessica replied, "I'm not trying to."

* * *

Nathan ascended the stair ladder to the Voss's command deck, making his usual one-eighty to the left to go around the railing that encircled the opening to the lower deck. His default duty position had become standing behind the flight pilots' seats and leaning against the backside of that railing. From there, he could see what his pilots were doing, watch the main sensor display on the center console, and have access to the comm-panel on the center overhead console. It wasn't ideal, but it worked for him.

Today, however, he found something different. "What's this?" he asked, pointing to some padding mounted along the railing where he normally leaned.

"We thought you could use a real duty station," Dylan explained from the copilot's seat, smiling.

Nathan took up his normal position, leaning back against the padding. "Not exactly a command chair, but..."

"There's more," Dylan interrupted. "Push that orange button on the overhead to the left."

Nathan glanced up, finding the button with ease. He pressed it, and a small panel deployed from a newly installed box behind the pilot's seat on the left. The panel reached its full height, about a meter off the deck, and then folded out into its fully deployed position in front of him. "What the heck is this?"

"We gave you an interface screen," Dylan explained. "That way, you won't have to keep bending over to see the overhead panel."

"A nice thought, but..."

"It's a fully functional touchscreen display," Dylan continued. "You can access just about any system on the ship. You can set it up however you want, just like an auxiliary station. This way, you can do anything you need to, without having to tell one of us to do it."

"How did you manage to do all this in one day?" Nathan wondered.

"Actually, Del's people started working on it nearly a week ago. It arrived this morning."

"Whose idea was this?"

Josh said nothing, just pointing at Dylan.

"Good thinking, Dylan," Nathan congratulated as he activated the display. "What's this button on the side?"

"It expands your back rest."

Curious, Nathan pressed the button. Padded sections extended out the sides of the pad against which he leaned, angling forward slightly to create a semi-wraparound cradle. At the same time, a piece extended upward, providing more back support.

"Next time we get pounded, that should keep you from falling," Dylan explained.

"Nice, but I'd prefer that we just avoid being pounded," Nathan joked.

"You and me both," Dylan agreed.

"We're ready for departure any time," Josh announced.

"The comm-panel on the overhead now folds down as well," Dylan added.

"Very convenient," Nathan replied, pulling the panel down for inspection. "Marcus," he called over the intercom. "Are we buttoned up and ready to go?"

"Ready to depart whenever you are, Cap'n."

"Take us out, Josh," Nathan instructed.

"You got it."

"Don't you look comfy," Jessica cooed as she entered the command deck.

"Pretty spiffy, huh?"

"Very," Jessica agreed. "I hope you don't mind, but I brought three additional crewmen on board."

"Why?" Nathan wondered.

"Since we're going into Jung space, I figured it would be better if we had enough hands to keep all guns manned instead of using Vlad, Marcus, and me."

"Do we have room?" Nathan wondered.

"Marcus created additional storage space in the missile bays, so we were able to clear the upper bunks."

"Who gets to double up?" Nathan asked.

"The Ghatazhak can double up," she replied. "They're used to it."

"Who are the other two?"

"These guys," Jessica replied, pointing at Josh and Dylan.

"What?" Josh complained.

"Most of the time, only one of you is up here," Jessica explained, "so you're naturals for hot-racking. Besides, would you rather bunk with Marcus?"

"Oh hell no," Josh replied. He looked at Dylan. "I call bottom bunk."

* * *

Nathan had taken advantage of their recharge layover to get some much-needed sleep. He had no idea how the next few days would go, let alone the next few hours.

Upon opening his cabin door, he found Dylan on the other side. "Come to get me for the final jump to Nor-Patri?"

"Not exactly," Dylan replied.

"What's up?" Nathan asked, sensing the young man's pensive mood.

"Can I speak with you a moment?" Dylan asked, looking to his right to confirm no one was within earshot.

"Sure," Nathan replied, stepping aside to let him into his cramped little cabin. The XKs, though far from small, did not offer much in the way of crew accommodations. Jessica often joked that the cabins on the Voss were smaller than the bathrooms in their quarters on the Aurora. It was an exaggeration, of course, but not by much.

"Something bothering you?" Nathan asked as he closed the door.

Dylan took a breath, obviously uncomfortable with whatever he was about to say.

"You're worried that you're not up to the task of filling Loki's shoes," Nathan surmised.

Dylan stared at him, shocked. "How did you know?"

Nathan laughed. "I've been there. Believe me, I know how you feel."

"I honestly believed that I could do this," Dylan explained. "I mean, I'm great in all the simulations."

"No matter how realistic a simulation is, it's still just a simulation," Nathan told him.

"It was real enough for you," Dylan pointed out.

"The first time, yes," Nathan agreed. "But that's because I didn't even know such a realistic simulation was possible."

"So knowing that it's a simulation makes you act differently?"

"Very much so. In the second sim, the one for the challenge, I took risks that I would not normally take, simply because I knew that it was a simulation."

"And because the stakes were so high," Dylan added.

"That too."

"Tekans believe that simulations are everything. That they are the key to intensive training, education, and preparation. Without them, our civilization would not be anywhere near as advanced as we are."

"Did you ever wonder if maybe your dependence on simulations, at least in some disciplines, might be holding you back?"

"I don't see how."

"The fact that you're standing here now is a perfect example," Nathan explained. "Would you have taken this assignment had you not honed your skills and built up your confidence in the sims?"

"Probably," Dylan admitted.

Nathan smiled. "At least you're honest."

"It's just that...I find myself hesitating. I mean, I know what to do, I'm just uncertain. I feel like I have to think about everything twice before doing it. In the sims, I just did it."

"Again, you didn't fear the consequences, because you knew they weren't real."

Dylan thought for a moment, then made another admission. "Don't tell anyone, but I always turn the simulated pain settings down to zero."

"Seems like that would compound the problem," Nathan told him. "Maybe you should try turning it back up?"

"I'm afraid to," Dylan admitted. "I don't think I'm cut out for this kind of assignment."

"I don't know," Nathan replied. "I think you're doing pretty well so far."

"Really?"

"There's room for improvement, but considering your age and your lack of actual experience, you're doing just fine."

"Then how come Josh is always on me?"

"That's just Josh," Nathan explained. "He did the

same thing to Loki, even though Loki was just as good a pilot as Josh; even better, in some ways."

"I don't see how that's possible," Dylan insisted. "Josh is an amazing pilot. Just don't tell him I said so."

"Yes, he is; and no, I won't," Nathan agreed. "His head is big enough as it is."

Dylan sighed, obviously still bothered by something.

"There's something else?"

"I don't think I'm the right guy to fly a Lightning," Dylan stated after a few seconds. "I think I'm too dependent on AIs. P-Seventy-Twos are much more manual...and..."

"And?"

"And they're so small."

"Small?"

"It feels like there's nothing between you and space."

"There's not much more between you and space right now," Nathan told him.

"I don't know, it's just different. I feel apprehensive in the Lightning sims. And that's in the sim. Can you imagine how I'd feel in the real thing?"

Nathan sighed. "It would have been nice to know this before we departed."

"I'm sorry about that, Captain. The last thing I want is to let you down. I just thought I could handle it." Dylan hung his head down in shame. "I guess I was wrong."

"You're not wrong, Dylan," Nathan insisted. "In fact, you're admitting your own shortcomings, and that's good. It would have been better to hear about it earlier, yes, but better late than never."

"What are you going to do with me?" Dylan wondered.

"Do you feel comfortable flying the Voss?" Nathan asked.

"For the most part, yes," Dylan replied. "I'm not sure about it when things get...you know..."

"Dangerous?"

"I get really scared."

"I'd be worried if you didn't," Nathan told him.

"Do you get scared?"

"Every single time," Nathan admitted.

"Really?" Dylan couldn't believe it. "You sure don't seem scared."

"Fear keeps you honest," Nathan explained. "Fear keeps you from doing stupid things."

"But how do you keep it from making you hesitate?"

"You just do," Nathan told him. "I wish I could give you some magic answer, but that's the truth of it. You just do. Maybe it comes with time and experience, or maybe one is born with that ability. Hell, maybe it's both. You just have to not let your fear control you. Recognize it; respect it; but continue on in spite of it."

"I'll try," Dylan agreed. "But when all this is over, I think I'd like to go back to AI coding. Who knows? Maybe I can come up with a simulation to help the user overcome their fears."

"Maybe," Nathan agreed. "In the meantime, we'll keep you on the Voss. I don't see us needing the Lightnings this trip, but if we do, Josh and I will fly them, and you can stay at the helm."

"I'd appreciate that," Dylan thanked, relief obvious in his voice.

"Now let's go say hello to the Jung, shall we?"

Dylan rolled his eyes. "I was feeling better until you said that."

* * *

Nathan and Dylan came up the stair ladder onto the Voss's command deck, moving forward past Jessica, who was sitting at the auxiliary station, her feet on the console as usual.

"How are we looking?" Nathan asked Josh.

"We were charged an hour ago," Josh replied. "We were just waiting for you."

"I told you to wake me when we were charged."

Josh pointed at Jessica.

"You needed your sleep," Jessica insisted.

Nathan just shook his head. "We all set?"

"Jump is plotted and loaded," Josh assured him. "All we have to do is push the little button, and bam, it's Hello, Jung!"

"Hopefully without the bam part," Dylan commented as he took his seat at the copilot's station.

"Should we man the guns?" Jessica asked.

"I suppose it wouldn't hurt," Nathan agreed. "But no one fires unless ordered."

"Hey, guys!" Jessica called out, her head leaning back a bit as if she were speaking toward the overhead speaker of the intercom. "Everyone man your guns but hold fire until ordered. We're about to jump to Nor-Patri."

"On our way," Kit replied over the intercom.

"What about shields?" Dylan wondered.

"Are they still set to automatically power up if attacked?" Nathan asked.

"Yes. I even programmed the AI to first raise only the shield toward the threat. That way, it can bring it up faster."

"What about the rest of the shields?" Josh asked.

"The rest of them still need a direct command to be raised," Dylan explained. "Unless, of course, attacks increase or come from multiple directions." Dylan looked at Nathan. "That is what you wanted, right?"

"It is," Nathan confirmed. "Well done."

Vladimir ascended the stair ladder, with Marcus coming up behind him. "I don't want to miss this," Vladimir stated.

"I would be just fine missing this," Marcus grumbled. "Are you sure you want to do this?" he questioned Nathan. "Remember, these people hate you."

"I know," Nathan assured him.

"I mean really hate you," Marcus continued. "Like you're the devil or something."

"I know," Nathan repeated.

"Like willing to start a Tonba-Hon-Venar over you just bein' alive...hate you."

"Marcus," Nathan said, becoming annoyed.

"Just sayin'."

Dylan leaned toward Josh. "What's a Tonba-Hon-Venar?" he whispered.

"You don't want to know, trust me."

Jessica pulled her feet down off the console and turned toward it, checking her displays. "All six main guns are manned," she stated. "Should they power up?"

"Not yet," Nathan insisted. "We need to look as non-threatening as possible."

"You're gonna jump into the Jung home system, unannounced, and hope they don't blow us out of the sky?" Marcus wondered. "Well that's just plain stupid."

"They're not going to blow us out of the sky, Marcus," Nathan insisted. "If anything, they're going to try to disable us so they can capture a jump-enabled ship."

"Oh that's so much better," Marcus grumbled. "Cuz we all know how accurate Jung weapons are."

"I'm with Marcus," Josh commented.

"Let's not forget that the Jung do not have jump technology," Nathan reminded them. "We'll be facing conventional ships and weaponry, so we should be able to evade them fairly easily."

"Famous last words," Marcus muttered as he took a seat at the auxiliary station next to Jessica.

"You people are making me nervous," Dylan admitted.

"We'll be fine," Nathan assured him.

"Is that why you wanted to be fully charged when we jump in?" Josh commented.

"Just make sure you always have an escape jump loaded and ready."

"No kidding," Josh muttered under his breath.

Nathan took a deep breath, letting it out slowly. The last time he had been in the Jung home system, he had been executed. His instincts warned him to stay as far away from the Jung as possible, but those instincts also told him that the Jung were their only hope at defeating the Dusahn. Furthermore, as long as the Jung remained an enemy of Earth, the birthplace of all humanity would remain in peril.

Again, fate had led him into the serpent's lair, and again he had no choice but to enter.

"Jump us in," Nathan instructed calmly.

Josh, too, took a deep breath as he activated the jump sequencer. "Jumping in three......two...... one......"

The jump flash washed over the Voss's command deck, translating through her windows and illuminating her interior for an instant. As expected, the stars shifted slightly. The distance they had jumped was only fifty light years, and the stars in the background were quite distant. The change was nearly imperceptible, but Nathan always noticed it, no matter how minute it was.

"Jump complete," Josh reported. "We are now in the Patoray system. There's a phrase I never thought I'd say."

"Set course for Nor-Patri," Nathan instructed. "Maintain current speed."

"At our current speed, it'll take us days to get there," Josh pointed out.

"I'm aware," Nathan assured him.

"Okay," Josh replied, entering the new course.

"You're not seriously going to spend days cruising in, are you?" Dylan wondered.

"Don't worry," Nathan assured him. "They may not have jump drives, but they can use their linear FTL systems well. They'll be intercepting us shortly."

"Then...shouldn't we take some sort of evasive action now?"

"We want them to know we are here," Nathan reminded him.

"Don't forget that the Jung are at war," Jessica reminded.

Nathan just shot her a look.

"Just sayin'," she defended, hands up.

Nathan flipped down the comm-panel, setting their array to transmit on all channels and frequencies.

"What are you doing?" Jessica inquired.

"Saying hello," Nathan explained.

"What kind of message?"

"Attention Jung Empire. This is the Karuzari Alliance ship Dalen Voss. We mean you no harm. We only wish to speak with your leaders. We are requesting permission to approach your world for the purposes of two-way communication. We eagerly await your response."

"It will be hours before anyone hears that message," Vladimir said.

"Assuming that no one closer hears it first," Nathan replied.

Dylan looked at his sensor display. "I'm not detecting anyone."

"That doesn't mean they're not there," Nathan said. "It just means we can't see them yet."

"Right."

"You get used to it," Josh assured Dylan.

"The last time we jumped into this system, we were met with about thirty missiles," Jessica stated. "And rather quickly I might add."

"Galiardi's attacks may have weakened their defenses," Nathan suggested, still not seeing any contacts on the sensor display.

"Or they just don't see us as a threat," Marcus said.

"More likely they want us to come further in so they can capture us," Nathan surmised.

"Maybe we should jump in and see," Jessica suggested.

"That doesn't sound like a good idea," Dylan insisted.

"If it's a trap, I'd rather find out now than waste a few days coasting across the Patoray system," Jessica stated.

"She's right," Nathan decided.

"She is?" Marcus asked in disbelief.

"What do you think their defense perimeter is?" Nathan asked Jessica.

Jessica thought for a moment. "We took out a lot of their ships last time around. And Galiardi has likely taken out quite a few since then; they can't have that many left."

"And those they do have left are likely spread all over the empire," Nathan surmised.

"Unless they immediately began moving them in to protect Nor-Patri," Jessica pointed out.

"Even if they did, some of them would take years to get back," Vladimir commented.

"If they recalled them," Nathan argued.

"Why wouldn't they?" Jessica asked.

Nathan sighed. "The Tonba-Hon-Venar."

"They cancelled that when you surrendered," Jessica reminded him.

"We can't be certain of that," Nathan replied. "It would take years to move enough ships into place to guarantee a victorious assault on Earth."

"They'd never get close enough," Jessica argued. "Galiardi's sensor nets and patrols would detect them."

"If they massed enough ships on the border and then charged in all at once, enough of them would get through to reach Earth. And all it takes is one ship carrying a big enough antimatter weapon," Nathan explained.

"Then why didn't they do that the first time?" Jessica challenged.

"Because they didn't want to destroy Earth, they wanted to remove us from it," Nathan explained. "Unfortunately, that changed when we attacked Nor-Patri."

"Then why did you attack it?" Dylan wondered.

"In retrospect, it may have been a mistake," Nathan admitted.

"It wasn't a mistake," Jessica disagreed, "not after Tanna."

"No use in debating old history at this point," Nathan decided. "What do you think?"

"If they're low on ships, they'll stay within a few million kilometers of Nor-Patri. Even that's a stretch to cover, especially against jump KKVs."

"What's a jump KKV?" Dylan wondered.

"I'm betting they're not even trying," Nathan postulated, ignoring Dylan.

"You think they sent everything toward Earth?" Jessica realized.

"Gospadee," Vladimir exclaimed under his breath.

"I'm sure they have a handful of ships protecting Nor-Patri," Nathan said. "But like you said, it's nearly impossible to defend against jump KKVs. Especially ones carrying antimatter warheads."

"What's a KKV?" Dylan repeated.

"Even a handful of ships is enough reason to stay the hell away from that planet," Marcus muttered.

"We didn't jump nine hundred light years to turn back now," Nathan insisted.

"Josh, plot a jump into high orbit above Nor-Patri."

"Are you sure?"

"Josh," Nathan urged.

"Just checkin'," Josh assured him, entering the destination into the jump navigation computer.

"Will someone please tell me what a KKV is?" Dylan begged.

"Kinetic kill vehicle," Nathan explained.

"It's like a jump missile but bigger," Jessica added.

"It's a heavy-mass weapon," Nathan continued.

"Once launched, it's accelerated to relativistic velocities, then jumped to its target. Its kinetic energy alone is enough to destroy just about any ship."

"And they put antimatter warheads on those things?"

"They call them planet killers," Marcus told him.

"And Earth is using them against the Jung?" Dylan wondered.

"Most likely," Nathan replied.

"No wonder they're pissed."

"Jump is ready, Cap'n," Josh reported.

"Heads up, people," Nathan announced so that his gunners would hear. "We're jumping to Nor-Patri. Execute your jump, Josh."

Josh reached for the jump button. "Here goes nothin'."

A few seconds later, the jump flash filled the command deck. Appearing before them was the Jung home world, Nor-Patri.

"Contacts!" Dylan announced. "Six of them! Two frigates, one cruiser, and three cargo ships!"

"What are they doing?" Nathan asked calmly.

"Nothing," Dylan replied. "They're just in orbit."

Nathan reached up for the comm-panel again. "Jung Empire, this is the Karuzari Alliance ship Dalen Voss. We come in peace and wish to speak with your leaders. Please respond."

"You don't really think that's going to work, do you?" Jessica asked.

"The warships just activated their weapons systems," Dylan warned. "The frigates are locking onto us...MISSILES! Six...no, twelve of them. Twenty seconds to impact!"

"I don't suppose you want me to activate point-defenses," Jessica said.

"Not yet," Nathan instructed.

"Our forward shields just came up," Dylan told him. "You want me to lower them?"

"Negative. Leave them up," Nathan instructed. "Pitch up and jump us ahead a few hundred kilometers."

"Five seconds to impact," Dylan warned.

"Pitching up and jumping three hundred kilometers," Josh reported as he pulled the Voss's nose up, adjusted the jump range, and then pressed the jump button.

"Hold course," Nathan instructed. "Keep an eye out for new contacts," he added as he reached for the comm-panel again. "Jung Empire, this is the Dalen Voss. Hold your fire. We only wish to speak with your leaders. We are no threat to you."

"Two new contacts," Dylan reported, his voice getting more tense. "Gunships...I think."

"Yup, those are gunships," Jessica confirmed after calling up the sensor display on her station. "I've got tactical and sensors, kid."

"Thank you," Dylan said, relieved.

"I'm going to need you to dial up the jump distances," Josh told him.

"I can do that."

"Gunships are closing fast," Jessica warned. "They're approaching our starboard side."

"Raise all shields," Nathan instructed.

"I thought you wanted to appear non-threatening," Jessica remarked as she raised the rest of their shields.

"I do, but I also don't want to be dead," Nathan replied.

"Shields are up," Jessica announced. "Weapons hold, boys."

"Bring us about," Nathan instructed. "We're going to jump back to Nor-Patri, but this time, I want to come out in a low orbit, below those warships."

"Coming about," Josh acknowledged.

"Gimme a minute," Dylan said.

"Gunships are firing," Jessica reported.

The starboard shields lit up, and the ship shook as the gunships opened up.

"Whoa!" Jessica exclaimed. "Jung gunships have energy weapons now!"

"Well, it has been seven years," Nathan said.

"Jump is ready," Dylan reported.

"On course back for Nor-Patri," Josh added.

"Execute the jump," Nathan ordered.

"Jumping," Josh announced as the jump flash washed over them.

"Pitch up and show them our forward tubes," Nathan instructed.

"Pitching up, bringing all tubes to bear."

"You want me to fire on them?" Jessica asked.

"Not yet," Nathan instructed as he reached for the comm-panel again. "I just want them to know that we can," he added. "Jung Empire, Dalen Voss! Hold fire! Hold fire! We just want to talk!"

"All three ships are locking onto us," Jessica warned. "Plasma cannons and rail guns."

Again the ship shook, this time more violently as larger, more powerful weapons found their forward shields.

"I don't think they're listening," Vladimir stated.

"Oh, they're listening," Marcus insisted. "They just don't care."

"More missiles," Jessica warned as the ship

continued to shake from the incoming fire. "Fifteen seconds."

"Josh," Nathan called.

"I'm on it."

"More contacts, dead ahead!" Jessica warned. "They just came out of FTL!"

"They're blocking our jump path!" Dylan warned.

"Watch this," Josh told him, pushing their nose down and jamming his throttles forward.

"Eight missiles inbound!" Jessica warned. "Five seconds."

"Any time, Josh," Nathan urged.

"We're entering the upper atmosphere," Dylan warned. "Our shields won't be able to withstand the heat at this speed!"

"They don't need to," Josh declared as he pressed the jump button.

The jump flash again washed over them, and they suddenly found themselves back in open space, riding quiet and smooth.

"Not bad, huh?" Josh said as he backed the throttles down. "Come about again?"

"Yes," Nathan replied. "Jess, how much of a threat are those ships?"

"Well, their rail guns are no problem. They don't drain our shields at all. Their energy weapons are run-of-the-mill plasma cannons. We can take quite a bit from them before it becomes a problem."

"What about those missiles?"

"They're a lot slower than the Dusahn's," Jessica insisted. "I can keep them off us if you let me use our point-defenses."

"Do it," Nathan instructed.

"Finally," Jessica replied, arming the automated

point-defense cannons. "Setting PDCs to widespread missile intercept mode."

"Queue up some shield busters as well," Nathan added.

"You got it," Jessica replied eagerly. "What are you thinking?"

"I'm thinking we need to show them that they're wasting their time and ordnance trying to take us out. Maybe that way, they'll agree to talk with us."

"When is the last time you met a Jung who wanted to talk," Marcus muttered to Vladimir.

"Back on course for Nor-Patri," Josh reported. "Where do you want us?"

"Head on with the cruiser," Nathan replied. "One hundred clicks out, just enough above her for a clear jump line if we need it."

"Working it," Dylan acknowledged as he entered the destination parameters into the jump computer.

"Jess?"

"Two shield busters in the tubes, two more in the ready racks."

"Whenever you're ready, Josh," Nathan instructed. "But this time, we stand and fight for as long as possible."

"Jump plotted," Dylan announced.

"Jumping," Josh added, pressing the jump button again.

When the jump flash subsided, they were once again looking at Nor-Patri, only this time, the three warships were too far away to be seen by the naked eye.

"Lock the first two shield busters on the frigates," Nathan instructed. "As soon as they're away, load two more and set them to snap jump as they leave the tubes. We'll be launching them from close range."

"Understood," Jessica replied.

"Launch the first two missiles when ready."

"Stand by to jump us in next to the cruiser," Nathan continued. "Ten clicks off her port side. You'll bring our tubes to bear as we jump."

"Ten clicks off the cruiser's port side. Tubes to bear as we jump," Josh repeated as he prepared to execute the maneuver.

"Launching the first two," Jessica announced. "Missiles away! Loading two more!"

Nathan watched out the front windows as the first two missiles jumped away. "Jump on my mark."

"Ready to jump," Josh confirmed.

"Two more shield busters loaded," Jessica confirmed. "Set to snap jump on exit. Two more in the ready racks."

"Jump!"

Again Josh pressed the jump button, immediately twisting the Voss's flight control stick to begin her yaw maneuver to port.

Nathan looked out the port cockpit window, spotting the small black object that was the distant Jung cruiser. He watched as their nose swung to port and the black object slid into the forward windows.

"I have a firing solution," Jessica announced. "On target in three......two......one..."

"Launch two," Nathan instructed.

"Launching two," Jessica replied.

The cockpit lit up, backlit by the jump flashes as the missiles left the tubes and vanished.

"Missiles have jumped," Jessica reported. "Confirmed impacts on the frigates. Both targets have lost starboard shields. Cruiser has lost starboard midship shields. Multiple missile launches. Both frigates. Twelve missiles inbound. Twenty seconds to impact. PDCs are hot."

The Voss's point-defense cannons, located on the upper and lower surfaces of each end of her nacelles, opened up in the direction of the incoming missiles. The cannons danced back and forth as they fired short bursts of bright yellow energy, creating a wave of energy bolts in the path of the incoming missiles. One by one, the missiles exploded, each of them intercepted by one of the hundreds of bits of energy flying toward them.

"All twelve inbounds are destroyed," Jessica reported triumphantly.

"Jung Empire, this is the Dalen Voss. We can take out your ships any time we wish, but we just want to talk. I suggest you stop wasting ordnance and answer us."

"New contacts," Jessica reported. "Uh-oh."

"What is it?" Nathan asked, not liking the sudden change in her tone.

"Two battleships," Jessica replied. "And they're launching fighters."

"They must have been further out in the system," Vladimir decided.

"Must have," Nathan agreed. "Jung Empire," Nathan called over comms again, "we will defend ourselves if forced to do so. Again, we just want to talk!"

"Minute thirty until their fighters are on us," Jessica warned.

"Gunners, if those fighters attack, you're weapons free," Nathan instructed. "But only if they fire first."

"Dalen Voss, Dalen Voss," a voice crackled over comms. "Identify or be destroyed!"

"Finally!" Nathan exclaimed. "This is the Karuzari Alliance ship Dalen Voss. We only wish to talk with your leaders. Please stop firing."

"One minute to fighters," Jessica warned. "The battleships are locking their big guns on us."

"Can they hit us from that distance?" Nathan wondered.

"Oh they can hit us," Jessica promised. "I'm not sure how much effect they'll have on our shields, though."

"I seem to remember taking a hell of a beating from those guns, myself," Marcus reminded them.

"Dalen Voss," the Jung voice repeated. "Who is your captain? Identify!"

"Why the fuck does he need to know who the captain is?" Marcus wondered.

"I have no idea," Nathan admitted.

"Dalen Voss, identify or be destroyed!"

Nathan looked at Jessica. "How long?"

"Thirty seconds," she replied, locking eyes with him. "Don't."

"I'm going to have to sooner or later," Nathan replied. "This is Nathan Scott, in command of the Dalen Voss. Cease fire and we'll do the same."

"Fifteen seconds," Jessica warned. "Everybody, lock onto a target."

"Are those battleships painting us?" Nathan asked.

"Hell yes," Jessica replied. "Here they come."

Nathan stared out the forward windows as dozens of streamlined, dart-like fighters, black with red piping, streaked over the Voss, passing on all four sides of the ship. But not one of them fired.

"They've broken into four groups," Jessica reported, watching her sensor display. "They're circling back around for another run."

"Hold your fire until fired upon," Nathan reminded them.

Again the fighters streaked past without firing a single shot. They passed from starboard, then from below. The third group to port, and then the final group passed overhead so closely that they almost collided.

"Jesus that was close!" Mori exclaimed over the intercom.

"Dalen Voss," the Jung voice called over comms. "State your purpose."

"I wish to speak with your kor-dom," Nathan replied.

"Why would the kor-dom wish to speak with you?" the Jung officer snapped.

"I know about your war with the Sol Alliance, and I believe I can help."

"You are from the Sol Alliance."

"I was but am no longer. I promise you the kor-dom will want to speak with me."

"The fighters are coming around again," Jessica warned. "The battleships are closing, but the frigates and the cruiser are moving away."

"Cuz we snuffed their shields," Josh chuckled.

"No, dumbass," Marcus snapped. "It's so those battleships will have a clear shot at us with their big-ass guns!"

Nathan keyed the mic again. "Look, we can jump away anytime we like, and there's not a damned thing you can do about it. And we'll just keep coming back until the kor-dom talks to me." After a moment, he added, "Or maybe I should broadcast my identity to your entire population."

The black fighters streaked past from all directions again.

"What's it going to be?" Nathan asked over comms.

"Those battleships are closing," Jessica reminded him calmly. "If they get much closer, they'll bring down our shields with just a few shots."

"Got your finger on the jump button, Josh?" Nathan asked.

"You thought I didn't?" Josh replied.

"Keep an eye on our jump line, Dylan," Nathan instructed. "Josh, if those guns fire, you jump."

"You got it."

"Dalen Voss," the Jung officer finally called. "Lower shields and power down all weapons. Kor-Dom Borrol is on his way."

"I'll be happy to power down my weapons, but I am not lowering our shields," Nathan replied. "Not while you've got those battleships bearing down on us."

Josh and Dylan kept their eyes on their displays, ready to take action. Jessica's eyes were glued to her tactical display as the fighters came about for another pass. Marcus and Vladimir stood quietly while Nathan continued staring out the forward windows, waiting for a response.

"They're turning," Jessica reported, breathing a sigh of relief. "The battleships are turning and moving away. Slowly, but they are moving away."

"What about the fighters?" Nathan wondered.

"Half of them are breaking off and heading back to their ships. The rest are taking up position on our six."

"Power down all weapons and lower shields," Nathan ordered. "But keep the shield buffers charged," he added. "I want to be able to bring them back up in a hurry."

"We can't hold the buffers at full charge for more than twenty minutes without causing them to overheat," Vladimir warned.

Nathan turned and flashed him a disappointed look.

"You wanted stronger shields, didn't you?" Vladimir defended. "That's how we gave them to you. Using the buffers."

"Well then," Nathan said. "Let's hope Kor-Dom Borrol calls us back by then."

* * *

The XK conversion yard had expanded considerably in the last few days. Now there were five of the old cargo ships lined up side by side, four of them currently being worked on.

The number of people and engineering droids working at the yard had increased as well. Not only were members of Subvert working on upgrading and renovating the ships, but regular citizens, skilled and unskilled, were volunteering their time in their off hours.

Robert Nash stood at the end of the makeshift production line, gazing at the XK before him. This was to be his next command. As expected, it was not the most impressive-looking ship. Its design, although well suited for its original purpose, seemed questionable considering its new role.

Even so, what they had done to the XKL series ships was nothing short of remarkable, especially considering how quickly it was all happening. In less than a month, they had converted two of the outdated cargo ships into well-equipped, multi-role, armed utility ships—in half the time estimated for the conversion of a single vessel. At their current rate, all twelve ships would be in service in five months.

Crews would be another issue altogether. There was no shortage of technicians and engineers capable of maintaining their new fleet. But full, properly trained crews would be a challenge. They didn't yet know exactly what the ships could do. Their strengths; their weaknesses—they could be predicted by SilTek's engineering AIs, but until people like him got them into space and put them through their paces, they could not be certain.

Luckily for Robert, he had been receiving copies of all the Voss's action logs and ship's telemetry to study. No pilot could push the edge of the envelope like Josh Hayes, and Robert had already gleaned valuable insight into the XK from the Voss's limited exploits.

"Can I help you?" a young woman asked as she approached Robert.

"You could point me to the man in charge," Robert replied.

"Are you here to volunteer?"

"Not exactly," Robert told her.

"Well, Del's a busy guy..."

"Apparently."

"Can you tell me what you want to see him about?" the young woman wondered.

Robert looked at her. "That's my ship," he told her, pointing at the completed XK sitting next to them.

The young woman's eyes widened. "You're Captain

Nash?" She suddenly straightened up, raising her hand in salute. "I'm your engineer."

Robert looked surprised. "How old are you?"

"Nineteen, sir!" she snapped back, smart and loud.

"What's that in Earth years?" Robert wondered.

"Uh..." Her eyes shifted back and forth. "I don't know, sir!" she barked.

"Relax, kid. You're going to hurt yourself." Robert offered his hand. "Robert Nash."

The young woman looked confused but reluctantly lowered her salute and shook her new captain's hand. "Cori Gammen," she replied.

"A pleasure to meet you, Miss Gammen."

"We weren't expecting you until tomorrow," Cori admitted.

"I just arrived an hour ago," Robert explained. "I thought I'd stop by and see my new command."

Cori looked uncomfortable. She looked at the XK, scratching her head, then back at Robert. "Well, she's mostly ready. Still a bit messy inside. Final adjustments and all."

"Don't worry," Robert told him. "I'm not going to hold it against you."

"Of course, sir," she replied.

The two of them stood silently for a moment.

"Shall we?" Robert suggested.

"Sir?"

"I'd like to see my ship," Robert explained.

"Oh of course!" Cori realized. "Follow me, sir."

* * *

"Both battleships are paralleling us from higher orbits," Jessica reported.

"How long are we going to just sit here?" Josh wondered. "We've got about a hundred cannons pointed at us right now, and our shields aren't even up."

"The moment we raise our shields, those hundred cannons will open fire," Jessica assured him.

"It's been fifteen minutes," Nathan reminded Josh. "Not exactly an eternity."

"It is when there are a hundred cannons pointed at you," Josh insisted.

"For once, I agree with him," Marcus added.

"I don't suppose you have a plan here," Jessica said.

"At this point, I'm making it up as I go," Nathan admitted.

"And sitting here, shields down, with one hundred cannons pointed at us seemed like a good plan to you?" Josh questioned.

"This is Kor-Dom Borrol," a voice suddenly called over comms.

"Finally!" Josh exclaimed.

"Hush!" Nathan scolded, reaching for the comm-panel.

"Kor-Dom Borrol, this is Nathan Scott, captain of the Karuzari Alliance ship Dalen Voss. Thank you for speaking with us."

"And for not blowing us to bits," Josh said under his breath.

"How do I know you are Nathan Scott?" Kor-Dom Borrol asked.

"How do I know you are Kor-Dom Borrol?" Nathan countered.

"Nathan Scott died seven years ago," Kor-Dom Borrol replied. "He was executed here on Nor-Patri for crimes against the empire."

"I died in one of your prison cells, the night before my execution, from a self-inflicted knife wound.

The body you dragged out for public execution was nothing more than a corpse... my corpse." There was no response. After a minute, Nathan added. "I can recite the menu for my last meal if you'd like. Corintakhat and ergin tota. Trever never told me what the dessert was called, but it was delicious."

After another long pause, the Jung leader spoke again. "Assuming for a moment that you are who you claim to be, why would I agree to speak with you?"

"So that I won't broadcast that I'm alive to your entire population," Nathan replied, playing his trump card.

"Doing so would only change the minds of those who do not support the Tonba-Hon-Venar," the kor-dom insisted.

"I suspect it would tip the balance of power among your leadership caste as well," Nathan told him. "Instability in government can be quite problematic in times of war."

Again there was silence.

"Do you really think threatening them is a good idea?" Josh wondered, pointing out the window. "One hundred cannons, remember?"

"It's only a conversation," Nathan called over comms.

Another minute passed.

"What takes this guy so long?" Jessica wondered.

"A good leader considers the consequences before he acts," Nathan said. "A good politician considers how his words will be received before he speaks them."

"What?"

"I will speak with you, whoever you are," Kor-Dom Borrol finally agreed. "But if we are to speak, it must be face-to-face, in my chambers."

Nathan smiled. "Not a chance," Nathan replied. "If we are to speak face-to-face, it will be on board the Voss."

"Then I will see that you have clearance to land at the spaceport nearby."

"I would prefer someplace remote; someplace as far away from defenses as possible."

"Nor-Patri has no such locations," the kor-dom replied. "However, I do know of a location which may be agreeable. My people will transmit the location. We will notify you when we are ready."

"Soon, I hope," Nathan replied. "And let's keep it private, shall we?"

Again there was no reply.

"I'm receiving a set of surface coordinates," Jessica announced.

"I guess that's a yes then," Nathan decided.

"You could have asked him to stop pointin' them cannons at us," Marcus commented.

CHAPTER SEVEN

Loki's eyes opened; slowly at first, the light causing him to squint. He was surrounded by unfamiliar voices and smells. And the air was different here... dry and cold.

Someone spoke but in a language he didn't understand. It sounded familiar, but he couldn't place it. He had experienced so many languages in his travels. He had even become fluent in Corinairan and Rakuen. But Angla had always been his native tongue.

The voices were all male except for one. The sole female voice spoke the same language as the others and seemed to be scolding them. The men laughed but appeared to fear her chastisements.

"Pay them no heed," the woman said to Loki in English. "They are only trying to scare you."

"They don't need to," Loki replied. "I'm already scared."

The woman placed a device on his head and then connected a set of cables to it.

"What are you doing?" Loki asked.

"Nothing that I wish to do," she told him. She put her hand on his shoulder, looking him in the eyes. "Forgive me, but times require such measures."

The woman departed, and a man who appeared unsympathetic stepped up. "You will feel pain... extreme pain."

The man's accent was familiar, but just as with their language, he could not remember from where. "What are you going to do to me?"

"We must know what is in there," the man said, putting his finger to Loki's forehead.

"Just ask," Loki told him.

"Machine is better," the man said. "Not for you, of course."

"What do you mean?"

"If you have a god, you should speak to him now," the man advised as he walked over to the device on the cart nearby.

Loki felt a wave of panic washing over him. His escape from the myriad of Super Eagles had been nothing short of miraculous, as had surviving the subsequent crash landing. Now, he would die strapped to a table, surrounded by men he did not know, for a reason he did not know.

Loki locked his eyes on the ceiling and recited an old Rakuen expression he had learned during flight school. "I embrace death as I embrace life, with heart and eyes open."

"I would suggest that you embrace life even more," the man said, turning on the device.

Loki felt nothing at first, but then his head began to tingle. The tingling intensified, quickly turning into a dull pain. That too increased, and in less than a minute, it became so bad that he cried out, begging for it to end.

The men in the room had grown quiet, undoubtedly silenced by the horrible screams. The woman was no longer heard from. For all Loki knew, she had left the room. The pain was so intense that he was losing touch with his senses. His sense of smell had left him first, followed by a decrease in hearing and blurring of vision.

If only his sense of pain would go away as well.

Suddenly, his wish was granted. The pain began to subside, lessening with each passing second.

Finally, it was gone. His senses returned.

Surprisingly, he found himself alone in the room, bathed in sweat, still bound to the table. His fingers and toes twitched, as did his eyelids. There was a sound...a door. Then someone touched him and removed the device from his head.

"It is over," the woman told him. "You survived. You are strong. It kills most men."

All Loki could say was, "Why?" He felt a prick in his arm.

"Like I said, it is a difficult time."

It was the last thing he heard as he drifted away.

* * *

"You do realize this is a trap," Jessica reiterated as she followed Nathan into the utility bay where the Ghatazhak were gathered, waiting for them.

"The thought had crossed my mind," Nathan assured her.

"But we're going through with it anyway," Jessica surmised.

"Don't worry, I have a plan."

"Care to let me in on it?"

"Gentlemen," Nathan greeted the Ghatazhak, ignoring Jessica's request. "I'm about to ask you all to take a huge risk. We are about to set down on the surface of Nor-Patri to welcome aboard the leader of the Jung Empire."

The Ghatazhak exchanged concerned glances but said nothing.

"To do so, I will have to set foot on a world that believes me justly executed years ago. Although I do not expect an audience, I doubt very seriously that Kor-Dom Borrol will be alone. At the very least, there will be a security contingent present."

"Can we extend our aft shields again?" Kit wondered.

"We'd still have to drop them to allow the kor-dom inside," Nathan pointed out.

"They'll have snipers," Mori stated. "Good ones."

"Which is why I need all of you," Nathan told them.

"You want us to protect you with our personal shields," Kit surmised. "I should point out that the six of us are not enough to encircle you."

"The Voss will be at my back," Nathan explained. "We'll drop the aft shield, and I'll walk out only as far as the shield perimeter. That will reduce my area of exposure by fifty percent. With the kor-dom in front of me, that should reduce it another twenty percent. I need you to cover the remaining thirty percent."

"More like forty percent," Jokay corrected.

"He's right," Jessica agreed. "Their snipers will be excellent."

Nathan nodded agreement. "The only reason the kor-dom agreed to meet is because he does not want the general population to discover that I'm still alive. My death was the only thing that prevented the Tonba-Hon-Venar seven years ago. Kor-Dom Borrol probably fears losing control if the public learns the truth. He may not even trust his own security forces."

"You should keep your identity hidden from everyone but the kor-dom," Jessica told him.

"I planned on wearing a hooded cloak," Nathan explained. "That's the best I can do. I do have to show my face to the kor-dom."

"And then what?" Kit wondered.

"We bring him aboard to talk."

"The longer we're sitting on the surface, the higher the risk," Kit warned.

"Which is precisely why the kor-dom must come

aboard," Nathan told him. "As long as he is on the Voss, they won't fire on us."

"And the moment he leaves?" Jessica wondered.

"We jump the hell out."

"They'll shoot us down before we get off the ground," Kit insisted.

"Which is why we're going to jump while we're on the ground," Nathan explained. "Before we even fire up the grav-lift."

"Can we do that?" Mori wondered.

Kit thought for a moment. "Technically, the planet's rotation gives us forward momentum. The trick will be to have a clear jump line. There're bound to be buildings, or mountains, or something in our way."

"We asked for a remote location as an LZ," Nathan explained. "Luckily, the location they chose is high enough in elevation to be above everything nearby. We'll have a clear jump line in all directions."

"How dumb are these people?" Kit wondered.

"They're not dumb," Nathan assured him. "Not by a long shot. They just don't have much knowledge about the jump drive or how it works."

"Won't they notice that we're not powering down our reactors?" Jokay asked.

"We'll be powering our shields, so they'll rightly assume that we need our reactors to be running," Jessica realized. "They've got to know that we're going to be skittish going into this meeting and that we'd never power down completely."

"Isn't there an energy surge just before a jump?" Mori wondered. "Won't that tip them off?"

"Like I said, we'll never get off the ground," Kit reiterated.

"That's why we're going to jump while the kor-dom

is still on board," Nathan explained, a mischievous look on his face.

Kit also smiled. "Oh I like this plan."

"I don't," Jessica disagreed.

"Suit up, gentlemen," Nathan instructed. "We set down as soon as you're ready."

The Ghatazhak said nothing further, going to their mark two lockers on the starboard bulkhead.

"Aren't we going to take a chunk of the planet with us when we jump?" Jessica questioned Nathan as they watched the Ghatazhak don their combat armor.

"Vlad has adjusted the jump calculations to compensate as best he can," Nathan explained. "And we're not jumping to a precise location, just back up to orbit."

"It would be better to jump further out," Jessica urged.

"The further we try to jump, the longer the detectable energy build-up," Nathan told her.

"We're only talking about a few seconds."

"A few seconds could make all the difference," Nathan replied. "This is the best plan under the circumstances. It mitigates all the risks to acceptable levels."

"Oh I've got no problem with risks," Jessica assured him. "I'm just trying to play Cam here."

Nathan looked at her. "She told you to keep an eye on me, didn't she?"

"She didn't have to," Jessica laughed.

"Josh?" Nathan called out as the Ghatazhak finished their automatic suit-up cycle. "How are we looking?"

Josh glanced across his flight displays, quickly scanning all critical systems. He then looked over at Dylan to his right.

"All set," Dylan assured him.

"We're good to go, Cap'n," Josh announced.

"Are you sure this is a good idea?" Dylan asked Josh.

"Of course it ain't!" Josh exclaimed. "That's what makes it so much fun!"

"I can hear you guys, you know," Nathan reminded them over the intercom.

"Sorry, sir," Dylan apologized.

"Starting our deorbit burn," Josh announced as he activated the ship's deceleration thrusters.

"Escort fighters are decelerating as well," Dylan reported, his eyes on the sensor display. "They're going to stay with us."

"LZ is on the far side of the planet at the moment," Josh told him. "I'll jump us down and then skip around to the LZ once we're in atmo. That'll shake'em for sure."

Vladimir checked the displays on the engineering console in the Voss's port nacelle. "I've finished segmenting the jump energy banks," he announced. "We should be able to jump back to orbit by using just the energy in the cells. One bank for the bubble and one to initiate the jump."

"And you accounted for the extra mass of dirt and rock we'll be taking with us?" Nathan inquired over the intercom.

"As best I could," Vladimir replied. "I do not know the composition of the LZ or what lies beneath it. I adjusted the bubble size to reduce the amount of matter we'll take with us, but it's all a guess at this point."

"Just tell me it will get us to orbit," Nathan asked.

"Da," Vladimir assured him. "I think."

"Which is it, Vlad?"

"It will work!"

"What about over here?" Marcus asked over the intercom.

"I've already configured the starboard nacelle from here," Vladimir assured him. "You just have to manually cross-connect circuit one five alpha to circuit two-seven bravo. Make sure the connection is tight..."

"I know how to hook up a jumper," Marcus snapped.

The utility bay shook suddenly as the Voss jumped into Nor-Patri's atmosphere.

"We shook the escorts," Josh reported over the intercom. "Two more jumps to the LZ. We should be gear down in less than a minute."

"You go out and line up on either side in an open, arrow-tip formation, just inside the shield perimeter," Jessica instructed the Ghatazhak. "Once we verify the presence of the kor-dom and that there are no immediate threats, we'll drop the aft shield. Once the shield is down, Nathan will come out and take position at the center of the formation. He will not remove his hood until the kor-dom is standing within your formation, face-to-face with the captain."

"What happens after that?" Kit asked.

"I'll try to convince him to come aboard to talk,"

Nathan told them. "The rest we'll have to play by ear."

"Nathan moves, you move," Jessica reminded them. "Adjust formation as you see fit. If we receive fire, return fire only as necessary to defend the captain and yourselves."

"LZ in sight," Josh reported over the intercom.

"How does the LZ look?" Jessica asked, tilting her head up to be heard clearly.

"Nine people, eight of them armed. Two ground vehicles," Dylan reported. "No other weapons within several kilometers."

"What about further out?" Jessica asked.

"I'm using a tight sensor band for resolution purposes," Dylan told her. "The entire planet is bathed in some sort of sensor-scattering field. Narrowband is the only way to see through it."

"That's new," Nathan commented.

"Let's hope that's the only trick they have up their sleeves," Jessica said.

"On final now," Josh reported.

"As soon as we're down, take main propulsion offline," Nathan reminded Josh.

"I remember," Josh assured him.

"Don't forget to drop the shields before you execute the jump," Vladimir chimed in.

"What?" Jessica exclaimed, surprised.

"We need the power in the shield buffers to make the jump without using the reactors," Vladimir explained. "Otherwise, we'd have to spin them up to at least sixty percent."

"And you didn't think this was worth mentioning beforehand?" Nathan wondered.

"I didn't mention it?"

"No you didn't."

"Huh, I could have sworn I did," Vladimir defended.

"The shields will only be down for a split second," Dylan pointed out. "A jump that short won't take more than a tenth of a second to execute, and I wrote a quick subroutine for the AI to drop the shields and initiate the jump. We'll only be vulnerable for zero point four seconds."

The ship rocked gently, a thud reverberating through the hull as its gear touched the surface.

"We're down," Josh reported. "Cutting mains; spinning reactor down to twenty percent to maintain shields."

"Is there anything else you forgot to tell us?" Nathan asked Vladimir.

"Nyet," Vladimir replied. "I don't believe so."

Nathan took a breath. "Let's do this," he told Jessica, putting his comm-set in his ear.

Jessica moved to the left of the cargo ramp, to the control panel. She waited, watching Nathan, who donned the hooded long-coat that he had brought with him, the one he usually wore as Connor when visiting rainy worlds like Palee.

Jessica activated the ramp, starting the opening cycle. The Ghatazhak took up their position; two groups of three abreast near the edge of the ramp.

No light came through as the ramp cracked open along its top edge and began folding open. It was nighttime, which was all the better. As the ramp came down past level and continued toward the surface, more details became visible. They were indeed on the top of a hill or small mountain and could see city lights as far as the horizon stretched. Nor-Patri was indeed a planet-wide city, at least from their vantage point.

The ramp stopped as it contacted the surface. All six Ghatazhak scanned the area, looking about and allowing their AIs to search for threats.

"Whatever their scattering field is, it screws up ours as well," Kit reported over the intercom, his suit-comms automatically connected to the Voss's intercom system.

"Dylan?" Jessica called. "Any points around us higher than us?"

"Negative," Dylan replied. "And we have a clear line in the direction of the planet's rotation."

"That will have to do," Nathan stated, his head covered with the hood of his long-coat, partially obscuring any direct view of his face.

"Move out," Jessica ordered.

All six Ghatazhak marched down the cargo ramp, getting into the open-arrow formation as they reached the ground. They came to a stop just shy of the aft shield line.

Kit, who was at the inside position of the left group, kept his eyes on the group of men standing in front of the vehicles parked ten meters distant. "Nine moving toward," he reported. "Eight armed, full combat gear, heavy weapons. Center subject is unarmed."

"That's got to be our guest," Jessica stated.

"Here goes nothing," Nathan said as he started toward the ramp. He walked down, maintaining an even stride. His father's voice echoed in his head. To win a negotiation, you must appear confident in your position from the start. Any sign of hesitation will be interpreted as weakness, inviting opposition even when such was not originally planned.

"Targets have stopped," Kit reported. "They are now nine abreast, one meter outside the shields."

Nathan kept his head down, not wanting to reveal his face until he was in position.

Jessica stood inside the cargo door next to the control panel, hidden from view.

"Captain is entering the pocket," Kit reported as Nathan came to a stop in the middle of the formation.

Kor-Dom Borrol took one step forward. "I am Kor-Dom Jung-Borrol, leader of the Jung-Borrol caste, ruler of the empire. Are you the one who wishes to speak with me?"

"Instruct your guards to move back," Nathan said, without revealing his face.

"So that you can strike me down?"

"If I wished to kill you, or even your entire world, I could have done so without putting myself and my people at risk," Nathan replied. "I ask that you move your guards back for your political well-being, not for our physical safety. After all, you may still choose to refuse my offer once it has been heard."

Kor-Dom Borrol observed Nathan for a moment. The man was about the right height and build, from best he could remember, but he could see nothing but the man's chin. However, he also knew that the man was right. His earlier communication with the man claiming to be Nathan Scott had been encrypted, with no one within earshot on his end. If the hooded man was Nathan Scott, and his guards recognized him as such, they would have to be killed. Although the kor-dom had no qualms in doing so, unnecessary killing was not the way of the leadership castes. Such was the purview of the warrior caste and was the sole reason they still existed within the empire.

The kor-dom turned slightly, speaking instructions to his men in Jung. The nearest soldier stared at his leader, uncertain at first, but heeding his leader's orders nonetheless.

In pairs of two, the kor-dom's guards peeled off, marching back to the vehicles that had brought them. The last two took their steps backward, carefully retreating to join their comrades, all the while keeping their eyes on their leader.

The kor-dom looked at the hooded man again. "I have done as you asked. Now reveal yourself."

"Step closer," Nathan instructed as he slowly removed his hood.

Kor-Dom Borrol's eyes widened in disbelief. It was the same face he had seen every day of the young man's trial those many years ago. The same youthful features, the same friendly eyes that nearly changed his mind about the murderous criminal's sentence. "My God!" he exclaimed under his breath as he slowly moved closer. "How can this be?"

"I can explain, but we must move inside," Nathan told him.

"Can we not speak here?" the kor-dom suggested. "Those men are the only ones in the area, and I trust them all."

"Do you?" Nathan challenged. "And do your people not have the ability to surveil one from great distances?"

"We do, but..."

"Do you trust the leaders of all your castes?" Nathan asked. "The Jung-Torret? The Dais? Or how about the Jung-Mogan? Or the Dusahn?"

"Your intelligence is flawed," the kor-dom replied. "The Dusahn caste no longer exists."

"Oh they exist," Nathan corrected. "In fact, they are the reason you are at war. That is why I am here. The enemy of my enemy is my friend."

Kor-Dom Borrol studied Nathan's face, looking for something that would belie his words. He saw nothing. Furthermore, the young man was correct. The longer the two of them stood on this hilltop, the more likely a spy for a rival caste, or even an independent contractor seeking to gain favor, would discover and witness their exchange. The smart move was to accept the invitation.

Kor-Dom Borrol sighed. "Very well, lead the way."

Nathan pulled his hood back over his head and turned around, heading up the ramp.

Kor-Dom Borrol followed, his eyes wide, taking in every little detail of the ship as he ascended the ramp. Should he return safely, what he witnessed this day might prove invaluable. Should he not return, his loss would seal his world's fate. The Tonba-Hon-Venar would continue, but with more dedication and passion than ever. That passion would ensure the survival of his people, despite the hardships they would have to endure once the war concluded. Whether he turned martyr or hero this day, Kor-Dom Jung-Borrol would become a legend in the history of his people.

Nathan reached the utility bay's forward hatch and turned to face the kor-dom as he approached the top of the ramp. As the Ghatazhak who followed breached the hull line on their way in, he nodded to Jessica.

Jessica activated the pressure shield.

Kor-Dom Borrol spun around, hearing the sudden hum of the pressure shield behind him as it activated. "What is this!" he demanded.

"Now," Nathan instructed.

The shields outside dropped as a blue-white flash filled the utility bay, temporarily blinding the kor-dom. Jessica immediately activated the ramp again, causing it to begin its close cycle.

"Hang on!" Josh warned over the intercom.

The ship began to rumble as both nacelles spun up power. The floor beneath their feet shifted slightly as they began to accelerate, the ship's inertial dampening systems not yet having reached full power.

"What has happened!" the kor-dom demanded, rubbing his eyes and blinking in an effort to recover his vision more quickly.

"No harm will come to you," Nathan promised. "Report, Josh!"

"We made it to orbit!" Josh exclaimed. "We brought a ton of Jung dirt with us!"

Kor-Dom Borrol turned around to look aft, his eyesight returning. The ramp had already passed the halfway point, continuing to close, but he could clearly see the stars and the edge of his planet just before it disappeared behind the ascending ramp. "What have you done!"

The blue-white flash returned, albeit more subdued now that the ramp was nearly closed.

"I apologize, Kor-Dom Borrol," Nathan said, removing his hood again. "I needed more time with you, more than I felt was safe to spend on the surface of your world. I promise that you will be returned to your people unharmed."

"This is an act of war!" the kor-dom insisted. "One that will not be forgiven!"

"Fine," Nathan agreed, removing his long-coat and tossing it aside. "Your people can attack mine after you've destroyed Earth, assuming you have any ships left." Nathan walked over to the counter and picked up the data pad he had brought in with him earlier. He then offered it to Kor-Dom Borrol. "Study this at length, and then we will speak."

Kor-Dom Borrol hesitated a moment, then took the data pad from him. "What is it?"

"It is everything you need to know in order to decide whether or not to accept our offer."

The kor-dom flashed through the first few pages. "This will take some time," he said. "My people will be looking for you. Once they find you..."

"Trust me, they won't find us," Nathan assured him.

The kor-dom looked around. "You have nowhere more comfortable?"

"We do," Nathan replied. "Please follow me."

Kor-Dom Borrol followed Nathan out the forward hatch of the utility bay.

"Two guards on him at all times," Jessica told Kit, "and don't underestimate the old fart."

* * *

Loki woke suddenly. The first thing he noticed was that he felt no pain, not even from the injuries sustained in his crash. The second thing he noticed was that he was alone.

He sat up slowly, unsure of himself. His head seemed to spin but settled down a few seconds later. He was in a room about four by five meters. Besides the bed on which he sat was a small table with two chairs, a sitting chair with a side table, and a kitchenette. There were also three doors and a window.

Loki rose and made his way to the first door. It was locked from the outside. The next door was a closet, and the third led to a bathroom. He then went to the window, pulling back the curtain to look outside. Below was a street that had been freshly scraped of snow, much of which was piled along the sides of the boulevard. There were buildings in all directions, with snow-covered mountains beyond. The window was also locked. Even if he could open it, the drop to the surface was more than his body could handle in his current state. He was still a prisoner. The question was: of whom?

He had been told that he was being given to the insurgents seeking to overthrow Admiral Galiardi. However, his experiences thus far didn't seem to support this. If his current captors were the insurgents, he was no safer with them than he had been with Udo. Perhaps even less so.

There was a remote on the table, but he saw no device that it might control. He went over and picked it up, pressing the power button. To his surprise, the painting hanging on the one bare wall disappeared, replaced by a live media feed.

Loki pressed another set of buttons, changing the programs displayed. Eventually settling on what appeared to be a news program, he stopped. The string of vid-footage clips being shown appeared to be from battles between ground forces of the Sol Alliance and the Jung, and in every clip, the Jung appeared to be losing...badly.

* * *

Kor-Dom Borrol had been sitting in the Voss's common room for nearly half an hour, reviewing the files on the data pad Nathan had given him. During this time, Nathan had waited patiently, making himself available should the Jung leader have any questions. Surprisingly, the elder man had none.

Finally, the kor-dom placed the data pad on the table in front of him, looking at Nathan. "Interesting read," he declared. "Very well presented."

It was not the reaction Nathan had expected.

"I am supposed to believe this?" the kor-dom questioned, motioning at the data pad. "All without evidence?"

"The fact that I'm willing to risk everything by returning to Nor-Patri should tell you something," Nathan insisted.

"It tells me that you want something bad enough to risk your life and the lives of your crew to obtain it," the kor-dom explained. "That is all that it tells me."

Nathan rose from his seat. "I guess we should return you to Nor-Patri then," he stated, turning to head forward.

"Assume for a moment that I believe what you have shown me," the kor-dom said. "Why is it that you were able to determine it was a false-flag operation, and the Sol Alliance, who has far more resources at their disposal, could not?"

"I believe that they do know," Nathan told him. "I believe that Admiral Galiardi is using it as a pretext to an all-out war against the empire."

"To what end?" the kor-dom wondered.

"Revenge, a means to power, both. I can't be sure."

"Can you even be certain that he does know that it is not us?"

"Given the evidence, I believe so," Nathan replied, pointing at the data pad.

"That will not be enough to convince the leaders of the warrior castes," Kor-Dom Borrol warned. "They will claim that it was fabricated by Sol Alliance intelligence to destroy public support for the Tonba-Hon-Venar. At the moment, I would be likely to agree with that assessment."

"If that is the case, then why are we even having this hypothetical discussion?" Nathan wondered.

"Because there is one other thing which I am curious about," the kor-dom explained. "Why are you here?"

"Lord Dusahn has threatened to destroy Takara if we attempt to invade," Nathan explained. "He even destroyed a world to prove that he could, sacrificing millions needlessly."

"Ah yes, the Chekta."

"What is the Chekta?" Nathan wondered.

"The chekta is a ferocious, serpent-like creature that lives in the marshlands of Nor-Patri. When two male chektas fight, the loser will often drive its venomous fangs into the victor. The venom then causes the victor to clamp down even tighter, guaranteeing the death of both. The Chekta protocol is the idea that one can still die as the victor by denying his attacker the prize they sought. It is considered the only way to die victoriously in the face of certain defeat. To the Jung warrior, victory is all that matters."

"Then you believe he is not bluffing," Nathan surmised.

"I am certain of it," Kor-Dom Borrol replied. "But that is not the reason you came to speak with me."

"I intend to challenge Lord Dusahn to a fight to the death," Nathan told him. "For the control of Takara."

"And what makes you believe he would accept this challenge?"

"I was hoping that if I broadcast my challenge to the people of Takara, including his own men, that his ego would not allow him to refuse," Nathan explained.

“Men do not become leaders of empires by acting foolishly,” Kor-Dom Borrol replied. “The Dusahn leader is indeed a proud man, as are all members of warrior castes. However, he is not stupid. In fact, his own people would consider him unfit to lead should he accept such a challenge without any legal precedent to do so.”

Nathan sighed, sitting back down. “I hadn’t thought of that.”

“Do you know how the current Dusahn leader came to power?” the kor-dom wondered.

“By killing off the heirs ahead of him in the line of succession.”

“No doubt his own brothers,” the kor-dom surmised. “That is good.”

“How so?”

“It means they still honor the old traditions of the Jung.”

“I’m not following,” Nathan lied.

“It means that, if the challenge is done properly, Lord Dusahn must agree or risk losing control of his own caste by default.”

“How?” Nathan asked, already knowing the answer.

“Only two people can challenge a dom for leadership,” Kor-Dom Borrol explained. “A member of the same caste or the leader of another caste. If either issues a challenge, refusing to accept that challenge would be considered a forfeit, bringing the ultimate shame upon him who refused. By Jung law, which governs all the castes, this would make him unfit to lead. If you wish to issue a challenge, one that Lord Dusahn cannot refuse, you must first be made a dom yourself.”

“How does one become a dom?”

"Of an existing caste, one must be appointed by the elders of that caste."

"What about of a new caste?" Nathan wondered.

"A new caste can only be created by a two-thirds majority vote by the leadership council."

"Can you make that happen?" Nathan asked.

Kor-Dom Borrol looked at Nathan. "You already know that I can, otherwise I would not be here."

"Forgive my subterfuge, Kor-Dom," Nathan apologized. "I needed to ensure that your answers were in earnest."

"I see you have inherited the skills of your father," the kor-dom commented. "I can submit the proposal and call for a vote, but that is all I can do."

"What are the chances the motion would carry?" Nathan wondered.

"Not good," the kor-dom warned. "However, I do have some influence over the other doms." He paused a moment before continuing. "It might help to know what the empire would get in return."

"An end to the attacks against the Jung Empire by the Sol Alliance," Nathan replied.

Kor-Dom Borrol laughed. "You will fire on your own people?"

"I had something else in mind."

"Such as?"

"The details are not your concern," Nathan told him. "Suffice to say that if the Jung Empire agrees to make me a caste leader and to back my challenge to Lord Dusahn, the Sol Alliance will no longer be a threat to them."

"As long as we are without jump drive technology, all those who possess it will be a threat to us."

"I cannot give you jump drive technology," Nathan told him.

"Yet you have willingly shared it with so many others."

Nathan sighed. "It was necessary at the time."

"As it is necessary now," Kor-Dom Borrol replied.

"You're asking me to share the technology that saved my people from destruction with those who tried to destroy us. Surely you can see how some might not consider that a good idea."

"Even if doing so prevents the destruction of both empires?"

Nathan leaned back in his chair, thinking. "The Jung Empire was built on the backs of the people they conquered. Sharing the jump drive technology with you would only enable you to continue that practice unchecked."

"The Jung Empire had to expand to survive," Kor-Dom Borrol insisted. "The limitations of linear, faster-than-light travel necessitated the acquisition of those worlds nearest us."

"I might believe that if you had just limited your expansion to a few worlds."

"Most worlds we encountered were in dire straits, having been unable to properly recover from the past ravages of the bio-digital plague. Our presence brought health and prosperity to those worlds."

"But at what price?" Nathan countered. "On most of those worlds, you forced your culture, language, and ideals on those people, eliminating those who were unwilling to accept them."

"I am not defending our past policies," Kor-Dom Borrol replied. "Nor do I feel the need to defend them. They are what they are, and I cannot change them. I can only change the future of my people."

"If I gave you the jump drive, what would you do with it?" Nathan wondered.

"I expect you have noticed that Nor-Patri has very little open land," Kor-Dom Borrol began. "Our world depends on the import of resources for its very survival and has for more than a century. The jump drive would relieve us of the need to control the resources of neighboring inhabited worlds."

"So your empire would spread across the galaxy," Nathan surmised.

"I will not deny that possibility," the kor-dom replied. "However, the events of the last seven years have caused a shift in the empire."

"What kind of shift?" Nathan asked.

"The number of caste doms supporting expansion through conquest has diminished. Until recently, it was in the minority. However, the unwarranted attacks by the Sol Alliance have swung that support back toward conquest."

"Even though it will surely lead to your destruction?"

"The Jung are a proud people," the kor-dom reminded him. "We would rather die fighting for what we believe than live subserviently."

"Yet you deny that to others."

"Which is why support of conquest has faded in recent years." Kor-Dom Borrol leaned forward, his elbows on the table. "Were you to share the jump drive with the Jung and end the attacks on our people, support would undoubtedly swing back in the other direction. There might actually be a chance for true peace."

"True peace meaning that the Jung Empire would stop conquering others and imposing their will upon them."

"Is that not the definition of peace?"

"There are many definitions of peace," Nathan insisted.

"If we had access to countless uninhabited, hospitable worlds, we would no longer need to conquer our neighbors."

"Until the resources of those worlds were depleted," Nathan replied.

"Which would likely take thousands of years."

Nathan paused, considering the kor-dom's position as if it were his own. "We would need assurances."

"What kind of assurances?" the kor-dom inquired.

"That you would not use jump drive technology to conquer more human-inhabited worlds or uninhabited worlds previously claimed by others," Nathan explained. "After all, you yourself stated that with the jump drive, you would no longer need to conquer others to survive."

"And how do you propose that we achieve such a détente?"

"You would need to join our alliance," Nathan replied.

"Your alliance?" the kor-dom wondered. "Then you wish us to become allies?"

"It would be better than being enemies."

"Perhaps," the kor-dom admitted. "I would require more details, of course."

Nathan picked up his own data pad, touching the screen several times before setting it back down. "Your data pad now contains a copy of our draft charter. A formal constitution will be created by a convention of the founding members. I am offering you the opportunity to be one of them."

"I see," the kor-dom replied, picking up his data pad again. "I shall consider your proposal."

"When can I expect a decision?" Nathan wondered.

"It will take time," Kor-Dom Borrol cautioned. "Several weeks, at least. Persuasion requires patience, especially when trying to change the minds of the devout. In the meantime, I would urge you to do what you can to end the attacks by your people against mine. That alone will go a long way toward convincing the doms to support the creation of a new caste with you as its dom."

"I need not remind you that time is of the essence... for both our worlds."

"I should warn you that even the most passive of the doms will not look kindly at the idea of bowing to the control of others."

"You don't find that ironic?"

"Nevertheless."

"Read the draft charter, Kor-Dom. You might be pleasantly surprised."

"I shall do so," Kor-Dom Borrol assured him. "After you return me to Nor-Patri."

"Of course," Nathan agreed.

"I do have one other question," Kor-Dom Borrol stated. "To end hostilities between our worlds, Admiral Galiardi will likely need to be removed from power. How exactly do you propose to accomplish this task?"

"I have a few ideas I'm working on," Nathan assured him.

CHAPTER EIGHT

The sound of footsteps in the corridor caused Loki to quickly switch off the broadcast on the wall-mounted view screen. Without delay, he returned to his bed as the door was unlocked.

A man in his forties appeared. His features were rugged, and his eyes told the story of the things he had done. Loki recognized this look, for he had seen it in the eyes of both the Ghatazhak and the Corinari. It was a look shared by men who had killed without regret.

"Not many survive the Jung memory extraction device," the man commented as he entered and the guard outside closed the door behind him. The man looked Loki over, assessing him. "I would not have guessed you to be one of them." The man pulled up a chair and took a seat. "What is your name?"

"Shouldn't you already know that?"

The man smiled. "Answering a question with a question. A wise tactic, but surely it cannot hurt to know how you should be addressed."

Loki studied the man for a moment. "Loki Sheehan."

"A pleasure to meet you, Mr. Sheehan. You may call me Joe."

"Just Joe?" Loki wondered.

"It is enough for now. I must say, the memories extracted seem rather difficult to believe, or should I say convenient."

"I'm not sure what you mean," Loki admitted.

"These memories tell us a story which seems designed to make us trust you," the man explained.

"It seems far more likely that these memories are false."

"Shouldn't your memory scans have revealed deception?"

"Yes, unless the memories that you carry were planted, in which case you would believe them to be true."

"If my memories were planted, then interrogating me would be of little use, correct?"

Joe smiled, shaking his finger at Loki. "An excellent response, but you are being evasive. If your memories are true, you have no need to be."

"What is it you want from me?" Loki wondered, becoming frustrated. "If you have extracted my memories, then you already know everything that I know."

"We did not extract all of your memories," Joe corrected. "To do so would most certainly have killed you. This is how the Jung got information. But you... Your surface memories are so intriguing I felt compelled to spare your life so that I could investigate further." The man stood back up again. "However, if you do not wish to answer my questions, then I will have no choice but to probe deeper. For your sake, I hope the inevitable coma comes sooner rather than later."

Loki sighed. "How do I know that you're not EDF?"

Joe laughed again. "If I were EDF, you would already be dead."

"Fair point," Loki nodded. "Do you have anything to eat?"

"You were watching the news for nearly an hour. You did not eat?"

"There is no food in the refrigerator."

Joe closed his eyes, shaking his head in disbelief as he turned toward the exit.

"You might want to bring some for yourself as well," Loki told him. "This could take a while."

* * *

After returning the kor-dom to Nor-Patri, Nathan decided it was best to execute the evasion algorithm, just to be safe.

"Did you find the relay station?" Jessica asked.

"It was right where we thought it would be," Nathan replied as he entered the Voss's common room. "I sent an update back to the Aurora and told Cam to keep the ship long jump ready, just in case we need them."

"Good idea," Jessica agreed. "So what's the plan?"

"Well," Nathan said as he took a seat at the table, "I figured the next step is to try to contact Aleksi Rusayev."

The name got Vladimir's attention. "Aleksi Rusayev?"

"Why do you sound so surprised," Nathan wondered.

"He never reads the daily intel reports," Jessica commented.

"I'm an engineer," Vladimir reminded her. "Besides, at the rate you people break things, when do I have time to read reports?" Vladimir moved from the kitchenette to the table, setting his plate down as he took a seat. "Why Aleksi?"

"You know you are a command officer," Jessica reminded him. "You're supposed to be aware of these things."

Vladimir dismissed her with a wave, his attention directed at Nathan.

"Then you know him," Nathan surmised.

"We went through basic together," Vladimir explained. "Russian Marines. It was a long time ago."

"Were you two close?" Jessica wondered, becoming curious.

"Back then, yes. But I haven't seen Aleksi for over a decade," Vladimir explained.

"Do you think he would remember you?" Nathan wondered.

"You don't forget someone who saves your life," Vladimir assured them.

"Maybe you can help us contact him," Jessica said.

"I'm still waiting for someone to tell me why," Vladimir said.

"Apparently, he's a leader of some sort of insurgency against Galiardi," Nathan explained.

"That makes sense," Vladimir said. "Aleksi despises the EDF, as well as the unification of Earth into a single global government. At one time, he even led the movement to separate Kamchatka from Russia."

"Do you have any idea where we could find him?" Nathan asked.

"Aleksi is from Klyuchi, a small city on the Kamchatka River south of Shiveluch. If he is operating an insurgency, it would be from somewhere in that area, as far away from any EDF installation as possible."

"Wouldn't the EDF also start there?" Jessica suggested.

"Aleksi's records show that he was born in Petropavlovsk, but his parents moved to Klyuchi when he was a baby. He ended up back at Petropavlovsk when his parents died in a car crash in the mountains. He was a teenager at the time and stayed with his aunt in Petropavlovsk while he finished school. But in his heart, Klyuchi is home."

"How is it you know so much about the guy?" Jessica wondered. "I went through basic with a bunch of people, and I don't know where any of them grew up."

"That is because you are not very social," Vladimir insisted.

"Hey, I'm social!" Jessica objected.

"We were stranded in the wilderness together for a week," Vladimir explained. "A training exercise that did not end well. Aleksi had a broken leg. I had to carry him out. We had plenty of time to get to know one another."

"That was a long time ago," Nathan pointed out. "How do we know he's still living in Klyuchi?"

"I went to visit him just before I started at the academy," Vladimir explained. "He was living in a small dacha on the outskirts of Klyuchi, very close to where he was raised. He had just been discharged from Russian special forces. He asked me not to tell anyone that he was not from Petropavlovsk. At the time, I got the feeling that he had done some pretty bad things in Spetsnaz and didn't want to leave a trail that led to him."

"If he didn't want to leave a trail, he should've gone to live someplace he'd never been," Jessica said.

"Like I said, Klyuchi is home to Aleksi."

Nathan looked at Jessica. "It sounds like our best option."

"I don't know," Jessica said. "It sounds like the guy has some skeletons."

"And you don't?" Vladimir asked.

"Is there anywhere near Klyuchi where we could

sit down without being noticed?" Nathan asked Vladimir.

"There is a volcano that has several lava tubes coming out from just above its base," Vladimir told them. "Aleksi told me about them. He explored them once with his father. They might be large enough to park the Voss inside."

"Might be?" Nathan wondered.

"The Aurora has fully detailed maps of the earth," Jessica reminded him. "Even subterranean ones. We can ask Cam to send them."

"Good idea," Nathan agreed. "With any luck, one of those tubes will be big enough for us to jump straight into."

"Did I just hear you right?" Dylan wondered, stopping suddenly as he entered the common room. "You want to jump us into a cave? Are you serious?"

Josh pushed past him. "Nothing I haven't done before."

* * *

Loki finally pushed the plate away from him. After days of barely enough food to keep him alive, it felt good to eat a full and hearty meal.

The conversation had turned out to be quite cathartic, which was something he hadn't anticipated. He had revealed virtually everything about himself, holding back only those things that he felt Nathan would not want revealed. Whenever Joe had pressed for more specific details, he played dumb, pretending to be just a pilot, without close associations to the leaders of the Karuzari Alliance.

Of course, he had no idea how much this man already knew. At times, the man appeared to know very little, so much so that Loki often found himself wondering if the Jung memory extraction device had worked on him at all. Loki knew very little about the device, only that the technology did exist. He remembered rumors from long ago about the technology being used on Admiral Galiardi. Many believed that it had been the real reason for the admiral's extended hospital stay after being liberated from Jung captivity.

While Loki had been feeding an overwhelming amount of personal information to Joe, his interrogator had been sharing a surprising amount of his own. Yet Joe had always been careful not to reveal any details that would confirm the identity of his organization or where they were currently located.

Still, it had been a pleasant conversation, not at all what he might expect from an interrogation. Even if the tone had been set on purpose, as a ploy to get him to reveal small details by accident, it was preferable to a more confrontational approach. In his current state, Loki was uncertain that he could have successfully navigated such an encounter.

"You have been through much," Joe admitted, pushing his own plate aside as well. "One can only wonder why you continue to fight."

"Honestly, I ask myself that same question nearly every day," Loki admitted. "Especially since Lael died. But when I look at my daughter's face, I cannot imagine what she would think of me if I turned my back on Josh and the others, if I walked away from the fight."

"Would she not appreciate that you did not want to risk leaving her fatherless?" Joe wondered.

"I would hope she would realize that my belief in our cause was great enough to risk never seeing her again. Besides, she is safe and likely in better hands with the Montrose family."

Joe nodded. "Perhaps." He stretched and leaned back in his chair. "You have been most forthcoming, Loki. I did not expect as much. However, there is one thing that you have not mentioned."

Loki pretended to be confused. "I'm pretty sure I've told you everything."

"Everything except who leads you."

"Like I said, I'm just a pilot..."

"The memories we did extract tell me otherwise," Joe insisted.

It was not the first time during their conversations that Joe had alluded to the memories they had extracted. Yet each time he had only hinted at what they knew, as if the memories had been distorted. "I believe General Telles is the leader of the Karuzari Alliance," Loki told him. "It might not be only him. There may be others with whom he shares leadership responsibilities. I can't be certain."

"And who is your commanding officer on the Aurora?" Joe asked.

"I told you. Captain Taylor."

"Yet there are very few memories of you taking orders from Captain Taylor, especially when under fire," Joe explained. "What about on the Voss? Who was your commanding officer then?"

"Commander Kamenetskiy," Loki lied.

"Yes, there are images and sounds of this man, quite recently in fact. However, there are memories of another man. One who frequently appears in your short-term memory. One who looks very much like someone who should not be alive."

"Maybe it would help if you told me who you think this person in my memory is?" Loki suggested, hoping to find out what the man actually knew, or at least what he suspected.

"Nathan Scott."

Loki chuckled. "Captain Scott was executed by the Jung seven years ago. It was all over the news."

"If we had gone into your long-term memory, you and I would not be having this conversation."

"Is it possible that I just thought of the captain recently? Maybe that's why he's in my short-term memory?" Loki suggested.

Joe sighed. "Anything is possible," he admitted. "I have seen stranger results from the device. I once scanned a man who believed he was a goat. He truly believed this. His visual memories were even from the eye-level of a goat, and he was walking around within the herd. Through interrogation, we determined that the memories were in fact from a recent dream the subject had experienced. One that he had remembered quite vividly."

"Wow, that is unusual."

"Not really," Joe said, dismissing it. "Turns out, the subject owned a small goat farm."

"So you're saying dreams can be picked up as memories?" Loki surmised.

"If they are recalled with enough clarity and are fairly recent, yes. To be honest, we don't really understand how the device works. We just know that it does."

"But wouldn't that make most memories suspect?" Loki decided.

"Most dreams are too unusual to be believed," Joe explained. "They are full of continuity errors and often violate the basic laws of physics. Like people flapping their arms and flying like a bird. So it is usually not difficult to tell them apart from memories of reality."

"Well, I do think about Captain Scott a lot," Loki insisted, hoping to coax Joe into believing that those memories were actually dreams.

"Perhaps, but you have many memories of Captain Scott," Joe pointed out. "Most of them fairly recent and quite clear. And those memories, while fantastic, do not seem to violate reality as we understand it."

"I don't know what to tell you," Loki lied. "I guess I'm just a realistic dreamer."

Joe leaned forward again, putting his elbows on the table and crossing his arms, a determined look on his face. "I believe I have a more logical explanation."

"I'd love to hear it," Loki invited.

"I believe that you are an excellent officer and are trying hard not to reveal that Captain Scott is alive and is leading the Karuzari Alliance."

"Your logical explanation is that a man whom everyone saw executed and buried is actually alive?" Loki rolled his eyes. "Yup, sounds completely logical to me."

"I have seen many things revealed by the memory extraction device," Joe insisted. "However, I have never seen memories so clear resulting from dreams, even recent ones."

"So you're accusing me of lying," Loki surmised. "Why would I do that? You have a machine that will get you the truth and turn me into a vegetable in the process."

"One can hide the truth without lying," Joe insisted. "Perhaps you believe what you are saying, or more likely, you are saying it in such a way that it does not feel like a lie to you...like a partial truth."

"I think you're giving me more credit than I deserve," Loki countered.

Joe assumed a less confrontational pose in his chair. "Let us assume, for the sake of discussion, that I am correct, and Captain Scott is alive. If this was revealed to the public, it could change the balance of power on Earth."

"How so?" Loki asked.

"As the son of a slain leader, Nathan Scott would have the legal right to act as president, at least until an election could be held. If he exercised that right, it would be the end of Admiral Galiardi's reign over us."

Over us, Loki thought. It was the first time that his interrogator had said something that might belie his allegiances. The question was, had he done so intentionally?

"From what I saw earlier, half the people on your planet like Galiardi," Loki stated.

"Like is a strong word," Joe insisted. "Many agree with his position on the Jung, for various reasons. However, many might not agree with him remaining in power should a legal heir to office appear."

"Which I'm betting Admiral Galiardi wouldn't like."

"Indeed," Joe replied, his expression revealing nothing about his feelings on the idea.

"What about you?" Loki pressed. "How do you feel about him?"

"I neither love nor hate the man. As far as I'm concerned, he has as many agreeable objectives as he has faults, assuming that the information that we have been given is the truth. Your memories seem to contradict that truth."

Loki shook his head in dismay. The man was

good. If Loki's suspicions were correct, and Joe was working for Galiardi, then life as he knew it was over. It was only a matter of time before they would put him back on the memory extractor, ending his life in the process.

* * *

The Voss had spent the night maintaining a position near the Sol comm-relay station, awaiting a response before planning their next move. During that time, Nathan had ample opportunity to reassess his options. Unfortunately, they were unchanged.

Nathan ascended the stair ladder to the command deck and made his way aft through the short corridor connecting it to the common room at the ship's center. Most of the crew had spent the short, simulated night in their racks, getting some rest while they could. As expected, most were gathered in the common room, sharing stories and insults over their morning meal.

"Morning, Captain," Kit greeted.

"Finally," Jessica exclaimed from the center table. "I was wondering when you were going to get up."

"Sorry," Nathan apologized as he made his way over to the kitchenette. "I didn't get much sleep last night."

"Funny, I could've sworn I heard you snoring," Jessica remarked.

"I'm pretty sure that was Marcus," Josh insisted, snickering.

Nathan removed a mug from the overhead cabinet and placed it into the beverage dispenser on the counter, pressing the button to activate the machine. "Any word from the Aurora?"

Jessica picked up her data pad from the table and then leaned back, handing it to Nathan with an outstretched arm. "Reply came back a few hours ago."

Nathan pulled his mug from the machine. "Anything interesting?"

"Not really," Jessica replied. "Cam's been keeping an eye on the Dusahn, but so far, they haven't left the Takar system. Intel shows they're putting every effort into upgrading the rest of their newly acquired ships, though."

Nathan took a careful sip of his beverage. It wasn't the same as the coffee back on the Aurora, but it was the closest thing SilTek had to offer, and it seemed to do the trick. "Did she send the maps?" he asked, studying the data pad.

"Yup," Jessica replied. "She also mentioned that she was surprised we weren't dead...especially you."

"Based on these timestamps, it looks like it took about four hours round-trip," Nathan said as he examined the comm-log. "Not too bad."

"The Aurora's comm-drones could make the trip in an hour," Vladimir insisted, his mouth full of food.

"Well, until we get a few more of the long-range variants, the relay system will have to do," Nathan commented. "Have you studied the maps yet?"

"I had to write a conversion algorithm to make the map files compatible with our holo-projector," Dylan told him. "I just completed the conversion as you came in."

"Load it up, and let's take a look," Nathan said as he moved toward the table, mug in hand.

Dylan pressed a few buttons on the remote for the common room's conference table, activating the holo-projector. A three-dimensional image of the volcano near Klyuchi appeared at the center of the table.

Nathan took a seat next to Jessica, studying the projection. "Zoom in on the base," he instructed.

The projection switched to a semi-opaque representation of the mountain, revealing several lava tubes branching out from the center of the volcano and opening around the base.

"That one looks to be the largest," Nathan said, pointing.

"The one on the near side is closer to town," Jessica suggested.

"Yes, but the opening is only about fifteen percent larger than the Voss," Nathan explained. "The other one is more like twice our size."

"That one is fifty kilometers from Klyuchi," Jessica pointed out. "It'll take us at least an hour to get there using the rover, depending on the terrain."

"Let's stick with the larger one," Nathan insisted. "For Dylan's sake. It's his first time."

"Thank you," Dylan said, relieved.

"Hell," Josh exclaimed, "I could make that jump with my eyes closed."

"That's the only way I would do it," Dylan commented. He looked at Nathan. "Just how accurate are these maps, Captain?"

"They were originally created to enable accurate targeting of Jung forces on the surface, as a precaution in case of invasion," Jessica explained. "So they're pretty damned accurate."

"The update stamps show them to be just over a year old," Nathan noted.

"How do we even know the tubes are still there?" Dylan asked. "What if someone has built something in there? What if it has caved in since these maps were made? What if..."

"I get it, Dylan," Nathan said, cutting him off.

"He's got a point," Jessica decided.

"What do you think, Josh?" Nathan said. "Care to do a little recon?"

"I'd love to," Josh replied. "I can jump in low to the northwest between the mountains and that volcano. In and out in about a minute, tops."

"Make sure you keep it to that," Nathan urged. "There probably aren't any air traffic sensors in the area. Only the higher altitude stuff. But if you're in there for too long, surveillance sats will detect you, no matter how low you fly."

"I'll keep it short and sweet," Josh promised. "Just long enough to verify our insertion point."

"When do we go?" Kit wondered.

"We'll move in closer now," Nathan explained. "We'll make the jump to Earth as soon as Josh gets back, assuming that tunnel opening is still there."

"I'll jump us to Proxima Centauri. I can jump into the system from there," Josh said, rising from the table. "Come on, kid. We've got work to do."

Nathan reached over and took a sausage from Vladimir's plate, taking a bite. "How sure are you that Aleksi is in Klyuchi," he asked Vladimir.

"The only way Aleksi would not live in Klyuchi is if he had no choice," Vladimir replied.

"Now that I know where the hell Klyuchi actually is, I think there's a good chance this guy might be there," Jessica agreed. "It's pretty damn remote. Not a bad place to run covert ops from."

"Well," Nathan said as he stole another sausage, "I guess we'll know soon enough."

Vladimir pulled his plate away from Nathan, wrapping his arm around it. "Get your own breakfast!"

* * *

After the events of the preceding day, none of the

caste leaders had been surprised when their kor-dom called an emergency session of the leadership council. What the leader of the Jung Empire had to say, however, was entirely unexpected.

The council chambers echoed numerous protestations of doms and caste representatives alike, so much so that one could barely hear themselves speak.

The banging of Kor-Dom Borrol's gavel rang so loudly, it was if it were amplified. Despite its ability to cut through the noise of the crowd, it took a dozen strikes to produce the desired effect. "Enough! Enough!" the kor-dom demanded. "Everyone will get a chance to speak!"

"The Tonba-Hon-Venar has already begun!" Dom-Jaya Jung-Mogan protested at the top of his lungs. "It has taken seven years to get our fleet into position! We are only days from vengeance!"

Several of the doms vehemently echoed the Jung-Mogan representative's sentiments, while others argued in opposition with equal fervor.

Kor-Dom Borrol banged his gavel repeatedly. "Do not make me clear this room!" he threatened with conviction. "I have called for a general assembly of all doms, regardless of rank and standing! But if we cannot have order, I will clear this chamber of all but the Leaders of Nine!" The kor-dom set his gavel down, determination on his face. Once the unruly occupants of the gallery had quieted down, he continued. "The council will hear Dom Jung-Viyakh."

The elderly leader of the ninth of the original Jung castes rose, allowing his gathered robes to hang freely before he began his oration. "We stand on the precipice of annihilation. This empire rose from disaster a millennia ago, when our founder saw an opportunity to save his people. Still, it required that he go against everything he believed. It is because of him that we all stand here this day. We now have the opportunity to show our people that we are not so foolish as to allow ego and tradition to cause us to forget the sacrifices of all those who came before us. Yes, this great empire can be rebuilt from the ashes of the Tonba-Hon-Venar, and in another thousand years, it will be bigger and stronger than it is today. But I ask you, what kind of leaders would we be if we allowed trillions of innocent people to die needlessly? Men, women, and children, all of whom trust us to protect and care for them." The old statesman paused a moment, his head hung low. "Kristoff Jung was no great leader of men," he continued, slowly raising his head again. "He was just the captain of an old cargo ship who did what was needed when it mattered most." Dom Jung-Viyakh paused again, looking around the council chambers, exchanging glances with as many of the caste leaders as he could before finishing his statement. "Who are we to let ego and politics stand in the way of the survival of this grand empire?"

"The Tonba-Hon-Venar must proceed!" someone yelled from the gallery. Immediately, several more joined him in voicing their opinions, both for and against.

Again Kor-Dom Borrol was forced to use his gavel. "Clear the gallery!" he ordered, pointing at the doors at the back of the gallery.

The arguing of the lesser caste leaders seated in the gallery became even more raucous. Half of them demanded that the Tonba-Hon-Venar continue, while the other half cursed them for ignorance in their call for violence and destruction. A few even demanded an immediate vote of no-confidence in Kor-Dom Borrol. More than a dozen of the empire's elite council guards were required to control the chaos and clear the gallery.

"Sequester them all until after this session has concluded!" Kor-Dom Borrol instructed his chief of security. It was an unprecedented step, even by a kor-dom, but their unwieldy behavior had left him little choice. Thus far, he had managed to avoid revealing the identity of the representative from the Karuzari Alliance; the man who wished to lead his own Jung caste. Were any of the doms to discover the truth, even those in the Leaders of Nine, they would get their vote of no-confidence. Even worse, there would be no turning back from the Tonba-Hon-Venar, and the empire would end.

The aide sitting beside Dom-Jaya Jung-Mogan tapped his caste's designated representative on the shoulder, leaning in close for a private conversation. "Sir, the combination of our cloaking technology and jump drive technology would give us a significant advantage over the Sol Alliance. We would be unbeatable."

Dom-Jaya Jung-Mogan considered his assistant's words. The Jung-Mogan caste had chosen to keep their cloaking technology a secret from the other castes. For too long, the isolationists had prevented them from achieving true glory. The defeat at the hands of the Sol Alliance and the destruction of Zhu-Anok had provided the isolationists with the political leverage they had needed to halt the expansion of the empire through conquest. Yet now they spoke of expansion, albeit peaceful. Such a reversal only served to confirm what the warrior castes had always suspected: that the isolationists were unfit to lead.

The words of Dom Jung-Viyakh echoed in his head. Especially one... Opportunity.

Dom-Jaya Jung-Mogan rose. "The Jung-Mogan caste again requests the floor."

Kor-Dom Borrol looked at the other seven members of the Leaders of Nine. Dom-Jaya Jung-Mogan had already spoken, which meant that he could only speak again if the other members of the council allowed it. When no one objected, he yielded the floor. "Dom-Jaya Jung-Mogan has the floor, but I caution you not to abuse the generosity of the members."

Dom-Jaya Jung-Mogan intentionally looked at the faces of the other eight members, lastly at Kor-Dom Borrol. "The words of Dom Jung-Viyakh have caused me to reconsider our position. The Jung-Mogan caste now supports the proposal put forth by the honorable Kor-Dom Borrol."

Soft mumbles of uncertainty, accompanied by suspicious glances between council members, followed as Dom-Jaya Jung-Mogan took his seat without another word. Kor-Dom Borrol was not fooled by Dom-Jaya Jung-Mogan's sudden change of heart, nor did he believe that it was prompted by the words of Dom Jung-Viyakh. The dom-jaya was up to something, and Kor-Dom Borrol was confident that the good of the empire was not his primary motivation.

Dom Immoritt was the next to stand.

"Dom Immoritt has the floor," Kor-Dom Borrol announced.

"I have but one question, my lord," Dom Immoritt began. "What happens if Lord Dusahn defeats this challenger?"

"The challenge cannot be made until the new

caste is created and that caste chooses its leader," Kor-Dom Borrol explained. "This cannot happen until these unwarranted attacks by the Sol Alliance have stopped and Admiral Galiardi has been brought to justice under the laws of their world. This alone would be enough reason to accept the Karuzari proposal. The challenge itself will likely be pointless unless our ships are there to enforce it. To do so, we must be provided jump drive technology, lest it take years for the challenge to be viable, at which point it might be too late. If, as I suspect, the challenge fails and Lord Dusahn remains in power, we will destroy Takara and withdraw to Jung territory. Either way, the current threat will be eliminated, we will have jump drive technology, the Dusahn will be neutralized, and this empire will prevail."

"The Karuzari will no doubt look upon this act unfavorably," Dom Immoritt warned.

"I do not care what the Karuzari Alliance favors," Kor-Dom Borrol stated. "I only care about the survival and the glory of the Jung Empire." The kor-dom kept his eyes focused on Dom Immoritt, waiting for him to speak further. When the dom took his seat, Kor-Dom Borrol looked to the other members of the Leaders of Nine.

It was time.

"As kor-dom, I call on the Leaders of Nine to cast their votes on the Karuzari proposal."

* * *

"That was fast," Dylan commented as Josh dropped into the pilot's seat on the left side of the Voss's cockpit.

"In and out quick; no one gets hurt," Josh replied. "Least of all, me."

"But you were only gone like five minutes. It

would've taken me that long just to get up the nerve to launch."

"We can't all have brass balls," Nathan joked as he came up the stair ladder to the command deck.

"Looks like it will take us two jumps," Dylan reported. "One to get into position, the other to jump into the cave." Dylan swallowed hard. "And I can't believe I just said that."

Nathan reached up and flipped down the overhead comm-panel, making sure that the ship-wide intercom was active. "Attention, all hands. Prepare for insertion jump."

"I don't get it," Dylan said. "How do you all stay so calm? I mean, we're about to jump two light years into a cave. Any normal person would be scared shitless."

"Don't worry, kid, you get used to it," Nathan assured Dylan as he patted him on the shoulder. "Are both jumps plotted and ready?"

"First jump is loaded and ready, and we're on course and speed," Dylan replied.

"Execute the first jump," Nathan instructed.

"Executing set-up jump," Josh acknowledged as he reached for the jump sequencer. "Jumping in three......two......one......jumping."

Now that the Voss had auto-darkening windows, the amount of light spilling into the interior of the ship was at more tolerable levels.

"Jump complete," Josh reported.

"Updating position," Dylan announced.

"Be sure you double-check our position," Nathan told him.

"Oh don't you worry," Dylan replied.

Nathan tilted his head slightly upward as he

leaned against the railing. "How are things looking, Vlad?" he called over the intercom.

"I've run full diagnostics and triple-checked everything," Vladimir assured him. "The jump drive and all related systems are in perfect working order."

"We are one point seven two seven five light years from Earth," Dylan reported. "Come to new heading one four zero, down fifteen point two five relative."

"Turning to one four zero, down fifteen point two five relative," Josh acknowledged as he initiated their course change.

"If it's all the same to you, Josh, I'd prefer the AI took this one," Nathan said.

"Hey, just cuz I got brass balls don't mean I'm stupid."

Nathan smiled.

"Course change complete," Josh announced. "Straight and true on one four zero, fifteen point two five down relative. Handing over flight controls to the AI." Josh pressed the auto-flight button on his control yoke, then released his grip. "AI has the controls."

"I assume you entered the parameters of the cave?" Nathan asked Dylan.

"Trust me," Dylan assured him, "the AI knows every rock, bump, and crack of that cave. I even uploaded the sensor data from Josh's recon flight and instructed the AI to create a three-dimensional representation of the interior."

"How long will it take us to decelerate to a safe insertion speed?" Nathan wondered.

"We're barely moving now," Josh insisted. "Hell, I can run faster than this."

"Actually, we're doing about fifty KPH right now," Dylan corrected.

"Maybe we should slow down even more?" Nathan suggested.

"It's going to take all available jump energy to get us there from this distance," Josh explained. "If we slow down by even a few KPH, we'll come out of the jump outside of the cave."

"Which will increase our risk of detection by surveillance satellites," Nathan deduced.

"Guarantee would be a better choice of words," Josh corrected.

"Maybe we should coast longer," Dylan suggested. "If we waited an hour, we might be able to slow down another ten KPH. We could bring our jump drive back up to full charge as well. That would get us even slower."

"According to Cameron, we'll be inside sensor range of the EDF's perimeter patrols if we do," Nathan warned. "There's already a chance that one of them will detect our jump, even from this far out. If they do, they can calculate our trajectory and determine our destination. That would mess up our mission real quick. Better that we don't make it any easier for them."

"Don't worry, Cap'n," Josh said. "I can slow us down before we run out of room."

"And smack into a wall," Dylan muttered to himself.

"I'm sure we'll be fine," Nathan assured Dylan. "Shall we get this over with, gentlemen?"

"Updating final insertion jump parameters," Dylan announced. "Update complete."

Josh reached over and pressed the button to activate the automated jump sequencer. "Hang on to your shorts, everyone," he warned over the intercom. "Insertion jump in three......"

* * *

The old man had been tracking his prey through the snow for hours. He had left his dacha before dawn, sure that his wife would disapprove of his desire to hunt.

But hunting was everything to him. Man against nature. Wits against instinct. It kept him alive and feeling young. The killing of a bear, a moose, or a snow sheep, and the subsequent ritual of turning it into sustenance, connected him to the forest. As long as he could hunt, he knew he was still alive.

But he also knew that he was getting on in years, and his senses were not what they had once been. Someday, his prey would get the better of him. However, the old man was not troubled by the thought. He could not think of a better way to meet his end than dying while doing the very thing that made him feel alive.

The snow had begun to fall again, threatening to erase the tracks that he had been following. He had already lost a previous shot that had taken him hours to set up. A strange little aircraft had buzzed overhead, skimming the treetops. He had cursed that pilot for alerting his prey. He lived where he did because it was as far away from technology as one could get.

As he trudged through the snow, he suddenly froze in his tracks. In the distance, something moved amongst the trees. Uncertain if it was the bear he had been tracking, he raised his rifle and removed the cover from its sights. Moving slowly so as not to alert his prey, he took aim, using the thumb buttons on his rifle stock to adjust the optics and increase his magnification. His digital rifle scope was one of the few technologies he had agreed to embrace, at the behest of his children. And it did help offset his failing eyesight.

He acquired his target, his pulse quickening. It was indeed the same bear he had been tracking. Just as he had expected, it had stayed close to the massive lava tube entrance, where bears often took shelter. Three days this week, he had snuck out to hunt and had brought home only excuses. Finally, he would have his kill.

The brown bear was much bigger than he had expected, which excited him further. His annual winter ritual was always the same. Take a bear first, since it provided the most meat. A moose was next, followed by at least two sheep. That was more than enough to get them through the Kamchatka winters.

The old man paused, taking note of the wind's direction and strength. The scope could automatically adjust for wind and range, but to him that was cheating, and he kept those features disabled. He only wished the scope to make him able to see the same as he once had in his youth.

The old man braced himself, carefully adjusting his aim as the bear continued to move through the forest from right to left. The bear lumbered along, maintaining a consistent stride, which was to the hunter's advantage. He slowly tracked the animal, keeping his crosshairs just forward of the bear's chest, instinctively leading him just enough. The best shot, the one that would drop the bear quickly and with mercy, would be when his front leg nearest the hunter was forward, allowing him to put the projectile through lungs and heart. The taking of the bear's life had to be done with respect.

He began counting off the bear's strides. His finger moved to the safety, switching it off, then to the trigger. He tightened his finger, advancing the trigger to the edge of firing, pausing just long enough for that leg to again swing forward...

A flash of blue-white light appeared from the base of the mountain to his right, followed by a thunderous roar. The bear, startled by the sound, broke into a run, departing with surprising speed.

"Chort!" the old man cursed, switching his safety back on as he lowered his rifle, watching the bear run off.

A second later, something else caught his attention. He turned to his right, just as a shock wave of displaced air slammed into him, knocking him on his ass.

* * *

All three men were silent, their hearts racing as they stared at the rocky overhang less than a meter outside of the Voss's cockpit windows.

"Told ya I could stop us in time," Josh finally said.

Dylan turned his head slowly to the left, staring at Josh but saying nothing.

"What?"

"I never doubted you for a moment," Nathan said, breathing a sigh of relief. "Except maybe those last ten seconds," he added as he released his iron grip on the railing. "Are we going to be able to get out of here in one piece?"

"If we can fly in, we can fly out," Josh assured him.

"We're still hovering," Dylan reminded them. "Like...half a meter above the deck."

"I know," Josh snapped.

"I'm just saying."

"Do we have room to turn around?" Nathan

wondered, looking out the overhead windows, noting how close the rocky ceiling was.

"We'll have to back up about sixty meters first," Dylan replied. "It's pretty tight this deep in."

"I can fly us out backwards as easily as I can forwards, Cap'n," Josh insisted.

"Might I suggest I program an auto-flight maneuver for that?" Dylan suggested. "Not that I don't trust you," he immediately added to keep Josh quiet, "but because we might be under fire...or worse yet, I might be the one who has to fly us out."

"Good thinking," Nathan agreed, "but I still want us to turn around. We may need to use the P-Seventy-Twos."

"Yes, sir," Dylan replied. "We won't be able to park as deeply into the cave, though. We're widest across our aft end."

"As long as our nose isn't sticking out, we'll be fine," Nathan assured him, patting him on the back as he turned to exit. "Park this thing, gentlemen."

"You got it, Cap'n," Josh replied.

* * *

Commander Jexx moved quickly through the mansion that had once housed the ruling family of Takara. Now it served as the home of Lord Dusahn, as well as the seat of power for the empire.

Since the facility had not been designed for such purposes, the commander often found himself walking long distances. The journey between the command center and his leader's private chambers was the longest of them. He often wondered why Lord Dusahn had chosen to be so far from the command center.

The only conclusion the commander had come up with was that his leader was not interested in the day-to-day decisions required to run his military. This task had always been delegated to subordinates. Such was the duty of generals and colonels with far more experience in the machinations and logistics of ships, weapons systems, and men.

The problem was, with each successive failure by his subordinates, fewer and fewer of them were left to manage the empire's forces. Commander Jexx often felt as if he had been cursed with his new-found position as the Dusahn leader's right-hand man. Not only were his responsibilities many, but so were the chances of failure for which he would be held responsible.

To make matters more complicated, his leader had become increasingly hostile as of late. Ever since his return from Infernum, his temper had been short, and his forgiveness sparse. Lord Dusahn had become less willing to listen to reason and more likely to be driven by his emotions rather than logic. The commander had been forced to develop an ability to phrase his presentations carefully as of late, to avoid his leader's wrath and guide him in the proper direction.

Today, however, was different. For the first time in what seemed like an eternity, the commander had news that he was certain would make the leader of the Dusahn Empire happy. For once, he wouldn't be dodging fire, attempting to weather the man's anger.

"Commander," the officer at the reception desk outside Lord Dusahn's private office greeted. When he realized the commander was not slowing down, he added, "I'm not sure our lord wants to be..."

It was too late.

Commander Jexx burst through the double doors

into Lord Dusahn's private office without knocking, something he had never done. "My Lord!"

As the officer outside had warned, Lord Dusahn did not appear to be in a mood to receive company. "Have you lost your mind, Commander?" his leader wondered. His tone was more of a warning than an inquisition.

"Apologies, my lord, but this cannot wait," the commander insisted, continuing toward his leader without slowing.

"For your sake, I hope so."

"We have found it, my lord," the commander explained, smiling.

Lord Dusahn's brow furrowed. "Please tell me you are speaking about the mysterious ally of the Karuzari."

Commander Jexx handed his leader the data pad. "They were only able to make one sensor pass, but they did so at low altitude, in their atmosphere, while under fire."

"A daring move," Lord Dusahn agreed as he examined the data.

"The sensor scans show many similar patterns and energy signatures as those used recently by the Karuzari," Commander Jexx told him. "They even detected the same missiles the Karuzari have been using to take down our shields. This must be it."

"I agree with your assessment, Commander," Lord Dusahn replied. "What is this world called?"

"SilTek, my lord. They gathered copious amounts of signals intelligence as well, including entertainment and news broadcasts. The ship that fought us in the Volon system comes from this world. They are arming them on the surface as we speak."

"Well done, Commander. Well done indeed."

"What are your orders, my lord?" the commander asked, knowing full well what would come next.

Lord Dusahn flashed a sinister smile. "I want this world SilTek erased from existence," he sneered. "Complete destruction. I want all who are invited to ally with the Karuzari against us to know precisely what they risk."

"Of course, my lord," Commander Jexx replied. "It will take some time, however. Our new long-range jump missiles have not yet been tested."

"Then the destruction of SilTek will be their test," Lord Dusahn snapped.

"My lord, our antimatter warheads are few. To risk them in this manner..."

"Risk is how empires are built, Commander," Lord Dusahn insisted. "Do as I command...immediately!"

"Yes, my lord."

CHAPTER NINE

Aleksi Rusayev was a nondescript man. Neither his size nor build was striking at first glance, nor were his features. Beard neatly trimmed, hair properly groomed; dressed in average work clothing, he did not stand out in a crowd.

That was by design.

The leader of the insurgency against Admiral Galiardi seemed more like a factory worker than a warrior. Few would peg him as a deadly killer of men. But Aleksi had seen more than his fair share of death. Death of family and the death of comrades; and of course, the deaths of many opponents. Yet he held no medals, was discharged from service without honors, and was never spoken of by his former commanders. He, like so many others in the special operations community, fought anonymously. Fame and fortune were not part of their lives.

Aleksi was content with that. He much preferred the true anonymity of the average man. While small, his distillery earned him a comfortable living and supported a small band of loyal employees. What most residents of Klyuchi did not know was how he spent the rest of his profits.

Aleksi had worked hard the last ten years, ever since he had left the service of the Russian military. He had built his company, invested his profits, and diversified his wealth in such a way that it was difficult to track. His little business had even managed to survive the Jung occupation and their subsequent attempt to glass the planet more than seven years ago.

It was one of the many advantages of living in a

remote city, far off the beaten path. He had loved Klyuchi as a child and still loved it as an adult. Were he to have his way, he would never leave it again.

Aleksi had been sitting at the conference table with his lieutenants for going on two hours. He was growing weary of the endless string of bad ideas. It was not that his subordinates were ignorant or uninspired; his organization simply lacked good options.

"Taking down the net would cost many lives," Anton argued. "And it would only take days to restore service."

"They would just switch most of the traffic over to the satellites," Dimitri insisted.

"The satellites cannot handle the load," Oleg protested.

"So the people would have slower net access for a while," Dimitri countered.

"For which they would blame us," Anton said.

"Anton is correct," Aleksi agreed. "While we might cripple data exchange, markets, and communications for a day or two, it would send shock waves through the global economy. They would blame us for the chaos and rightfully so."

"We must seize control of the nets," Oleg suggested. "Force Galiardi to step down or hold an election."

"It is impossible to seize control of the entire net," Dimitri insisted. "There are too many redundancies. You would need an army, and a well-equipped one at that!"

"A vast army," Aleksi added. "You'd have to hold those assets to control it."

"We need to get our message out to the people," Oleg said.

"And what would that message be?" Aleksi wondered. "That we despise Michael Galiardi? That we believe he assassinated Earth's first family? Without evidence, we would be labeled as just another group of conspiracy theorists."

Dimitri smiled. "Aren't we?"

"Technically, yes," Aleksi agreed. He always enjoyed Dimitri's ironic sense of humor. "I fear the best we can hope to do is to continue hitting small targets. Take out as many assets on the ground as possible."

"That will not stop them," Oleg insisted.

"No, but it will feed talk on the net. It will get people thinking about Galiardi and questioning his motives and honor. We are fighting a propaganda machine, gentlemen, and an effective one at that."

"I still say we should get our message out on the net," Oleg reiterated. "The more people hear something, the more they believe, with or without proof."

"Then we would be no better than Galiardi," Dimitri argued.

"Again, we do not have the resources to seize control of the net long enough to get our message to everyone," Aleksi insisted. "Even if we did, the cost in lives would be too high."

"We are willing to die," Dimitri insisted.

"I know you are," Aleksi assured him. "I know that all of you are. But this insurgency is still tenuous, and our losses have been few thus far. The surgical methods of our strikes are what draws people to our ranks. They know that we are not reckless."

"Galiardi is taking us into a full-blown war with the Jung," Anton stated.

"I am well aware," Aleksi assured him.

"Gentlemen," he declared, having reached his limit for the day. "Please bring me a list of viable targets. Ones you have actionable intelligence on. I do not wish to waste my time on speculation. We will meet again in three days. I expect better ideas by then."

Aleksi rose from his chair, heading out of the conference room and down the corridor. The day was half over, and he still had a business to run.

"Aleksi," his friend, Igor called.

Aleksi stopped, turning back toward the voice of one of his trusted, right-hand men. Igor had a young man with him, one whom Aleksi did not recognize.

"Aleksi, this is Evgeni, Lula's boy," Igor said, introducing the young man.

"A pleasure," Aleksi said, shaking the young man's hand. "Your mother has worked for me for many years. I would be lost without her."

"Thank you, sir," Evgeni replied. "She speaks highly of you as well."

Igor looked both ways up and down the corridor, checking that no one was within earshot. "Evgeni is one of many locals who act as our eyes and ears."

"Is he now?"

"He is one of my most trusted," Igor assured Aleksi.

"Of course."

"Tell him what you told me, Evgeni," Igor urged the young man.

"An hour ago, an old man came into the clinic where I work. His face was covered with small lacerations. He said he was hunting near Papiva Cavern when a flash of light came from the cavern, startling his prey. He also said there was a thunderous echo from deep within the cavern, and then he was knocked down by a fierce wind...like a shock wave. The doctor believes the lacerations were from small bits of lava rock, probably ejected from the cavern, assuming the old man was being honest."

"You have reason to suspect he was not?" Aleksi wondered.

"He was on pain medication," Evgeni explained.

"Sounds like a cave-in, or a gas pocket deep within the lava tube opened up causing the ejecta," Aleksi surmised.

"The old man swears otherwise," Evgeni told him. "He claimed to have seen gas pockets rupture within the lava tubes, and the smell of sulfur was not present today."

"I suspect the old man was mistaken," Igor said, making a gesture indicating an imbibe.

"There was one other thing," Evgeni added. "He said that a small jet, perhaps a fighter, flew over him no more than ten minutes prior. He said it had come out of nowhere. A small crack of thunder, and it was streaking over his head, just above the treetops. It disappeared less than a minute later, or so he said."

Aleksi exchanged a glance with Igor. "Thank you for the information, Evgeni," he said, handing the young man a credit chip.

"Thank you, sir," Evgeni replied, happily turning to exit.

As soon as the young man was gone, Aleksi looked at Igor. "What do you think?"

"I think it was a drunken old man in the woods who wanted an excuse for why he was unable to provide dinner," Igor decided.

"If it were just the blast from the cavern, I might agree with you."

"You think it was an EDF fighter?" Igor wondered, a bit surprised.

"More likely a small recon ship."

"You think Vasyli was captured?"

"We have not heard from him in over a week," Aleksi stated.

"Vasyli is too careful to be caught," Igor insisted. "Someone spooked him, and he has gone into hiding. He will turn up. You will see."

"I hope you are correct," Aleksi agreed. "In the meantime, send Sasha and his men to check out Papiva Cavern, but tell them to keep a low profile."

"I'll speak to Sasha directly," Igor promised.

* * *

"You wanted to see me, Ken?" Cameron asked as she entered the Aurora's intelligence office.

"We got some disturbing data from one of our recent recons of the Takara system," the lieutenant commander began. "At first, we thought it was a missile launch, but the configuration was wrong."

Cameron stepped up to the display table at the center of the compartment, looking at the data displayed on its surface. "Wrong, how?"

"Well, to begin with, its jump drive signature resembles one of our comm-drones. The original routable variants with series-jump capabilities."

"I thought the Dusahn didn't have any of those?"

"Neither did we," the lieutenant commander agreed, "until now." He pressed a few buttons on the control console at the table's edge, calling up a different set of images. "I'm thinking they took the comm-drones that were originally servicing the Pentaurus sector and either reverse-engineered them or just adapted a few for their purposes."

"Well I guess we can't get too upset if they're just communicating with neighboring systems."

"They may be doing more than that."

Cameron shot him a concerned look. "I don't like the sound of that."

Lieutenant Commander Shinoda sighed. "I showed these scans to Lieutenant Parsa in engineering. It looks to him like the Dusahn combined four jump comm-drones, probably to increase their range."

"If they're series-jump capable, why would they need to?" Cameron wondered.

"The original jump comm-drones were series-jump capable, but they were powered by fusion reactors," the lieutenant commander explained. "It took them several minutes to recharge for the next jump. That problem was solved when they replaced them with mini-ZPEDs. Four separate jump drives would allow for shorter intervals between jumps, allowing the drone to reach its final destination more quickly."

"If they wanted to send a message someplace far away, why not just replace the fusion reactor with a mini-ZPED? Seems like it would be easier than cobbling together four comm-drones."

"We took out their ability to manufacture ZPEDs when we attacked Rama a few months back," he reminded her. "They're probably in short supply."

"So they must've really wanted to send a message badly. But to where?"

The lieutenant commander reached for the control console again, calling up a three-dimensional holographic star chart that hovered over the table. "The original departure course was in the general direction of both the Orswellan and the Rogen systems," he informed her as the departure trajectory drew its way across the holographic map.

"You think they still have operatives in those systems?" Cameron wondered.

"Possibly, but even one of the fusion-powered

comm-drones would make the trip in a few hours. So why go to the trouble of building one with a shorter trip time?" The lieutenant commander adjusted the controls again, expanding the star map to include additional sectors. "It wouldn't be a huge course change to steer them toward SilTek."

Cameron felt a sinking feeling. "Are you suggesting that the recon pass was a diversion so that they could put operatives on SilTek?"

"Or worse," the lieutenant commander replied. "Maybe those aren't comm-drones at all, but weapons."

"I'm assuming you didn't detect any warheads?"

"That doesn't mean they didn't have them." The lieutenant commander called up the image of the comm-drone again, this time zooming in tightly on its forward half. "The nose has been altered. According to Parsa, it's big enough to be heavy shielding to hide a nuke or even an antimatter warhead. If it is, the target world wouldn't even realize it was a weapon until it was too late."

Cameron felt that sinking feeling getting worse. "That's a lot of assumptions," she said, hoping that the lieutenant commander would start shooting holes in his own theories, thus easing her concerns.

"That's what you pay me for."

Cameron sighed. "How many did they launch?"

"Four that we know of," he replied. "All of them on the same departure trajectory."

The sinking feeling was quickly turning into a knot in her stomach. "We need to find those things, whatever they are."

"If they split up, it's going to be difficult," the lieutenant commander warned.

"We'll start with the Falcon," Cameron said,

undaunted. "They've got the best long-range sensors. Send them along the departure trajectory, short intervals, checking for old jump light along the way. If they are weapons, it's more likely they're headed for SilTek than Rogen or Orswella."

"Let's hope you're right," the lieutenant commander stated.

"Let's hope you're wrong," Cameron insisted, "and they're just comm-drones after all."

* * *

Josh took a seat at the Voss's starboard auxiliary console, a cup of hot tea in his hand. There was nothing worse than standing watch while on the ground. The away team had only been gone for an hour, and he was already bored.

Josh sipped his tea, savoring its intense flavor. He activated the comm-channel, connecting the command deck intercom with the comm-sets the two Ghatazhak standing guard at the mouth of the cave were wearing. "So you guys freezing your asses off yet?"

"Nope. We're Ghatazhak, remember?" Mori replied over comms.

Josh smiled. "You brought your bodysuits, didn't you."

"Damn right, we did."

"I gotta get me one of those," Josh commented.

"They're too big for a runt like you."

"Ha, ha." Josh took a long, loud sip of his tea. "In case you were wondering, that sound was me taking a nice big sip of my steaming hot, spiced marajin tea."

"You're such a dick, Josh."

"What's the matter, Jokay?" Josh chuckled. "Forgot your bodysuit?"

"No, but my nose is fucking frozen," Deeks replied. "We should've worn our full combat gear. Helmet, visor, and all."

The proximity alert indicator flashed, beeping several times. Josh leaned forward, calling up the ship's sensors on the console display. "Uh, guys?" he called, his brow furrowing. "I'm picking up movement out there."

"Probably just that bear coming back again," Mori opined.

"If it is, he brought friends." Josh adjusted the sensors, reducing the range of the scans to increase the resolution. "I count four contacts moving toward you. Looks like they're about three hundred meters out." The contacts suddenly disappeared from the sensor display. "Wait... Shit, they're gone."

"What do you mean, they're gone?" Jokay asked.

"I mean they've dropped off the screen. Probably a dip in the terrain. Plus these damned sensors don't work for shit from inside this cave. Something in the mountain messes with them."

"How the hell did you get a scan of the interior before we jumped in?" Mori wondered.

"I kicked her sideways as I passed the entrance. Got my full array on it."

"You must've been awfully low."

"You bet I was. It was a sweet move." The contacts appeared on the screen again, except now they were further apart. "They're back. Still moving toward you. They're spreading out."

"How far out are they?" Mori asked.

"Two fifty. Looks like they've picked up the pace a bit."

"Are they randomly paced, or grouped in pairs?"

Josh studied the sensor display a moment. The

screen refreshed, then beeped another warning as the four contacts suddenly became eight. "Oh shit! There're eight of them, not four! Four pairs, still advancing. Spreading out line abreast."

"Better wake the troops, Josh," Jokay suggested over comms. "It looks like we've got company."

Josh switched on the ship-wide intercom. "Heads up, everyone! We've got company!"

"You might want to consider powering up the forward shields," Mori suggested.

"No can do," Josh replied. "Not inside the cave. We don't know how stable it is."

"Then put Marcus on the nose gun, just in case."

"Marcus!" Josh called over the intercom. "Man the nose gun!"

"What have you got, Mori?" Specialist Grimard asked over comms.

"No visual yet, Effi," Mori replied. "Josh picked up eight unknown ground contacts, two hundred meters and closing. They're moving in pairs, line abreast."

"Sounds like an organized advance to me," Effrin remarked.

"It isn't a hunting party, that's for sure."

"We're on our way out," Effrin assured Mori. "We'll have your six in thirty seconds."

Josh continued studying the display as the four pairs of contacts spread out even further, continuing to advance. "One fifty, still closing. Outer pairs are spreading out to the sides. Middle pairs are staying the same distance apart."

"We need to take them outside of the cave," Mori announced over comms. "I'm going right."

"I'm going left," Jokay followed.

"We'll go up the middle and force an engagement fifty meters out," Effrin told them.

"What the hell's going on?" Marcus asked, coming up the stair ladder behind Dylan.

"Visitors," Josh replied. "Ghatazhak are going out to say hello." Josh turned to Marcus, who was only halfway up the stair ladder. "I told you to man the nose gun!"

"I'm going! I'm going!" Marcus grumbled, heading back down the stair ladder.

Dylan moved past Josh, going to the copilot's seat. "They know not to kill them, right?"

"Of course," Josh snapped. He pressed the comms transmit button. "You guys know not to kill them, right?"

* * *

The city of Klyuchi was larger than Nathan had expected. Like many of the more remote cities and towns on Earth, it had managed to survive the Jung invasion and the subsequent battle for its liberation nearly eight years ago. Very little of it appeared to be newly built or renovated. In fact, although still in good repair, it seemed a century old.

Nevertheless, he could see why the residents might like Klyuchi. Unlike so many of the cities and worlds he had visited, this place was not yet saturated with technology. It was there, but it was well integrated into their society. If you ignored the subtle signs of technology, one could imagine living in a time before the Ark had been discovered, and the devices of their ancestors had come flooding in.

Kit pulled the vehicle to a stop at a small park with a statue at its center, surrounded by a cluster of official-looking buildings. "This looks like the city center," he announced.

Vladimir climbed out of the vehicle, looking around to get his bearings.

"Where should we start?" Nathan wondered, also climbing out of the vehicle. "Are we just going to ask people if they know Aleksi Rusayev?"

"We could go into the tavern over there," Jessica suggested, pointing. "Start asking about."

"No one would speak with you unless you drank with them." Vladimir insisted.

"Oh they'll speak to me," Jessica boasted.

"Not unless you drink with them," Vladimir told her.

"Fine, so I'll have a few drinks with them."

"You do not want to get into a drinking contest with these people," Vladimir insisted. "Trust me."

"Well what are we going to do?" Nathan asked.

"When I came to visit Aleksi, the bus dropped me off here, at the center of Klyuchi. Aleksi's home was to the east. A few kilometers at least. I believe I can find it."

"Sounds as good a place to start as any," Nathan decided, climbing back into the vehicle.

* * *

Three Ghatazhak, in cold weather gear and carrying specialized energy rifles, moved swiftly from the mouth of the massive cavern. With skill and precision, the men moved from one concealed firing position to the next as they advanced toward the approaching threat.

Effrin Grimard, the most senior of the three Ghatazhak who had joined the Voss's crew for this mission, led the way as each man took turns advancing.

"The two side pairs dropped off sensors," Josh informed them over comms. "They're probably beyond the sides of the cave mouth and outside of her beam width."

Effrin ran in a crouch, weapon at the ready, across the open, snow-covered ground, moving to an outcropping of rocks sticking up through the blanket of snow. "We are in position, concealed," he announced, looking to either side to check on the position of the other two Ghatazhak.

"Copy that," Mori replied over comms. "Two in sight."

Mori moved quickly through the woods, double-timing it from one concealment position to the next. Rocks, trees, snow-covered berms; all were used to remain hidden from those he meant to intercept.

Finally, he stopped, taking position behind the root end of an old fallen tree. He peeked around the twisted root ball, spotting two men in white snowsuits designed to make them blend in with the snowy landscape. Both were carrying projectile assault weapons and large knives on their hips. The men were attempting to get into their own firing positions, hoping to provide cover fire for their cohorts approaching the cavern from the center.

Mori carefully threaded his rifle through the entangled roots of the fallen tree before him, moving slowly so as not to attract the attention of his targets. Once in position, he activated his scope, placing his crosshairs on the man to the left. He waited several seconds, timing the man's steps and body motion to place the shot perfectly. It was not necessary, since the stun setting on his weapon would work equally well regardless of where it hit, as long as it hit the target's torso.

Mori pressed the trigger, sending the first shot off with a zing. He immediately shifted slightly right, putting his crosshairs on the next target and firing again, all before the first man hit the ground.

Jokay had two targets of his own in his scope, firing twice the moment he heard the report of Mori's shots in the distance. Both men in his scope dropped, motionless in the snow.

Jokay quickly rose and ran over to the stunned men, deftly picking up their weapons. In a smooth, practiced motion, he removed the magazine from the first weapon and ejected its chambered round, letting the round drop into the snow at his feet. He tossed the magazine into the woods, then repeated the process for the second rifle.

Confident the men were no longer a threat, Jokay checked them both to ensure they were still alive and then proceeded to bind their hands and legs.

"Two pairs still coming up the middle," Josh reported over comms.

"Two down, securing them now," Jokay announced over his comm-set.

Mori quickly moved in on the two downed men, discovering that one of them was still conscious and fumbling with his weapon. The man clumsily attempted to point his weapon at his assailant but was having difficulty controlling his hands.

"Bad idea," Mori told the man, pointing his weapon at him.

The partially stunned man dropped his own weapon, showing his hands and surrendering.

Mori quickly collected the weapons and began unloading them, rendering them harmless.

"Who are you?" the man asked, his hands trembling sporadically, but still held up in a show of surrender. "What are you doing out here?"

Mori ignored him, binding the man's feet.

"I am injured. I am bleeding."

Mori pulled away the man's torn pant leg, spotting a large, deep gash in his leg. "You'll be fine," he told him, as he bound his hands and then moved to restrain the other, unconscious man.

"You cannot leave me here," the man protested. "I will bleed out."

"I thought you Russians were supposed to be tough," Mori said as he finished binding the second man's hands. "Besides, you're not bleeding that badly." Mori reached into his thigh pocket and pulled out a small med-kit. From it, he pulled a spray bottle, gave it a shake, and then sprayed its contents on the open gash on the man's leg.

"What is that?"

"Nanites," Mori replied as he put the bottle back in the kit. "You should heal up in a few hours."

"Nanites do not work that fast," the man insisted.

"These ones do," Mori replied, rising to depart.

"Wait," the man pleaded. "You cannot leave me here. I will freeze to death."

"That part might be true," Mori replied as he pointed his weapon at the injured man and fired again, this time stunning him completely. Mori tapped the side of his comm-set. "Two secure. Moving to next intercept position," he reported as he headed further out into the woods.

Effrin crouched down behind a large boulder with a section of an old decaying tree trunk lying over it. From his position, he could see the four men approaching: one pair to the right and one to the left. All four of them were dressed in white snow gear and were carrying projectile assault weapons. "Stop where you are or we will fire!" he yelled out at the approaching men.

The four advancing men scrambled for cover, looking around but still not spotting the source of the warning cry.

After a few seconds, one of the men yelled. "Who are you?"

"Who we are is not your concern!" Effrin yelled back. "Retreat or you will be fired upon! There will be no further warnings!"

"These are our woods! No one orders us to leave our woods!"

Effrin rolled his eyes. "As you wish!"

Four blaster shots were heard, two from the right and two from the left. Effrin peered over the tree trunk, just in time to see the men fall face-first into the snow. "Took you long enough," he said over comm-sets as he stood.

* * *

Nathan, Jessica, and Kit stood on the street next to the rover, staring at the unimpressive home. Like all the homes on the street, it was mostly shrouded by overgrown shrubs and well-placed fences. While the landscape was not precisely manicured, it was apparent that someone still lived there.

Vladimir came back through the front gate, carefully closing it behind him before joining his cohorts. "He does not live here."

"Are you sure this is the right place?" Jessica asked.

"I am certain."

"How do you know he doesn't live here?" Jessica challenged.

"Because the lady who answered the door said he did not. She also said she has owned this house for three years."

"Did she say where the original owner went?" Nathan asked.

"She bought it through a broker. She never met the seller," Vladimir explained.

"You think she was telling the truth?" Nathan asked.

"I believe so."

"I guess my bar idea is starting to look better," Jessica decided.

"Maybe if we ask a few of the neighbors?" Vladimir suggested. "Perhaps they know where Aleksi moved to."

"We're running out of daylight," Nathan said, looking up at the overcast sky. "I'd like to avoid navigating those mountain roads in the dark, especially if it starts snowing. We can return first thing in the morning and spend the whole day looking for Rusayev."

* * *

"Jump eighty-seven, complete," Ensign Lassen reported from the Falcon's copilot seat.

"This is a proverbial needle-in-a-haystack

search," Sergeant Nama complained from the sensor station directly behind the pilot's seat.

"More like a glowing needle-in-a-haystack," Lieutenant Teison corrected.

"Negative scans," the sergeant reported.

"Jump eighty-eight, coming up," Ensign Lassen announced, tiring of the monotony.

"Why can't they just use recon drones for this kind of crap?" Sergeant Nama complained.

"You know we've got better sensors than the drones do, Riko," the lieutenant replied.

"Then they need to put better sensors into those things."

"Jump eighty-eight, complete."

Sergeant Nama sighed. "Scanning."

* * *

Eight unconscious men sat on the deck of the Voss's utility bay, propped up unceremoniously against the forward bulkhead and each other. Their snowsuits had been removed, as had the body armor they had been wearing underneath them.

Mori knelt down in front of the first man in line, pressing a pneumo-ject into the man's neck and activating it. He studied the man's face, waiting for signs of a response. After a moment, the man's eyes began to open.

"He's coming around," Mori said, standing.

The man looked around, struggling to focus. He tried to move his hands and feet, but they didn't seem to be functioning properly. Eventually, he stopped struggling and just glared at the man standing before him. "Where am I? Who are you?"

"You're safe for now," Jokay assured him.

"Release me," the man insisted, growing impatient.

"In good time."

The man looked at Mori and Effrin, noticing their similar dress. "Who are you people?" he asked calmly. "Where is this place? Are we inside Papiva?"

"That depends," Jokay replied. "What is a Papiva?"

The man eyed his captor with suspicion. "The great cavern. It is called Papiva. How can you be here and not know this?"

"Why did you and your men come to Papiva?"

"We are hunters," the man said, leaning his head back against the bulkhead. "We hunt bear."

"With heavy assault rifles?"

"Big bears."

"Every one of you had four fully loaded fifty-round magazines," Jokay reminded the man. "That's one hundred rounds each, for a total of eight hundred rounds. All for hunting bears?"

The man smiled more broadly. "Many bears."

"And you were all wearing body armor under your snowsuits."

The man shrugged. "Russian bears have big claws."

"Right." Jokay pulled up a chair and sat down in front of the man. "I am Jokay Deeks. What should I call you?"

The man smiled again. "Bear Hunter."

Jokay chuckled to himself. "Okay, Mister Hunter, answer me this. Why were eight heavily armed men closing on Papiva Cavern line abreast, in pairs, using cover-and-advance tactics?"

The man smiled again, finding his own sarcastic responses entertaining. "We are very good bear hunters."

"Except when the bears are armed," Mori chuckled.

"You will awaken my men."

"Again, in good time," Jokay replied. "First I need to know why you were advancing on our position with obvious ill intent. How did you know we were here?"

"We did not," the man replied with a shrug. "We expected bears."

"This is going nowhere," Mori decided. "Let's just dump them in the snow and be done with them."

"More will follow," the man insisted.

"We don't even know who they are," Effrin added.

"He just told us," Jokay corrected. "They're bear hunters, and their leader's name, by an amazing coincidence, is Bear Hunter."

The man sighed, leaning his head back again. "An old man reported a sudden flash of light from Papiva Cavern, followed by a shock wave. My friends and I came to investigate."

"The guy has a lot of friends," Mori commented.

"A flash of light?" Jokay wondered. "You came to investigate a flash of light? With eight armed men?"

The man smiled again, sensing another opportunity for sarcasm. "Russian bears are very dangerous, and they...like...caves."

"I'm pretty sure you and your fellow hunters expected something other than bears."

"If we did, then we were right."

Jokay thought for a moment. "Who is it you think we are?"

"I do not know, but to have this kind of facility inside a mountain, far from civilization? It raises questions, yes?"

"We're wasting our time here," Mori insisted. "The guy won't even tell us his name, let alone who sent him."

"Did anyone even ask him?" Effrin questioned.

Jokay sighed. "Do you work for the Earth Defense Force?"

"I told you...we...hunt...bears."

"Let's just stun him and wake up the next guy," Mori suggested. "Sooner or later, one of them will tell us what we want to know."

The man suddenly became uneasy. "They will tell you nothing."

"Oh that wiped the smile off his face," Mori realized. "Let's do it. I'm tired of this guy's smart-ass answers anyway."

Marcus stepped through the forward hatch, passing between the two groups of prisoners. "You find out who they are yet?"

"He's not exactly being cooperative," Effrin replied.

"What a shocker," Marcus grumbled as he headed aft toward the cargo ramp controls. He pressed a button, and the pressure shield snapped on.

The man's eyes widened, surprised by the glowing, pale blue, semi-opaque wall of light that had just materialized across the opposite end of the bay.

"What are you doing?" Mori asked Marcus.

"The away team is back," Marcus replied as he activated the cargo ramp to start its deployment cycle.

The man watched with curiosity and concern as the massive ramp cracked open along the top edge and began lowering out and away from the bay. "What is this place?" he asked as he watched the ramp deploy. His eyes suddenly grew wider as he spotted the walls of the cavern outside. "Why is it not cold in here?" he wondered, realizing that there was no rush of cold air coming in from outside.

"Magic," Marcus grumbled.

The cargo ramp hit the floor of the cave with a thud, kicking up dust. A moment later, a six-wheeled, all-terrain vehicle rolled up into the bay, its headlights shining in the man's eyes.

The man squinted from the rover's lights. "Who are you people?" he asked when the lights shut off. He watched as three men and a woman, all clad in cold-weather gear, climbed out of the rover.

Jessica walked over to Jokay and Mori as she removed her coat. "You guys having a party?"

"A couple of hours ago, these guys approached the mouth of the cavern," Effrin explained. "They advanced in pairs, line abreast. They were heavily armed and wearing body armor. We ordered them to retreat, but they did not comply."

"Did they say who they are?" Jessica wondered. "Or who they're working for?"

"We've only spoken with this guy so far," Jokay told her, "but he's not telling us much."

"He did tell us they were hunting for bears," Mori added, smiling.

Jessica squatted down in front of the man they had been interrogating, staring him in the eyes. "That's cute."

Vladimir came over, tossing his jacket onto a nearby cargo container. He looked at the man and began speaking to him in Russian. The man replied in the same language, appearing to speak more freely than he had with Jokay, but still sounding less than cooperative.

"What is he saying?" Mori asked.

"Shush," Jessica warned Mori, listening to Vladimir's conversation.

Nathan and Kit came up to stand beside Jessica

and Vladimir. "Is he telling you anything?" Nathan asked as he removed his coat.

The man suddenly looked as if he'd seen a ghost. "Bozhe moi."

Jessica noticed his reaction. "I'm pretty sure he just recognized you," she told Nathan, looking at him.

Nathan waved. "Hi there."

"You are supposed to be dead," the man exclaimed, still in shock.

"If I had a nickel for every time I've heard that," Nathan joked.

"How is this possible?" the man asked.

"That's a long story," Nathan replied.

The man finally got his wits back, and curiosity took over. "Why are you here?" He looked around at the others. "Why are all of you here?"

Nathan looked at Jessica. "Should I ask him?"

"Couldn't hurt," Jessica shrugged.

Nathan sighed. "We're looking for Aleksi Rusayev. I don't suppose you know him?"

The man cast a suspicious look toward Nathan. "Why are you looking for this man?"

"I believe that we have similar goals. Do you know him?" When the man did not respond, Nathan spoke again. "It's a simple question. Answer it, and you'll be one step closer to being released. Do you know Aleksi Rusayev? Yes or no?"

"Mozhesh yemu doveryat," Vladimir added.

The man studied Nathan, still uncertain.

"What did he say to him?" Effrin wondered.

"He told him he could trust Nathan," Jessica replied.

Finally, the man decided to answer. "Da. I know him."

"Great," Nathan exclaimed. "Now we're getting somewhere. Can you take us to him?"

"Da," the man replied, realizing that playing along with them was his best chance at escape. After a pause, he added, "But you must release my men."

"Fair enough," Nathan agreed.

"And return our guns to us," the man added.

"Nice try, bear hunter," Jessica laughed.

"I'm afraid I'm going to have to agree with her," Nathan said. "However, I'll be more than happy to return them to you after we meet Aleksi."

Jessica leaned in closer to Nathan, keeping her voice low. "We'll have to keep them overnight."

"That's right," Nathan sighed.

"If we do not return, they will send others," the man insisted, having overheard Jessica's comment.

"Our rover isn't really equipped for icy roads," Nathan told the man. "We have to wait until morning."

"We have an air shuttle just over a kilometer from here," the captive explained.

"Well then," Nathan exclaimed, "let's go meet Mister Rusayev, shall we?"

* * *

General Telles stepped up to the open hatch to the captain's ready room aboard the Aurora. "Am I intruding?" he asked before entering.

Cameron looked up from the view screen on her desk. "Of course not," she assured him, gesturing toward the chair opposite her.

"I heard about the drone launches from Takara," the general began as he entered. "I assume you are making every effort to locate them."

"We've dispatched the Falcon to search for them," Cameron told him. "I've also notified Rogen

Command to put defenses on alert for both the Rogen and Orswellan systems."

"What about SilTek?" the general asked as he sat.

"I sent word to them myself," Cameron sighed. "For what good it will do."

"Then you do not believe defense is possible?" the general surmised.

Cameron leaned back in her chair. "Possible? Yes. Unfortunately, it depends on how far away from the target the weapon comes out of its final jump."

"Then you are assuming it is a weapon?"

"I don't see how we have much choice."

"Agreed."

"Honestly, the best chance we have is to find the drones first and destroy them en route," Cameron told him. "If we wait until they are terminal, our chances of intercept drop dramatically."

"Have you informed Captain Scott?"

"Not yet," Cameron admitted. "I figure he's got enough on his mind at the moment. Besides, we aren't even certain the drones are weapons."

"I believe he would want to know either way."

"Yes, but there is nothing he can do about it at the moment."

"What do you intend to do?"

Cameron took a pause. "If they are comm-drones, then technically we're already doing the only thing we can. Nathan ordered the Dusahn to stay within their own territory. He said nothing to them about comm-drones."

"And if they are weapons?" the general asked.

"Then we destroy them. Hopefully before they reach their targets."

"Should we not destroy them even if they are only comm-drones?" General Telles suggested.

"Trust me, I'd love nothing more," Cameron agreed, "but I don't think that would sit well with the other worlds. If the entire idea of our alliance is to allow all worlds to govern themselves as they see fit, should we not allow the Dusahn to govern their world as they see fit?"

"A fair point," the general agreed. "However, I am not certain that it applies in this instance."

"Perhaps."

"Why would the Dusahn wish to communicate with the suspected target worlds?" General Telles wondered. "Other than to contact covert operatives of course."

"We're not even certain what their destinations actually are at this point."

"Well, if they are bound for either the Rogen or Orswellan system, contact with operatives is their most likely goal. They may even be planning on deploying a covert jump comm-relay satellite. That could be what is contained within the additional mass at the front of the drones."

"I hadn't thought of that," Cameron admitted.

"If the destination is SilTek, and the drones are not weapons, then they may be trying to make diplomatic contact with SilTek."

"To what end?" Cameron wondered.

"To acquire the same technologies that SilTek has provided us," the general explained.

"You think they would try to purchase tech from SilTek? How would they even know they're in the business of selling technology?"

"I know we are assuming the Dusahn followed the jump trail of one of our cargo ships back to SilTek," General Telles said. "However, for the sake of discussion, let us assume that they already had intelligence on SilTek. Perhaps they already knew about SilTek's corporate society. If so, they may hope that offering them a higher price than we can afford to pay would procure them favored status, as well as a technological advantage over us."

"That would not be very Dusahn-like," Cameron opined.

"Neither is struggling to survive," the general countered, "or allowing someone to make overt threats against them without retaliation."

"So we've essentially backed them into a corner," Cameron surmised. "They have no choice but to try to negotiate their way out."

"I should remind you that the tarka is at its most dangerous when it is trapped and feels threatened."

Cameron looked at him a moment. "I'm guessing a tarka isn't exactly a fluffy bunny?"

"Most definitely not," General Telles replied.

CHAPTER TEN

The ride in the air shuttle reminded Nathan of the first time he had ridden in a Corinari air shuttle. In fact, he was pretty sure that the technology had come from Corinair, since he hadn't remembered anything like the shuttles on Earth when he was a cadet.

Although Nathan had initially agreed to release all the prisoners, Jessica had convinced him to keep them in custody as a safety net. The only reason they had released more than one of them was because Sasha, the man who had agreed to take them to meet Aleksi, did not know how to fly the air shuttle. Rather than figuring it out for himself, Nathan decided to play it safe and wake up Sasha's pilot as well.

Nathan looked out the window, catching a glimpse of their destination. The sun was already behind the nearby mountains, and the approaching city of Klyuchi was twinkling in the twilight.

Kit leaned forward from the seat behind Nathan, speaking in hushed tones. "Has anyone considered that this might be a trap?"

"You see, I'm not the only one," Jessica whispered to Nathan.

"You saw the guy's reaction when he recognized me," Nathan reminded them.

"He could just be a good actor," Kit suggested.

Vladimir leaned forward as well. "Aleksi will not harm us."

"You mean he won't harm you," Jessica corrected.

"I'm with Vlad on this one," Nathan insisted. "There is no reason for Aleksi to harm us. He's bound to know what a threat my existence is to Galiardi."

"Pretty good reason to hold you hostage," Jessica explained.

"Come on, Jess."

"That old 'enemy of my enemy' stuff doesn't always work, you know," Jessica added.

"We will be landing shortly," Sasha warned from the cockpit.

"I guess we'll find out soon enough," Nathan told them.

"I am telling you, he will not harm us," Vladimir reiterated.

Nathan looked out the window again as they passed over what appeared to be an industrial area. They came to a hover above a large, fenced-in area behind a large building, then descended straight down, kicking up dust as they landed.

"I don't like the looks of this," Kit said, noticing how dimly lit the area was.

The air shuttle's ducted fans spun down, and once the dust had begun to settle, the two men in the cockpit opened their doors and climbed out.

Jessica was the first of the away team to step out of the air shuttle, pausing to look around the yard where they had set down. There were barrels stacked along one side of the yard next to a couple of large delivery trucks, with a half dozen cars parked on the opposite side.

"How does it look?" Nathan asked as he stepped down next to Jessica.

"Like a perfect place for an ambush."

"You are so suspicious," Vladimir said, climbing down next.

"That's why I'm still alive." She turned back toward Kit as he climbed out. "Eyes open, head on a swivel, Kit."

"Always," Kit assured her as he jumped down.

"You will leave your weapons in the shuttle," Sasha directed.

Jessica smirked. "Not a chance."

"This is not negotiable," Sasha replied, standing firm.

"We still have your friends, you know."

Sasha glared at her. "They are ready to sacrifice themselves to protect Aleksi."

Jessica stepped up, getting in Sasha's face.

"Jess..." Nathan said, urging her to back down.

"No......weapons," Sasha repeated, standing firm.

Jessica stared him directly in the face for a moment. "Fine," she finally agreed, taking her sidearm out and placing it on the floor of the shuttle's cabin. "I can kick your ass just as easily without them, bear boy."

Sasha smiled and laughed. "I like this one," he declared. "Follow me."

"Bear boy?" Nathan commented as Jessica passed, following Sasha.

Sasha and the pilot led them across the yard and through the back door of the building. Inside, there was a large main room full of distilling equipment. The facility seemed devoid of workers, all of whom had probably gone home for the night.

"What is this place?" Kit wondered.

"It looks like some sort of distillery," Nathan commented.

"Aleksi was always making his own vodka," Vladimir explained. "Maybe this is all his?"

"Makes for a pretty good cover," Jessica added.

Sasha and the pilot led them to a connected room, stopping at the open door.

"You will wait here," Sasha instructed.

The away team entered what appeared to be a small break room, complete with tables, chairs, and a small kitchenette.

Sasha turned to leave, intending to close the door, but Kit stopped him, grabbing the edge of the door.

"The door stays open," Kit warned him.

"This is not negotiable," Jessica added, smiling.

Sasha smiled back. "As you wish," he replied, turning and walking away.

Kit moved to the door, watching the men leave. "We're going to need a plan if this goes sideways."

"Nothing is going sideways," Vladimir insisted.

"I'm sure you're right, Vlad," Nathan said, "but a plan in case it does wouldn't hurt."

"Kit and I will flank the door," Jessica told them. "If they come in armed, Kit and I will deal with them."

"What do you want us to do?" Vladimir asked.

"Duck." Jessica moved over to the door next to Kit. "Someone's coming." She stepped back so as not to be noticed, briefly peeking back around the door frame. "I count four. Sasha, the pilot, and two others."

"Weapons?" Kit asked, taking position up against the wall on the right side of the door.

"None visible," Jessica replied, positioning herself on the opposite side.

A man in his forties entered. He was followed by another man of the same age, along with Sasha and the pilot. The first man smiled broadly upon seeing Vladimir. "Vlad!" he exclaimed, his arms outstretched.

"Lyoha!" Vladimir replied, hugging his old friend.

The man pulled back to look at Vladimir. "I could not believe it when Sasha told me you were here! Now I understand how your people were able to find me!

You look well, my friend," he added, patting Vladimir on the cheek.

"As do you, Lyoha. I see you found a way to make a living from your little hobby."

"It is nothing. It pays the bills and keeps me out of trouble." He turned to Nathan. "I see you brought a ghost with you."

"Aleksi, this is Nathan Scott. Nathan, this is Aleksi Rusayev."

Aleksi stepped over to Nathan, taking his hand. "I have never before met a dead man," he commented, shaking Nathan's hand vigorously. "It is an honor to meet you."

"The honor is mine, Mister Rusayev," Nathan replied.

"Ah! Call me Aleksi!" Aleksi insisted with a dismissive wave of his hand. He looked at Jessica and Kit, standing on either side of the door. "And who are these two standing by the door, ready to pounce?"

"This is Lieutenant Commander Nash, my chief of security and tactical officer," Nathan introduced. "And this is Sergeant Vasya of the Ghatazhak."

"The Ghatazhak?" Aleksi said, surprised. "I have never met a Ghatazhak before, either." He nodded politely to them. "It is an honor to meet you both as well."

"I have to admit, I am quite surprised that you are so willing to meet with us," Nathan told Aleksi.

"Who am I to ignore fate?"

"Fate?" Nathan asked.

Aleksi put his arm around Vladimir's shoulders. "The only person in the galaxy who would know where to find me, and he just happens to be working with the one man who could save our world...again?

If that is not fate, what is?" He released his friend and moved over to a nearby table, leaning against it. "Tell me, Captain, why have you sought me out?"

"I was hoping we could help one another," Nathan replied.

Aleksi crossed his arms. "How can I possibly help you?"

"Intel has it that you lead a group of insurgents who oppose Galiardi's rule," Jessica explained. "They say you have been attacking EDF assets on the surface."

"You are mistaken," Aleksi insisted. "I am but a simple businessman."

"Lyoha," Vladimir objected, "we do not have time for this..."

"If I were this leader you seek," Aleksi began, interrupting his friend, "I would be suspicious of you all, even you, my old friend. How do I know that you are not EDF spies?"

"Because I say so, Lyoha," Vladimir told him.

Aleksi began pacing across the room, thinking.

"How do I know that you are not a spy?" he asked Vladimir. "Surgeons can make a man look like any other these days. Even like dead men."

Vladimir stepped over to Aleksi, leaning in close and speaking in hushed tones. "Would a spy know that you peed your bed until you were eight?"

Aleksi shot Vladimir a sidelong glance.

"And would he keep his voice down so as not to betray his friend's trust?"

Aleksi looked over at Nathan, thinking. "Suppose I was this leader you speak of. What would you ask of me?"

"I was hoping that you might have some ideas

about how to bring down Admiral Galiardi," Nathan told him.

One of Aleksi's eyebrows shot up. "Then it is all true," he surmised.

"What is true?" Nathan wondered.

"That the attack by the Jung was a false-flag operation," Aleksi explained. "Executed by a long-exiled Jung caste, to prevent the Sol Alliance from interfering with their conquest of the Pentaurus sector."

Nathan suddenly became suspicious. "How exactly did you come to know this?" he asked, his brow furrowed.

Aleksi nodded to the man by the door, who immediately departed.

"Where is he going?" Jessica inquired, suspicious of the subordinate's sudden departure.

"Your captain wishes to know how we acquired this information, does he not? I am merely going to show you."

Jessica exchanged a look with Kit, who immediately changed positions, allowing him to see out the door.

Aleksi began pacing again. "Bringing down Admiral Galiardi is a difficult task. Not only does he command all Sol Alliance forces, but he also has control of the media. He fills it with an endless stream of propaganda designed to inspire support for his cause, and it is quite effective. Even the people of Klyuchi, most of whom, like myself, do not believe in a global government, are becoming brainwashed by the constant onslaught. I did not believe it was possible to defeat this man and reverse the damage he has done. Even if I had equal access to the media, I would be branded a fanatical conspiracy theorist like so many others." Aleksi stopped pacing, turning to look at Nathan. "Until now."

"Why until now?" Nathan wondered.

"Now we have an heir-to-office," Aleksi said, pointing at Nathan. "One that Galiardi cannot refuse."

"And if they do not believe that I am Nathan Scott?" Nathan asked.

Aleksi nodded agreement. "You have a good point," he said with a sigh. "Perhaps you have evidence that will prove the Jung Empire is not to blame and that Galiardi already knew this but continued attacking them anyway."

A suspicious look crossed Jessica's face. She glanced at Kit, who also looked curious. "You have frighteningly good intel, Mister Rusayev," she said. "I'm afraid I'm going to have to insist on knowing how you obtained it."

Aleksi smiled. "We have our sources."

Jessica stepped forward, facing off with Aleksi. "What...sources?"

Aleksi smiled, then pointed toward the door.

Jessica turned around, her eyes widening and her jaw dropping in disbelief. "Loki!" she exclaimed, running over to him and throwing her arms around his neck.

* * *

Ensign Lassen was operating in fully automatic mode. Plot the jump, execute the jump, and when Riko said 'no contacts', repeat. So it had been for over three hundred jumps.

Lieutenant Teison was fully reclined in his pilot's seat, eyes closed and mouth open, snoring.

"How the hell does the LT sleep so easily?"

Sergeant Nama wondered as he studied the sensor screen.

"I've heard you sawing logs back there yourself," the ensign reminded his sensor officer as he plotted the next jump. "Anything?"

"Listen, Tomi, if I see something, I'll let you know, trust me. Otherwise, just keep plotting and jumping."

Ensign Lassen glanced at the ship's clock. "In another hour, it's going to be my turn to snore."

"You don't snore," Riko laughed, adjusting his sensors. "You make little chirping noises, like one of those annoying little birds in the morning."

"Very funny," Tomi said. "Executing jump three forty-seven."

"You do!" Riko teased, making chirping noises himself. "It's just weird."

"At least I don't drool like some people," Tomi countered. He let out a long sigh as he calculated the next jump.

"You're just jealous because you wish you could sleep that deeply," the sergeant replied as he began his next sensor sweep.

"I sleep fine, thanks," the ensign replied as he transferred the jump plot to the sequencer. "I also don't wander around like I'm in a drunken stupor for the first hour after I wake."

The sergeant did not respond, choosing to concentrate on his displays.

"Jump three forty-eight plotted and locked. Jumping in five."

Sergeant Nama's brow furrowed, and he reached for his sensor controls. "Wait..."

"What?"

"I said wait," the sergeant quickly followed. "I may have something."

Tomi reacted automatically, canceling the jump and starting a recalculation at the same time. "Holding jump." He turned to look at his friend. "Please tell me you found it."

Sergeant Nama smiled. "Better wake up the LT."

* * *

"Josh is going to be so happy to see you," Nathan said as he hugged his friend.

"I'll be happy to see him, too," Loki replied. "I didn't think I'd see any of you again."

"Come here," Vladimir insisted, his arms wide.

Loki complied, receiving a massive hug from his big, Russian friend.

"Good to see you alive, Sheehan," Kit said, shaking Loki's hand.

Nathan looked at Aleksi, dumbfounded. "I don't know what to say," he said, shaking his head, still in disbelief. "I don't even know how this is possible."

"The man who delivered him to us said he had crashed in the northern Japanese islands ten days ago," Aleksi explained. "He was rescued by two farmers who hid him from the EDF."

"Why would they take such a risk?" Jessica wondered, suspicious as usual.

"Not everyone likes the EDF."

"Japan?" Nathan said, surprised.

"My jump drive was damaged, but I managed to jump anyway," Loki explained. "It was either that or get blown out of the air. I think I clipped the top of the mountain on the way out. I came out of the jump on the edge of space, somewhere out over the ocean. I was losing pressure, and I was pretty much out of control. Thrusters were firing randomly...I was lucky just to get my ship headed back toward the surface, so I took another chance and jumped again, just to get back down into the atmosphere. From that point, I had about zero control. Next thing I know, I'm in a bed in a barn loft over a bunch of cows, with two brothers taking care of me."

"How long were you down before they found you?" Nathan wondered.

"From what Udo told me, they found me less than an hour after I crashed."

"You must've been out for nearly a week then," Nathan surmised.

"Actually, I'm pretty sure I woke up about a day and a half after I crashed," Loki corrected. "It's a good thing you made us take those nanite boosters," he said to Kit. "Otherwise, I'd probably be dead."

Jessica noticed Nathan's expression. "What is it?"

"It doesn't add up," Nathan explained.

"What doesn't add up?" Vladimir wondered.

"The incident in Monterey was fifteen days ago, not ten." Nathan turned to Aleksi. "Maybe your intel is bad?"

"The incident in Monterey was your people?" Aleksi asked.

"Yes, unfortunately."

Aleksi laughed. "We were blamed for that."

"Sorry."

"I thought the leader of our Monterey cell was lying to me. I owe him an apology."

"Is it possible that..." Jessica looked at Loki, "what did you call him?"

"Udo?"

"Yeah. Is it possible that Udo just lost track of time?"

"Doubtful," Loki insisted. "He seemed very smart, and I have been keeping track of the days since I first awakened. By my estimates, it has been nine or ten days. I could be off a day, but not by five days."

"We have his wreckage," Aleksi told them. "But we could not figure out how to access its systems. The technology is foreign to us."

"Dylan should be able to," Vladimir suggested.

"Then perhaps you can solve this riddle?"

"Is the wreckage here?" Nathan asked.

"It is," Aleksi replied. "Sasha will take you to it if you wish."

"See what you can find," Nathan told Vladimir.

Vladimir nodded, following Sasha and the pilot out of the room.

"So, Aleksi," Nathan began. "As I said before, we were hoping you might have some plan, or at least some ideas, about how to bring down Galiardi. Preferably without having to kill any more of our own people."

"When something as great as the fate of an entire world is at stake, one cannot worry about killing their own," Aleksi said. "I would expect you of all people to understand this."

"I do," Nathan assured him. "However, the more of our own that we kill, the more opposition we will be creating going forward."

"A week ago, I would not have agreed with you," Aleksi told him. "A week ago, I would not have had a plan, either. But now, you are standing here, and what once seemed impossible is no longer."

* * *

"Captain, Comms," Ensign Keller called over the intercom. "Flash traffic from the Falcon."

Cameron reached for the intercom panel on her desk. "Go ahead."

"The Falcon reports they have found the drones,

and they are definitely headed for SilTek. They are maintaining their track and have transmitted a suggested intercept point."

"Distance from target?" Cameron asked.

"Falcon reports two hours, based on current jump patterns."

"Understood. Set general quarters," she ordered, rising to exit the ready room. Before she had even passed her desk, the trim lighting had changed to red, and the alert klaxons were sounding. Much to her surprise, it was not Naralena's voice calling the Aurora's crew to action stations, it was Ensign Keller's.

Cameron exited the captain's ready room, pausing at the comm-station at the aft end of the bridge. "Ensign Keller, flash traffic to Rogen Command. Notify them of the situation and request that they put all alliance worlds on alert. Also, request that they prepare a strike package to Takara, Orochi and Gunyoki, targeting all surface-based jump missile launchers, and await word."

"Aye, sir."

Cameron continued forward to her command chair.

"All weapons are charged and ready," Lieutenant Yuati reported from the tactical station as she passed.

"Very well," Cameron replied. "Helm, prepare to break orbit for SilTek. I want a single jump to destination ready ASAP."

"Single jump to SilTek, aye," Ensign Tala acknowledged from the helm.

"Question, Captain?" Lieutenant Yuati asked.

"Yes, Lieutenant?" Cameron replied, turning back toward him as she stood next to her command chair.

"Are we not going to intercept the drones?"

"We are, but we can get word to SilTek much faster than our comm-drones can," she explained, "and the more time they have to prepare, the better."

"Understood," the lieutenant replied. "My apologies for questioning your orders."

"No apology necessary, Lieutenant," Cameron assured him as she took her seat. "I shudder to think about the things Captain Scott might have done had I not questioned his decisions on occasion."

"Thank you, sir," the lieutenant replied.

"All departments report general quarters," Ensign Keller announced. "Chief of the boat is in damage control."

"Very well."

"Jump to SilTek is plotted and ready," the Aurora's navigator reported from the helm.

"Break orbit and jump us to SilTek," Cameron ordered. "Ensign Keller, make sure that transponder is squawking. We're jumping in unannounced, and I don't want another mistake by their automated defenses."

"Transponder is squawking at full power," the comms officer assured her.

"On course for SilTek. Jump point in ten seconds," Ensign Tala reported.

"Execute when ready," Cameron instructed.

"Jumping in five..."

"Comms, I'm going to want a connection to SilTek Security the moment we come out of the jump."

"Three..."

"Aye, sir," the comms officer replied.

"Two......one......jumping."

The blue-white light of the jump briefly illuminated the interior, transmitted through the wrap-around spherical view screen surrounding the forward half of the Aurora's bridge. What was once a blinding flash had been reduced to a mere signal that a jump had occurred.

"Jump complete," the navigator reported. "We're entering high orbit over SilTek."

"I have SilTek Security, General Pellot on the line, Captain," the comms officer announced.

Cameron tapped her comm-set, activating the link to the comm-channel. "General Pellot, Captain Taylor of the Aurora. The Falcon has located the drones. All four are on course for SilTek. If they maintain their current rate and range of jump, they should arrive in approximately six hours."

"Have you confirmed that they are indeed weapons?" the general asked.

"Not yet," Cameron admitted. "However, I doubt they would send four comm-drones to the same target."

"Agreed," General Pellot replied. "We shall put all defense systems on active alert."

"We are about to attempt an intercept," Cameron told him. "I just wanted to give you as much lead time as possible. I'll update you once we have more information."

"Understood."

Cameron tapped her comm-set again, ending the connection. "Helm, set course for the intercept point suggested by the Falcon and jump when ready."

"Setting course for intercept point," Ensign Tala acknowledged.

General Telles entered the bridge, heading to the command chair at its center as the image of the planet on the wrap-around view screen fell away. "SilTek?"

"I figured it would be faster if we warned them personally," Cameron explained. "We're headed for the intercept point now."

"Good thinking," the general agreed.

"On course for intercept," the helmsman announced. "Jumping in three..."

* * *

Aleksi pulled out a chair from one of the nearby tables and sat down. "There has been an ongoing debate among my lieutenants about seizing control of the net long enough to get a message out to the people. To inform them that all is not as it seems. Unfortunately, the cost in lives would be high, and the effectiveness of the message itself would be questionable."

"That's an understatement," Jessica quipped. "You'd have to strike all of them at precisely the same moment. If just one of those installations went on alert before the others, they'd all go on alert, and your people wouldn't get anywhere near them. Even if you managed to capture most of them, unless you get them all, your message wouldn't reach everyone. At best, you'd only reach half of the people on Earth."

"Actually, we only need to control one of the hubs. The others would be attacked at the same time so that net-control wouldn't know which hub was transmitting."

"One hub?" Jessica challenged. "How does one hub get you access to the entire population?"

"The hubs automatically synchronize at zero hundred hours, Earth Mean Time," Aleksi explained. "Our people have devised a hack that will slave all the hubs to the one that transmits the hack."

"Local controllers will pull their hubs off the main

grid," Jessica insisted. "Your message still won't get out."

"That was the second reason to attack every hub," Aleksi explained. "We would only need to maintain control of them for a few minutes. Once the message spreads through all the secondary nodes, it will be too late for net-control to block or censor the message. But as I said, the cost in lives would be high, and the effectiveness of the message would be questionable."

"It was my understanding that the people were pretty much split on Galiardi and the war with the Jung," Nathan commented.

"This is true."

"Then we're halfway home," Jessica decided.

"I wish it were that easy," Aleksi said. "The nets are full of conspiracy theories, many of them quite creative. Their sheer number decreases the credibility of them all. Yet another reason that I have thus far chosen not to pursue this idea. However, if we can prove to the people that Galiardi knew the Jung had not violated the cease-fire agreement, the balance of opinion would shift in our favor." Aleksi pointed at Nathan. "And now that you are here..."

"I'm a clone," Nathan told him, knowing what he would suggest next.

"Nathan!" Jessica snapped, shocked at his sudden admission to a man they had just met.

"Bozhe moi," Aleksi exclaimed.

"He just gave us Loki," Nathan reminded Jessica. "Right now, he's probably the only man on this planet we can trust."

"Then you are not Nathan Scott?" Aleksi wondered.

"I am Nathan Scott," Nathan assured him. "My

consciousness was copied into a device before my execution and then transferred into this body."

"Like the Nifelmians?"

"Precisely. So my claim for the right to assume my father's position might be legally challenged. Unless there has been some clarification as to the rights of clones passed in my absence."

Aleksi sighed, realizing that matters had just become more complicated. "Not to my knowledge, no." After a moment, Aleksi continued. "If I may ask, where have you been all these years?"

"That's a long story," Nathan told him. "The short version is that it took several generations of cloning me to create a version that could accept my consciousness without severe memory loss. That took a few years."

Aleksi looked confused. "Then you have only just been revived?"

"About seven months ago, so to speak," Nathan told him, not wanting to go into the details.

"Then why have you waited until now to return?"

"We've been a little busy," Nathan replied.

"Ah, yes...the Dusahn. Mister Sheehan's memories were less exact on that topic."

Jessica's expression changed, becoming angry. "You used the Jung memory extractor on him?"

"We were careful not to probe too deeply," Aleksi responded. "I assure you we did him no permanent harm."

Jessica glared at him. "You'd better hope you're right, for your sake."

Aleksi turned his attention back to Nathan, paying little heed to Jessica's threat. "How many people know that you are a clone?"

"Not that many," Nathan replied.

“Then perhaps we can conceal that fact long enough to achieve our goals.”

“Galiardi is not going to give up control without some sort of proof. After all, just like everyone else, he saw me buried.”

“But if you are a clone, will not your DNA be a match?”

“Not exactly,” Nathan replied with a sigh. “The consciousness transfer device was designed for Nifelmian DNA, which is somewhat different than humans’ as a result of being altered incrementally over hundreds of generations of clones. The Nifelmian scientists who resurrected me altered my DNA as well, over four or five cloning cycles. So my DNA will show that I am a clone.”

“But if our laws do not explicitly denounce the rights of a clone...”

“It won’t work,” Jessica insisted, interrupting Aleksi.

“We don’t know that,” Aleksi argued.

“Oh yes, we do,” Jessica told him. “Think about it. His consciousness was copied the night before his execution, and Nifelm was under Jung rule for years and had only been liberated shortly before Nathan’s surrender. It won’t take long for Galiardi to insist that Nathan was resurrected by the Jung and sent to Earth to weaken support for the war against them. Hell, they even have memory extraction technology. It won’t be much of a leap for most people to believe they have the technology to create their own clone of Nathan.”

Aleksi nodded his agreement, staring at Jessica. “You have special operations training, yes?”

“Yes.”

Aleksi thought a moment. "Perhaps the evidence alone will do the trick. What can you provide?"

"Sensor logs from the Aurora show that several of the same ships that violated Sol Alliance space later fought in service of the Dusahn back in the Pentaurus sector," Jessica offered.

"Might that not be interpreted as collusion between the Jung and the Dusahn?"

"We can also show that the Dusahn are the ones who invaded the Pentaurus sector and that Galiardi knew it was the Dusahn and not the Jung."

Aleksi looked unconvinced.

"There is one other point that you are both overlooking," Nathan mentioned. "If the Jung and the Dusahn were working together against the Sol Alliance, why has Galiardi been able to continue attacking Jung assets with impunity? If the Jung and the Dusahn were working together, or if they were one and the same, wouldn't the Jung have jump drives as well? And if they did, we wouldn't be having this conversation. The Earth would have been destroyed months ago. After all, the Jung Empire still has a considerable fleet. If they had jump drive technology, they would have been able to plow right through the Sol Alliance defenses."

"He's right," Jessica agreed.

"Perhaps," Aleksi said. "However, it would be better if we could offer an heir-to-office. That would seal Galiardi's fate."

Jessica looked at Nathan.

"There is something else?" Aleksi asked, noticing the knowing glance exchanged between them.

"No," Nathan stated firmly.

"Nathan..." Jessica urged.

Nathan gave her a stern look.

"It's the only way, and you know it," Jessica insisted. "Besides, you know what she'd say."

"What who would say?" Aleksi wondered, confused.

Nathan sighed, turning back to Aleksi. "My sister Miri is alive."

Aleksi smiled. "Then there is hope after all."

* * *

Waiting had never been Cameron's strong suit, and pacing was a habit she had never been able to break. It helped her think, burn nervous energy, and maintain her focus.

"One minute," Kaylah reported from the Aurora's sensor station.

Cameron stopped pacing a moment. "Hold fire until we confirm that the drones are, in fact, weapons."

"Aye, sir," Lieutenant Yuati acknowledged. "However, does it matter at this point?"

"Probably not," Cameron agreed, returning to her pacing. "But I prefer to know what I'm shooting at."

"Weapons are fully charged and ready. Awaiting your orders to fire."

"Twenty seconds."

Cameron returned to her command chair, standing beside it as she faced forward again. They were about to see for themselves precisely what the Dusahn had sent to SilTek. While a small part of her hoped for the best, she was certain that the drones were weapons.

Four small jump flashes appeared on the semi-spherical main view screen, directly ahead and slightly above their flight path.

"Four contacts," Kaylah reported. "Scanning."

"Shall I lock weapons on the targets?" Lieutenant Yuati inquired from the tactical console.

"Not yet," Cameron replied.

"Lieutenant Parsa was right," Kaylah realized as she studied her sensor displays. "They're definitely modified Takaran jump comm-drones. It looks like they clustered four complete drones together and added a central control unit tucked into the space between their noses."

"What about the mass in front?" Cameron asked.

"It's pretty big, nearly the diameter of the cluster of drones itself," Kaylah continued. "Some kind of shielding; I'm having a hard time penetrating it with our sensors."

"The drones are closing fast," the tactical officer warned. "At their current speed, they will reach us in two minutes."

"Collision risk?" Cameron asked.

"Unless they change course, they will pass over us with about five hundred meters of separation. However, if we do not fire soon, our chances of hitting them will decrease significantly."

Cameron took her seat as she considered the situation. If, as she suspected, the drones were weapons, this could be their best opportunity to neutralize them. However, if they were just communications drones, she could be escalating things with the Dusahn.

She immediately dismissed her concerns over escalation, as it seemed impossible to escalate beyond the destruction of entire worlds for the sake of example, something the Dusahn had done on multiple occasions.

"Lieutenant Yuati," Cameron called. "Lock all weapons on the drones and prepare to fire."

"Locking forward plasma cannons and point-defenses on the drones," the tactical officer acknowledged as he prepared to fire.

"I'm adjusting sensors to try to penetrate the shielding," Kaylah reported.

"Weapons are locked on targets," Lieutenant Yuati reported. "Ninety seconds until they pass over us."

"Captain!" Kaylah interrupted urgently. "I'm picking up traces of antimatter from within the shielded forward mass. A lot of it! Targets are raising shields."

"Weapons free! Fire at will!" Cameron ordered without hesitation.

"Firing all weapons!" the lieutenant replied.

Flashes of reddish-orange filled the bridge as bolts of plasma energy streaked away on either side of the view screen.

"Targets are changing course!" Kaylah reported. "They're spreading out!"

"Keep firing," Cameron urged.

"Energy spikes!" Kaylah warned. "All four! They're armed!"

Four yellow bolts of energy lashed out at the Aurora's forward shields, causing them to flash brilliantly with each impact.

"What the hell?" Cameron exclaimed as the Aurora shook more violently than expected with each impact.

"Some sort of energy weapons," Kaylah reported. "Similar to the ones on the Dusahn octos, but far more powerful."

"Why didn't we detect any weapons?" Cameron demanded.

"Their cannons were embedded in the nose of the

forward shielded mass," Kaylah replied. "They only became detectable when they deployed to fire."

"Nice trick."

"That means they will not be able to defend against an attack from astern," Lieutenant Yuati opined.

"Keep pounding them, Lieutenant," Cameron instructed. "Helm, prepare to come about as they pass," she added as the ship rocked from the weapons impacts against their forward shields. "Kaylah, are you detecting any weapons in their stern?"

"Impossible to tell," Kaylah replied. "Their reactors are interfering with my scans, especially from this angle."

"Our weapons are not getting through their shields," Lieutenant Yuati announced.

"I'm detecting only a ten-percent drop in the targets' shield strength!" Kaylah added.

"Thirty seconds until they pass over us," the lieutenant reported.

"Keep your weapons on the targets as we turn," Cameron instructed. "Helm, come about now."

"Coming about, aye," Ensign Tala replied from the helm.

"Tracking through the turn," the tactical officer acknowledged.

The drones filled the main view screen, spreading out and continuing to fire as they passed overhead.

"Targets have passed over us and are spreading out further," Kaylah reported as the violent shaking from the weapons impacts ceased.

"Concentrate fire on the nearest drone!" Cameron ordered.

"Targets are turning to different vectors!" Kaylah warned.

"Stay with the middle target, Ensign Tala," Cameron instructed.

"Targets are jumping!"

Four flashes of light appeared across the view screen, just as the Aurora finished her turn.

"Targets are gone," Lieutenant Yuati reported.

"Based on their new trajectories at jump, I'd bet they're splitting up and taking different routes to SilTek," Kaylah suggested.

"Damn it," Cameron cursed to herself. "Comms, contact the Falcon and tell them to go after the missile on the most direct heading for SilTek. We'll go after the others."

"Aye, sir."

"Captain," the ship's AI called over the intercom speakers. "If I may offer an observation?"

Cameron did not care much for talking with the Aurora's AI. Its voice was so similar to her own that it made her feel as if she were talking to herself. "Yes, Aurora?"

"The tactics employed by the targets strongly support your belief that Dusahn artificial intelligence is being used. I have studied all intelligence on the Dusahn AI capabilities. I believe that I can anticipate their tactics more reliably than any human. No insult intended."

"None taken," Cameron replied. "Recommendations?"

"While I believe that I can assist in locating the missiles, I am but one ship."

"The Nighthawks," Cameron said, realizing where their AI was going.

"Correct. Their AIs would be able to do the same. Also, they can carry the miniaturized version of the shield-penetrating jump missiles. Once the targets' shields have been disabled, the Nighthawks should be able to destroy the missiles before they reach SilTek."

"But they can't get here fast enough," Cameron surmised. "Helm, jump us back to Corinair ASAP."

"Setting course for Corinair," Ensign Tala replied.

The navigator turned to face his captain. "Sir, jumping back to Corinair and then back here again will take us below minimum jump reserves."

"Will we have enough to get back to SilTek?" Cameron asked.

"Yes, sir," Ensign Dorsay replied, "but it will be four hours until we're able to jump back to any alliance world."

"All other worlds will be defenseless until then," Lieutenant Yuati added, concerned.

"Not defenseless," Cameron corrected, "just not as well defended. Unfortunately, we're out of options." She tapped her comm-set. "Engineering, Captain. Run all reactors at one hundred and twenty percent, and channel all available power to recharging the jump drive."

"Parsa here. Understood."

"Drop shields and shut down all weapons," Cameron instructed her tactical officer. "I want all available power going to the jump cells."

"Dropping shields and shutting down all weapons," Lieutenant Yuati acknowledged.

"Jump to Corinair plotted and ready, Captain," Ensign Dorsay reported. "If we took a few minutes to further accelerate before jumping, we could lessen the drain on our jump cells."

"A few minutes could be the difference between life and death for the people of SilTek," Cameron told him. "Jump us back, Ensign. Comms, scramble all

Nighthawks the moment we come out of the jump. I want them on our decks as quickly as possible. And tell the deck boss to be ready to load them with mini-shield busters."

* * *

Nathan and the away team hiked up the Voss's aft cargo ramp with Loki, Aleksi, and several of his men in tow. Marcus and Dylan were there to greet them, their mouths dropping open in surprise.

"Holy crap," Marcus said, spotting Loki.

"Oh my God," Dylan added in disbelief.

Loki came up the ramp, smiling as he received handshakes from Mori and Jokay.

Marcus threw his burly arms around Loki, hugging him with all his might. "Josh is going to be so happy to see you."

"Josh is going to be happy?" Dylan exclaimed. "Hell, I'm happy! Now I don't have to be his copilot!" Dylan shook Loki's hand as soon as Marcus released him. "Honestly, I don't know how you put up with him."

"It takes practice," Loki laughed.

"Josh!" Marcus yelled over the intercom. "Get your skinny ass down here pronto!"

"I'm busy!" Josh objected over the intercom speakers.

"Get down here NOW!" Marcus barked.

"As soon as I finish eating!"

Loki smiled, happy to hear father and son bickering again. "I'll go surprise him," he told Marcus, heading forward.

"This is Aleksi Rusayev," Nathan introduced. "Aleksi, this is everyone."

"A pleasure," Aleksi replied, nodding respectfully.

"You can cut our prisoners loose," Nathan

instructed the Ghatazhak. "Dylan, we brought back the data core from Loki's P-Seventy-Two. Can you access its flight logs?"

"Sure," Dylan replied, taking the satchel offered to him by one of Aleksi's men. "I'll just plug it into..." Dylan stopped, pulling the damaged unit from the bag. "I'll figure something out."

"Top priority," Nathan urged.

"Yes, sir."

Aleksi watched Dylan depart. "He is just a boy," he said to Nathan under his breath.

"A very smart boy from a very advanced world," Nathan explained.

The first of the freed prisoners came up to Aleksi, his head hung in shame. "Please forgive us, Aleksi..."

Aleksi placed his hands on the man's shoulders. "You were bested by Ghatazhak, Pyotr. There is no shame in this."

Mori and Jokay exchanged knowing glances.

"Marcus, can you pull one of our comm-drones and program it to jump between this cavern and the relay station?"

"Sure, but how the hell do you plan on launching and recovering it?" Marcus wondered.

"I'm sure we can construct a launch track of some sort," Aleksi assured them. "As for recovery..."

"If we program the comm-drone to travel at only a few meters per second, we could snag it with a recovery net," Vladimir suggested. "We could string it across the mouth of the cave, connected to four tracks with some sort of a deceleration system."

"Just make sure you keep the net down unless you're conducting a comm-relay," Nathan instructed. "Just in case we need to return unannounced."

"I will see to it," Aleksi assured him. "How long until we hear from you again?"

Nathan thought for a second. "As soon as we're off, I'm sending the intelligence you provided to General Telles of the Ghatazhak for analysis. Meanwhile, I will talk with Miri. I should have an update for you in a few days. Just make sure you have that recovery net ready."

"It will be ready," Aleksi assured him. "And we will keep the cavern well guarded at all times, to ensure your ability to return at will."

"Thank you," Nathan replied. "Regardless of how we proceed, knowing that we have a safe way to get to and from Earth will be invaluable."

"Come, Lyoha," Vladimir said, patting his old friend on the back. "We will discuss your launch and recovery systems before we go."

Nathan watched as Vladimir, Aleksi, his men, and the freed prisoners headed down the ramp into the cavern.

Mori stepped over closer to Nathan. "Are you sure we can trust this guy?"

"Vladimir does," Nathan replied.

"Is that enough?"

Josh's joyous voice suddenly came across the intercom speakers. "I told you he was alive!"

Nathan smiled. "And he did bring Loki back to us."

CHAPTER ELEVEN

Cameron continued to pace, repeatedly passing between her command chair and the Aurora's helm. It wasn't a fast pace, but rather a slow, thoughtful stroll, as if she was contemplating all options.

The funny thing was that she had not always been this way. She had, in fact, paced on occasion, but not as frequently as in recent weeks. It made her wonder if she were losing her edge. She had commanded the Aurora for seven years, but that had been during peacetime. The only stress she experienced back then was either simulated or political.

She had commanded warships in combat before, and in far more stressful situations, but the stakes never seemed to lessen. Today, there were millions of lives at stake, and her one thought was why she didn't think to bring the Nighthawks with her to begin with. She had been certain that the Aurora could deal with a handful of drones, but she had been wrong, and it was causing her to second-guess herself.

"Thirty minutes to terminal attack leg," Lieutenant Yuati updated.

Cameron glared at him. She didn't mean to; it was just a response. She was well aware of how much time they had left to locate and destroy those drones; she glanced at the time display on the view screen with each leg of her pacing. But the lieutenant was just doing his job. He had too little experience in his station to realize how attentive she was to such details.

The lieutenant got the message but chose not

to respond, lest he draw additional ire from his superior.

Cameron changed her course, moving up to the communications console at the back of the bridge. "Anything?" she asked.

The young ensign at the comm-station looked up apologetically. "No, sir."

* * *

"Anything, Les?" Talisha asked her wingman.

"Negative," he replied over comms. "I don't know how Teison and his crew do this kind of shit day in and day out."

"How many jumps have we made so far?" another pilot wondered. "I've lost count."

"It's only been twenty-seven jumps," Talisha replied. "Twenty-eight coming up."

"Jesus," the pilot of Red Three exclaimed.

"Come on," Talisha said. "We do three times that many jumps on an average patrol."

"Yeah, but we're not actually hoping to find anything, so it's not disappointment with every negative scan," Les pointed out from Red Two.

"Less talk, more scanning," Talisha joked as she prepared to jump again. "Leader to group; jump twenty-eight in five seconds."

* * *

"Report!" General Pellot barked as he entered SilTek Security's defense command center.

"All defenses are charged and ready," the weapons officer reported. "All missile launchers are loaded with two shield busters and two fragmenting interceptors each. Any of them can be launched with split-second notice."

"Make sure all targeting systems are set to low orbit intercepts by default," the general ordered his chief weapons officer. "If those drones get through, they'll come out as close to the planet as possible, so we're only going to get one shot at them."

"Yes, sir!" the weapons officer acknowledged. "Recommend all launches start with shield busters, with the frag-interceptors launching five seconds after."

"Very well." The general turned to his tracking officer. "Tracking?"

"All surface and space-borne tracking arrays are online," the tracking officer reported. "I've taken the inner system arrays and pointed them inward toward us, to increase the coverage and light up any dead zones."

"That will leave the outer system inadequately covered," the general commented.

"As you said, sir, if any of the drones get by, they'll arrive terminal close in."

"Very well."

The general's second came up next to him, leaning in. "We're ready, sir. I've had diagnostics run on every system, just to be certain we are running at one hundred percent efficiency."

"Of course," the general replied. "I just hope it's enough." The general sighed. "Sometimes, I hate jump drives."

* * *

"New contact," Kaylah reported from the Aurora's sensor station. "Comm-drone."

"Receiving data stream," the communications officer reported.

Cameron paused her pacing, turning toward the comms officer, hoping for good news.

"Red and Blue flights reporting negative contact,"

Ensign Keller reported. "Nothing yet from Green or Gold."

"What about the Falcon?"

"Their next comm-check isn't for three more minutes."

Cameron sighed, growing frustrated with each passing moment. "This isn't working. They've been searching for over an hour and haven't even caught a glimpse of old light." After thinking a moment, she tilted her head up as if talking to the ceiling. "Aurora, any chance we've missed something?"

"Current search patterns are based upon known Dusahn jump trace evasion tactics and the performance parameters of the old Takaran jump comm-drones. All search teams are currently searching along the most likely evasion paths."

"Then why haven't they found anything?" Cameron asked. "Is it possible that their AIs are using random patterns?"

"It is possible but highly unlikely. An AI cannot be truly random; rather, it introduces enough choices into an algorithm to appear to be random."

"That's not helping," Cameron insisted.

"My apologies, Captain," the Aurora's AI replied. "I am only able to make decisions based on available data."

No statement had ever rung truer for Cameron. Her entire career had been about making the most appropriate decision based on available data. Long ago, she had learned that it was impossible to always make the correct decision, since the information itself was always fluid. Even her hunches were based on available data. Not once had she ever just gone with her gut, except for one time, which was why she was here now.

"Aurora," she called again. "Do we have enough data to determine how far the drones jumped the last time we had solid tracks on them?"

"Based on velocity, course, and intensity of jump flash, we can determine the location of their first jump to an accuracy of three-point two five light hours," Aurora replied.

"And we determine their course change based on the position of their next departure flash in comparison to their original arrival flash," Cameron stated.

"Correct."

"What if that departure flash was a ruse?" Cameron suggested.

"Generation of a jump flash that does not initiate a transition out of our dimension is theoretically possible. However, it would require another recharge cycle, the same as if the transition had actually occurred. As an evasion tactic, it is sound, but not under the current conditions."

"Why not?" Cameron wondered.

"It would increase the risk of redetection," Aurora explained. "With only four weapons, it would be illogical to take such a risk, especially when there are multiple options that provide a greater chance of successfully reaching the target."

Cameron thought for a moment, imagining herself in the cockpit of a Nighthawk, talking to the same type of AI. "The Nighthawks don't search very far, do they?"

"They do not," Aurora confirmed. "Instead, they execute micro-jumps of two light minutes, then spend a minute on station scanning in all directions."

"So all the drone would have to do to prevent redetection is to initiate a fake jump flash, then go dark for a few minutes...maybe even make a low-burn turn before jumping."

"Current search patterns would have detected the drones even in the scenario you have described," Aurora defended.

For a moment, Cameron felt as if the ship's AI had taken offense. "What if they accelerated as well?"

"They would have to turn to terminal course before doing so," Lieutenant Yuati interjected, seeing where his captain was going.

"Aurora, calculate likely positions on the following assumptions," Cameron began. "One; the first departure flash after their initial escape from our track was a decoy, and no jump actually occurred. Two; the drones went dark at the same time and stayed dark long enough to ensure that they would be outside of detection range by a ship attempting to follow their jump path. Three; they executed a turn to terminal intercept course with SilTek once past detection range. Four; they jumped one time, then accelerated as quickly as possible to maximum speed, burning all available propellant to do so."

"Parameter four is illogical," Aurora argued. "The drones would be unable to adjust course for final intercept."

"They don't have to," Cameron insisted. "They're carrying antimatter warheads. Close is good enough."

"Calculation complete, plots are on the viewscreen," Aurora reported. "I should point out, Captain, that this tactic is extremely unlikely for an AI."

"That's why I'm going with it," Cameron said, studying the new drone course and position predictions displayed on the main view screen.

"Comms, flash traffic. Redirect the Falcon to search along the new track prediction for target three."

"Aye, sir."

"You believe the Dusahn know about the Sugali AIs," Lieutenant Yuati surmised.

"I have no idea," Cameron admitted. "But if they did, then they'd use it against us."

Lieutenant Yuati also studied the new track predictions. "If you are correct, then the drones are less than twelve minutes from SilTek."

Cameron said nothing. Part of her hoped she was wrong. At least then they'd have more time.

* * *

"Still nothing?" Lieutenant Teison asked.

"Nothing," the sergeant replied. "Wait... comm-drone."

"Don't do that!" Ensign Lassen snapped.

"Do what?"

"You know damn well what!"

"You need a break, Tomi," the sergeant commented, smiling.

"We all need a break," the lieutenant added. "What's the message?"

"You're not going to believe this," Tomi told him.

Lieutenant Teison leaned in, reading the communications display on the top of the center console. "You've got to be joking."

"What is it?" Sergeant Nama wondered.

"They're redirecting us to grid Delta Two Five, direct SilTek," Ensign Lassen said.

"Delta Two Five?" the sergeant repeated in disbelief. "The only way they'd be in Delta Two Five would be if they turned terminal after the first jump and hauled ass. That doesn't make any sense."

"Like any of this makes any sense," the lieutenant commented as he prepared to change course.

"We've been searching this track for the last hour!" the sergeant complained. "For all we know, we could find something in the next few grids!"

"He's right, Jasser," Ensign Lassen agreed. "If we bail on this track now..."

"And if she's right?" the lieutenant interrupted. "Do you want the deaths of millions on your conscience? I sure as hell don't. Not for a lieutenant's pay."

"Jasser..."

"Shut up and plot the jump, Tomi," the lieutenant insisted. "It's not our call, and you know it."

* * *

"Why four drones?" Lieutenant Yuati asked, breaking the relative silence.

"Excuse me?" Cameron replied, her pacing interrupted.

"Why four?" the lieutenant continued from the tactical station. "Why not two, or six, or even eight?"

"What does it matter?" Cameron countered.

"If the intent is to destroy SilTek, more weapons would increase the probability of success."

"Antimatter is not an abundant commodity," Cameron told him. "I doubt they have much capacity for manufacturing it."

"Didn't the Takarans use antimatter?"

"Yes, but they shut down production shortly after developing zero-point reactors."

"Then where are the Dusahn getting their antimatter?" the lieutenant wondered.

"Probably from the reactors of destroyed ships," Cameron explained. "When their warships are lost, their antimatter cores automatically eject so they can be recovered and reused."

"Is that why they did not send any such weapons toward the Rogen system?" the lieutenant wondered.

"Probably," Cameron agreed. "They didn't need to destroy your worlds, they just needed to punish you. Besides, at the time, most of their warships were still intact, so they probably didn't have any to spare."

"So by defeating all those battleships at once..."

"We gave them quite a bit of antimatter to recycle."

"Then you believe they sent four weapons because that is all the antimatter they had to spare," the lieutenant surmised.

"It took four warheads to destroy Ancot," Cameron told him. "There have got to be at least that many wired up to take out Takara."

"Then they wish to destroy SilTek," the lieutenant concluded. "It seems wholly unnecessary. A single antimatter event in the atmosphere would likely be enough to cause the people of SilTek to reconsider their support of this alliance."

"That's not enough for the Dusahn," Cameron insisted. "Especially since we've boxed them in and threatened to attack any ships they send out, armed or not. The Dusahn, just like the Jung, rule by fear of consequences."

"All human civilizations have been ruled by fear of consequences," the lieutenant pointed out. "It's only a matter of degrees."

"I'm sure you and Captain Scott could have a lively discussion on that topic," Cameron told him.

* * *

"Jump complete," Ensign Lassen reported.

"Starting scans of grid Delta Two Five," Sergeant Nama announced.

Lieutenant Teison felt a glimmer of hope as he quickly performed his post-jump systems check. He and his crew had spent over thirty hours searching for the drones, only to have to try and find them again. Nothing was more tiresome than trying to pick up a jump trail. Although they had flown many missions that lasted twice as long, the monotony of the task was far more tiring. Add the fact that millions of lives hung on their success, and the pressure was enough to drive the strongest of men over the edge.

"And...nothing," Sergeant Nama reported, disappointed, but not surprised.

"What the hell are we doing here?" Ensign Lassen exclaimed. "We never should have left our original search track," he added, looking at the lieutenant.

"What do we do now, LT?" the sergeant wondered.

Lieutenant Teison sighed, that glimmer of hope having faded away. "We launch a comm-drone to report negative contact on this grid and request instructions."

"So we just sit here until then?" Ensign Lassen wondered in disbelief. "Time is running out, Jas."

"I know."

"At least we can jump ahead to the next grid," Sergeant Nama suggested. "We can probably search two or three more while waiting for a response from the Aurora."

"We can tell them to send the response a few grids ahead," Ensign Lassen added, indicating his agreement with the sergeant's suggestion.

"Very well," the lieutenant agreed. "Tomi, prep a comm-drone. Report negative contact at Delta Two Five, and let the Aurora know we are progressing on this track until further orders. Add that we expect a reply from them by grid Delta Two Nine."

"And if we don't hear from them by then?" Tomi

asked as he began prepping the comm-drone for launch.

"Contact!" Sergeant Nama exclaimed. "Dead astern! Close in!"

The Falcon suddenly rocked violently, as if something twice their size had slammed into them from behind.

"It's the drone!" the sergeant continued. "It's firing at us!" he added as the ship lurched again.

"NO SHIT!" the lieutenant exclaimed, grabbing his flight controls to take evasive action.

"We just lost aft shields!" Ensign Lassen reported as the ship took another hit astern.

"Flight controls aren't responding!" the lieutenant announced.

Warning indicators began lighting up, and alarms filled the cockpit.

"Jump drive is offline!" Ensign Lassen reported. "Maneuvering is down!"

A million thoughts raced through Lieutenant Teison's mind; every option and possible outcome flooding in so quickly that he could barely keep them sorted. Only one option stood out.

Another impact kicked their stern to port.

"We just lost main propulsion!" the ensign reported as the ship rocked again. "Crap! We're fucking coming apart, Jas!"

The lieutenant looked to his copilot. "Update the message. Positive contact at Delta Two Five. Include course and speed data...and a Mayday."

Ensign Lassen looked at the lieutenant.

"Tell them we're ejecting."

The ensign immediately went to work.

"Punch out, Riko," the lieutenant ordered, lowering his helmet visor.

"Not until you guys do!" the sergeant insisted as the ship rocked and sparks erupted from his console.

"Comm-drone updated!" Ensign Lassen announced. "Launching!"

The ship rocked again. There was a deafening sound of shearing metal, and a whoosh of escaping air headed aft. Lieutenant Teison turned to look over his shoulder as the aft bulkhead was torn away. Behind them, the main body of their ship was breaking apart as another volley of energy tore through it.

"Eject, eject, eject!" the lieutenant ordered, reaching down for his own ejection handles in between his legs at the base of his seat. He grabbed the handles and pulled them up sharply with all his might. There was a long pause, so long in fact that he wondered if his ejection mechanism had failed. The cockpit filled with smoke and bright flames as the other two members of the Falcon's crew activated their own ejection systems and were shot from the doomed wreckage. A split second later, the lieutenant felt something hit him hard in the ass. The impact was so hard that it knocked the wind out of him. Before he could comprehend what was happening, he found himself no longer in the Falcon's cockpit but hurtling through open space.

A few seconds later, the rocket motor propelling him away from certain death ran out of propellant, and he found himself coasting silently through space. He drifted a minute, slowly tumbling. With each revolution, he could see the wreckage of his own ship in the distance, lit only by the occasional flashes of light as the last of its systems signaled their end. However, try as he might, he could not spot Tomi or Riko.

On his next revolution, he spotted the drone passing beneath the wreckage of his ship. A moment later, there was a flash of blue-white light, and everything was gone. He could no longer see anything but the distant stars surrounding him. But other than the stars, there was no light anywhere. The only reason he could see his own gloved hands was because of the light spilling out from his helmet.

"Tomi?" the lieutenant called over his helmet comms. "Riko?" When there was no response, he felt incredibly alone. "Guys? If you copy me, check in."

"I'm here, Jas," Tomi finally replied.

"Oh, thank God," Jasser exclaimed, breathing a sigh of relief. "Riko, you out there, buddy?"

"What a fucking ride that was!" Riko answered.

Jasser smiled. Their situation was still dire, but at least they were all still alive. "Tomi, please tell me you got that drone away."

"I got positive confirmation that it launched just before we ejected," Tomi assured him.

"Riko, did you see the comm-drone jump?"

"Sorry, LT," Riko replied. "I lost sensors just after we lost aft shields."

"I'm sure it got away," Tomi insisted. "That drone only had one gun, and it was firing at us at regular intervals. It had to get away."

"What do we do now, LT?" Riko wondered.

"We wait, and we pray that Tomi's right."

"New contact!" Kaylah announced. "Comm-drone."

"Drone ID shows it's from the Falcon," Ensign Keller reported from the Aurora's comm-station.

"Receiving message... They found it! Course and speed data included!"

"Aurora, can you predict the positions of the other three drones based on the Falcon's target track data?"

"Calculating," the Aurora's AI replied.

"There's more," Ensign Keller added. "They declared a Mayday, sir!"

"Launch the SAR Reaper," Cameron ordered as the projected drone positions and course plots appeared on the main view screen. "And send these course plots to all four Nighthawk attack groups."

"Aye, sir," the comms officer acknowledged.

Lieutenant Yuati studied the new drone position predictions, doing the calculations in his head. "Based on those positions, we have five minutes before impact."

"Four minutes and twenty-eight seconds," Aurora corrected.

"At least we have a chance now," Cameron stated, finally returning to her command chair.

"That's fifteen light years away!" the pilot of Red Two exclaimed.

"Those are the orders," Talisha replied.

"How the hell could we have been that far off?"

"The actions of the Dusahn AIs are not following predictable logic patterns," Talisha's AI stated. "Their decisions seem more human than AI, which would indicate that the Dusahn automation systems are not truly artificial intelligence at all."

"Did you just called us stupid?" Talisha laughed as she prepared to jump to the new search grid.

"I believe I was calling the Dusahn AIs...stupid," Leta corrected.

"Les, you and I will jump to the left side of the grid. Munro and Roddi will jump to the right side. We'll get a wider scan that way."

"Copy that," Munro acknowledged.

"If anyone makes contact, don't wait for the others. Put a pair of shield busters into it. We'll have two minutes to bring down its shields before it jumps again."

"Incoming message," Ensign Keller announced from the Aurora's communications station. "Green Leader reports contact...and a confirmed kill!"

"Yes," Cameron said, more to herself than anyone else. "Did they confirm destruction of the antimatter warhead?"

"Yes, sir," the comms officer replied. "Lieutenant Cruthers reports that the antimatter detonation nearly took them out as well."

"It sounds like they got lucky," Lieutenant Yuati opined.

"Hunting antimatter weapons is a dangerous business," Cameron said. "Luck is sometimes all you have."

"I never did congratulate you on guessing the location of the drones, Captain," the lieutenant said.

"It's too soon for congratulations, Lieutenant. There are still three more to go."

"I have a contact!" Les called from Red Two. "Edge of sensor range; old light. Looks like a jump flash."

"I've got it as well," Talisha confirmed. "What do you think, Leta?"

"Ninety seconds old," her AI replied. "Based on known decay rate, I estimate that the drone executed a ten-light-year jump. Recommend you jump ahead twenty light years to intercept as it comes out of its next jump. Anticipate ten-degree change in heading."

"Listen up," Talisha called to her group. "We jump twenty. We go ten to port, Munro and Roddi go ten to starboard. Jump in ten."

"Got it, Leader," Munro acknowledged.

"Lead pops busters, wing pops killers," Talisha added as she turned ten degrees to port. "Jumping in three......two......one......"

The stars shifted slightly, her fighter jumping ahead twenty light years. She immediately flipped over, pointing her nose aft, arming her missile launch systems. "You with me, Les?"

"I've got two killers hot on the rails."

"You launch five seconds after I do," Talisha reminded her wingman.

"My finger is on the button."

A moment later, the contact alert light on her sensor display lit up.

"Contact," her AI reported. "Drone at one seven five, ten up relative. Range four hundred thousand kilometers and closing. Target is initiating a turn to starboard and pitching downward."

"Locking two busters on target," Talisha announced as she prepared to launch. "Good locks! Launching two!" She pressed the launch button, sending two missiles streaking forward. A split second after they launched, both weapons disappeared behind small, blue-white flashes of light. "Two busters away!"

"Red Two, launching two!" her wingman reported. "Two killers away!"

Talisha glanced to her left, just as the missiles launched by her wingman jumped away. "Jumping ahead three hundred and ninety thousand klicks," she reported as she dialed up a new jump range and activated her jump drive.

"New range to target; ten thousand kilometers and closing rapidly," Leta reported. "Target has lost forward shields."

"What about the kill shots?" Talisha inquired.

"I'm detecting damage to one of the drone's propulsion modules. I'm also picking up debris from a missile detonation one hundred meters ahead of the target."

"Leader to Red Group!" Talisha called. "They've got point-defenses! I repeat; the drone has point-defenses!"

An energy bolt suddenly slammed into her forward shields, rocking her fighter.

"Forward shields down to forty percent," Leta warned. "One more direct hit and forward shields will fail."

"Evasive!" Talisha called out. "Going port!" she added as she rolled into a hard left turn. Another bolt of energy streaked past her.

"I'm hit!" her wingman cried out.

"Going hot with two killers!" Talisha reported. "Les, evade!"

"I'm trying!"

"Target is continuing to fire," Leta warned.

Talisha killed her main propulsion and swung her nose to starboard, going into a sideways slide to bring her nose onto the target. "Red Leader, launching two!" she reported as she pressed the launch button again. "Two killers away!"

Another bolt of energy streaked to her right. She turned her head to follow it, just as it broke through her wingman's shields and cut through his port side. "LES!" she cried out as her wingman's ship exploded. "Two is down!" she yelled over comms.

"Roddi is gone!" Munro reported over comms from Red Three.

"Missile impact," Leta announced. "Target has lost another drive module."

"Munzi!" Leta called over comms. "Form up on me! We'll jump ahead and attack at the next intercept point!" After a moment, she called out again. "Munzi, do you copy?"

"I have lost contact with Red Three," Leta reported. "The only contact I have is the drone, which is attempting to target us."

"Did he jump?"

"Negative," Leta replied. "I am detecting debris at his last known location."

"Son of a bitch!" Talisha exclaimed as she pressed her jump button to get away. "Leta! Pop a comm-drone to the Aurora. Lost three; target damaged but still operational. Continuing pursuit. Include tracking data and warn them that the drones have point-defenses and a stern gun."

"Blue reports a kill!" Ensign Keller reported from the Aurora's comm-station.

"Two down, two to go," Lieutenant Yuati commented.

"And they're two jumps from terminal," Cameron

added. She glanced up at the drone track displayed in a window on the lower right side of the Aurora's wrap-around view screen. Luckily, their orbit had them on the same side of SilTek as the inbound drones. "Ensign Keller, take us to a higher altitude. At one minute before the drones make their terminal jump, we'll yaw to port twenty-five degrees and roll forty-five to starboard to bring more weapons to bear. Lieutenant Yuati, at that point, we'll start laying down a flak field with the main rail guns."

"Depth of field?" the lieutenant wondered.

"Split the range between us and the drones' expected arrival point into five layers, with a flak field between each layer. One gun for each layer."

"If we restrict our roll to forty degrees, I can get both starboard ventral rail guns in action. That will allow us to increase the density of at least two of the flak fields."

"Good thinking," Cameron agreed. "We'll use them on the two flak fields closest to us. That will help thicken the field a bit. And if those drones make it that far, we're going to need every bit of flak we can create."

"By that logic, would it not make more sense to use fewer fields?" the lieutenant wondered. "Perhaps two or even one?"

"We can't be certain about their arrival points," Cameron explained. "Make sure each layer is offset from the others. The less empty space there is between the drones and SilTek, the better the chance of intercept."

"New contact!" Kaylah announced from the sensor station. "Comm-drone...Red Group!"

"Incoming message," Ensign Keller added. "From Red Leader. Drone Four is damaged; no forward shields. Red Group has lost three, but is continuing pursuit."

"Damn," Cameron cursed under her breath. "Launch another SAR Reaper and send them to Red's last engagement grid. The Nighthawks' AIs may have saved them."

"According to the telemetry included in the last communication, Red Leader has no missiles left," Lieutenant Yuati advised.

"There's more, sir," the comms officer continued. "The drones have point-defenses and a stern energy cannon."

"That qualifies them as gunships instead of drones," Lieutenant Yuati surmised.

"Gunships with antimatter warheads strapped to their bows," Cameron added.

Talisha came out of her jump, arriving in the next grid where she expected the drone to conduct its brief recharge layover. She quickly flipped her ship over, then jammed her throttle to full power.

"Based on your aggressive deceleration attempt, I must assume that you plan on jumping inside the drone's shields," Leta surmised.

"We've got no missiles left," Talisha replied. "You got a better idea?"

"Two of the drone's drive modules have been damaged and are unusable. I recommend that you concentrate on the remaining modules, preferably the one with the highest charge, since it will be the next one used to jump."

"The next jump is the last one," Talisha reminded her AI. "The drone will be terminal after that."

"I am aware of that," Leta assured her pilot. "However, it may buy us some extra time. If we are lucky, we may be able to take out both drives."

The use of the word lucky made Talisha nervous. AIs didn't believe in luck, just statistical probabilities. "Just how lucky will we need to be?"

"You do not want to know," Leta assured her.

"Gold reports a kill!" Ensign Keller reported from the Aurora's comm-station.

Cameron said nothing, preferring not to get too excited. There was still one more drone headed their way. While a single drone couldn't destroy SilTek, it could kill millions and cripple the Karuzari Alliance to the point of being unable to keep the Dusahn Empire contained, which may have been their intention from the start.

Cameron glanced at the intercept clock on the view screen. "Time to execute your maneuver, Mister Tala," she instructed. "Lieutenant Yuati, prepare to lay down flak fields. We need to stop that last drone."

"Now that we know the exact approach trajectory of the last drone, I recommend we narrow our intercept fields so that we can increase their density, thereby improving our chances of intercept."

"Good idea, Lieutenant," Cameron agreed. "And the moment the drone appears, turn all guns onto it. Don't wait for me to give the order."

"Yes, sir."

"Contact," Talisha's AI reported. "Two one five; fifteen up relative; range five hundred twenty-five thousand kilometers. Aspect change; target turning to port and pitching up. I suspect that it is lining up for its terminal jump."

"How much time do we have?" Talisha asked as she prepared to jump in to attack the drone.

"Scans show that they will have enough energy for terminal jump in forty-eight seconds," Leta reported.

"Then we'd better work quickly," Talisha said as she ended her deceleration burn and flipped the ship back over.

"We're going to pass through the drone's shields right at the edge of the penetration envelope," Leta warned.

"Can't be helped. No time left." Talisha pressed the jump button on her flight control stick. Her fighter decelerated further with a sudden jolt, as if they had hit water. The projection canopy flickered a moment, then came back to life as warning lights flashed and alarms sounded.

"Forward and port shields are down to twenty percent," Leta warned.

"Target their shield emitters, Leta, and open fire!" Talisha instructed her AI as she twisted her flight control stick to the left to bring her nose around toward the drone. "We're inside their damned shields!"

Her Nighthawk fighter's nose swung around, and Talisha pressed and held her firing button, opening up with the plasma cannons in her ship's twin noses. As her fighter yawed about, her first few volleys glanced off the drone's port upper drive module, causing little to no damage. But as she came around and her firing angle became less oblique, the damage inflicted with each energy impact became more pronounced. Within seconds, her bolts of energy were tearing open the drone's drive module, sending debris flying.

"The drone's AI has shut down the upper port drive module to prevent an explosion," Leta reported.

The ship rocked violently as weapons fire from three different point-defense cannons found their shields, lighting them up.

"Target has lost starboard shields," Leta reported as the ship rocked. "Our port shields are down to fifteen percent; forward shields at ten percent. Estimate shield failure in fifteen seconds."

Talisha ceased firing as she rolled her ship over and immediately translated upward, trying to slip under the drone to target its remaining drive section. Again she swung her nose back onto the target, pitching slightly to get her nose cannons lined up.

"Drone is powering up for a jump," Leta warned.

"Already?" Talisha exclaimed.

"The drone's jump fields only extend one point five meters from its surface," Leta warned.

"Fuck!" Talisha exclaimed, her options dwindling and her time about to run out. Blue-white light began spilling out from the drone's jump emitters. Talisha flipped her ship back over so that her topside was toward the drone, jammed her throttles forward, and pitched up toward the drone...hard.

"Collision alert," Leta warned.

"Don't you dare take control!" Talisha ordered as the blue-white light covering the drone flashed just as her fighter slammed into the underside of the drone's last functioning drive module.

Talisha felt her restraints digging into her shoulders as she was thrown to one side. Her canopy flickered several times, turning permanently clear just as her forward console also began to flicker.

More warning alarms sounded, and critical failure lights began flashing.

"We have partially jumped, along with the drone," Leta announced. "We are now on terminal intercept for SilTek and approaching a flak field created by the Aurora."

"Start an overload on the reactor and get us the fuck out of here!" Talisha ordered.

"Initiating immediate reactor overload," Leta acknowledged. "Critical failure in twelve seconds."

Talisha closed her eyes and grabbed the side rails of the cockpit. A split second later, the small doors along the outside of the cockpit opened, and the clamps holding the module in place released.

"Ejecting," Leta announced as the separation boosters kicked in, propelling the cockpit away from the doomed fighter and the drone cruising alongside it.

"Contact!" Kaylah announced from the Aurora's sensor station. "Drone inbound! And a Nighthawk! It's damaged!"

"The drone or the Nighthawk?" Cameron wondered.

"Both!" Kaylah replied. "The drone has no propulsion or maneuvering, and its main power is about to fail."

"Drone is headed for the flak field," Lieutenant Yuati announced.

"What about the Nighthawk?" Cameron asked her sensor officer.

"It's badly damaged," Kaylah replied. "It looks like it collided with... The Nighthawk's reactor is going critical! The pilot is ejecting!"

A white flash appeared on the main view screen some distance away.

"Report!" Cameron demanded.

"The Nighthawk's reactor went critical, taking out the back half of the drone. The warhead is still inbound... Adrift but inbound."

"Target that warhead with everything you've got, Lieutenant," Cameron insisted.

"Targeting warhead," the tactical officer acknowledged. "Firing!"

Within seconds, there was another flash of light on the wrap-around view screen, this one a hundred times larger and significantly brighter.

"Warhead destroyed," the lieutenant reported calmly.

"Threat estimate on the antimatter event?" Cameron asked Kaylah.

"The force of our weapons prevented the device's antiprotons from completely mixing with protons in its reaction mass. There will be some additional gamma radiation filtering down to the surface, but not enough to do much damage. Maybe a few burnt out circuits and some interrupted comms. SilTek's atmosphere is pretty thick."

"What about us?" Cameron wondered.

"Our shields will protect us."

"What about the Nighthawk's cockpit module?" Cameron inquired.

"If her ejection thrusters worked properly, they should propel her far enough away."

"Any sign of her?"

"Not through all of these gamma rays," Kaylah explained. "We're going to be blind for a few minutes."

Cameron sighed. "Comms, let's launch another SAR Reaper to look for her. Hopefully, she was as lucky this time as she was over Volon."

CHAPTER TWELVE

Nathan entered the Voss's common room after squeezing in a nap during the first recharge layover. The last twenty-four hours had been just as tiring as the previous twenty-four, and the drain was beginning to catch up with him.

Nevertheless, he found it hard to sleep for more than a few hours aboard the Voss. His cabin was even smaller than it had been on the Seiiki, and the bed was uncomfortable. He wondered if the XK series had been staffed by Tekans of smaller stature, or if the population was generally of smaller size. Nathan himself was of average height, at least for Terrans. But he was starting to realize that on SilTek, most of the people he had met were a bit shorter than him. He wondered how Loki, who was the tallest among them, was able to sleep in the Voss's racks.

"You didn't get any sleep?" Nathan asked Jessica, who was sitting at the table talking to Loki.

"Loki and I have been swapping stories," she replied. "Catching each other up."

"It's been mostly her catching me up," Loki admitted. "I've been lying in bed for the last week or two while you people have been having all the fun."

"You and I have very different ideas of fun," Nathan joked. "Any word back from the Aurora?"

"About an hour ago," she replied. "You're not going to like the news," Jessica warned, handing her data pad to Nathan.

"Why?" Nathan wondered, taking it from her.

"Apparently, Griogair decided to call your bluff."

Nathan studied the reports on the data pad, his expression becoming more concerned as he read. "I guess it was to be expected," Nathan sighed. "We're going to have to retaliate, though."

"Swipe ahead a few pages," she suggested.

Nathan did so, and his expression changed again. "Nice."

"Four Orochi with full loads," Jessica summarized. "Took out every surface missile launcher they had left. Gunyoki took out two of his new ships as well. They're down to four now, none of them Dusahn."

"How much collateral damage was there?"

"By our brief recon scans, not much," Jessica told him. "Telles is still waiting to hear from his operatives on Takara to confirm. Meanwhile, Griogair is playing it off as an unwarranted act of aggression by an alliance that would see the people of Takara perish as retribution for the revolution against the oppression of the Ta'Akar family."

"Griogair and Galiardi should get together sometime," Nathan commented. "They'd probably have a lot in common."

Vladimir came bursting through the port hatch that led from the port forward bay, with Dylan close on his heels. "Nathan!" he called, spotting his friends at the table. "Bozhe moi!"

"What's wrong?" Nathan asked, a bit worried by his friend's sense of excitement.

"We got the core from Loki's ship working...or Dylan did...or at least the data chip," Vladimir tried to explain.

"Calm down," Nathan urged.

"We swapped the data chip from Loki's flight recorder into one of our Lightnings and then uploaded it into a data pad," Dylan explained. "There was a lot of lost data, but we got enough."

"You are not going to believe what happened,"

Vladimir insisted, taking a seat at the table next to Loki. "How are you feeling, my friend?" he asked Loki, looking him over.

"Uh, okay...I guess."

"Vlad, what the hell is going on?" Nathan inquired.

Vladimir looked at Nathan, taking a deep breath. "Loki was in the jump for five days."

"What are you talking about?" Nathan asked.

"Is that even possible?" Jessica wondered.

"An hour ago, I would have said no," Vladimir admitted. "The flight data from Loki's P-Seventy-Two is chronologically exact up to the moment that he jumped through the mountain. The very next entry, which notes the moment that he came out of that jump, every data point's time stamp is one hundred and thirty-seven hours and eighteen minutes off. He was stuck in that jump the entire time."

"Wait, you said he jumped through the mountain," Nathan realized. "I thought he just grazed the top of it."

"No, he jumped through it," Vladimir insisted. "His navigation logs show that he struck the mountain at least fifty meters below its summit, and he struck it at the precise moment of his jump."

"That's not possible," Jessica argued. "You can't jump through solid matter."

"That's not entirely correct," Vladimir pointed out. "We jump through matter every time we jump. It's just that the mass of that matter is insignificant compared to our own mass."

"I'm no physicist, but that doesn't make sense to me," Loki argued. "That mountain had a lot more mass than my Lightning."

"Your jump drive was going in and out of about six different failure modes just before your jump,"

Vladimir explained. "That could have something to do with it."

"How could a failing jump drive make it able to jump through a mountain?" Nathan wondered.

"I don't know," Vladimir admitted. "Truth be told, I don't really understand how the jump drive actually works; at least, not from a physics standpoint. Just don't tell Abby I said that. It could have something to do with when the jump fields actually formed around Loki's ship. Perhaps they interacted with the mass of the mountain in some way. Maybe some of the mountain was included within his fields."

"Wouldn't some of the mountain come out of the jump with me, then?" Loki theorized. "There was no debris around me that I remember."

"I don't know."

"If you don't know, then how can you be sure of anything?" Jessica postulated. "How do we even know the time stamps on that log are correct?"

"Could the jump have screwed up his ship's chronometer?" Nathan suggested.

"Time isn't kept by a chronometer," Vladimir replied. "It's calculated by the ship's computers. If something affected his fighter's computers enough to put it that far out of time-sync, all kinds of other problems would have been occurring."

Nathan sighed. "It just seems far more likely that Loki was out longer than he thought."

"I know how long I was out," Loki insisted. "Udo told me."

"He could've been lying," Jessica suggested.

"He could have, but to what end?" Loki challenged.

"You aren't understanding what I'm saying here," Vladimir insisted. "The time stamps are accurate. If they weren't, we'd be able to tell."

"He's right, Captain," Dylan agreed.

"How can you be sure?" Jessica challenged.

"It's a computer thing," Dylan explained. "Trust me on this."

"So not only did Loki jump through a mountain, but he also traveled forward in time," Nathan surmised.

Vladimir became excited again, his friend finally realizing what he was trying to tell him. "Precisely!"

Nathan still wasn't as excited as Vladimir. "We'll forward all of this to Abby and see what she makes of it," Nathan decided.

Vladimir rolled his eyes. "At least Abby will be properly excited."

"Oh I'm properly excited," Loki assured him.

"Why?" Jessica wondered.

"Are you kidding?" Loki chuckled. "I finally did something more impossible than Josh. I can't wait to rub it in his face."

* * *

"I take it you've read Nathan's latest communiqué," Cameron said as General Telles entered her ready room.

"I have," he replied, closing the hatch behind him. "Excellent news about Mister Sheehan."

"Yes it is," Cameron agreed. "What did you think of Mister Rusayev's idea?"

"It is an ambitious plan."

"Then you don't think it's a good idea?"

"The Ghatazhak can seize control of the network hubs, and we can hold them long enough to get the message out. The real question is how the people of Earth will react. If our current intelligence is correct, and the population is split, this may not solve anything."

"Heir-to-office has never been challenged since it was instituted over a century ago," Cameron insisted. "I can't imagine it would be now."

"There are many variables at play at the moment, none of which were ever in play before," the general explained. "The lingering hatred of the Jung being the most influential."

"As powerful as hatred and vengeance can be, I believe that most people prefer peace and security over violence and uncertainty."

"While I certainly hope you are correct," the general assured her, "in my experience, humanity is more often ruled by emotion than by intellect."

Cameron sighed, thinking for a moment. "If Miri steps up to claim heir-to-office rights, Galiardi will undoubtedly challenge her, and he'll tell any lie possible to avoid having to hand over power."

"Which is why her claim must be backed up by threat of force," the general replied.

Cameron was caught off guard. "What force?"

"We must bring everything we have to back her," he explained. "Then, if Admiral Galiardi chooses to risk the very forces that the Earth would need to defend itself against the Jung rather than step down while the courts decide, he will be committing a criminal act himself. Under Sol Alliance fleet regulations, his own officers would be forced to arrest him."

"Assuming he hasn't got them all in his back pocket by now."

"Was it not you who expressed faith in your fellow Terrans?" the general stated.

"We may not have enough firepower to challenge the Sol Alliance," Cameron told him. "And Nathan is not going to want to fight our own people."

"If Nathan truly believes in what we are trying to

achieve, he will find it within himself to do whatever is needed. Even if that means killing fellow Terrans."

Cameron sighed again. "That's an order I hope I never have to give."

* * *

Shortly after the Voss touched down on SilTek, at what was now being referred to as the 'XK yards', Nathan, Jessica, and Loki disembarked.

"Welcome back, Cap..." Del stopped mid-sentence, disbelief on his face at the sight of Loki coming down the Voss's ramp. "I thought..."

"Long story," Nathan told him. He turned to Jessica. "I've been saying that a lot lately, haven't I?"

"Well I'm glad to see you're not dead after all, Loki," Del congratulated.

"Can you arrange transport to your nearest medical center?" Nathan asked Del. "I'd like Loki to get examined and treated."

"Of course," Del assured him, turning to one of his assistants. "Jader, get Mister Sheehan to the health center."

"Right away," Del's assistant promised. "Mister Sheehan, welcome back. Follow me."

"Don't leave without me," Loki told Nathan.

"Not a chance," Nathan promised. "Get back as soon as you can." Nathan looked about the yard, noticing that the second XK was gone. "You already launched the second XK?"

"She launched four days ago. Captain Nash has been conducting training maneuvers. He should be back later today. He named his ship the Ancot."

"Wasn't that ahead of schedule?"

"Like I said the last time you were here, we've got volunteers showing up by the dozens. Captain Roselle's XK should be ready in three days. He plans to name her the Ellison. Captain Kainan's ship, the Lawrence, will be ready by the end of next week. With the number of volunteers we have now, we should be able to put out one XK per week."

"That may present a problem," Nathan admitted. "We may not be able to come up with qualified crews that quickly, let alone train them."

"I may be able to help you with that," Del replied. "Just about every person working in this yard is willing to serve as crew on these ships. Many of them know every system in the XK like the backs of their hands. There's really only one crew position that we lack qualified people to fill: commanding officers."

"Those I can provide," Nathan assured him, smiling. "What about pilots? Can your people fly these things?"

"The XKs' AIs can fly the ships as well as any human, probably better. So they can learn as they go."

"Don't say that around Josh," Jessica warned.

"How are we going to get everyone trained so quickly though?" Nathan wondered.

"We used our AIs to adapt the Night Runner game sim into a training sim. Roselle's crew is using it as we speak. It's about as real as you can get. We've got the bugs in the P-Seventy-Two sim hammered out as well. We just needed help programming combat tactics for the simulated opponents."

"Needed?" Nathan wondered.

"I contacted Captain Taylor, and she loaned us Commander Verbeek for a couple of days. Now we have realistic simulations for Dusahn, Jung, EDF, you name it. He also helped us set up training regimens to teach our Lightning pilots basic combat tactics."

"That was good thinking," Nathan complimented.

"We've even started installing sim hubs in all the bunks, so that crew members can train as much as they want."

Nathan shook his head in disbelief. "You're constantly surprising me, Mister Shelton, and in a good way."

"Thank you, Captain," Del replied. "I'm just excited to be doing something positive to protect my world. We've been harassed by the Benicasi and their like for far too long. Just being able to do something...I can't even describe how good that feels. If you hadn't come to our world, I don't know if we ever would have gotten that bitch Batista to take action."

Nathan put his hand on the young man's shoulder. "Hopefully, someday, such concerns will be long forgotten...by everyone."

* * *

Commander Jexx was afraid to speak. He had never seen such anger on his leader's face. He had just murdered one of his servants with his bare hands upon hearing of the failure to destroy SilTek, and he looked as if he was ready to do it again.

The commander stood silently as Lord Dusahn slowly regained his composure. His leader looked down at the servant's lifeless corpse without a single glimmer of remorse. It was as if killing someone had brought him balance; as if he needed it in the same way as one needs air, water, and food. Such was the way of the Dusahn. A warrior caste where killing was life and death held honor.

The commander had never understood the Dusahn philosophy. It was so different from that of his Truunian mother. She, like all Truunians, was a devout pacifist. Life was all that mattered to them, and no crime, no matter how heinous, warranted death. Truunians would rather die than take the life of another.

Of course, their devotion to non-violence had been their undoing. The Dusahn had swept through the Truunians's non-lethal defenses in minutes, extracting resources from their world for years before moving on. It was their way. The strong took all that they needed from the weak, without regard to life.

Commander Jexx had been taken from his mother by his Dusahn father at an early age, before his mother's Truunian beliefs could take permanent hold. But his father had little interest in raising a child, even a male child. In fact, the only reason he had been taken was because Lord Dusahn ordered it. All the half-breed sons of Dusahn fathers were taken and raised by pure-blooded Dusahn women.

But Commander Jexx had secretly studied the Truunian culture. It was his only connection to his mother. He had always felt more Truunian than Dusahn. As a half-breed, he had always been relegated to the lower classes of the empire. It was only recently that he had been promoted to lieutenant, and even then, only because the empire was running out of pure-blooded officers.

And now he stood before the leader of the empire, trying not to appear terrified. Somehow, he had managed to escape the same fate as those who had come before him, despite the string of failures the empire had suffered in recent weeks. The best he could figure was that his ability to tell his leader the truth, rather than what he wanted to hear, was what had kept him alive.

But doing so was becoming increasingly difficult. Today was the first time his leader had killed someone else, an innocent servant, when it was obviously the commander who had been the object of his anger. For that, he felt an incredible amount of guilt.

But had he not been complicit in other far more hideous acts?

"We will make more drones," Lord Dusahn finally said, still seething.

"We barely have enough comm-drones left to stay in touch with the worlds we still control." The commander's response had been automatic and surprising.

"Then we will fit fighters with antimatter warheads."

"We have no more antimatter," Commander Jexx replied. There was no use in lying to his leader at this point. He would either be executed or not. Lately, he was finding it difficult to care.

"Then we will make more of it."

"That will take time, my lord. Perhaps years."

"Then we will use nuclear warheads," Lord Dusahn stated.

"We have very few of those as well," Commander Jexx replied. "The only way we would be able to get them in close enough to avoid intercept would be to have our pilots jump them into the atmosphere at extremely low altitudes. It would take dozens of warheads to interrupt their industry and support of the alliance. We would be sacrificing our only means of defense against an all-out attack for nothing more than to mend our wounded pride."

"Careful, Commander," Lord Dusahn warned.

"It is my duty as a Dusahn officer to speak honestly with my superiors, regardless of the consequences," the commander replied, hoping to avoid joining the servant on the floor. "To do less would dishonor both my father and the empire I serve."

Lord Dusahn glared at the commander a moment, studying him. "I take it you have more to say?"

"I do," the commander admitted. His gaze shifted to the dead servant.

Lord Dusahn noticed the young man's hesitation. "Speak without fear of retribution," he ordered.

Commander Jexx took a deep breath, summoning all his courage. "There are two ways to ensure that our empire survives," he began. "Either we throw everything we have at our enemy and hope for the best, or we play the long game, building up our forces and our technology to the point that our future is assured. The Takar system is rich with resources. We have everything we need, including a highly technical industrial infrastructure and workforce. All we have to do is keep those we rule happy and productive, and in time, we will prevail."

Lord Dusahn's eyes narrowed. "He threatened me," he replied. "He threatened me. I cannot let that challenge go unanswered. I will lose credibility as a leader."

"I am not suggesting that you do, my lord," Commander Jexx explained. "I am simply asking that you wait until you can answer that challenge without risking the empire. Our people wandered the galaxy for centuries in search of worlds from which to build an empire. This system is the first that can do more than just keep us alive. It was a mistake for us to attempt expansion too quickly. We must hold this world long enough to rebuild our forces and make ourselves invincible."

Lord Dusahn stood there, seething with anger. "We cannot allow our enemy to believe that they have us backed into a corner. We will rebuild our ZPED manufacturing capabilities, and we will create new drones capable of reaching SilTek more quickly." He looked the young commander directly in the eyes. "I will see SilTek destroyed."

Commander Jexx had no choice. "Yes, my lord," he replied, bowing his head as he backed toward the door.

A wave of despair washed over the commander as he exited his leader's office and closed the door behind him. He had failed to reason with him. He had managed to survive, but he had accomplished nothing. The empire he served was headed for disaster, and he knew it. Even worse, it seemed there was nothing he could do to stop it. And now that he was Lord Dusahn's right-hand man, his own death was certain, either at the hands of their enemy or at the hands of his own leader.

* * *

Nathan followed Miri out onto the back patio of her residence on SilTek. "Wow," he muttered.

"What?"

"I didn't realize how nice it was out here," Nathan admitted.

"You haven't been out here before?" Miri wondered.

"I haven't. I was always pressed for time."

"And you're not now?"

"No, I am," Nathan replied. "We're jumping to the Aurora in the morning."

Miri led him out to the lounge chairs under the gazebo next to the pool. Nathan offered his hand, expecting her to have difficulty sitting down, but she waved him off.

"I see you're getting better," Nathan commented, taking a seat himself.

"I'm getting about more easily," Miri explained. "I still get tired more quickly than I'd like, but that's getting better as well. Luckily, the physical therapy people here are absolute slave drivers."

"Well it's good to see you making such progress."

"I heard about Loki," Miri said. "Such wonderful news."

"Who told you about Loki?" Nathan wondered.

"Jessica came by earlier to check on security. I was surprised that you hadn't come with her."

"I had to review the latest draft of the alliance charter with Caitrin," Nathan explained, looking around as if looking for a way to lead into the next topic.

His uncertainty didn't go unnoticed. "Yes," Miri stated.

Nathan looked confused. "Yes, what?"

"Yes, I'll do it."

Relief washed over him, quickly replaced by irritation. "Jessica?"

"Of course."

"I swear, that girl has never understood chain of command."

"Oh she understands it," she insisted. "She just doesn't care." Miri noticed Nathan's frustration. "She knew you'd struggle to ask me."

"You may want to give it some thought before you decide," Nathan urged.

"I have, and the answer is still yes."

"It's a lot of risk and a lot of hard work."

"I was chief of staff, remember?" Miri said. "I know exactly how hard the job is. Besides, there's less than a year before the next scheduled election. If it's too much for me, I don't have to run."

"It's not just the stress of the job that I'm worried

about. The mission will be risky. We're talking about jumping to a heavily defended planet for the purpose of overturning its government. And don't think for a moment that your rights under heir-to-office will stop them from killing you if they can."

"The Ghatazhak will protect me."

"Yes they will," Nathan agreed. "But they can't protect you from everything. If Galiardi decides to play rough and send a battlefield nuke at you, it's over, and your kids will have no one."

"They'll have you," she insisted.

"Assuming I survive."

"You always do."

"You need to be realistic about this, Miri."

"I'm just trying to keep it light, Nathan."

"There's nothing light about it."

"Look," she told him, "I know exactly what I'm getting into. And I damn sure know the risks."

"Then I guess I just don't understand why."

"I guess it's my way of avenging pop's assassination."

"The chances of being able to prove that Galiardi ordered his assassination are slim," Nathan warned. "If we're lucky, he'll just step down once you exercise your rights."

"You think he might refuse?"

"I think he'll do anything possible to avoid having to relinquish power before he accomplishes his ultimate goals."

"Which are?"

"At the very least, the destruction of the Jung Empire," Nathan replied.

"And at the most?" Miri inquired.

Nathan thought for a moment, letting out a long sigh. "I don't rightly know," he admitted. "However, nature abhors a vacuum, and history is full of examples where military leaders used their victories as a stepping-stone to greater power."

"You think he wants to create his own empire?"

"I don't know what he plans to do," Nathan told her. "All I know is that he is willing to do whatever he feels is necessary. Even worse, he believes he's justified in doing so. That's what makes him so dangerous."

"Perhaps that is why I want to exercise my rights of heir-to-office," Miri surmised. "You know, our father went to great lengths to prevent Galiardi from starting another war. It was a constant battle between them."

"Do you really want to have to deal with that?" Nathan asked.

"Are you kidding? My first act will be to fire his ass and then open up an investigation into the assassination of our father and sisters."

"You do realize what a shitstorm you'll be creating if you do so."

"Tough," Miri replied defiantly. "From what you said, our people are already divided. At least this way, they'll be divided because of the truth instead of a pack of lies."

Nathan smiled.

"What are you smiling about?" she wondered.

"My spitfire of a sister is back."

* * *

Nathan entered the Aurora's command briefing room, heading directly to his seat. "As you were," he instructed before anyone had the chance to rise. "I'd like to thank all of you for coming on such short notice," he began. "I know you are all busy, and some of you had to travel a considerable distance to be here."

"Not like it took that long," Deliza commented, smiling. "Thanks to Captain Nash."

"It was on my way," Robert said, tipping his head toward Nathan.

Nathan smiled as well. "Nevertheless, I appreciate that I may have interrupted your demanding schedules." Nathan took a breath before continuing. "I'd like to start by announcing, for any of you who might not have heard the news, that Loki Sheehan is alive and well. He has been cleared by both SilTek and Rakuen medical and is currently spending time with his daughter on Rakuen while he recovers from his injuries." Nathan looked around the room, expecting at least a few surprised looks, but saw none. "I guess the news got around faster than I thought."

"Commander Kamenetskiy sent me the logs from Loki's P-Seventy-Two," Abby explained.

"And Abby shared them with me," Deliza added.

Nathan turned to Commander Verbeek, his CAG, who also did not appear surprised by the news. "Commander?"

"Are you kidding?" the commander replied. "When a lost pilot turns out to be alive, every pilot in the fleet hears about it within minutes. It's a morale thing."

Nathan nodded his understanding, turning to Abby as he moved on. "Any idea what caused him to be stuck in the jump for so long?"

Abby laughed. "Not a clue. There are so many variables to consider, I don't even know where to start. The mass of the mountain, the timing of the jump in relation to his impact with the mountain, the various failure modes of his jump drive, the fact that his reactor was surging at the time—it could take a lifetime to figure out. I'm more interested in how he managed to pass through the mountain, let alone why his jump field decay rate was so drastically extended."

"Is it worth pursuing?" Nathan wondered. "Are there any practical applications?"

"Most definitely," she assured him without hesitation. "Thus far, we've been extending our jump range by increasing the amount of power dumped into the jump field at the moment of transition, under the assumption that doing so slows the decay rate. The longer it takes for the jump field to decay to the point of collapse and conversion, the farther the jump. The data from Loki's logs brings all of that into question. What if we could slow the decay rate without having to increase the amount of energy used? The distance we could jump could be infinite for all we know."

"Sounds like it will take quite some time to figure out," Nathan surmised.

"Yes," Abby agreed, "but the sooner we get started the better. We've already reached the maximum amount of instant power we can create. The only way we currently have to increase our jump range is to install multiple jump drives and energy banks. Imagine being able to jump any distance and then jump back, all without having to worry about recharge times. The Aurora could literally protect every member system at the same time, even if those worlds were thousands of light years apart."

"I understand the implications, Doctor," Nathan assured her. "Trust me, it will be researched, but not until after the current situation has been resolved."

Abby nodded her understanding, saying nothing further.

Nathan turned to General Telles next. "General, have you had a chance to look over the intelligence from Rusayev's people and review their suggestions?"

"Mister Rusayev's assessment that the risks outweigh the possible rewards is correct," the general replied with his usual measured demeanor. "Were the Ghatazhak to take on this task, the risks would be greatly reduced. I assume you have spoken with your sister?"

Nathan sighed. "I have. She insists on claiming her right of heir-to-office."

"That definitely changes the risk-reward balance. However, the plan does present several challenges. First, there are twelve hubs that must be taken simultaneously. If any one hub avoids capture, the message will take considerably longer to propagate to that part of the world from the other hubs. This delay would make it possible for Galiardi's people to intercept the message and block its distribution or even alter the message, creating further confusion. Second, it will take a minimum of seventy-two Ghatazhak, which leaves us with very few reserves should something go awry. Lastly, extrication, should it become necessary, will also be difficult. The Earth Defense Force has an ample supply of Super Eagle fighters stationed on the surface, which they will undoubtedly dispatch the moment they learn of our arrival."

"That's why I think we need a diversion," Nathan stated.

"Maybe we can use the insurgents? Have them attack a different target?" Jessica suggested.

"You're thinking too small," Nathan replied.

"Besides, I thought we might use the insurgents to coordinate the assembly of crowds to surround the net-hubs. The presence of hundreds if not thousands of civilians would greatly limit Galiardi's options out of fear of negative publicity. Furthermore, he might have a hard time getting his officer to execute an attack against their own people."

"The presence of civilian crowds might be useful," General Telles agreed. "Many on Earth still distrust the Ghatazhak due to that one unavoidable incident. However, I have to wonder how much we can trust Rusayev and his people, considering the stakes."

"We can trust him," Vladimir insisted.

"I am aware of your history with Mister Rusayev, but the question still stands," the general insisted. "If those crowds take even the slightest hostile action, it will give Galiardi's forces the excuse they need to use deadly force."

"Lyoha will not betray us."

"I believe Vladimir is correct," Nathan stated. "However, using them to coordinate crowd support poses a lower risk to our forces than if they were fighting with us side by side."

General Telles nodded agreement.

"He will not betray us," Vladimir repeated.

Nathan chose to push past the issue. "We should also have the insurgents set up vid-cams at all sites and transmit their feeds to each hub. We need to show the presence of the crowds to the public. That will further prevent Galiardi from conducting strikes against them. The whole purpose of capturing the hubs is to replace Galiardi's propaganda with truth."

"What if the people still want Galiardi to destroy the Jung?" Cameron wondered.

"I'm betting they won't," Nathan replied. "Either

way, Galiardi has to be removed from power before it's too late."

"The crowds will need to be staged close enough to the hubs to get to them before Galiardi's QRT units arrive, but still be far enough way so as not to be noticed," Jessica pointed out.

"That could be a problem," Cameron stated. "Some of those hubs are nowhere near a population center."

"Rusayev's people will have to figure that one out," Nathan told her. "Maybe they can arrange buses or something? Have them pre-loaded and rolling. Even if we only take control of half the hubs, it's better than nothing. Yes, it will take a lot longer for the message to get to everyone, and yes, Galiardi will have time to block, alter, or at least counter the message, but the message will get out."

"The more time it takes for the message to get out, the greater the chance that force will be needed to take down Galiardi," the general warned. "It is my understanding that the Earth's president has the authority to use such force against a military leader who refuses to follow orders."

"Yes, but it's never been needed," Nathan replied. "At least not since the original formation of the Earth Defense Force."

"Currently, half of the Earth's population is against Galiardi and his campaign against the Jung Empire," the general explained. "The legal claim of heir-to-office may be enough to force the admiral to step down, or for one of his aides to place him under arrest until the situation can be sorted out."

Nathan looked at Cameron. "If you were a subordinate standing next to Galiardi when Miri exercised her right of heir-to-office, and the admiral refused to honor her claim, would you arrest him?"

"Of course," Cameron replied. "But I'm a stickler for procedure. However, the result of that action would depend on whether or not the officers around me supported my decision."

"It may become necessary for your sister to order the use of force against her own military," the general warned. "Is she capable of issuing that order?"

"Let's hope it doesn't come to that," Nathan replied.

"There is also the problem with insertion," General Telles continued. "Two recent intrusions are going to put the EDF's sensor net on full alert. They are likely to have increased patrols in the planet's atmosphere as well. If we jump in multiple insertion ships at once, they will notice, and they will put all their forces on alert. Even if we are able to get boots inside every net-hub's defense perimeter, holding them long enough to get the message out may prove more difficult and will increase the risk to Miri. If we are to insert the Ghatazhak covertly and maintain the element of surprise, we will have to conduct space jumps from well outside the system."

"You want to space-jump from outside the Sol system?" Nathan asked in disbelief.

"I believe I said well outside the system."

"Is that even possible?" Nathan wondered. "Weren't the mark two suits designed for micro-jumps?"

Mister Ayseron leaned forward, holding up a single finger. "If I may, Captain?"

Nathan nodded.

"The AIs in the mark two CAP systems are perfectly capable of calculating jumps of any distance," the SilTek engineer began. "In this case, as long as the jumpers are put on the proper trajectory at the proper speed by the deployment vessel, accuracy is not the issue, since the insertion jumps would terminate in Earth's upper atmosphere. The problem is power. The mass of enough energy cells to power such a jump would exceed the safe carrying capacity of the jumpers' parachutes, even with the shock protection of the CAP system."

"Couldn't they drop them during freefall, before they open their chutes?" Cameron suggested.

"Some of them might survive the impact," Lieutenant Commander Shinoda pointed out. "That would put advanced jump tech into the hands of Galiardi's people."

Talisha Sane had been silent the entire time. She had never attended a command briefing and felt a little intimidated. "Could the power packs be detonated during freefall?" she managed to get out. "After separation of course."

"The detonations might be detected," Cameron replied.

"But we're only talking about seconds, right?" Talisha continued. "They arrive, jettison their energy packs, pop their chutes, and then jump down to the hubs. The detonations could take place after the attack has already started."

"That could work," Jessica agreed.

Talisha suddenly felt a little more confident.

"Or you could just leave the energy packs behind to begin with," Deliza interjected.

Mister Ayseron was shocked. "That makes no sense whatsoever," he sputtered. "We need the additional energy banks to make the jump."

"The energy in the packs, yes, but not the packs themselves," Deliza defended.

Mister Ayseron was still confused by her idea. "What?"

Deliza rolled her eyes. The solution seemed so obvious to her. "Detach the packs from the jumpers but leave them connected with a tether. The tether gets cut by the jump event, leaving the packs drifting in space. The energy transfer is near-instantaneous, so most of the energy will reach the mark two's emitters before the power umbilical is severed."

"That's insane!" the engineer exclaimed.

"Is it?" Deliza challenged.

"You could even umbilical them to the delivery ship," Abby suggested. "Then you wouldn't even need the energy packs."

"Each XK has to deploy three teams," Nathan explained, "each of them at a different position in space. So it would have to be energy packs, since the teams have to coast for some time before jumping." He looked at Ayseron. "Can this actually work?"

Mister Ayseron thought for a moment. It was obvious he didn't like the idea. "We'd have to calculate the percentage of energy transfer loss due to the severing of the umbilical a split second before the jump..."

"And adjust the jump calculations accordingly," Deliza added, finishing his thought.

"Assuming testing proves the loss rate to be consistent, yes. It might actually work. It's still insane, though."

"Sometimes insane ideas work. I assume you three can figure it out?"

"We'll get started immediately," Abby promised.

"There is still the matter of a diversion," General Telles reminded Nathan.

"The diversion will come one minute after your

forces touch down," Nathan explained. "That will give Galiardi time to go into domestic terrorism mode. Then we jump into the system with everything we can muster. The sudden shifting of gears will cause confusion and conflict among division and unit commanders. With any luck, he'll believe the attacks against the hubs are the diversion, and that the diversion is the real attack."

"The forces used to defend the hubs are different than those used to defend the system," General Telles pointed out.

"Only partially," Nathan replied.

"He's right," Cameron interjected. "If we send a few hundred Gunyoki and Nighthawks at them, backed up by the Aurora, the Glendanon, and the Orochi, he'll likely divert the Super Eagles being used to fly cover for the QRTs to help with the intercept, especially if the majority of our fighters jump close in."

"As soon as the initial broadcast is out, we demand that Galiardi step down as acting president and immediately hand power to Miri, or we will take him out with force," Nathan stated.

"You don't really plan on using force against our own people, do you?" Cameron inquired.

"Not if I can avoid it," Nathan assured her. "That's where we need to get creative. We need to figure out how to take EDF forces out of the game without killing anyone, and preferably without inflicting too much damage. The last thing I want is to disable their fleet and leave them defenseless."

"That's not going to be easy," Cameron warned.

"We should consider using Subvert's swarm-bot technology," Deliza suggested.

"Aren't those designed to take out shield emitters?" Jessica wondered.

"Yes, but you can program them to attack any system, as long as you know where it is located. Shield emitters, jump field emitters, sensor arrays, even guns. Their only downside is that they must receive their target programming before release."

"Our current shield-penetrating missiles carry standard explosive warheads," Cameron stated. "They're not so much designed to take out a shield as they are to just inflict general damage to the target, which usually leads to the collapse of the shield segment. If we could modify them to carry swarm-bots instead, we could take out just their shield emitters without damaging the rest of the target."

"Take out enough of their shields, and they'll think twice about standing their ground," Jessica stated. "What if we take out their jump drives as well?"

"I'd prefer to only take down their shields," Nathan insisted. "Once they realize their shields won't protect them, there's a chance they may withdraw. Each of those captains still has a duty to protect Earth, and they can't do so if they're out of commission."

"It all sounds great, but the Cape Town has two complete shield arrays," Lieutenant Commander Shinoda warned. "That's over two hundred shield emitters. Her jump array has a redundant backup as well."

"Swarm-bots are cheap and quick to replicate," Deliza told them. "If we task all our replicators, we can crank out tens of thousands of them in a matter of days."

"Could the swarm-bots be programmed to take out the Cape Town's main guns?" Cameron wondered.

"I don't see why not," Deliza replied. "We'd need the specs on her guns so we could figure out the most efficient way to disable them. I assume you want them disabled with as little total damage as possible."

"That's the idea," Nathan replied.

"We have the basic specs on the Cape Town. Just not the classified stuff," the lieutenant commander stated.

"The Cape Town's big guns are still projectile-based rail guns," Cameron explained. "They have incredible range and accuracy, and can fire a wide array of projectile types, but nothing about them is classified."

"What about their point-defenses?" Jessica wondered.

"Standard point-defense, pulse plasma, just like ours," Cameron replied. "But they also have the new Scorpion missile defense cannons. Extremely high fire rate and very good tracking systems. We're going to have to jump our shield busters in extremely close to get past them."

"We don't know what the Cape Town's shield expansion range is, either," the lieutenant commander added. "That's still classified."

"I have a friend who was on the development team for those shields," Abby said. "He never spoke about the project, but I had several meetings with him to discuss the effects of sustained, high-energy fields running in close proximity. They may have been working on multi-layered shielding."

"For all we know, that second shield array I spoke of may be part of that," Cameron suggested.

"Perhaps we should broadcast the message to the Cape Town as well?" Lieutenant Commander

Shinoda suggested. "Maybe her captain or her senior officers will be swayed, and she'll stand down."

"It certainly won't hurt, but I wouldn't count on it," Cameron warned.

"You're probably right," Nathan agreed. "But we should consider broadcasting the message to all EDF forces. The more doubt we can create, the better." Nathan noticed that Commander Verbeek looked concerned. "Something on your mind, Verbee?"

"I'm worried about our Super Eagles mixing it up with theirs. Even with some sort of customized IFF transponders, the risk of misidentifying someone will be high. That extra hesitation can get people killed."

"Actually, I was thinking of having your pilots fly the P-Seventy-Twos down low to provide air support for the Ghatazhak."

"That would help, but you're still asking us to go up against people we once flew with. The Eagle-driver community is pretty close-knit."

"Hopefully it won't come to that," Nathan replied. "Besides, if my plan works, most of the EDF's Eagles will be busy chasing the Gunyoki."

That caught Vol Kaguchi's attention. "How many Gunyoki will you require?"

"How many do you have?"

"Three hundred and twelve are in service. Two hundred of them have been fitted with grav-lift systems. Fifty of those are currently stationed on Orswella."

"We'll take them all," Nathan replied.

"That will leave the Orochi without escorts," Vol warned.

"The Orochi are coming with us."

Aiden looked at Nathan. "We are?" He turned to

Commander Verbeek, who was sitting next to him. "I was wondering why I was here."

"The Orochi will be the key to avoiding a full-blown gunfight," Nathan explained. "We'll load up your ships with shield busters loaded with swarm-bots. But your ships will be launching from the engagement area. The more ships they see, the better chance we have of getting them to stand down without a shooting war."

"My ships?" Aiden wondered.

"Captain Nash says you're ready for a little more responsibility," Nathan replied. "With Nash, Roselle, and Kainan flying XKs, you're the most experienced Orochi captain we have."

"Well that's frightening," Aiden muttered to himself. He looked at Captain Nash. "Thanks a lot."

Robert smiled. "You're welcome."

"You'll do fine," Nathan assured him.

"So the Rogen and Orswellan systems will be completely undefended," Vol surmised.

"Both systems have surface-based jump missile launchers and complex detection grids," Nathan reminded him. "The Dusahn's newly acquired ships are all in the Takar system at the moment, most of them undergoing upgrades. After our recent retaliatory attack, they don't dare move them out of the Takar system. Even if they did, it would take them days to reach the Rogen system, by which time we'll be back."

"Their octos can reach us in just under a day," Vol pointed out.

"They've only got about thirty of them left," Lieutenant Commander Shinoda told him. "That's not enough firepower to attack a planet, especially one that's got jump missiles and anti-aircraft batteries. They're not going to risk them just to harass someone."

"We will make sure the Glendanon and the Aurora are both fully charged before the mission begins. That way, we'll have enough energy to jump back to defend any member world should the need arise," Nathan assured the Gunyoki commander.

"I assure you, Captain, the Dusahn aren't going to go on the offensive any time soon," the lieutenant commander insisted. "Based on our recon flights, it will take them a few weeks to finish the upgrades on just their first two ships."

"Could they not send drones, like they did to SilTek?" Vol wondered.

"They don't have any left, and it will take time to build them," Lieutenant Commander Shinoda insisted. "Now is the safest time for our forces to be away."

"I pray that you are correct, Lieutenant Commander."

"If we're going to take down the Dusahn, we all have to take risks," Nathan insisted.

"Of course," Vol agreed, bowing his head respectfully.

"Based on all available intel, the only world at risk of attack during our brief absence is Corinair," Lieutenant Commander Shinoda stated confidently. "The Dusahn could easily jump over, launch a bunch of missiles, and jump back, and there's a good chance that some of them could make it to their targets. Corinair is still a long way from having a complete defense grid."

"Lord Dusahn is an egomaniac and a narcissist, but he isn't stupid," Nathan insisted. "He knows that if he keeps lashing out at our allies, sooner or later we're going to put a missile right down his chimney and take our chances with those antimatter doomsday warheads he's got the planet wired with."

"How are we going to get all these forces to the Sol sector?" Robert wondered.

"Gunyoki, Nighthawks, and Lightnings will be ferried using the Glendanon, Quawli, Manamu, Inman, and Gervais," Nathan explained. "The Forenta will be coming along as well. You can never have too much propellant available. The flatbeds Magruder, Kenna, Golity, and Scroggin have all finished their refits and will be serving as gunboats. Each has been fitted with four plasma turrets and a single quad jump missile launcher. All of these ships and the Orochi will be departing four days ahead of us and should be in position at the rally point by the time the Aurora and the Glendanon jump out to meet them. That will keep a significant amount of our Gunyoki here until hours before mission zero."

"I would suggest that we load the Nighthawks and Gunyoki stationed on Corinair onto the Glendanon, and do so at the last possible moment," Commander Verbeek suggested. "That way, Corinair will be without fighter cover for as brief a time as possible."

"Good thinking," Nathan agreed.

"We intercept about ninety percent of the Dusahn's recon flights," Lieutenant Commander Shinoda reported. "They fly fairly direct routes and rarely recon the far side of Corinair. If the Gunyoki and the Nighthawks jump in close to the Glendanon while she is on the far side of Corinair, the chances of the Dusahn recon flights detecting their departure will be low."

"What about when they don't see them on the ground?" Jessica wondered.

"The Corinari erected blast shelters over all the fighter parking spots on the airfield," Commander Verbeek reported. "The Dusahn haven't been able to detect which ones are or are not occupied for more than a week now."

"Work up an op for that," Nathan instructed. "Gunyoki and Nighthawks will go to the Glendanon. We'll pick up all the Lightnings from SilTek."

"We have a few more Corinari pilots than we have ships," the commander added. "I can check them out in our Eagles before we go. It won't be much, but they'll be better than nothing."

"See to it," Nathan agreed. "We brought a Lightning training simulator with us from SilTek. Get your pilots plugged into it as soon as possible."

"Yes sir," the commander replied.

"What role will the XKs play?" Robert asked Nathan.

"The XKs will be responsible for deploying the Ghatazhak strike teams as well as extracting them should it become necessary," Nathan told him. "They are perfect for hot LZ extraction. They can take a pounding, and their aft shields can be dropped independently of the other shield segments, keeping the ship protected during the extraction."

"So we're not going to be committed to the shooting war?" Robert surmised. "Assuming it comes to that, of course."

"After deploying the Ghatazhak, the XKs will return to the rally point and jump in with the rest of the fleet. Again, the greater the show of strength, the better," Nathan explained. "But if any of our strike teams on the ground call for extraction, that will be the XK's priority." Nathan looked around the room, noticing the worried looks on everyone's faces. "I'm not going to pretend this doesn't have the potential to turn ugly really fast. In fact, we're bringing the Mystic Empress along as well, in case we do take heavy casualties. But the fact is, we can't defeat the Dusahn without the help of the Jung, and that means we have to stop Galiardi's assault. If we don't, the Jung will execute the Tonba-Hon-Venar, and the Earth and Nor-Patri will be destroyed. We cannot let that happen."

"I doubt that anyone here disagrees with you, Captain," General Telles assured him.

"Damn straight," Jessica agreed. "Let's go kick Galiardi's ass."

* * *

"Sasha just returned," Igor reported as he entered Aleksi's office. "A comm-drone has arrived."

"I take it the capture system worked correctly."

"Perfectly," Igor replied. "Sasha said the cavern filled with blue-white light and a thunder that scared the hell out of them. Before they realized what had happened, there was a comm-drone hanging in the capture net at the end of the track run." Igor handed his data pad to Aleksi.

Aleksi read the message on the data pad. It had not been what he had expected. "Crowds? That's all?"

"That's enough," Igor insisted. "They need hundreds at every net-hub. Perhaps thousands. How are we going to get that many people to show up at the hubs at precisely the right moment in twelve different locations all over the world?"

"We will pay them," Aleksi replied.

"What do we tell them we are paying them to do?" Igor wondered.

"We tell them they are being hired to protest

something. People always like a good protest, especially the young."

"What do we tell them they are protesting?"

"Whatever works best for each area," Aleksi insisted. "But we do not tell them it has anything to do with the net-hubs."

"Then how do we get them to the hubs?"

"We load them into leased buses and take them to the hubs at just the right time."

"How do we know when that time is?" Igor wondered.

"I'm sure Captain Scott will find a way to let us know."

Igor sighed. "Do you know how many buses we will have to lease? It will be very expensive."

Aleksi smiled. "We will worry about the cost later, Igor. I have a feeling it will be the least of our worries."

CHAPTER THIRTEEN

Kor-Dom Borrol stood on the observation deck at the summit of Mount Lona, gazing down at the city. Lights twinkled as far as the eye could see. His world was beautiful in its own way. No other human civilization had ever created such a wonder. He could not help but wonder if they would be able to build it all again.

A clap of thunder and a flash of blue-white light briefly illuminated the summit park, followed by a wash of displaced air at the kor-dom's back. He turned around to see the Voss hovering three meters above the grassy summit, its landing struts deploying as it descended.

Kor-Dom Borrol was amazed at the precision of their arrival, as well as the fact that there was no thrust wash keeping the ship in the air.

The Voss rotated around so that her aft end faced the kor-dom and his guards as the cargo ramp came down. As the ship touched down, its shields glowed and sparkled along the bottom edge.

Four soldiers in black combat armor jumped down from the ramp as it passed the horizontal position, quickly taking up positions on either side. Nathan was next, heading down the ramp as it touched the grassy surface.

Kor-Dom Borrol and his men moved toward the Voss, stopping a meter from its still-glowing shield. A moment later, the aft shield section disappeared, and they continued forward.

Nathan stopped at the bottom of the ramp, waiting for the Jung leader. "Kor-Dom."

"Captain," the kor-dom greeted. He looked at one

of his men, signaling for them to hold position, after which he continued toward Nathan.

"Would you like to come inside?"

"We can talk here," the kor-dom replied.

"Are you certain?" Nathan wondered, looking around.

"The area has been evacuated out to ten kilometers," the kor-dom explained. "It seems there has been a hazardous materials leak in the area. A transport accident, I believe."

"As you wish. Have you reached a decision?"

"The leadership council has agreed to proceed with your plan under certain conditions," the kor-dom replied.

"What conditions?" Nathan asked.

"First, I need to know how you plan to remove Galiardi from power."

"I'm afraid I cannot discuss the details for security reasons," Nathan replied. "For all we know, someone on your council could be feeding intel to Galiardi."

"The council has already approved your proposal. The decision now rests with me alone. Perhaps that will assuage your concerns."

"Not fully, no," Nathan admitted.

"I'm afraid I must insist."

Nathan thought for a moment. "Let's just say there is a legal claim on the office of president that we intend to enforce."

"And you believe Admiral Galiardi will honor this claim," the kor-dom surmised.

"We weren't planning on giving him a choice," Nathan assured him.

"Then you believe you have enough firepower to force him to comply?"

"Sometimes it's better to be clever than strong," Nathan replied.

"As long as you have the strength to back your play, yes."

"We do," Nathan told him.

"Interesting."

"What are the other conditions?" Nathan asked.

"We will require jump drive technology prior to making you a caste leader."

Nathan smiled. Even with the fate of trillions of people in his hands, the kor-dom was trying to haggle. "The deal was that we get rid of Galiardi and put an end to the attacks on your forces, and you create a new caste, so that its leader can challenge Lord Dusahn."

"Unseating Galiardi serves your interests as much as it does ours," Kor-Dom Borrol insisted. "It will be difficult enough to stop the current Tonba-Hon-Venar, let alone the one that will be called for once the general population learns that you are alive. The only thing that can prevent that is for both sides to be on equal footing. Otherwise, we will have no choice but to destroy your world."

"I agree," Nathan replied, "but I will not hand over jump drive technology until Lord Dusahn is defeated."

"You mean when Lord Dusahn accepts your challenge," the kor-dom corrected.

"You believe Griogair Dusahn will be victorious. That's why you want the jump drive technology first."

"If you die, how do I know that your subordinates will honor your word?" the kor-dom wondered.

"If I give you jump drive technology, you could destroy Takara with ease, no matter who wins."

"If you lose, the Dusahn will become even more

powerful. Without jump drive technology, we will not be able to stop them ourselves."

Nathan's brow furrowed. "How will they become more powerful?"

"If you lose, all the assets of your clan become the property of the Dusahn." Kor-Dom Borrol noticed the surprised look on Nathan's face. "You were not aware of this?"

"No I was not, but I guess I should have expected it."

"If you wish this plan to happen, you will need to act soon, before it is too late," Kor-Dom Borrol warned.

"Why the hurry?"

"With every day that passes, we lose more assets to Galiardi's attacks. It is only a matter of time before he attacks Nor-Patri directly. Once he does, I will be unable to stop the Tonba-Hon-Venar."

Nathan thought for a moment, remembering the kor-dom's earlier words. "You said the current Tonba-Hon-Venar will be difficult to stop."

"A slip of the tongue."

"Politicians at your level don't make such errors," Nathan insisted. "There is already a Tonba-Hon-Venar in progress." When the kor-dom did not reply, Nathan pressed further. "For how long? Weeks? Months? Years?"

"As I said, you must act quickly."

"If you want jump drive technology before we defeat the Dusahn, I've got conditions," Nathan told him.

"Such as?"

"First you must join our alliance."

"To what end?"

"The Jung Empire values honor. If your empire

expects to thrive in the interstellar political arena, your word will need to be golden. If you join our alliance, you cannot attack us. Not without going back on your word and ruining your standing with all other worlds."

"Is that all?"

"You must also tell me how long the current Tonba-Hon-Venar has been in progress."

It was the kor-dom's turn to think a moment. "It began the moment you destroyed Zhu-Anok. Ships were recalled from all over the empire and put on a course for Sol, with orders to travel covertly and penetrate as deeply into Sol Alliance territory as possible."

"How close are they?" Nathan wondered.

"I have no way of knowing, but seven years is more than enough time for even our slowest warships to traverse our empire and travel to Earth."

"The Sol Alliance would detect them," Nathan insisted.

"Space is vast," Kor-Dom Borrol replied, "and our captains are both clever and patient."

Nathan was confident that Kor-Dom Borrol was not being forthright, but there was little he could do about it at the moment. "Can the Tonba-Hon-Venar be stopped?"

"Before or after the council learns that you are still alive?"

"You didn't tell them?" Nathan wondered, surprised.

"It would have complicated matters."

"Then both I guess," Nathan stated.

"That is also complicated." Kor-Dom Borrol took a breath before continuing. "There is much hatred toward your people, especially in the warrior caste.

They shouldered much of the blame for the failure to defeat the Sol Alliance. Had you not surrendered, the empire might have collapsed from within by now. Since the destruction of Zhu-Anok, it has been a constant struggle to control them. The Tonba-Hon-Venar has been the only thing preventing them from turning on the leadership and seizing control for themselves. It is how they will restore their honor, and without that honor, the people will not see them as fit to lead."

"Then honor is important to the Jung," Nathan concluded.

"Honor is everything to us. The honor of one's words, the honor of one's actions, and the honor of responsibility. They are hallmarks of the empire."

"Yet your empire has committed countless atrocities."

"For which we are willing to be judged by our maker."

"I've heard that excuse before," Nathan replied.

"There are many definitions of honor, Captain," Kor-Dom Borrol stated, "just as there are many definitions of truth."

"You still haven't answered my question," Nathan reminded him.

"The warrior castes have given their word. They will abandon the Tonba-Hon-Venar if ordered to do so."

"But what about their honor?"

"There is just as much honor in accepting disgrace for the sake of your people as there is in avenging the fallen, perhaps more so," Kor-Dom Borrol assured him. "The Jung Empire was built on the conquering of those who had what we needed. But that practice should have ended when our homeworld became self-sufficient. Instead, the warrior castes, which were in power at the time, used it as an excuse to expand the empire further. Their conquests provided for the people of Nor-Patri, allowing our population to grow to unimaginable heights. That is why our world is what it is."

"Surely your people had to realize that Nor-Patri was becoming overpopulated and dependent upon other worlds to survive."

"You'd be surprised how much a life of luxury and excess can influence the average person. The warrior castes knew this. They built a utopian society where the people were happy and fulfilled. In exchange, they were free to build countless warships to protect the opulence that is Nor-Patri. When questioned about their conquests, they vowed that they had sought to bring the same to all humanity."

"And no one noticed how many people they were slaughtering to do so?"

"Having only linear FTL made it easy to control what the people of Nor-Patri actually knew," the kor-dom explained.

"Your people cannot be that blind."

"They are not," the kor-dom assured him. "However, opulence tends to reduce the number of questions asked."

Nathan sighed. "And still I have no answer."

"You needed the proper context. As a student of history, you should understand this."

"Forgive me, Kor-Dom, but standing in the open on top of a hill, on a world where everyone sees me as the devil himself, makes me a bit anxious."

"The jump drive technology is the key to stopping the Tonba-Hon-Venar," the kor-dom explained. "The honor of the warrior castes will be restored by swallowing their pride, as their sacrifice will open the galaxy to us."

"Then it can be stopped," Nathan surmised.

"I believe so."

Nathan didn't find his response entirely reassuring. "But you cannot promise it."

"Humans are fickle creatures, Captain. This is precisely why honor is so valued in Jung society."

The kor-dom's words reminded Nathan of those times he had listened to his father giving speeches. Politicians could talk for what seemed like hours while never actually saying anything of substance. "I'm not sure your assurances are enough, Kor-Dom," Nathan warned.

"Then let us return to opulence," the kor-dom suggested. "Members of the warrior castes are human, just like the rest of us. They have wives, families, and careers, all of which they would like to keep. For most, the promise of being able to continue practicing for war with their toys will be enough. Only a perverse few still seek glory through conquest."

"The proposition remains unchanged," Nathan insisted, standing his ground. "You get jump drive technology once the Tonba-Hon-Venar has been stopped and after the Dusahn have been dealt with, and then only if the Jung Empire joins our alliance."

"You expect us to trust you at your word, despite the fact that you somehow managed to avoid death at your execution?"

"You and I both know that I committed no crime," Nathan insisted. "My execution was to appease your public and buy you time to covertly position your forces to destroy my world. Besides, when I surrendered, I had no plans of escape. That came later and not by my request. You, on the other hand, have intended to go back on your word to honor a cease-fire for seven years now. By your own admission, your ships are already in Sol Alliance space, which is a violation of that agreement. Technically, Galiardi has the right to attack you. He just happens to be doing it for the wrong reasons at the moment."

"I made no such admission," Kor-Dom Borrol insisted. "I only implied."

"Call it what you like, Kor-Dom. The point is that neither of us has any reason to trust the other. What we do have, however, is a shared motivation. You wish your empire to survive, and we wish all of humanity to survive. Now, we can continue to live with the barrels of guns pointed at one another, or we can move beyond our mutual hatred and distrust, and find a way to coexist in peace. But the deal stands as originally offered."

Kor-Dom Borrol eyed Nathan a moment. "Striking a deal with us is the only way you can save your world, let alone these Takarans you care so much for."

Nathan sighed again, growing tired of the conversation. Like every other negotiation, it seemed more of an attempt to wear down one's opponent than to reach a reasonable compromise. "Have you ever heard of a doomsday ship?" he asked the kor-dom.

"I have not."

"It's a simple concept, really," Nathan explained. "It's a big, ugly-looking ship. Slow, poorly defended, and not very maneuverable. At first glance, you'd think it was just a massive cargo ship. But the truth is, it's an insurance policy. You see, it's full of one thing: jump-capable kinetic kill vehicles designed specifically to destroy your entire empire. These ships jump to a new location every few hours, and twice a day, they send a jump comm-drone back to Fleet Command requesting permission not to launch their weapons. If their request is granted, they carry on. If not, they launch, and then they find some quiet little corner of the galaxy to start their own colony."

Although he was trying to hide it, Nathan could tell that his little story had affected the kor-dom in the way he had hoped.

"We suspected that such ships existed," Kor-Dom Borrol finally admitted.

"Then you know that the Tonba-Hon-Venar is a no-win scenario."

Kor-Dom Borrol looked at Nathan. "It is not about winning, Captain, it is about sacrifice. When the people call for the Venar, they know the risk they are taking."

"And you are comfortable with that risk?"

"If I was, you would not be alive," Kor-Dom Borrol replied. "The question is, are you willing to take that risk?"

"If I must."

"You are an impetuous young man, aren't you?"

"It's part of my charm," Nathan replied, smiling.

"I know your type," Kor-Dom Borrol stated. "We have people like you on our world as well. Children of the wealthy and powerful, believing that charm and an enchanting smile will get them out of trouble, only to fall back on their father's name when it fails."

"My father's dead," Nathan replied, not amused. "He and all but one of my sisters were assassinated by Galiardi."

Again the kor-dom's expression revealed his state of mind. The fact that he did not know about the assassination of Nathan's father told him that the

Jung Empire's current intelligence about Earth was weak, if not non-existent. "It's time for you to decide the fate of your empire, Kor-Dom."

Kor-Dom Borrol studied Nathan very carefully before continuing. "If you are successful at removing Galiardi from power and at stopping the attacks against the Jung Empire, I will do everything within my power to stop the Tonba-Hon-Venar. However, to do so, I will need to accompany you."

"Why?"

"To witness your success firsthand," the kor-dom explained, "and to communicate my orders to abort the attack on your world myself. It is the only way to be certain my instructions are followed."

"It would help if you would at least put a hold on the attack. That would give us more time to prepare to take down Galiardi."

"Or to find our ships and destroy them."

"And I thought we were beginning to trust one another."

"Trust is earned, Captain."

Nathan took a breath, looking out at the city lights. "I don't suppose there will be time to issue the abort order before your forces attack?"

"Ships assigned to a Tonba-Hon-Venar have no need to communicate with the empire," the kor-dom replied. "They already have all the orders they require. This is why I must be present."

Nathan looked at the kor-dom again. "I'm beginning to wonder if it wouldn't be better to just glass the Dusahn and let you and Galiardi destroy one another."

"But you will not, as you are unwilling to inflict that level of destruction. If you were, you would not have surrendered to us the first time."

"I don't suppose that would work again?"

"Not likely."

Nathan sighed again. "Alright, you can come with us. But only you."

"As kor-dom, I am not allowed to travel without at least one guard. Especially after your last stunt."

"I suppose I had that coming," Nathan admitted. "Very well, but only one, and I get to pick him."

Kor-Dom Borrol suddenly became suspicious. "You have friends on Nor-Patri?"

Nathan smiled again. "Friend might not be the right word."

* * *

"Update from the Aurora," Dylan reported as he entered the Voss's common room. He squeezed in between Josh and Marcus, smelling the steaming pot on the table. "What is that? It smells great!"

"Give me that," Jessica said, snatching the data pad from Dylan's hand.

"Teeten stew," Nathan replied.

"I call it slop stew," Marcus corrected.

"One of Neli's recipes," Nathan explained. "She programmed it into the auto-chef for us."

"She thinks we actually like it," Josh laughed.

"Shut up and eat your slop," Marcus grumbled, handing a bowl of stew to Josh.

"It's actually not that bad," Josh admitted, digging in.

"How much longer are we going to wait out here?" Kit asked as he took a seat at the table.

"What, you don't like it here?" Mori joked.

"In between two empires who both want to see our fearless leader here cut up into tiny pieces and set on fire?" Kit replied. "What's not to like?"

"We jump back in the morning to pick up the kordom," Jessica stated.

"I can't believe we're cutting a deal with the leader of the Jung Empire," Marcus commented as he served another bowl of stew to Vladimir.

"It's the only way," Nathan insisted.

"Yeah, but you're giving them jump drive technology," Jessica said.

"They would have gotten it eventually," Nathan defended.

"I'm surprised they don't already have it," Vladimir said, scooping up a spoonful of stew.

"At least this way, it will be on our terms."

"You don't really think they're going to be good little members of our alliance, do you?" Kit asked.

"I think they have no intention of honoring their commitment with us," Nathan admitted. "That's why we're taking him back to the Pentaurus sector with us. The more he sees what's really going on and how much membership in our alliance has to offer the Jung Empire, the more they might actually become real allies."

"You're dreaming," Jessica insisted as she accepted a bowl from Marcus. "Telles reports the test of the prototype was a success," she said, reading the data pad. "They've already started production and expect to have enough in a few days."

"If you lose, the Jung will just glass Takara," Kit pointed out. "There's no way they let the Dusahn survive."

"I still think we'd be better off glassing Takara ourselves and let Galiardi take care of the Jung," Marcus said.

"Hey, that's our homeworld you're talking about, old man," Kit warned.

"Don't be so sensitive, soldier-boy."

"Whoa!" several of the Ghatazhak jeered, teasing their comrade.

"Did they say anything about the swarm-bots?" Nathan asked.

"Just that SilTek is cranking them out like crazy," Jessica replied, setting the data pad aside and digging into her dinner.

"Sooner or later, the Jung will turn on you," Marcus told Nathan. "You know that."

"The only way to save Earth and Takara is to make the Jung an ally," Nathan insisted. "Yes, they may betray us down the line, but not until after the Tonba-Hon-Venar has been canceled and Takara has been liberated."

"Hear, hear," Kit agreed. "About the liberating Takara part, anyway."

"Did you consider surrendering again?" Marcus joked.

"Shut up and pass the pepper sauce," Nathan scolded, accepting the bowl of stew handed to him.

"This is all moot anyway," Jessica reminded him.

"Why do you say that?" Vladimir wondered.

"No way in hell Nathan beats Griogair," Jessica replied.

"I can always count on you for support, can't I," Nathan commented.

* * *

Kor-Dom Borrol strolled up the base of the Voss's aft cargo ramp, a single guard trailing him. The rest of his security detail stood just outside the shield boundary, their commanding officer appearing uncomfortable with what was occurring.

"I'm not certain your choice was a wise one," the

kor-dom told Nathan as he approached. "Thus far, Cento Soray has shown nothing but disdain for you."

Nathan looked at Trever. The man had aged quickly and lost a few kilograms. The kor-dom was right; the man did not look happy. "Cento Soray," he greeted.

The man said nothing, choosing just to glare at Nathan.

"There is an additional requirement," Nathan stated, his eyes locked with Cento Soray's. "Mister Soray was not to blame for my suicide."

"He left a blade in your cell."

"Was a blade found?" Nathan asked, looking at the kor-dom.

"No, but the count was short the next day, and you were dead," the kor-dom explained.

"It was the blade of General Bacca that took my life that night," Nathan explained. "He was the one who provided access to the team sent to rescue me that night. His condition was that he would be the one to take my life."

"General Bacca took his own life with that blade."

Nathan pretended to look surprised. "I was not aware of this."

"Cento Soray admitted to leaving a blade in your cell," Kor-Dom Borrol stated.

"I suspect he did so to gain a lesser punishment," Nathan argued.

"Perhaps."

"Mister Soray's record is to be absolved of any blame in that incident," Nathan insisted. "He is to be restored to his previous rank and pay, and is to be awarded any promotion that would have been due him during the last seven years."

Kor-Dom Borrol studied Nathan a moment,

his brow furrowed. "Why would you make such a demand, considering all that is at stake?"

"Mister Soray showed me kindness during my darkest hour," Nathan explained. "He treated me with the respect due my rank, despite his utter hatred for me and my people. I believe him to be a man of exemplary honor, and I do not wish him to suffer on my account."

After a moment, Kor-Dom Borrol signaled the officer of his security detail who was still waiting just beyond the shield perimeter. The man came over, and the kor-dom spoke a few commands to him in Jung. The officer removed the rank insignia pin from his own collar, using it to replace the one on Trever's collar. "Cento Soray is now Preto Soray," the kor-dom told Nathan. "That is probably a higher rank than he would have achieved had you never existed. I trust that will suffice?"

"Thank you," Nathan replied, nodding respectfully. He stepped aside, allowing Kor-Dom Borrol and Preto Soray to head up the ramp. He wasn't sure, but he thought he detected a faint look of gratitude on the older soldier's face as he passed.

Nathan followed the two men up the ramp, the four Ghatazhak standing guard outside only a few steps behind.

"These men will escort you to the common room for the journey," Nathan stated as the ramp closed behind them.

"How long will the journey be?" the kor-dom asked, suspicious.

"The jumps will be instantaneous," Nathan explained. "However, there will be a four-hour recharge layover between them."

"I was under the impression that your ships had

more than enough range to jump between Nor-Patri and Sol," Kor-Dom Borrol stated.

"We're not going to Sol just yet," Nathan told him. "We're heading for the Aurora in the Pentaurus sector, about nine hundred light years away."

Kor-Dom Borrol tried to disguise his disbelief but without success. "I was under the assumption that we were going to Earth."

"Our forces are not yet ready," Nathan explained. "And the more you know about us, the Dusahn, and the state of the rest of the galaxy, the better informed you will be."

Kor-Dom Borrol continued forward, commenting as he passed. "We shall see."

* * *

Kor-Dom Borrol and his guard, flanked by Kit and Mori, followed Nathan and Jessica onto the Voss's command deck. It had been some time since the kor-dom had left Nor-Patri, let alone stood on the bridge of any spaceship. "Not exactly what I was expecting," he commented, looking about.

"The XKs are actually old cargo ships that the Tekans have been converting into armed utility ships for us." Nathan's eagerness to share information with the Jung leader drew a look of disapproval from Jessica, which he ignored. "They're not much to look at, but they're tough as hell and get the job done."

"And what job would that be?" the kor-dom asked, doing his best to appear innocently curious.

"Their primary mission will be to make contact with as many worlds as possible and invite them to join our alliance," Nathan explained. "However, we can use them for just about anything."

"How many of these XKs do you have?"

"Four at the moment. We expect to have twelve in service within a few months."

"Captain?" Jessica interrupted, obviously displeased with his willingness to share.

"We about ready?" Nathan asked his flight crew.

"Jump to Corinair is plotted and ready," Loki reported.

"On course and speed," Josh added.

"Execute when ready," Nathan instructed.

"How far are we about to jump?" the kor-dom wondered.

"Loki?" Nathan said, passing the question to him.

"Four hundred and twenty-seven point three two five seven light years," Loki replied.

"Incredible," the kor-dom stated, unable to hide his amazement. "And you are not worried about hitting something along the way?"

"Our jump path avoids any systems, so there's very little chance of colliding with something," Nathan explained.

"Yet space is not empty," the kor-dom insisted.

"Something to do with our mass versus the mass of whatever might cross our path," Nathan replied. "I don't understand most of the physics to be honest."

"Jump point in ten seconds," Loki reported.

"The mere thought of it is unsettling," the kor-dom admitted.

"You get used to it," Nathan assured him.

"Jumping in three......two......one..."

Kor-Dom Borrol and Preto Soray stared out the front windows as blue-white light spilled out across the bow of the ship like water flowing from a faucet. In a split second, the entire bow was covered, the coating of light flashed, and the planet Corinair appeared before them. "Incredible," the kor-dom repeated.

"Jump complete," Loki reported. "Corinair, dead ahead."

"Aurora Flight, Voss," Loki called over comms. "Request permission to land."

"There she is," Nathan said, spotting the tiny sliver of gray moving across the planet in the background.

"Voss, Aurora Flight. Welcome back. Approach port bow high. Cleared to land, port aft pressure deck."

"Let them know we have a VIP," Nathan told Loki.

"Aurora Flight, Voss. Approaching port bow high, clear to land, port aft pressure deck. Be informed we have a VIP on board."

"Voss, Aurora Flight. Understood."

Kor-Dom Borrol continued staring out the window as the planet, and the Aurora orbiting it, rapidly increased in size. "I was not aware the Aurora was large enough to accommodate a ship this size."

"We're not exactly going to be inside of the ship," Nathan explained.

The Aurora quickly grew from a sliver, taking on the familiar form as they closed.

"Turning base," Josh announced, adjusting his course slightly to port, allowing them to intercept the Aurora perpendicular to her flight path. "Decelerating," he added, easing the deceleration throttles forward.

"Your pilots fly manually?" the kor-dom wondered, surprised.

"Not all of them," Nathan admitted, smiling.

Josh increased his throttles smoothly, watching his deceleration rate climb sharply as he increased thrust.

"Plus two hundred," Loki reported, also watching their speed in relation to the Aurora.

The Aurora slid to their right, moving from their front windows to the starboard ones.

"Turning final," Josh snickered.

"This isn't an airport, Josh," Loki stated, knowing it wouldn't do any good. Josh was having fun, and there was no stopping him. "Plus one-fifty."

Josh twisted his flight control stick, yawing the ship to starboard and causing the Aurora to move back from the starboard windows into the forward windows once again. Another deft adjustment of his controls and the Voss was on the same flight path as the Aurora, only slightly higher and just off her port side.

"Plus one hundred," Loki updated.

Nathan and Kor-Dom Borrol watched as the Aurora filled the front windows, slowly sliding down and left as the Voss started her final landing approach.

"I see the Aurora has seen considerable action as of late," the kor-dom commented, noticing the patches to her hull as the massive ship slid past.

"Griogair has kept us busy," Nathan replied.

"Interesting."

Nathan looked at the kor-dom.

"Griogair is not a name that a parent gives a child," the kor-dom explained. "It is a sacred name among our people. The great-great-grandson of our founder. It was Griogair Jung who brought the warring houses of Nor-Patri together to form the empire."

"Plus fifty," Loki informed Josh.

"How did he manage that?" Nathan wondered.

"By taking the heads of all the leaders."

"By 'taking the heads', you mean..."

"Early Jung history is quite brutal," the kor-dom stated. "The plague caused men to do horrific things to ensure the survival of their castes."

The back slope of the Aurora's forward section fell away, and Josh adjusted his flight controls, firing the Voss's dorsal thrusters to translate downward. At the same time, he fired his forward docking thrusters, slowing down the ship further to match the Aurora's track.

"Plus ten," Loki updated. "In the lane. Touchdown in twenty seconds. Plus five."

"Voss, Aurora Flight. Deck gravity at ten percent. Transferring deck control to you."

"Voss has the deck," Loki replied. "Plus five; ten down to the deck."

"Got it," Josh replied.

"Plus two......plus one......matched and on the mark."

"Did you have any doubt?" Josh chuckled.

"Three......two......one......"

There was an almost imperceptible thud as the main gear touched the Aurora's deck.

"Thrusting down," Josh reported, adding a little dorsal thrust to hold them to the deck while Loki dialed up the deck gravity.

"Mag-locks activated," Loki announced. "Deck gravity at point seven five."

"Dorsal thrusters off, shutting down the mains," Josh announced as he started shutting down the main propulsion system.

"Maneuvering to standby," Loki reported. "Purging docking thruster feeds."

Josh took his hands off the controls, then turned

his head back toward Nathan. "We're down and locked, Cap'n."

"Kor-Dom," Nathan said, gesturing aft.

Kor-Dom Borrol looked out the windows, seeing only the forward slope of the Aurora's aft section. "Did we dock?"

"Not exactly," Nathan replied.

* * *

Kor-Dom Borrol and his bodyguard stood at the top of the Voss's aft cargo ramp, staring out across the open landing deck of the Aurora.

"Something wrong, Kor-Dom?" Nathan asked, noticing the apprehension of both men.

"The area outside doesn't appear to be...enclosed."

"I guess that depends on your definition," Nathan stated. He looked over at Marcus, who was standing to the left side of the hatch.

"Good pressure outside," Marcus confirmed.

"Drop the shield," Nathan ordered.

The pale blue, nearly transparent pressure shield covering the open end of the Voss suddenly disappeared, its gentle hum going silent.

Kor-Dom Borrol's eyes widened. "Is this wise?"

"Wise, no," Nathan admitted. "But it's what we've got," he added as he headed down the ramp.

"Gives me the willies too," Marcus muttered as he passed the kor-dom and his bodyguard, following Nathan down.

Seeing that Nathan and Marcus had suffered no ill effects, the kor-dom took a deep breath and proceeded down the ramp himself, followed by Preto Soray. Both men moved cautiously at first but quickly realized that they were safe for the moment.

As they got halfway down the ramp, the kor-dom's pace slowed, his eyes widening in disbelief. Above and to his left was open space...nothing but stars. “Incredible,” he said to himself.

Preto Soray said nothing but shared in his leader’s awe.

“Pressure shield,” Jessica commented from behind the preto. “Pretty slick, huh?”

“Can you pass through it?” the kor-dom wondered.

“Yes, but you’ll pick up a heck of a static charge if you do,” Jessica explained. “You can fly through it, though.”

“Astonishing.” Kor-Dom Borrol looked forward again, noting that Nathan was standing a few meters from the bottom of the ramp alongside two officers, one male and one female.

“Kor-Dom Borrol,” Nathan began as the Jung leader approached. “Allow me to introduce Captain Cameron Taylor of the Earth Defense Force and General Lucius Telles of the Ghatazhak. This is Kor-Dom Borrol, leader of the Jung Empire.”

“It is an unprecedented honor, Kor-Dom,” General Telles stated, bowing his head slightly to show the Jung leader the respect due his position.

“The honor is mine,” Kor-Dom Borrol greeted. “The exploits of the Ghatazhak have reached Nor-Patri. You are likely as hated on my world as is Captain Scott.”

“I’ll take that as high praise,” General Telles replied.

“And the legendary Captain Taylor,” the kor-dom continued, turning his attention to Cameron. “It is rumored among our intelligence analysts that you are the true genius behind Captain Scott’s creative tactics.”

“More like his voice of reason,” Cameron corrected. She too bowed her head, despite the fact that the man was the leader of an empire that had once nearly destroyed her world. "An honor."

Four Ghatazhak soldiers in full combat armor came marching out of the Aurora onto the deck.

"What is this?" Kor-Dom Borrol inquired, eying the approaching soldiers suspiciously.

"These men will escort you and Preto Soray to our high-security VIP quarters on A deck, just below the command deck," Nathan explained.

"Are we prisoners?" Kor-Dom Borrol wondered.

"No, sir," Nathan assured him. "They are for your protection. Half the people on this ship probably despise you as much as your people do me. The last thing we need right now are complications."

"You do not trust your people?"

"I do, but I also know that grief can cause people to do terrible things. We will provide all that you need to ensure your comfort during your time with us. Lieutenant Commander Nash will provide you with all the intelligence you require. I would like to meet with you as soon as you are ready."

"It has been a long and eventful day," Kor-Dom Borrol replied. "Perhaps in the morning. That will give me time to review your intelligence."

"As you wish," Nathan agreed. "Lieutenant Commander," he added, turning to Jessica, "see to it that Kor-Dom Borrol has access to all of our intelligence."

"You mean all of our intelligence about the Dusahn," Jessica assumed.

"I mean all of our intelligence," Nathan corrected.

Jessica did not look happy. "Including Vlad's recipe for glopsy?" she remarked as she passed, following the kor-dom and the Ghatazhak.

"Holy crap," Cameron said, once the kor-dom was

out of earshot. She turned to look at Nathan. "Are you insane?"

"We need him on our side," Nathan insisted. "This is the best way to achieve that goal."

"By sharing everything?"

"Yes."

"I believe the captain is correct," General Telles agreed. "There is extreme distrust between Terrans and Jung. If we wish the Jung leader to be forthright, we must be so as well."

"Trust is earned," Nathan reminded her.

"It's bad enough you want to give them jump drive technology," Cameron stated as she headed toward the hatch.

* * *

Dom Mogan stood at the gallery window, staring out at the stars. Between FTL and cloaking fields, the stars were distorted, in a constant dance of shifting and stretching.

"You are spending a lot of time star-gazing these days, Penta," Admiral Korahk commented as he entered.

"What must it be like to blink your eyes and be somewhere else," Dom Mogan said. "Somewhere far from where you were." He turned to look at his trusted friend. "Have you ever contemplated the possibilities, Jero?"

"On many occasions."

Penta turned back to the stars. "We take from those nearest to us because of our limited reach. It is necessary, and it is logical, but it is also easy."

"It was not always so," Jero reminded him.

"And that is the problem. We once found glory in the conquering of others for the sake of our own. But when the prey fights back, we declare them criminals, unworthy of mercy or respect. We declare a Tonba-Hon-Venar, not for the purpose of justice, but for national pride. Pride for which we are willing to sacrifice all that we are and all we have built."

"We will build again," Jero insisted. "We will learn from our mistakes, and the new empire will be even more glorious."

"Will it?" Penta wondered. "Humanity has advanced to the point where we are capable of the complete destruction of worlds, not just the decimation of their inhabitants. How are we to rebuild our world once it has been turned to dust?"

"We go to a new world."

"And when does it end?" Penta sighed. "Something needs to change." He continued gazing at the stars. "The answer is not here; it is out there," he stated, gesturing to the distant stars. "Worlds not yet discovered. Secrets not yet revealed. That is where we should be going. New frontiers are what we should be conquering, instead of trying to reshape that which already exists into what we wish it to be."

"We have had this discussion before, Penta. What you propose takes centuries with our current technology."

"That is the key," Dom Mogan stated, looking at his subordinate.

Admiral Korahk's left brow raised. "I know that look, Penta. What are you planning?"

"We attack in two days, do we not?"

"We do."

"The Terrans will be taken by complete surprise. However, their defenses are strong. Even if our entire first wave of missiles makes it through their defenses, they will send everything they have at us. Their jump missiles, fighters, gunships...everything. There will be chaos, ships jumping around everywhere." Penta paused, looking his friend in the eyes. "All we need is one."

"You wish to capture one of their jump ships?"

"All three battle platforms attack. We hit them with everything, then the Ton-Mogan falls back while the Ton-Orso and the Ton-Joja complete the task. In the fog of war, we capture one of their gunships or even a fighter. Anything with a jump drive."

"Our intelligence indicates their jump ships are equipped with a self-destruct system. Their captains are under strict orders to destroy their ships if capture is imminent. They may even have tamper-prevention sensors."

"It is a risk we must take," Dom Mogan insisted. "It will take us four years to get out of Sol Alliance space. Longer, if we intend to return to Nor-Patri. That is plenty of time to reverse-engineer the captured technology and incorporate it into this ship."

"Assuming we don't blow ourselves up in the process."

"We can conduct the initial examinations aboard one of our cargo shuttles, far from the Ton-Mogan."

"The empire has been attempting to capture a jump drive for years, Penta."

"We have never had an opportunity such as this. We would be fools not to take advantage of it."

"Agreed, but..."

"We must figure out how to disable their self-destruct system," Dom Mogan insisted. "An EMP, a gamma burst, a digital virus, something."

"We know nothing about it," Admiral Korahk pointed out. "How are we to devise a way to disable it?"

"I do not know, Jero," Dom Mogan admitted. "All

I know is that we have two days to come up with something."

Admiral Korahk sighed. He knew the leader of his caste was a dreamer. It was both his inspiration and his downfall. "And suppose we are successful. Suppose we managed to give this vessel the ability to jump between the stars. What do you suggest we do with that ability?"

Dom Mogan turned to face the stars again. "The Tonba-Hon-Venar will go on for years after the Earth is destroyed. Perhaps decades. There may even be retribution from subsequent generations. All of this will make the rebuilding of the Jung Empire slow and difficult if not impossible. We will initiate the attack, steal a jump drive, and continue on our way without changing course. We will go beyond all that is until we find a new frontier that suits our needs. There, we will build an empire the likes of which no human has ever imagined. And we will build it so far away that by the time humanity catches up to us, we will be invincible."

"All this in two days," Admiral Korahk commented.

"You've always been a clever man, Jero. That is why you are an admiral."

* * *

Nathan sat down across the table from Kor-Dom Borrol, uncertain of why he had been called to the Jung leader's quarters. In the corner, Preto Soray stood, silent as usual, watching over the kor-dom.

"You are probably wondering why I requested to speak with you at so late an hour," the kor-dom began.

"The thought had crossed my mind," Nathan replied.

"I have reviewed all of the intelligence your

Lieutenant Commander Shinoda provided. He is a very thorough officer."

"That he is."

"I must say, you have accomplished much. If the Dusahn had not managed to recover so many of their antimatter cores after you defeated four of their battleships at once, Takara would probably already be liberated, and you and I would not be having this discussion."

"Yeah, I've kicked myself more than once over that one," Nathan admitted.

"One of the keys to being a leader is not to second-guess oneself. It serves little purpose."

"I'll try to remember that," Nathan promised. "But surely you didn't call me here to offer leadership advice."

Kor-Dom Borrol paused a moment, examining the young captain. "Have you not wondered why I agreed to come with you?"

"I believe you insisted," Nathan corrected. "Honestly, I agree that your forces are more likely to stand down if you are personally giving the order. However, I also suspect you see this as an opportunity to gather intelligence on the state of the galaxy."

"Or the state of the Dusahn."

A light went on in Nathan's head. "It isn't Earth you fear, it's the Dusahn."

"Actually, it's both," Kor-Dom Borrol corrected. "The Tonba-Hon-Venar is only acceptable to our people because we know that it is not the end but rather a new beginning."

"I have to be honest with you, Kor-Dom. The fact that your people see it that way is somewhat disturbing."

"Perhaps. The Dusahn, however, complicate matters."

"How so?"

"The Tonba-Hon-Venar will obliterate the civilizations of both our worlds and will decimate both fleets. The survivors will be desperate and willing to follow anyone who provides them with the basics of life. Neither fleet will be capable of mounting a significant defense, should a third party attempt an invasion."

"Oh my God," Nathan exclaimed. "You believe the Dusahn intend on being that third party."

"I believe that Lord Dusahn orchestrated the false-flag operation to guarantee a Tonba-Hon-Venar would occur, after which the Dusahn caste would finally take control of the Jung Empire."

"So this is all about revenge?"

"The Dusahn believed themselves to be the rightful leaders of the empire. When the Leaders of Nine decided to elect a kor-dom instead of continuing the practice of selection by combat, the Dusahn threatened to destroy all nine ruling castes. What followed were the bloodiest days in the history of our empire. I believe that Lord Dusahn intends to succeed where his ancestors failed centuries ago."

"Then he has no interest in Takara or the Pentaurus sector," Nathan surmised.

"As a stepping-stone to Nor-Patri, perhaps. Beyond that, I cannot be sure."

"How can you know this?" Nathan wondered.

"Had he simply wished to be welcomed back into the empire, he merely had to offer us jump drive technology. The fact that he did not make such an offer, but rather set our two empires at war with one another is what originally made me suspicious.

Then once I learned he had taken the name Griogair, I was certain. The intelligence you provided only confirms my suspicions. For example, why did the Dusahn need so many ships? Takara had almost no defenses, and Corinair had but a single capital ship. The element of surprise alone would have guaranteed their victory. They needed the extra ships in order to seize control of what was left of the Jung Empire once the Sol Alliance had reduced our fleet to a manageable level."

"How could your people follow him, knowing that he was the one who had brought on the death and destruction?" Nathan wondered.

"Desperate people will believe whatever you tell them, as long as you provide them that for which they are desperate."

Nathan leaned back, the weight of the realization hitting him hard. "The entire Pentaurus cluster is disposable to him."

"Had you not decimated his forces before his plan came to fruition, yes," Kor-Dom Borrol confirmed. "Now, however, he cannot succeed without Takara."

Nathan thought for a moment. "I don't see how this changes anything."

"Probably not," the kor-dom agreed. "However, it would suggest that, were you to challenge Lord Dusahn to personal combat, he would accept. If he is going to this much trouble to avenge the honor of his caste, he would not dare refuse your challenge and risk losing face in the eyes of all those whom he intends to rule."

Nathan sighed. "I'm not sure any of this is making me feel any better."

"It was not intended to do so," Kor-Dom Borrol replied. "I just thought you should know." He observed Nathan a moment before speaking again. "You might want to reconsider your plans."

"Which one?" Nathan wondered.

Kor-Dom Borrol took a slow, measured breath, giving his next words careful consideration.

Nathan noticed the older man's hesitation. "There is something else."

"You cannot defeat Griogair Dusahn in hand-to-hand combat. I'm not even certain one of your Ghatazhak could beat him."

"I've found that the best way to beat someone who is unbeatable is to outsmart them," Nathan stated.

"I'm afraid Griogair Dusahn has you in what your people call...checkmate."

"Then you believe he will destroy Takara rather than lose it."

"I have no doubt."

Nathan paused a moment. "I didn't realize the Jung played chess."

"We call it skorate," the kor-dom replied. "It may be time to accept that you cannot save Takara and that by continuing to try, you place all at risk."

"I am aware of this," Nathan assured him. "Believe me, I've had little else on my mind."

"Then you realize that the Jung Empire cannot tolerate the rise of a Dusahn Empire."

"I do."

"If you challenge him and lose, we will have no choice but to glass the planet," Kor-Dom Borrol stated.

"You won't have to," Nathan assured him. "If we fail, we will obliterate all military forces on the surface of Takara, without regard to collateral damage."

Kor-Dom Borrol looked doubtful. "You would do that to innocent civilians?"

“Do I blame the burglar for robbing me or myself for giving him the opportunity by leaving my door unlocked?” Nathan stated, a faraway look in his eyes.

“An interesting phrase.”

“Something my grandfather used to say,” Nathan explained. “I didn’t understand it at the time, but I do now.”

“He was speaking of social responsibility,” the kor-dom surmised.

“Actually, I believe he was speaking about the true cost of a free society. The Takaran people ignored their responsibility for far too long. Nevertheless, I will do everything in my power to protect them, even if from themselves. But be assured, I am prepared to sacrifice the few to save the many.”

“Just as you did when you attacked Zhu-Anok?” the kor-dom asked, looking Nathan in the eyes.

Nathan took a slow and steady breath before responding, not wanting to appear defensive. “Zhu-Anok was a purely military asset. The collateral damage it caused on Nor-Patri could not have been anticipated.”

“I agree.”

Nathan was taken aback. “You do?”

Kor-Dom Borrol leaned back in his chair. He looked at Preto Soray. “Excuse us, Preto.”

Preto Soray nodded and exited the kor-dom’s quarters.

“What I am about to tell you must never be repeated,” the kor-dom explained, taking another breath before continuing. “Do I have your word on this?”

“You have my word,” Nathan replied after a moment’s hesitation.

“While your attack on Zhu-Anok may have been

the trigger, it was not the cause of its destruction, and by extension not the cause of the disasters that befell Nor-Patri."

Although he tried, Nathan could not contain the grin that formed on his face.

"Not the reaction I expected," Kor-Dom Borrol stated, one eyebrow raised.

"I had a lot of time to think about this during my trial," Nathan reminded him. "I may not be a scientist, but I know that moons don't blow up like that. Come apart sometimes, but not like that. Not with that much force."

"Then why did you not say as much during your trial?"

"The purpose of my trial wasn't justice, it was appeasement. For both our worlds to survive, your people needed a scapegoat, and I fit the role."

"A noble sacrifice."

"As much as I'd like to accept the compliment, the truth is that I just wanted a way out."

"Out?" the kor-dom wondered. "Out of what?"

"Everything. The war. The responsibilities. The death and destruction. I wasn't ready for any of it. It was just thrust upon me."

"You could have resigned at any point along the way, could you not?"

"I considered it," Nathan admitted. "Nearly every day of my command."

"Yet you did not."

"Just as you have not," Nathan replied.

Kor-Dom Borrol's brow furrowed.

"Your world is headed for certain destruction. You can't even be certain that there will be anyone left to rebuild. Some men would simply give up and enjoy what time they had left. Instead, you are here, going against all that you and your people believe. Only to bet that my skinny ass is somehow able to save both our worlds."

"It appears to be the only option remaining."

Nathan laughed. "No insult, Kor-Dom, but I find that hard to believe."

"Allow me to rephrase. It is the only option I find acceptable. Like many, I find the Tonba-Hon-Venar an archaic concept. It was intended to create fear in the hearts of our enemies, back in the early days of our people, when our conflicts were still limited to the castes of Nor-Patri."

"If it is so archaic, why do your people hold onto it?" Nathan wondered.

"There is comfort in traditions," Kor-Dom explained. "Even ones that no longer make sense. Since the Zhu-Anok disaster, favor has been swinging back toward the warrior castes and their philosophy of strength and conquest."

"And you do not agree with that philosophy," Nathan surmised.

"It had its place at one time," Kor-Dom Borrol admitted. "But advances in technology have caused many of the old traditions to become obsolete. The trick is in knowing when to let go. This is where my people have failed. I hope to correct that error."

"To do so is going to require a great leap of faith on your part," Nathan warned. "I hope you have it in you to trust me."

"So do I," Kor-Dom Borrol agreed. "You may be our only hope."

Nathan sighed. "Great. So no pressure then."

* * *

Nathan stepped into the corridor from the kor-dom's quarters after a lengthy and wide-ranging discussion. Nathan had shared all he that knew about the Dusahn and the various worlds he had visited as both Connor Tuplo and as Nathan Scott. If Jessica had been present, she would have bound, gagged, and dragged him from the room an hour ago.

As much as he had shared, the kor-dom had shared equally as much, if not more. The Jung leader had been in office for more than two decades and had spent the entire time trying to shift the empire away from their expansionist ways. The Jung Empire had grown tremendously during the century that had preceded his administration. While the growth of their fleet had done wonders for their economy and their imperial pride, it had cost them dearly. Infrastructure on Nor-Patri, as well as on several of their older expansion colonies, was suffering from old age, having been long ignored.

The takeaway for Nathan had been that the kor-dom was tired of fighting both the Sol Alliance and his own warrior caste leaders. In facing his empire's inevitable demise, his only solace had been that, in the end, they would all know his prognostications had been correct. They would not admit it, but they would know.

When the kor-dom had stated that Nathan might be their only hope of salvation, he had been speaking of more than just staving off destruction under the Tonba-Hon-Venar. The course of their conversation brought forth the realization that the Jung leader had been envisioning what his empire could become with jump drive technology for years, possibly since learning of its development. Nathan was actually amazed that the Jung had not yet acquired it, especially considering how quickly it had spread across the Pentaurus sector.

Nathan had thought long and hard about his decision to share the technology with the Jung. In the end, he had concluded that eventually they would acquire it, and that offering it to them now was just as likely to turn them into an ally as it was into the galaxy's eventual rulers. So many arguments could be made against his decision, as Jessica had pointed out on so many occasions. However, just as many could be made in favor, and she knew it.

"Captain," Preto Soray greeted. He had been standing in the corridor, along with the two Ghatazhak guards posted outside the kor-dom's door, the entire time.

"Mister Soray," Nathan replied.

"I would speak with you," the preto said. It was more of a statement than a request. The preto shot a glance at the two Ghatazhak. "In private."

Nathan exchanged looks with the Ghatazhak, nodding at them. "Walk with me?" he suggested to his old jailer.

The two men strolled away, despite the disapproving glances of the Ghatazhak still guarding the kor-dom's quarters.

"I'm glad to have the opportunity to speak with you," Nathan said, starting the conversation. "I wanted to apologize for all that you and your family have probably been through. I also wanted to thank you for the kindness you showed me that night. I feel guilty that I betrayed it."

"You committed no crimes. You were a soldier trying to defend your people against unwarranted aggression. The fact that you surrendered to save billions of lives on both sides, knowing full well that it meant your death, speaks to your character."

Nathan looked at the preto, surprised. "Your English has improved."

"I've had a lot of time on my hands these last seven years."

Nathan sighed. "It must have been hard on your family."

"It has been difficult for them, yes. But they understood why I did what I did and agreed that it was right," Trever explained. "You see, it is not only the kor-dom who believes our old ways no longer serve us. He is also not the only one who believes you might be our only hope."

Nathan was surprised again. "You were listening?"

Trever tapped his left ear. "I hear everything the kor-dom hears. Even now, I hear the water running in his bath."

"Does the kor-dom know?"

"It is standard procedure for an imperial bodyguard."

"I see."

"I should thank you for that as well," Trever added. "Assuming they do not throw me back into a cell when this is over, the position will all but assure the restoration of my family's honor and their future. Protector of the kor-dom is a high honor."

"And if I fail?" Nathan wondered.

Trever smiled. "Then it will not matter."

Nathan said nothing, the weight of Trever's last statement weighing heavily.

Trever himself noticed Nathan's worried expression. "May I offer some advice?"

"Of course," Nathan replied. "I believe you've more than earned that right."

"Try not to worry so much about the result and concentrate on the efforts themselves."

Nathan looked confused.

"You see, there are so many variables in life that are beyond one's control. You can do everything correctly and still not achieve the desired result. Even coming close is, in itself, a miracle. So you concentrate on the effort, always striving to do your best, but accepting your own failures along the way." The preto paused in his tracks, turning to look at the captain. "Most importantly, you learn from your failures and try harder the next time. The only true failure is in the resignation that you cannot do better."

"Considering the stakes, I don't see how I cannot worry about the result," Nathan admitted.

"What you must realize is that even if you fail, life will go on. Unfathomable losses there will be, yes. But there will still be civilizations that will not be affected. Humanity will continue on those worlds, perhaps for the better."

Nathan smiled, continuing along. "All this wisdom from a jailer?"

Trever smiled back at him. "As I said, I've had a lot of time on my hands as of late."

CHAPTER FOURTEEN

The look in her children's eyes nearly broke Miri's heart. "I'll be back in a few days," she promised. "Mind Neli, and don't give her too hard a time."

"Why do you have to go?" her daughter, Melanie, wondered.

"I have to finish what your grandfather started," Miri told her.

"What if something happens to you?" her son, Kyle, asked.

"I've got the toughest men in the galaxy protecting me," Miri said, gesturing toward Kit, Mori, and the other Ghatazhak. "Besides, I'll be on board the Aurora most of the time, with your Uncle Nathan."

"Why can't someone else finish grandpa's work?" Melanie wondered.

"Because I'm a Scott," Miri replied, exchanging glances with Nathan. "Scotts always do the right thing."

"Why can't Uncle Nathan do it?" Kyle suggested. "He's a Scott."

"Because I'm the next in line," Miri reminded him. "We talked about this, Kyle."

Kyle looked at Kit and Mori, both of whom he knew quite well from their time on Sanctuary. "You'll protect her?"

"With our lives," Kit promised.

"You'd better," Kyle warned, "or you'll have to answer to me."

Kit smiled. "Fair enough, little man."

Miri kissed her daughter on her forehead, then her son. "See you both soon," she told them.

Nathan took Miri's hand, helping her to stand

again. She had made significant progress over the last few weeks, but she was still not entirely herself, and it worried him.

Miri headed for the door, escorted by the Ghatazhak. Nathan watched her go, then turned back to Kyle and Melanie. “I won’t let anything happen to your mother,” he assured them.

“You can’t promise that,” Kyle insisted.

“No I can’t,” Nathan admitted. “But I can promise that they’ll have to kill me to get to her. And I came back from the dead, remember?”

It wasn’t enough to bring a smile to Kyle’s face. But his niece trusted him implicitly. “I know you’ll protect my mommy,” Melanie told Nathan. “You’re Na-Tan. You can do anything.”

Nathan grabbed them both, pulling them in close. “I love you both,” he whispered. Nathan then stood and turned to Neli but didn’t know what to say. Instead of speaking, he just hugged her as well.

“Like they were my own,” Neli whispered in his ear.

Nathan turned and headed out the door, following his sister.

“Keep Marcus out of trouble!” Neli added as he exited.

Nathan walked out the door and down the path to the front landing pad, where their shuttle was waiting. Kit and Mori were standing on either side of the hatch, keeping watch on the surrounding area, more out of habit than necessity. Nathan went inside and headed aft to sit with his sister for the ride up to the Aurora. As expected, he found his sister teary-eyed. “You’ll see them again,” he promised.

“I’d better,” she joked, taking her younger brother’s hand.

* * *

Nathan had instructed the pilot to cruise all the way up to the Aurora instead of jumping. Miri was still rather upset about having to leave her children behind, and the extra time would do her good. She was stepping into a completely different life now. Not only different from what she had known for the last few months, but also different from the years she had spent as their father's chief of staff. The responsibility for trillions of lives was about to be placed squarely on her diminutive shoulders.

But Miri was strong; she always had been. And she possessed the ability to see a problem from all sides with perfect clarity. Growing up, Miri had been the one Nathan had always turned to when facing an important decision. He often wondered what she would have advised had he consulted her before enlisting.

"We'll be landing in a few minutes," the pilot's voice announced over the cabin speakers.

Miri watched out the window, taking in the view of the Aurora as they approached. "I still marvel at how big she is."

"The Aurora?"

"Yes."

"And she's not even that big," Nathan reminded her. "Not in comparison with some of the other ships we've seen. Heck, the Glendanon's nearly twice her size."

"Yes, but we didn't build the Glendanon," she pointed out. "Pop always said the Aurora was an example of how much we could accomplish when we all worked together toward a common purpose."

"Funny thing is, the Aurora is only as big as she

is because of the limitations of the technology used to build her."

Miri looked at him, skeptical. "How so?"

"Well, for starters, she's got an incredibly thick hull because we didn't have shield technology at the time. Because of the extra mass, she needed massive engines to get her to accelerate at an acceptable rate. If you took her internal deck space and stuck it inside a ship built with current technology, you'd have a ship half her size. She's actually a terrible design for what her mission turned out to be. In fact, I'm finding the Voss to be better suited for our current needs."

Miri looked out the window again, appreciating the graceful lines of the Aurora. "But the Voss is ugly and doesn't inspire confidence when you see her."

"I suppose not," Nathan agreed. "But her smaller size and modularity make her far more flexible."

"You just miss the Seiiki," Miri teased.

"Damn right I do," Nathan agreed. "She was a fine ship."

"And a hell of a lot more attractive than the Voss."

"Okay, fine, the XKs are ugly," Nathan conceded. "But they were free, and we really needed some decent expedition ships."

"I just thought of a benefit of exercising my heir-to-office rights," Miri decided.

"What's that?"

"You'll finally have to do what I say," she explained, smiling.

The cabin darkened as they entered the Aurora's starboard landing bay, their shuttle no longer bathed in the light reflected off of SilTek. Moments later, their landing gear kissed the deck, and they started their entry roll. The starboard flight complex had yet to be fitted with pressure shields and still relied on transfer airlocks to move ships in and out.

"Stand close as I disembark," Miri told Nathan. "I still have a little trouble going downhill."

"Always," Nathan promised, taking her hand.

A few minutes later, their shuttle came to a stop.

"Ready?" Nathan asked.

Miri said nothing, merely rising from her seat with a little help from her kid brother. The two of them moved forward as Kit and Mori headed down the side ramp. Miri followed them out but stopped at the hatch, taken aback by what she saw outside.

The entire crew of the Aurora was assembled in the hangar bay. Their uniforms were mixed, but they stood as proudly as any unified group of people could. In front of them stood the Aurora's command staff, fronted by Captain Taylor and General Telles.

Miri glanced to her left as Kit stepped to the side of the ramp. The Ghatazhak, clad in full mark two combat armor, had formed a line on either side leading from the base of the debarkation ramp to the assembled crew.

"Company, ah-ten-shun!" Cameron barked, causing all assembled to snap to attention.

"Company, sah-lute!" she added.

In unison, every man and woman assembled snapped their hands to their brow in salute. Though half the crew were not Terran, the Aurora was a ship of Earth, which made Miri their leader.

"President of Earth, arriving," a voice announced over the loudspeakers.

Miri looked at Nathan. "Are you trying to make me cry again?"

"Don't look at me; I didn't arrange this," he assured her.

Miri smiled, taking his arm as the two of them started down the ramp and into her new life.

* * *

Kor-Dom Borrol stared at Nathan in disbelief, then at General Telles and Miranda Scott-Thornton. "This is your plan?" he asked. "Twelve six-man teams, jumping into small compounds from several light years away...in spacesuits?" He looked to Cameron next. "Please tell me there is some element you are not disclosing at the moment. After all, I am hanging the fate of my people on it."

"The fate of our people," Cameron corrected, "and no, there isn't more to it."

"We have successfully executed insertions before," General Telles assured the kor-dom.

"One time and from a much closer range," Kor-Dom Borrol reminded him. "Unless the intel you provided me was incomplete."

General Telles nodded, confirming the kor-dom's point.

"Our fleet will be within striking distance in days," Kor-Dom Borrol reminded them. "Might it not be better to wait until they arrive? Perhaps the threat of immediate annihilation, combined with Miss Scott-Thornton's legal claims to the presidency, will be enough to sway your people and force the admiral's resignation."

"More likely it will be seen as a Jung plot to overthrow the Sol Alliance," Jessica commented.

Nathan glanced around the conference table in the Aurora's command briefing room, wondering if it had been a mistake to bring the kor-dom into the pre-mission briefing. "As fantastic as it seems, this is our best option," he insisted. "And the pending arrival of your fleet leaves us no time to cultivate alternatives."

This time, it was the kor-dom who nodded concession. "Nevertheless, your entire operation depends on predicted reactions by Admiral Galiardi and his forces. This is, by far, your most dangerous gamble."

"Not the seventy-two men jumping several light years in nothing but spacesuits?" Jessica commented.

Kor-Dom Borrol ignored Jessica's sarcasm, having already learned of her personality despite the brevity of his association with her.

"War is nothing more than a string of gambles," General Telles stated. "Each a bet that the gains will be worth the cost. The key to victory is not only in the daring of the bet but also in the careful calculation of its risks. This is where the Ghatazhak excel."

"I take it you are trying to tell me that you believe this plan will work?" Kor-Dom Borrol surmised.

"I would not be betting the lives of my men on it if I did not."

Kor-Dom Borrol sighed, turning to Miri next. "You have been silent since this briefing began, Miss Scott-Thornton. Have you no opinions on the matter?"

"I trust these people," she replied. "If for no other reason than the fact that they have repeatedly risked their own lives to protect us all...even when it is against ourselves."

"You will be risking your life as well," Kor-Dom Borrol reminded her. "As well as the futures of your children."

"I do not need you to remind me of those facts," Miri snapped back. She had only met the Jung leader an hour ago and did not yet see why her younger brother trusted him.

"Forgive me," the kor-dom apologized. "I only meant to point out that, should the reactions of the admiral and his forces not be as expected, your life will likely be at greater risk than anyone. You and your brother, after all, pose a real threat to his power."

"Assuming power is what he is after," Nathan stated.

"All humans seek power," Kor-Dom Borrol noted. "It is in our genetic code. It is what ensures our survival."

"Not everyone wants power," Miri disagreed.

"Your mistake is in the understanding of what is meant by power," Kor-Dom explained. "At its core, it means control, of which there are many levels. Control over one's home, one's environment, one's life, one's world. There is control over the individual, over the members of one's family or tribe, and so on up the ladder. The question is, what level of power does Admiral Galiardi seek? If it is simply to protect his people's future, releasing control to someone who can better assure that future would be acceptable to him, provided he believes that you can deliver. However, if the admiral's goal is to remodel the Terran Empire into something he believes to be more promising, things might become...complicated. Unfortunately, based on the intel provided me, I can only assume the latter."

"Respectfully, Kor-Dom, the mistake you are making is that you are betting on the reaction of one," Nathan explained. "We are betting on the reactions of many, and that those reactions will carry more weight than that of the one. This is what makes a society free. The fact that the many can overcome the one, no matter how powerful the one may be. It is not something that exists in charters or constitutions, for it is far more than words. It is a belief within each of us. A belief that, no matter how restrictive our leaders may become, we still hold control of our own destiny. Even the act of acquiescing to the control of others is a choice that affects one's destiny. So you see, we're not betting on Galiardi, we're betting on the people of Earth."

"So you're betting on billions of unknowns," the kor-dom surmised.

"No, we're betting on the results of thousands of years of human history," Nathan insisted. "A history where one thing has always remained consistent: that people do not want to be told what to do, what to think, or what to believe."

"I hope you are correct," Kor-Dom Borrol stated. "For the sake of both our worlds."

"Well, if I'm wrong, half the galactic human population dies, and something else rises from its ashes," Nathan concluded.

"You just described the Tonba-Hon-Venar," Kor-Dom Borrol noted with a wry smile. "The only difference is that it would be the result of a loss, rather than of a victory."

"Well now you're just being insulting," Jessica commented.

Kor-Dom Borrol's smile broadened. Despite all that was at stake, he was beginning to like these people. "And where will I be during all of this?" he questioned, turning back to Nathan.

"Aboard the Mystic Empress," Nathan replied. "It is the only ship in the fleet that will not be in harm's way."

"I am not to take the same risk as the rest of you?" the kor-dom wondered. "That hardly seems fair."

"I appreciate your sentiments, Kor-Dom," Nathan assured him. "However, you are the only one who can stop the Tonba-Hon-Venar. You must be protected at all costs."

Kor-Dom Borrol silently nodded his understanding.

"Want to trade places?" Jessica asked.

Again, Kor-Dom Borrol found himself amused.

* * *

Kor-Dom Borrol stood beside the Aurora's tactical station, gazing at the semi-spherical view screen that wrapped around the front half of the bridge. "An interesting display," he commented. "I imagine it impresses visitors; however, I fail to see much use for it beyond that."

"I've always wondered about the logic behind it myself," Nathan admitted.

"I must admit, I never expected to set foot on this ship, let alone on her bridge." The kor-dom turned to face Nathan, who was standing to his left. "I do appreciate the opportunity to witness this jump firsthand."

"I just thought you might like a demonstration of the technology which will hopefully transform your empire."

"I imagine Lieutenant Commander Nash did not agree with your decision."

"She rarely does," Nathan replied.

"Flight reports all Nighthawks and Gunyoki from Corinair are on board," Ensign Keller reported from the comm-station at the back of the bridge.

"Very well," Cameron replied from the command chair. "Signal the Glendanon that they're clear to jump."

"Aye, sir."

"Mister Dorsay?" Cameron inquired.

"Single jump to the rally point is ready, Captain. One minute to the jump point."

"Very well," Cameron replied. "Execute jump as planned."

"Aye, sir," the navigator replied. "Fifty seconds to jump."

Kor-Dom Borrol leaned in closer to Nathan, keeping his voice low. "You are not in command of this vessel?"

"Technically, Captain Taylor is the Aurora's commanding officer. My responsibilities are a bit difficult to categorize. I believe Lieutenant Commander Nash refers to me as a rogue admiral who thinks he's a frontline officer."

"Then you do not lead your forces from the Aurora?"

"I never much cared for that," Nathan admitted. "This time around, I decided to be a bit more involved."

"Is that not risky?"

"How do I ask others to take risks if I am not willing to take them myself?"

"Is that not the job of a leader?"

"Sharing that risk not only makes me more comfortable sending others into harm's way, but it also makes those I send more willing to accept that risk since they know I am willing to take it as well."

"Ten seconds to jump," Ensign Dorsay reported.

"Glendanon has jumped," Kaylah reported from the sensor station.

Kor-Dom Borrol mentally braced himself, uncertain of what to expect.

"Jumping in three......two......one..."

Kor-Dom Borrol watched the view screen as blue-white light spilled out from the emitters along the bow of the Aurora. In less than a second, the glow covered the hull, then quickly brightened into a flash that illuminated the interior of the bridge for a split second, despite the view screen's attempt to subdue its brilliance.

The view of Corinair was immediately replaced with a completely different set of stars, some of which seemed awfully large.

"Jump complete," the navigator reported.

"Multiple contacts," Kaylah added. "It's our fleet."

Nathan pointed to the right, slightly high, causing Kor-Dom Borrol to turn his head in the indicated direction. Just above them and to starboard, the front half of the Glendanon loomed nearby, having jumped to the same location only a few seconds before them.

Kor-Dom Borrol shook his head in disbelief. "Incredible."

"Are all ships present?" Cameron asked her sensor officer.

"Thirty contacts," Kaylah confirmed. "All ships are present and accounted for."

"All your ships have such range?" the kor-dom wondered, surprised.

"Only the Aurora and the Glendanon," Nathan explained. "The other ships departed a few days ago and had to make a series of jumps with multiple recharge layovers along the way."

"Take us to the point position in the fleet formation," Cameron instructed her helmsman.

"Aye, sir," Ensign Tala acknowledged.

"Message from the Mystic Empress," Ensign Keller reported. "They have launched a shuttle to retrieve the kor-dom. ETA is fifteen minutes."

"Well, Kor-Dom," Nathan said. "I guess it's time I went to work. I'll see you in about five hours."

"I truly hope so, Captain," the kor-dom replied. He bowed his head in respect, then turned and headed off, his Ghatazhak escorts in tow.

"Good luck to you, Captain," Preto Soray stated, also bowing, before following the kor-dom.

Cameron rose from the command chair and walked over to stand beside Nathan as the kor-dom's party left the bridge. "That was surreal."

"It's not like you to understate things," Nathan quipped.

"Are you sure it was a good idea?"

"Just reminding him of what his empire has to gain in this arrangement."

"Do you really think he doesn't know?"

"Of course not," Nathan agreed. "But it's hard to fully comprehend the magnitude of the jump drive's capabilities without witnessing it for yourself."

"I noticed you made sure he was gone before we pulled in alongside the fleet," Cameron added.

"Yeah, better he doesn't see how ragtag we truly are," Nathan chuckled. "Which reminds me, make sure we pull up close to the Mystic before his shuttle launches. It's got windows."

"I'll make sure his pilot knows to keep the kor-dom's eyes off the fleet," Cameron promised.

Nathan took a deep breath and sighed. "Well, I've got a ship full of Ghatazhak who are just dying to be set adrift in space."

"Good luck," Cameron wished.

"To all of us," Nathan replied as he turned to depart. "We're going to need it."

* * *

"On course and speed for the first deployment,"

Loki announced over the intercom speakers in the Voss's aft cargo bay. "One minute to deployment."

"Team One!" Lieutenant Brons barked from his position near the aft end of the bay full of Ghatazhak. "Prepare to deploy."

"How did we end up being first out?" Corporal Moskol complained as he closed his mark two CAPS helmet visor and picked up the auxiliary power pack tethered to his back.

"At least you'll have time for a nap," the lieutenant joked.

"A three-hour coast is more than a nap," the corporal replied as he and the rest of their team walked through the aft pressure shield and out onto the ramp.

"How are we looking, Loki?" Nathan asked over the intercom.

"AI has us on track for insertion point one, at a slow crawl. We couldn't be more perfectly aligned if we tried."

"The AI is flying the ship?" Miri asked, in awe of all that was happening.

"It can do it far more accurately than a human pilot," Nathan explained, "even Josh."

"I heard that," Josh stated over the intercom.

The six Ghatazhak walked out onto the ramp, spreading out into an evenly spaced formation, each of them setting their auxiliary power packs down behind them.

"Twenty seconds," Loki updated.

"How do they do it?" Miri wondered. "How do they just walk out there knowing the danger they are putting themselves into?"

"They are well trained," Nathan explained.

"How does that help?"

"Each of them knows what to do in every possible scenario."

"Ramp gravity off in three..."

"They also know that their comrades know what to do, same as them."

"Two..."

"It breeds the confidence that the risks they face have been reduced as much as humanly possible," Nathan continued.

"One..."

"Still," Miri added, shaking her head.

"Ramp gravity off," Loki reported.

The six Ghatazhak standing on the ramp outside the cargo door stood perfectly still, avoiding anything that might alter their trajectory. The mark two combat suits carried limited maneuvering thrust. At this distance, even a millimeter of course change could result in being hundreds of miles off target when they came out of their jump.

"It is hard to understand if you haven't been through similar training," Nathan told her. "I've had combat training, and they still impress the hell out of me."

"Thrusting down and away," Josh announced.

The Voss's thrusters fired briefly, and the six Ghatazhak began to float up and slightly away from the ramp.

Miri watched in fascination as the six men continued to drift away from the ship, their tethered power packs trailing behind them. "How long do they have to drift out there?"

"Coast," Nathan corrected. "Drift implies that they are not on any particular course, just a random heading."

Miri cast a sidelong glance at her younger brother.

"Just over three hours," he explained. "The second group will coast about two hours, and the third group for about an hour."

"Why can't we just deploy them more closely together?" Miri wondered. "That way, they wouldn't have to coast for so long."

"It takes time to get the ship onto the proper course and speed for each insertion trajectory," Nathan explained. "We could probably narrow the timing down a bit, but there are always unexpected variables to deal with, especially when deploying twelve teams."

"So better not to rush it," Miri surmised as the first team disappeared from sight.

"The first team is deployed," Loki reported. "Maneuvering onto course and speed to jump to the next insertion waypoint."

"One down, two to go," Nathan said, turning to head back to the common room.

"Where are you going?" Miri wondered.

"To get something to eat," Nathan replied.

"What about the rest of them?" she asked, gesturing toward the other twelve Ghatazhak still sitting about the bay.

"They know where the food is," Nathan replied as he disappeared through the forward hatch.

* * *

Four busses stood in a well-lit parking lot as lines of people waiting to board began to form. Organizers made their way down the sparse lines, taking names and account numbers through which to pay those who completed their tasks this night.

A vehicle pulled up next to the assembled leaders of the gathering, and two men climbed out. The leader of the group did not recognize the two men and looked on them with suspicion. "The lines are over there," he told the two men.

"Tento Nori," one of the two men stated.

The leader of the gathering became even more suspicious. "Allon Nori," he stated, providing the agreed-upon response.

"Garret Natta?" the approaching man asked.

"And you are?"

"Aleksi Rusayev," he replied, offering his hand.

"Aleksi?" Garret replied in disbelief. "Should you be here?"

"This is precisely where I should be," Aleksi assured him. "Not much of a turnout," he said, looking about.

"It is still early," Garret defended. "I assure you; we have a high reservation count. The buses should be filled."

"The Winnipeg Wolves?" he asked, noticing the banners and how many people in the lines were wearing team jackets and t-shirts.

"The Wolves have a playoff game in Minneapolis tomorrow night. It makes for a pretty good cover, don't you think?"

"Won't the authorities become suspicious when the buses do not go toward Minneapolis?" Aleksi wondered.

"The route to Minneapolis takes us within one kilometer of the Winnipeg net-hub," Garret explained.

"What about the capitol complex?" Aleksi asked.

"We have two more groups forming to the northeast and northwest, both of which will travel a route that takes them near the complex. We even bought several thousand tickets to the game to make our cover story look legit." Garret looked guilty. "I hope you don't mind, as they were not cheap."

"Send the tickets to our cell in Minneapolis, and have them attempt to scalp them at the game," Aleksi suggested.

"Already done," Garret assured him.

"Then it appears you have everything well in hand, Mister Natta," Aleksi congratulated, observing the lines of people. "And the turnout at the other two locations you spoke of?"

"The last report showed them to be at good reservation levels as well," Garret reported.

"Very well," Aleksi stated, turning to return to his vehicle. "Carry on."

* * *

General Telles and his team walked across the Aurora's open port aft flight deck toward the Voss just as Nathan and Miri came down her aft ramp. "I trust the deployments went as planned?"

"Absolute perfection," Nathan replied. "Right down to the nanosecond. You have to love those AIs."

"I doubt Mister Hayes would agree with you," Lieutenant Rezhik commented, walking alongside the general. "Gentlemen, store your gear and prepare for departure," he instructed the two four-man squads who accompanied them.

"Good to have you back on board, gentlemen," Nathan said, welcoming Kit and Mori as they passed by him on their way up the ramp.

"Are this many men necessary?" Miri wondered. "I'm just one person, after all."

"You're currently the most important person in the entire sector," Nathan corrected.

"Had I more men to spare, I would have brought them as well," General Telles assured her.

"How are ten or even twenty men going to protect

me any more than one man while I'm aboard the Voss?" Miri wondered.

"You're assuming that you will not have to leave the Voss," General Telles reminded her.

"Leaving the Voss wasn't part of the plan," Miri argued.

"If the plan works, you'll eventually have to leave the Voss and take charge at the capitol complex," Nathan pointed out. "I'm with the general. The more men, the better."

"I have three six-man, quick-response teams loaded onto Reapers. In addition, I have a platoon of one hundred Corinari special forces, sitting in the cargo pod of a pod hauler. If we need more men, we'll have them."

"The Corinari volunteered?" Nathan wondered, surprised.

"Insisted would be a more appropriate term," the general replied, glancing at his watch. "We have just under ten minutes until mission zero. Perhaps we should continue this conversation while underway?"

"You're the general," Nathan agreed, turning to head back up the ramp.

Miri took a deep breath, letting it out in a long sigh.

"Are you certain you're up for this, Miss Scott-Thornton?" the general inquired politely.

"Honestly, no, I'm not certain." Miri looked at him. "Are you ever certain?"

"Rarely," the general admitted, offering her his arm.

"Then let's get this over with," she decided. "I'd like to go home. My real home."

"As you wish, Madam President."

* * *

Six bodies clad in black armor coasted through deep space, barely visible against the black, starry backdrop. Each man was followed by an external energy pack, tethered to his back by an umbilical.

Lieutenant Brons checked the display on the inside of his visor. "One minute, gentlemen. Check in."

"Moskol, green."

"Tokarski, green."

"Close, green."

"Siewert, green."

"Kjelland, green."

"Wow, I expected Tokarski to be asleep," the lieutenant joked.

"I was until a few minutes ago," Tokarski admitted. "Nothing like a zero-G nap."

"Twenty seconds to upper atmosphere insertion jump," the lieutenant's CAPS AI warned.

"Stun only, boys," the lieutenant reminded the other five in his team. "Don't kill unless we have no choice."

"Yes, mother," Corporal Moskol replied.

"Has it occurred to anyone that this extended-range system has never been live tested?" Specialist Siewert asked.

"We're testing it now," the lieutenant replied. "Jumping in three......two......one......"

Six small flashes of light appeared, and the team of Ghatazhak coasting toward the Earth two light years away disappeared. All that was left were their auxiliary energy packs, their tethers severed by the very jump fields they had dumped their additional energy into.

Four buses, their sides decorated with the logo of the team they were pretending to support, exited the highway and pulled onto the service road leading to the Winnipeg net-hub.

Inside the lead bus, a man sitting behind the driver rose and turned toward the fifty passengers behind him. "Five minutes, people. Time to earn your credits. Signs and banners are in the cargo bays below. Grab something on your way out. And remember to remove your team gear before you disembark. We don't want to get our Wolves involved."

Six tiny flashes of light appeared in the upper atmosphere, fifteen kilometers above Earth's North American continent. Six Ghatazhak in full mark two combat augmentation and protection suits fell toward the surface in formation. The men spread out as they fell, using their bodies to steer themselves toward their final destination far below. At eleven other locations around the planet, similar teams arrived, making their own controlled, covert descents toward the surface.

Less than a minute after their arrival, small drogue parachutes spilled out of the packs on their backs, trailing out behind them. Once deployed, the small parachutes slowed their descent enough to safely deploy their main chutes, putting them into controlled descents that enabled their suit AIs to more precisely control their approach to the small compound still seven kilometers below.

Six buses pulled into the lighted parking lot

in front of the shopping center, joining the buses already unloading their passengers.

"Form up into lines beside your bus," the man called over the handheld loudspeaker as disembarking passengers grabbed protest signs from the buses' cargo bays. "The protest location is half a kilometer away. We will begin our march in three minutes."

"How many do we have?" the man with the loudspeaker questioned his cohort.

"Looks like we filled every seat," his cohort replied. "Should be about nine hundred people."

"Excellent," the man with the loudspeaker stated, looking satisfied. "That should make a believable protest."

"Are they staging similar protests at the other hubs or just this one?" his cohort wondered.

"Our instructions only referred to this hub. What might be happening at the others is no concern of ours."

"The insurgency calls, and we obey," his cohort commented, unconvinced that they were doing the right thing. "And if Galiardi's marines show up?"

"They won't fire on an unarmed crowd of peaceful protesters," the man with the loudspeaker assured his cohort.

"I hope you're right," his cohort replied, "for their sake."

"Just remind all unit leaders that no one is to make any moves that could be misinterpreted as violent acts."

"Trust me, they know."

Lieutenant Brons kept his eyes on the display inside his helmet visor. It had taken less than thirty seconds for his suit's AI to maneuver him onto a precise course for the Winnipeg net-hub. He had been descending under canopy for two minutes now, and after initial course acquisition, he had yet to veer from it even one hundredth of a degree. As much as he hated to admit it, the AI was far better suited for the task than even a Ghatazhak.

"Twenty seconds to final insertion jump," his AI warned. "Are you ready, Lieutenant?"

"Don't be a wiseass, Capsi."

"I'll take that as confirmation of your readiness," his AI replied.

Although he was certain it was his imagination, Lieutenant Brons could swear he heard a faint bit of sarcasm in his AI's voice.

"Disconnect in three......two......one......"

The lieutenant pulled his arms in close to his body and tucked his legs together as his parachute's main lines suddenly disconnected. For a brief moment, he felt himself falling.

"Jumping," his AI announced.

The lieutenant closed his eyes, counting off a single second as his AI jumped him the rest of the way down to the surface. Opening his eyes, he spread his arms back out for balance, and bent his knees in preparation for touchdown.

The lieutenant glanced downward. As planned, his AI had executed a micro-jump that had transitioned him to a position only ten meters above the surface, an altitude from which his mark two suit could easily absorb the impact of landing.

He braced himself, landing with no more force than if he had ridden his parachute all the way down.

A quick glance at the tactical map displayed on the inside of his helmet visor revealed twelve targets. One in each corner guard tower, two at the entrance to the main building, and six more patrolling the compound in pairs. It also showed him the positions of the other five men on his strike team, all of whom had jumped to the surface at the same time and were already swinging into action.

The red icons on the lieutenant's display began changing to yellow, indicating the targets had been stunned by members of his team and were not currently a threat. He raised both arms, cocking his wrists downward and touching the sides of his index fingers to fire the blasters mounted on his forearms. Two shots, and the two guards at the entrance to the main building were down, rendered unconscious by the energy charges. The lieutenant then turned left, bringing his arms together and firing again, dropping the two guards charging toward him. Corporal Moskol, who had landed to the lieutenant's right, took out the only other pair of guards within range.

Both Ghatazhak immediately moved to the entrance of the main building as the other four members of their team dealt with the rest of the EDF personnel trying to defend the net-hub. As expected, the sudden change in the guards' states of consciousness automatically triggered the alarm. In less than a minute, there would be twenty more guards emerging from the main building, and it would be the responsibility of himself and the corporal to deal with them.

The lieutenant glanced at his mission clock in the upper right corner of his helmet visor display. They had been on the ground for twenty seconds and had less than three minutes left to take control of the facility and upload the hack provided by the insurgents before the auto-sync occurred.

Piece of cake, he thought to himself, remembering the Terran phrase from his time on Earth seven years ago.

The officers and technicians at Net Control were accustomed to sudden interruptions in their normal routines. However, the alerts were always drills, not indicators of real assaults against the data-com network that connected every person and every thing on the planet.

"Intrusion alarm at the Winnipeg hub," the officer monitoring that particular facility reported.

The duty officer in charge of the facility immediately took notice. "Set condition three," he ordered. The lighting in the room changed, indicating the change in defense condition.

"Intrusion alarm at the Moscow hub," another officer announced.

"Intrusion alarm at the Beijing hub."

"Intrusion alarm at the Guinea hub."

"Intrusion alarm at the Brasilia hub."

"I've got it, people," the duty officer stated, halting the stream of reports before the remaining officers could sound off. "Set condition two," he added, tapping a button on his console. "Command, Net Control, Commander Persei. Condition Two. Intrusion alarms on all hubs. This is not a drill. Dispatch QRTs to all hubs."

Without communication, Lieutenant Brons and Corporal Moskol took up positions on either side of the building's front entrance, readying themselves. As expected, EDF Marines came charging out. The first group of four ran a few meters before dropping to one knee to take up firing positions. Within seconds, the marines spotted two of the other Ghatazhak charging toward them from the north side of the complex and opened fire. What the EDF Marines had not expected was for the intruders to have personal shields.

The two charging Ghatazhak purposefully missed, firing all around the kneeling marines. Their feint had the desired effect, drawing reinforcement soldiers out of the building. Once the additional troops were in the open, the attacking Ghatazhak stopped missing their targets, again firing with precision. At the same time, the lieutenant and the corporal also opened fire, and in seconds, all twelve EDF Marines lay unconscious on the ground.

"North side, secure," the lieutenant announced. It was the first communication between him and his men since entering Earth's atmosphere.

"South secure," Specialist Tokarski reported.

"Close and Siewert, sweep east," the lieutenant instructed. "Tokarski and Kjelland sweep west. Moskol and I will secure the building. Once you finish your sweeps, man the towers. Those QRTs will be here in two minutes."

Nathan stood at his makeshift station on the Voss's command deck, trying not to watch the mission clock on his display and failing miserably. "Plus three minutes," he stated. "Anything?"

"Not a peep," Jessica replied from the starboard auxiliary station.

"Didn't Telles say the net-hubs would be relatively easy to seize?"

"Relatively," Jessica reminded. "Wait... Message from the Aurora. All twelve hubs are under our control."

Nathan glanced at the mission clock again. "They've got thirty seconds to upload that hack. That's cutting it awfully close."

"They've got this, Nathan," Jessica stated confidently.

"I wish I had your confidence," Nathan admitted.

"If you'd trained with these guys for the last seven years like I have, you'd have just as much confidence in them as I do."

"Another signal from the Aurora," Jessica continued. "We jump in twenty seconds."

Two EDF Reapers appeared behind blue-white flashes of light, three hundred meters above the city of Winnipeg and half a kilometer from its net-hub.

The lead QRT Reaper's pilot looked out his window as they approached and started their circle to land, noticing the stream of protesters marching toward the Winnipeg net-hub, signs in hand. "Command, QRT One Five. We've got about a thousand civilian protesters approaching the facility. Estimate they'll have it surrounded in one minute."

"QRT One Five, Command. Are you saying protesters have taken control of the Winnipeg hub?"

"Command, One Five," the pilot replied. "I'm saying that there are protesters approaching. We're circling the facility now."

Several bolts of energy weapons fire streaked up at the circling Reaper, slamming into its starboard shields and rocking the ship.

"What the fuck?" the pilot exclaimed, taking evasive action. "Hold on, boys," he warned the marines in the back.

"Did you get eyes on?" the senior marine in the back asked over the intercom.

"I was too busy evading," the pilot answered as he came back around.

"I've got him," the copilot reported as more energy bolts lashed out at them. "Shooters are in the towers. Black combat armor. The energy bolts are coming from something on their forearms!"

"Those sure as hell aren't your run-of-the-mill protesters," the pilot stated as he took more evasive maneuvers.

"Can you drop us in the center?" the senior marine asked.

"Negative," the pilot answered. "We'd be sitting ducks the moment we dropped shields to let you down. Command, One Five. We're taking fire from the guard towers."

"One Five, Command. Can you take out the towers?"

"Command, One Five, not without killing civilians."

"One Five, Command. Are civilians in the towers?"

"Negative, Command," the pilot advised. "Civilians are on the ground, outside the facility. They are unarmed. Troops in black combat armor are in the towers. Please advise."

"One Five, Command. Stand by."

"Figures," the senior marine in the back complained. "Drop us a few blocks away. We'll hoof it in."

"And if those civilians get in your way?" the pilot asked.

"They won't," the senior marine assured him.

The pilot swung the Reaper's nose around, turning away from the net-hub to find a place to set down safely and unload his ambitious passengers. "No chance this goes south," he remarked sarcastically.

The door to Admiral Galiardi's office at the capitol complex in Winnipeg burst open as his aide and two plainclothes bodyguards entered the room in a rush.

"What is it?" the general demanded.

"All twelve net-hubs have been seized," his aide reported.

"By whom?"

"We do not know. Initial quick-response teams report protesters at all the net-hubs and soldiers in black combat armor in the towers, shooting at our QRT Reapers to keep them away."

"Protesters?" the admiral wondered as he quickly dressed. "How many?"

"Numbers vary. A few hundred to a few thousand. Moscow has the most. Winnipeg is right in the middle at around a thousand. There are two QRTs on the ground at each hub, trying to find a way in from the outside, but the protesters are getting in the way."

"Are the protesters armed?" the admiral asked, hoping for an affirmative answer.

"Not that we know of," his aide replied. "But that could change at any moment."

"Have we sent in reinforcements?"

"Commander Denton sent a second wave of QRTs, as well as squadrons of Super Eagles to each hub. They should be on scene in a minute or two."

Admiral Galiardi glanced at the clock on the wall. "Why now?"

"Cover of darkness?" the aide suggested.

"That is only true on half the world," the admiral pointed out.

"You are wanted in the command center," his aide insisted.

Admiral Galiardi rose from his desk. "Tell Commander Denton to dispatch a full platoon of marines to each net-hub for crowd control," he instructed as he headed for the door. "We need to reestablish control over those hubs, pronto."

"Tell me something good, Corporal," Lieutenant Brons urged as he looked over the unconscious control room staff, ensuring that all of them had been adequately stunned.

"I'm running the hack now," Corporal Moskol reported as he typed away at the keyboard.

"We've got twenty seconds until the auto-synch," the lieutenant reminded him.

"I'll make it," he assured him.

"You had better," the lieutenant warned.

"What is it about you officers?" the corporal wondered as he typed.

"What do you mean?" the lieutenant asked as he checked the time display on his helmet visor again.

The corporal stopped typing, leaning back in his chair and looking at the lieutenant. "Always reminding us of the obvious, as if that would motivate us more so than we already are."

"Shouldn't you be typing?" the lieutenant wondered.

"Why?" the corporal replied, smiling. "The hack was uploaded fifteen seconds ago."

"You suck, Moskol," the lieutenant stated as the mission clock on his visor reached the plus four-minute mark.

"I try."

Twenty-nine flashes of blue-white light decorated the night sky as a collection of ships both great and small, led by the Aurora, arrived in high orbit above the Earth.

"Admiral on deck!" the EDF guard at the entrance to the capitol complex command center barked as Admiral Galiardi and his aide entered.

"Status report!" the admiral barked.

"We just lost control of all the net-hubs," the duty officer reported.

The admiral glanced at the row of time displays across the top of the room's far wall, each showing a different time zone on Earth. Oddly enough, it was less than a minute after zero hour, Earth Mean Time. "At what time did we lose control?"

"Zero hundred and three seconds, Earth Mean

Time," the duty officer reported. "We believe that one of the strike teams uploaded a program that spread to the other hubs during the auto-synchronization process that takes place at zero hundred EMT."

"And the program severed our control of the network, transferring it to the distributing hub," the admiral surmised.

"We believe so, yes."

"I don't suppose there is a way to tell from which hub the network is now being controlled?"

"We're working on it, sir," the duty officer reported.

"Sir!" the communications officer barked. "Flash traffic from Fleet Command! Twenty-nine ships have just jumped into high orbit above us! One of them is the Aurora!"

"Signal Fleet Command," the admiral replied. "Set condition one. Immediate recall of all combat-ready vessels."

"Admiral," the duty officer interjected. "If the Aurora is with them..."

"The Aurora has been AWOL for months," Admiral Galiardi revealed, shocking the duty officer. "For all we know, she was captured and has been under the control of the Jung the entire time."

"Shouldn't we attempt to contact her?"

"She'll contact us," the admiral insisted. "Trust me."

"Are you ready back there?" Nathan asked over the Voss's active intercom system.

"We're ready," Dylan assured him.

"Miri?" Nathan asked.

"I'm ready," she replied.

"It's showtime, Josh," Nathan stated.

"Time to have some fun," Josh replied, pitching down and pulling away from the fleet formation. "Decelerating," he added, pushing two of his four engine throttles forward.

The Voss lurched slightly, its inertial dampening fields not able to fully compensate for the abnormally abrupt change in their forward momentum.

"This will be two jumps," Josh announced. "One into the upper atmo to slow down further and the second to take us to direct contact range with the hub."

"I know the plan, Josh," Nathan reminded his pilot.

"I was explaining it to everyone else," Josh defended. "Ready, Lok?"

"Both jumps are plotted and ready," Loki replied.

"Okay," Josh stated. "Jumping in three......two..."

"Shut up," Loki complained, realizing that Josh was mocking him.

"Jumping," Josh announced, smiling.

The jump flash washed over them, and the ship began to buffet violently, suddenly finding itself in the Earth's upper atmosphere.

"Twenty seconds to final jump," Loki reported. "Grav-lift is operating, speed is falling fast."

"How does the Winnipeg hub look?" Nathan asked.

"Four Reapers buzzing around," Loki replied. "No fighters as of yet."

"There will be," Nathan commented.

"Final jump down in three......two......"

"You have no sense of humor," Josh stated, knowing that his friend was only counting down to irritate him.

"One."

Josh pressed the jump button, and the Voss's forward windows suddenly filled with the view of the city of Winnipeg coming up at them rather quickly. "Net-hub, dead ahead."

"Initiate the link, Dylan," Nathan instructed.

Dylan entered commands into the makeshift console set up on the table in the middle of the common room, connecting the three-dimensional broadcast vid-cam setup in front of the curtain that separated the med bay from the rest of the compartment to the encrypted receiving unit set up by the Ghatazhak at the Winnipeg net-hub. "I've got it!" he exclaimed, receiving the confirmation signal from the ground unit.

General Telles activated the camera, then looked at Miri, nodding.

"People of Earth," Miri began. "This is Miranda Scott-Thornton, daughter of the late President Dayton Scott. I have survived the attempted assassination of the entire Scott family and am here to claim my rights under the heir-to-office clause of the United Earth Constitution. I am transmitting my DNA to the entire world to prove my identity. I call upon Admiral Michael Galiardi to stand down all EDF forces and relinquish power to myself as my father's sole heir. Together, we will finish what my father started and return our world, and all the worlds of the core, to peace. Admiral Galiardi, I await your response."

General Telles pressed the stop button on the camera. "We are off." He looked at Dylan next.

"I'm looping the broadcast," Dylan announced.

"It will keep repeating as long as we remain within contact range of the hub."

"What do we do now?" Miri asked the general.

"We transmit your DNA and await the admiral's response," General Telles replied. "And we pray that he is an honorable man."

"Together, we will finish what my father started and return our world, and all the worlds of the core, to peace. Admiral Galiardi, I await your response."

Admiral Galiardi looked away from the view screen, doing his best to hide his anger. "Shut down the net."

"Sir?" the duty officer replied, confused.

Admiral Galiardi looked at the officer, reading his name plate. "Commander Hetchin, shut down the global network."

"Admiral, with all due respect, doing so is a violation of Earth law."

"The net can be shut down in times of global emergency," the admiral insisted.

"Not without support from Congress," the commander reminded the admiral.

"I gave you a direct order, Commander."

"And I'd love to follow it, sir, but my oath is to the constitution of our world, as is yours, Admiral. Besides, the primary hubs cannot be shut down remotely. They can only be shut down on site."

"Then order the QRTs to retake control of the primary hubs at any cost," the admiral instructed.

"Admiral, it is also illegal for us to use military force against our own people. If the protesters stand their ground..."

"Then they will become a direct threat to the security of Earth..." the admiral insisted.

"Admiral, I must protest..."

Admiral Galiardi raised his right hand and snapped his fingers, causing two armed guards to step forward. "You are relieved of duty, Commander Hetchin."

"Admiral..."

Admiral Galiardi looked at the commander. "Would you like to be placed under arrest as well?"

Commander Hetchin stood fast, his eyes locked with the admiral's. His leader was wrong, he was certain of it. But he was also certain that opposing him further would accomplish nothing and likely render him unable to do anything in the immediate future if things worsened, which he suspected they might. "I stand relieved, Admiral," he acquiesced, saluting before departing the command center.

"Second officer of the watch," the admiral barked.

Another officer stepped forward. "Lieutenant Commander Perrin, sir.

"Lieutenant Commander Perrin, order the QRTs to retake control of the primary net-hubs."

"They will need rules of engagement, sir."

"Weapons free, deadly force against armed persons is authorized, civilians included," the admiral replied.

"And unarmed citizens?" the lieutenant commander asked, forcing his leader to clarify his instructions. "And before you answer, I respectfully remind you that a knowing violation of the Earth's constitution is a violation of an EDF officer's oath and is grounds for immediate arrest, under both the constitution and EDF procedures."

Admiral Galiardi cast a sidelong glare at the

lieutenant commander. "Are all duty officers so bold as you and the commander?"

"Duty at this particular level requires more intestinal fortitude than most assignments," the lieutenant commander replied confidently, not allowing the admiral's glare to cower him. "As our leader, I doubt you would want it any other way."

Admiral Galiardi took a breath, rethinking his position. "If the civilian protesters attempt to stand in the way of our QRTs, our troops are authorized to use non-deadly force as needed to control the situation and achieve their objectives."

"And if the protesters are armed?" the lieutenant commander inquired, making sure there was no ambiguity.

"Deadly force is authorized against armed civilians as needed to maintain the safety of our troops," the admiral explained. "Will that suffice, Lieutenant Commander?"

"Perfectly, sir," the lieutenant commander replied, turning to issue his leader's commands.

"And one more thing, Lieutenant Commander," the admiral said. "If you'd be so kind as to determine where that transmission is coming from, I'd greatly appreciate it."

"Yes sir."

"Captain," Ensign Keller called from the Aurora's comm-station. "I'm receiving calls from all the net-hub strike teams. They are under attack from EDF quick-response teams. They are holding for now but anticipate the EDF will increase their forces."

"What about the civilian protesters?" Cameron asked.

"The Ghatazhak report that the EDF are avoiding engagements with the protesters, but they are using non-lethal force to get through the civilians when needed."

"Kaylah, how long will we have sensors on Winnipeg?" Cameron asked her sensor office.

"Five minutes and twenty-eight seconds," Kaylah reported. "Thus far, QRTs at the Winnipeg hub don't have any air cover, but Super Eagles are being scrambled from the Merida spaceport. They should be airborne and jumping to station in about a minute."

"Perhaps it is time?" Lieutenant Yuati suggested.

"He hasn't violated any laws yet," Cameron pointed out. "He's playing it right to the line."

"They did go to condition one," Ensign Keller reminded her.

"Only because twenty-nine armed ships jumped into orbit unannounced," Cameron explained. "Again, he's following protocols."

"Attacking the Ghatazhak is evidence that he is attempting to retake control of the net-hubs for the purpose of sequestering Miss Scott-Thornton's assertions from public knowledge," Lieutenant Yuati stated. "Isn't that an illegal act?"

"He is attempting to regain control over an asset that he is tasked with protecting," Cameron argued. "Against an armed force, I might add. Until he either publicly refuses Miri's claims or does so by overt action, he has not crossed the line, and my hands are tied."

"Then why are we here?" her helmsman wondered.

"To remind Galiardi that there is a line and that we are standing on the other side of it."

"Admiral," the lieutenant commander called, "four of the QRTs report an armed ship circling their respective net-hubs. Each is transmitting a data-com carrier signal. The design of the ships matches the one that was engaged over Carmel Valley a few weeks ago."

"Which hubs?" the admiral wondered.

"Moscow, Beijing, Brasilia, and Winnipeg," the lieutenant commander replied. "Fleet Command has routed a squadron of Eagles to each of those hubs. Coincidentally, those are also the hubs with the greatest numbers of protesters, and their numbers are growing."

"Then one of those four ships is the source of the transmission," the admiral concluded. "Figure out which one."

Ensign Soboleski ran frantically through the corridors of the capitol complex's medical division, data pad in hand. "Where is Doctor Hellinger?" he asked a passerby in the hall. The frightened woman pointed down the corridor but said nothing.

The ensign continued running down the corridor, yelling the doctor's name until he came to the end of the hall, stopping suddenly when he spotted the doctor standing in the cafeteria, watching the looped broadcast from Miranda Scott-Thornton. "Doctor Hellinger!" he yelled, running inside.

Doctor Hellinger looked puzzled, not recognizing the man at first. Ensign..."

"Soboleski, from communications."

"Ah yes..."

"It's her!" the ensign exclaimed, handing his data pad to the doctor. "I mean, this is her DNA. We just received it. You can compare it to her DNA on record, right?"

"I can," Doctor Hellinger confirmed, tapping some instructions into the data pad. "Oh my God," he exclaimed, his eyes becoming as wide as the ensign's. "It is her."

"I knew it!"

"I have to get this to Admiral Galiardi," the doctor declared, heading out.

Commander Verbeek's Lightning came out of its jump just above the treetops of Winnipeg, only a few kilometers from the net-hub. Although he had spent hours in the simulator, it was his first actual flight in the tiny, Tekan fighter. The first thing he noticed was that it did not slice through the thicker atmosphere of Earth as smoothly as the Eagles did. The P-Seventy-Twos used grav-lift instead of aerodynamic lift and had a lot of drag to overcome. That drag made for a bumpy ride.

The second thing he noticed was that the Lightning's inertial dampeners were weak at best. You felt every bit of turbulence, and the force of turns, banks, and acceleration was brutal to say the least. It reminded him of the jet trainers used by the EDF academy twenty years ago.

He dialed in the EDF comm-channels used by the QRT Reapers and started his broadcast. "EDF Reapers, this is Commander Verbeek. We do not wish to engage you, but your presence threatens our mission to see the rightful heir take the office of President of the United Earth Alliance. Disengage and withdraw, and we will not pursue. Continue your attack, and we will be forced to disable your ships. This is your only warning."

"You think that will convince them?" his wingman wondered.

"Would it convince you?"

"Not likely."

"I'll take the one to the north, you take the one to the east," the commander instructed.

"I was afraid you'd say that."

"Try for one of their engine pods," the commander suggested. "They can safely land with three."

Flashes of blue-white light lit up the Voss's cockpit, and a second later, her shields flashed from incoming weapons fire.

"Eagles!" Loki warned. "A lot of them!"

"Evasive," Nathan ordered.

"No shit," Josh replied, already twisting and turning with wild abandon.

"Hang on, everyone!" Nathan called over the intercom. "We've got Eagles on our ass. Gunners, do your best to keep them off us, but try not to kill anyone."

The ship rocked violently as more energy bolts slammed into their shields.

"Maybe you should tell them that!" Josh exclaimed.

Nathan reached up to the overhead comm-panel, switching to the Aurora's comm-channel. "Aurora, Voss! We're getting pounded by Eagles down here. We need more air cover!"

"All four XKs report they are being attacked by EDF Super Eagles!" Ensign Keller reported from the Aurora's comm-station.

"Well that didn't take long," Cameron said. "Dispatch Nighthawks and Gunyoki to provide air cover, and prepare to broadcast on all EDF command channels, including those used by UEA Command in Winnipeg. I want to make sure Galiardi can hear me."

"You're patched in, sir."

"Admiral Galiardi, this is Captain Cameron Taylor, commanding officer of the UES Aurora. You are attacking a ship carrying the daughter of the late President Dayton Scott, who has broadcast her claim of heir-to-office. This attack is in direct violation of the United Earth Constitution, as well as EDF policy one seven five, section four, subsection B. This policy demands that you verify the identity of the claimant. Furthermore, by failing to do so, any junior officer near you is required to place you under arrest and assume your responsibilities. I call upon any EDF officer in the position to do so to follow EDF procedures in this matter and place Admiral Galiardi under arrest. If you do not, the admiral and all the forces that follow him, will be considered members of an armed insurrection and will be met with all the force at my disposal, which is considerable. I beg of you, Admiral, do not force me to spill the blood of my own people."

Talisha Sane pushed her Nighthawk's nose downward, pressing the jump button on her flight control stick. A moment later, she found herself deep in the Earth's atmosphere, skimming the tops of buildings and dodging trees as she snaked her way toward the Winnipeg net-hub.

"Multiple contacts," her AI reported. "Six EDF Super Eagles are attacking the Voss, and six more are defending the QRT Reapers against our P-Seventy-Twos."

Talisha glanced at her tactical display, checking that the other five Nighthawks in her flight had jumped in behind her. "Alright, people. Let's get those Eagles off the Voss's back. Weapons free but try to disable only. We don't want to kill anyone."

"So we're just going to play tag with them?" her wingman surmised.

"That's the idea."

"That's a rotten idea."

"Don't I know it," Talisha agreed, adjusting her course to intercept the nearest Super Eagle.

"Cape Town has just jumped into the system," the tactical officer in the capitol complex command center announced.

"Order her to intercept the Aurora and destroy her," Admiral Galiardi immediately ordered.

"Admiral, with all due respect, perhaps we should attempt to disable her instead," Lieutenant Commander Perrin suggested. "She is a considerable asset."

"Captain Taylor has already demonstrated that she is complicit in this insurrection attempt and has threatened military action against her own people!" the admiral barked.

"More accurately, she begged not to have to fire on her own people."

Admiral Galiardi glared at the lieutenant commander. "An armed insurrection during a time of war is an act of treason. For all we know, this is an attempt by the Jung to weaken us from within. Now, are you going to follow my orders, or do I need to replace you as well?"

"Cape Town is moving to intercept," Kaylah warned from the Aurora's sensor station.

"She's painting us," the tactical officer added. "She's bringing her big guns to bear."

"He's just trying to scare us," Cameron stated.

"Incoming message from the Cape Town," Ensign Keller reported from the comm-station.

"Stettner?" Cameron asked.

"No designator," the comms officer replied. "Message reads: Aurora, lower shields and power down weapons, or you will be fired upon. Prepare to receive boarding party."

"He's awfully confident," Cameron decided.

"Cape Town is firing!" Kaylah warned.

"Big guns," Lieutenant Yuati reported. "Clean miss across our bow." He looked at the captain. "A warning shot, I'd guess."

"Next one won't be," Cameron surmised.

"Surely he knows that we'll be difficult to destroy," the lieutenant commented.

"This is Stettner's chance to make a name for himself," Cameron explained. "Besides, he doesn't have to destroy us. He just has to keep us from backing Miri's claim." Cameron glanced at the Cape

Town's track on the tactical display superimposed on the bottom right corner of the main view screen. "Comms, prepare to drop a stealth comm-drone aft, so the Cape Town doesn't see it."

"Destination?" Ensign Keller asked.

"Orochi strike group," Cameron replied. "Send them targeting data for the Cape Town for an immediate missile strike, shield busters only."

"Loading message," the comms officer acknowledged.

"Let's see how cocky Stettner is without shields," Cameron stated.

"Our shields won't stand up to her big rail guns for more than a few shots," Lieutenant Yuati warned.

"I don't plan to let them," Cameron replied.

"Where the hell are all these Eagles coming from?" Josh exclaimed as he jinked the Voss hard to port and rolled her over to avoid an incoming air-to-air missile. "I thought we had air cover."

"They've got a lot more fighters than we do," Nathan reminded Josh. "And Gunyoki fly like tanks in the atmosphere."

"I have a feeling Galiardi has figured out where your sister's transmitting from," Loki surmised as the ship rocked from incoming weapons fire.

"Are our gunners doing anything?" Josh exclaimed.

"Not exactly a picnic for us, either," Corporal Vasya defended over the intercom.

"Incoming from the Aurora," Jessica reported from the auxiliary station. "Cape Town is challenging her. Cam's going to take down Stettner's shields to teach him a lesson."

"This is going to escalate quickly," Nathan sighed, holding on tight as the ship rocked from more weapons fire. "Miri," he called over comms. "Time for your second broadcast."

"Holy crap," Aiden exclaimed from the bridge of his Orochi. "I never thought I'd be ordering a missile strike against an EDF capital ship."

"I'm so glad I'm just your XO," Ledge opined.

"Pass the word to all Orochi," Aiden instructed his comms officer. "Ledge, prepare a full strike package, busters only."

Ledge took a long breath as he programmed the missile launch control computer. "I can't believe I'm doing this."

"Secure comm-link from Captain Tegg on Orochi Three," Ensign Yamma announced from the comm-station. "Sending it to your comm-set."

Aiden tapped the side of his comm-set. "What's up, Char?"

"Are you sure about this, Aiden?" she asked over comms.

"Above our pay grade, Char," he answered. "Besides, we're just taking out their shields."

"Thirty seconds to launch point," Ledge warned from the tactical station.

"Don't be late, Char," Aiden added, tapping his comm-set again to end the call.

"I call upon all command-level officers of the

Earth Defense Force to honor their oath to protect the Constitution of the United Earth Alliance and obey the orders of their commander-in-chief. I have broadcast my DNA to the entire world, and I offer to provide a live sample for your testing. I only ask that you lay down arms long enough..."

"Turn that off!" the admiral barked.

The communications officer in the capitol complex command center immediately switched off the speaker, silencing the transmission being heard by the entire world.

"What happens if we take out the net-hubs?" he asked his subordinate.

"That would cripple all data comms around the world," Lieutenant Commander Perrin warned.

"But we'd still have the satellites, right?" the admiral surmised. "We'd still have command and control?"

"Yes, but the planetary economy would come to a standstill. Banking, stock markets, civilian air navigation, law enforcement, and emergency services all depend on the net," the lieutenant commander insisted. "Not to mention that doing so would be an act of treason in itself."

"Do it," Admiral Galiardi ordered.

"Admiral..." the lieutenant commander began to object.

"Admiral!" another voice called from the doorway as he entered.

Admiral Galiardi turned toward the exit, spotting Doctor Hellinger held up at the entrance by security. He waved his approval at the guards, allowing the doctor to enter.

"Admiral," Doctor Hellinger continued as he approached. "I have received Miss Scott-Thornton's

DNA transmission. It is a perfect match to her DNA profile on record. She is Miranda Scott-Thornton."

"Those results could be faked," the admiral insisted with a dismissive wave.

"Perhaps, but not without great difficulty," the doctor argued. "The tests were performed using standard EDF medical DNA scanners. The device ID encoding matches the ID on file for the Aurora's medical department."

"It could be from a hair sample," the admiral argued. "A hair from an old hairbrush or something."

"The DNA scan was performed on a live being, not a tissue sample. The equipment used for samples is completely different from the equipment used on a live person. The ID coding would show that. It is her."

"You cannot be certain of this!" Admiral Galiardi barked, nearly losing control of his normally calm demeanor.

"Of course not," the doctor admitted, "but I am certain enough to testify in court that at this moment in time, it was reasonable to assume that she is who she claims to be."

Admiral Galiardi glared at the doctor. "Are you challenging me, Doctor?"

Doctor Hellinger stood his ground. "I am merely doing my duty as a doctor and an officer, by providing you with information. What you choose to do with it, I cannot control. However, I should remind you that, as the chief medical officer for the United Earth Alliance, I have certain authorities that you should consider before making your decision."

Admiral Galiardi turned away from the doctor. "I don't like challenges, Doctor. Especially during times of crisis." The admiral raised his hand and snapped his fingers, summoning the guards. "Place the doctor under arrest."

"On what charge?" Doctor Hellinger demanded.

"Sedition, treason, aiding the enemy...I'll decide later."

"Admiral, you cannot do this!" the doctor objected as the guards dragged him away.

Lieutenant Commander Perrin stepped closer to the admiral, keeping his voice low so that only the admiral could hear him. "With all due respect, Admiral, you are violating several EDF policies as well as several laws," he warned, hoping to persuade his commander to take a more reasonable position. "Doing so could work against you once the current situation is resolved."

"I will not risk the safety of Earth and the entire alliance on the basis of a single unverified DNA transmission," Admiral Galiardi replied, his voice equally as discrete.

"Admiral..." the lieutenant commander pressed.

Admiral Galiardi raised his hand, cutting the lieutenant commander off. "You are about to cross a line, Lieutenant Commander, one from which there is no return."

The tone of the admiral's voice and the look in his eyes were all the lieutenant commander needed to convince him.

The Cape Town slid into position directly ahead of the Aurora on the same orbital plane. At more than three times the Aurora's size, she easily dwarfed the ship she was training her main guns upon.

Dozens of flashes of blue-white light appeared on

all sides of the massive Protector-class warship, none of them more than a few hundred meters from her shield perimeter. A split second later, the inbound missiles were penetrating the target's shields.

Flashes of energy inside the Cape Town's shield perimeter bathed the ship in brilliant, yellow light. The massive dump of energy reached her shield emitters, overloading them until they exploded in showers of sparks. All around the ship, their shields shimmered momentarily, then disappeared.

"Cape Town has lost all shields!" Kaylah announced from the Aurora's sensor station.

"I guess she doesn't have layered shields after all," Cameron surmised.

"Her big guns are locking onto us!" Lieutenant Yuati warned. "They're charging rails!"

Several pale-blue flashes appeared all about the front of the Cape Town on the main view screen.

"Cape Town is firing!" Kaylah announced.

The view screen flashed as the Aurora's forward shields took repeated direct hits from the incoming, explosive rail gun rounds, violently rocking the ship.

"I guess we're not getting any more warning shots," Cameron stated.

"Forward shields down thirty percent and falling fast!" Kaylah warned.

"Channel all available power to forward shields!" Cameron instructed. "Helm, hard to starboard. Mister Dorsay, jump us twenty kilometers past them as soon as you get a clear jump line. Comms, order the Orochi to launch the second strike, and inform the Voss that we are taking live fire from the Cape

Town." Cameron paused a moment, taking a breath. "This just became a shooting war."

"My God," Ensign Yamma exclaimed from the Orochi's comm-station. "The first strike took out all the Cape Town's shields!"

Aiden said nothing, equally shocked. He knew the shield busters worked, but they had never taken out all of a target's shields in a single strike.

"They're ordering the second strike," the ensign added in equal disbelief.

Aiden sighed. "Pass the word to the rest of the group," he instructed. "Second strike in one minute."

"Aiden," Ledge objected. "Taking out their shields is one thing, but..."

"Again, above our pay grade," Aiden reminded him.

"But..."

"We have our orders, Commander."

"Yes sir," Ledge acknowledged, calling up the second strike package.

The Aurora lurched violently as a flash of light from their shields filled the bridge.

"Shields down to forty percent!" Lieutenant Yuati warned. "Suggest we target the Cape Town's big guns!"

"Helm, jump us past the Cape Town!" Cameron ordered. "Her main guns won't be able to track that fast. They're for distance, not close-in combat. That'll buy us half a minute."

"Cape Town is jumping!" Kaylah warned.

"Belay that!" Cameron instructed, glancing at the mission clock.

"Jump flashes!" Kaylah added. "Second strike! A clean miss! Missiles are headed for the planet."

"Tactical!" Cameron barked. "Override codes! Detonate those missiles!"

"Detonating second strike missiles," the tactical officer acknowledged.

"Kaylah, where did the Cape Town jump to?"

"I show her one hundred kilometers ahead, slightly higher orbit," the sensor officer replied.

"Helm, jump us to a position twenty kilometers off her stern, same altitude," Cameron ordered. "Comms, another broadcast on all channels and frequencies. I want the whole damn planet to hear this one!"

"All channels and frequencies, aye!" the comms officer replied. "Tied in, ready to broadcast!"

"Admiral Galiardi, by refusing to submit to a legal claim of heir-to-office, and by ordering your forces to fire upon vessels attempting to enforce this rightful claim, you have committed an act of treason against the people of Earth and have, just as you did when you failed to provide support to our allies in the Pentaurus sector, violated your oath as an officer of the Earth Defense Force. Surrender yourself to your junior officers and submit to the rules of the worlds you are sworn to protect, or we will use deadly force against you and all those who defend your illegal actions. To all officers of the Earth Defense Force, I urge you to honor your own oaths and refuse the admiral's illegal orders. Do not force us to attack you further!"

"Jumping in three..." the navigator began to count.

"Comms, direct channel to the Cape Town," Cameron ordered.

"Two..."

"I want to speak to Stettner," she added.

"One..."

"One moment," her comms officer replied.

"Jumping!"

Blue-white light flashed across the bridge as the Aurora jumped past the massive Protector-class vessel, taking up a new position twenty kilometers past her, still in Earth orbit.

"Tactical, target her aft main guns, but don't fire until I give the order," Cameron instructed.

"Helm, ninety to port and roll twenty, if you please," Lieutenant Yuati instructed.

Cameron tapped her comm-set again. "Cape Town Actual, Aurora Actual!" she called.

"Ninety to port and roll twenty," the helmsman acknowledged.

"Aurora Actual, Cape Town Actual," Captain Stettner's voice crackled over comms. "Taylor, have you lost your mind!"

"Stand down!" Cameron insisted. "Galiardi has been lying to everyone! The Jung didn't violate our space! It was a false-flag op by the Dusahn to keep us busy while they invaded the Pentaurus sector!"

There was no response.

"Their main guns are coming around," Lieutenant Yuati warned. "They'll have us locked in again in fifteen seconds."

"Stettner! For once in your life, don't be a pawn!" Cameron yelled over comms. "No matter how you look at it, Galiardi is committing treason! If you continue to support him, you'll be just as guilty as he is!"

Again there was silence.

"Cape Town's aft rail guns have locked onto us," Lieutenant Yuati reported. "I have targeted key sections of their jump arrays with our point-defense cannons. We should have no problem taking out their jump drive."

"Goddamn it, Stettner, don't make me disable you!"

"The universe is not black and white, Taylor," Captain Stettner finally replied over comms. "That's always been your problem."

"Their aft guns are charging rails," the lieutenant warned.

"Take out their jump drive," Cameron solemnly ordered.

"Firing."

Jessica braced herself with her left hand while her right hand adjusted the comm-channel selector on her console. "What the hell is wrong with the inertial dampeners?" she wondered as the ship lurched and rolled, making it difficult to do anything.

"They're at minimum settings!" Nathan explained as the ship shook from incoming weapons fire. "I'm shunting all available power to shields! Better we get airsick than fried!"

"I'm not even maneuvering that hard," Josh defended.

"Maybe that's why we're taking so much fire?" Jessica suggested.

"We're taking so much fire because there are a couple dozen fighters gunning for us!" Josh insisted.

"Nathan," Jessica said, ignoring Josh's reply, "The Aurora is exchanging fire with the Cape Town. Cam's taken out their shields, and now she's targeting their jump drive."

"Great."

"I take it things aren't going as planned," Miri surmised as they entered the Voss's command deck, stumbling forward from handhold to handhold.

"As planned? No," Nathan admitted. "As expected...?"

"Two squadrons of Gunyoki are about to face off against a hundred Super Eagles," Jessica added. "It doesn't look like anyone's going to turn on Galiardi any time soon."

"I have to speak to Galiardi," Miri insisted.

"I can make a connection, but I can't guarantee he'll talk to you," Jessica warned her.

"It has to be in person," Miri added.

Nathan turned to look at his sister. "He'll have you gunned down."

"Isn't that why you brought the Ghatazhak along?"

"Miri..."

"It's the only way, Nathan, and you know it," Miri insisted. "I can't allow our people to kill one another, not when I can stop it."

"You don't know that you can," Nathan warned.

"I'm giving you an order, Nathan," Miri told him.

"I'm not EDF," Nathan reminded her. "My commission ended when I died."

"Nathan," Miri stated firmly.

Nathan sighed. "We have to get all these fighters off our backs first. Jess, tell those two squadrons of Gunyoki about to face off against the Super Eagles to jump down here and give us a hand."

"I'm on it," Jessica assured him.

"I'll notify our reserves," General Telles stated. "I take it we are about to head to the capitol complex?"

"Ask her," Nathan replied, pointing to Miri. "Apparently she's in charge."

"Target's primary jump drive array is offline," Kaylah announced from the Aurora's sensor station as the ship rocked from impacts against their shields by the Cape Town's big rail guns.

"Get their secondary array down, Lieutenant," Cameron instructed.

"A few more impacts, and he would have overwhelmed our shields," Lieutenant Yuati stated.

"They're jumping again!" Kaylah reported.

"He's afraid of another missile strike," Cameron commented.

"I've got her," Kaylah added. "Eighty clicks, same altitude."

"Helm, jump us forward again. Same relative range," Cameron instructed.

"Jumping forward," the navigator acknowledged.

"Why do they not jump further?" Lieutenant Yuati wondered as he prepared to reacquire the target.

"He's trying to stay within striking distance of Winnipeg for as long as possible," Cameron explained. Port Terra won't be coming over the horizon for another ten minutes, and Galiardi's afraid of an all-out assault on his position." Cameron glanced at the window on the main view screen showing the Cape Town's current orbital track in relation to the North American continent below. "Comms, prepare a comm-drone."

"Message?"

"No message," Cameron replied.

"Jumping forward in three..."

Ensign Keller looked up from his station. "Who are we sending no message to?"

"Two..."

"The Orochi strike group."

"One..."

"Preparing a jump comm-drone, no message, to the Orochi strike group," the ensign acknowledged.

"Jumping."

"Launch when ready," Cameron added as the jump flash washed over the bridge.

"Jump complete," Ensign Dorsay reported.

"Comm-drone away."

"Reacquiring target," Lieutenant Yuati announced. "Targeting secondary jump array."

Cameron glanced at the display on the lower edge of the main view screen noting the time. "Resume firing when ready."

"New contact," Ali announced from the Orochi's sensor station. "Jump comm-drone."

Aiden turned to Ensign Yamma at the comm-station, expecting a message.

Ensign Yamma looked at her captain, shrugging. "It's not transmitting anything."

"Is it broken?" Aiden wondered.

"Sensors show it to be working normally," Ali assured him.

"Weird," Aiden decided. "I hope this isn't an ominous sign."

"Message from General Telles," Ensign Keller reported from the Aurora's comm-station. "He is requesting immediate launch of the Ghatazhak QRTs. He's ordering them to the capitol complex."

"That can't be good," Cameron commented.

"We've taken out another of the Cape Town's main guns," Lieutenant Yuati reported.

Cameron tapped her com-set. "Flight, XO. Launch the QRTs and route them to the capitol complex."

"Missile launch!" Kaylah warned. "From the Cape Town! Eight inbound! Fifteen seconds!"

"Helm, ten to port and jump ahead twenty clicks past the Cape Town!"

"Ten to port, aye," the helmsman replied, immediately initiating the course change.

"Ten seconds!" Kaylah warned.

"Jumping twenty past target!" the navigator reported.

The blue-white flash washed over them again as the Aurora transitioned forward to avoid the incoming missiles.

"Jump complete," the navigator reported.

"We'll have to reorient to get our guns on them," Lieutenant Yuati warned.

"Not yet," Cameron stated.

"Captain?" the lieutenant asked, confused.

"Target is jumping," Kaylah announced.

Cameron glanced at the time display again. One minute had passed. She smiled. "Let me guess, sixty clicks?"

Kaylah looked at her. "You got it."

"How the hell did that guy get command?" Cameron muttered. "Comms, another comm-drone. Strike orders for the Orochi."

Talisha rolled her Nighthawk to the right, pushing her nose down and backing off her main propulsion throttle. Once in a dive, she pulled back hard on her flight control stick and jammed the throttle back to full power as she pulled her nose back up. Within seconds, her maneuver paid off, and four EDF Super Eagles were directly in front of her, passing right to left as they chased her wingman.

"Any time now, boss," her wingman urged over comms.

"Leta, target their drives and fire four," Talisha instructed her AI.

"Targeting drives, four away," Leta responded in her usual calm demeanor.

Talisha waited just long enough for all four missiles to clear her nose, then pulled up to a forty-five-degree climb and pressed her jump button, instantly transitioning to a position several kilometers above her current altitude and just as many downrange.

Once out of the jump, she pushed her ship into a tight left turn, preparing to return to the engagement area over the Winnipeg net-hub.

"Two of the four missiles missed," Leta reported. "The other two have found and disabled their targets. Their pilots ejected safely."

"Razor Leader, Voss Actual," Nathan called over comms.

"Go for Razor Leader," Talisha replied.

"Take all Razors to the capitol complex and take out their air defenses. Notify when complete."

"Understood," Talisha replied. "What about the Eagles harassing you?"

"Gunyoki will keep them at bay. We're done broadcasting for now."

"On our way," Talisha assured him. "Razor Leader to all Razors. New mission. Capitol complex air defenses. Alpha group takes north and east targets, Beta takes south and west. Let's do this." A moment later, she changed course and jumped, putting the capitol complex directly ahead of her and only a few kilometers away. "Leta, target the nearest air-defense batteries and launch when ready."

"There is a twenty-two percent risk of collateral damage, including civilian casualties," Leta warned. "Confirmation of launch order is required."

"Confirmed. Launch when ready," Talisha replied. "I'm sure Captain Scott is aware of the risks." I hope, she thought.

"Launching missiles," her AI announced.

The Aurora shook violently as explosive rail gun rounds slammed into her port shields.

"Port shields down to forty percent!" Lieutenant Yuati warned from the tactical station.

"How many more guns does she have on us?" Cameron wondered as another volley shook the ship.

"She still has two guns on her aft side that can reach us," the lieutenant replied.

Cameron glanced at the clock. Another minute was about to pass. "Don't let me down, Stettner," she muttered to herself.

"They're jumping again!" Kaylah reported.

Cameron kept her eyes on the main view screen as the flash from the Cape Town appeared, followed a split second later by the flash of her arrival further ahead of them. Then, as expected, smaller flashes appeared all over the place; some ahead and some behind the location where the Cape Town had arrived.

"More contacts!" Kaylah announced. "It's the third missile strike! Eleven impacts!"

"Jump us ahead to stay with the target, Mister Tala," Cameron instructed her helmsman.

"Jumping to target."

"Detonate the weapons that missed, Lieutenant," Cameron instructed her tactical officer.

"Jumping in three..."

"Detonating the jump missiles that missed their target."

"Two..."

"Confirming all missiles have detonated," the lieutenant reported.

"One..."

"Reacquire and open fire when ready," Cameron added.

"Jumping."

The jump flash washed over the Aurora's bridge once again, and the Cape Town appeared before them; a small dot at the center of the main view screen, still ten kilometers away.

"Damage to target?" Cameron inquired.

"She's lost her secondary jump array!" Kaylah replied. "She's not jumping anywhere, sir."

"If they fire another of their big guns at us, take that gun out, Lieutenant."

"Aye, sir."

"New contacts!" Kaylah warned from the sensor station. "Destroyers. The Tanna and the Nagoya. Wait! I've got gunships jumping in directly astern, about two thousand kilometers. About ten of them."

"Comms, all EDF channels again," Cameron instructed.

"You're hot!" Ensign Keller replied.

"All EDF ships, this is Captain Taylor commanding the Aurora! We are attempting to enforce a legal heir-to-office claim by Miranda Scott-Thornton. Admiral Galiardi has refused the claim and has taken illegal, hostile action against Miss Scott-Thornton and the vessels backing her. I strongly urge you to stand down and refuse the order. You may have us in numbers, but we have superior technology. If you don't believe me, just look at the Cape Town. Do not fire on this ship, or you too will be committing an illegal act, and we will return fire." Cameron took a breath. She was getting tired of this awfully fast. "Do not test me, for I will use deadly force if necessary. You have been warned," she concluded, signaling her comms officer to end the broadcast.

"I hope it has the desired effect," Lieutenant Yuati stated.

"We're not about to sit here and find out. Mister Dorsay, be ready on that escape jump button. Random escape jump ranges from one to ten light minutes. It's high time we started dancing."

"Nighthawks have taken out the capitol complex's outer air defenses," Jessica reported from the starboard auxiliary station on the Voss's command deck.

"What do you mean outer air defenses?" Nathan asked.

"The complex has a shield, and there are eight air-defense batteries inside the shield."

"When the hell did that happen?" Nathan wondered.

"We must disable that shield," General Telles stated. "Regardless of the cost."

"This is not going the way I'd hoped," Nathan admitted as he reached up to the comm-panel. "Razor Leader, Voss Actual," he hailed over comms.

"Go for Razor Leader," Talisha replied.

"I've got a mission for you, but it's a tough one."

"Anything would be easier than trying to shoot down Super Eagles without killing their pilots," the commander replied. "It's a tahkah's nest here!"

"I need you to jump through the capitol complex's shields and take them out."

"You're talking about that slow-speed maneuver that Josh did?" Talisha surmised. "At treetop level?"

"That would be the plan, yes," Nathan confirmed.

"I stand corrected," Talisha replied. "On our way."

"That's a suicide mission," Jessica pointed out.

"No choice," Nathan replied. "A standard buster strike would probably level the place, and swarm-bots can't function in the atmosphere. They'd just fall to the ground."

"I vote we level the place, myself," Jessica stated.

"Perception is the only truth that matters," Miri commented.

"What?" Jessica wondered.

"She means that leveling the place won't play well in the court of public opinion," Nathan explained.

Jessica shook her head in disgust. "I hate public opinion."

Talisha glanced at her fighter's tactical display,

noting the position of all the Nighthawks in the engagement area. “Broc, Chaim, you two are in the best position. You get the first run.”

“Lucky us,” Broc replied over comms. “Chaim, you want to lead?”

“Rolling in now,” Chaim reported.

“Remember to slow to about five meters per second, or you won’t make it through their shields,” Talisha reminded them.

“We’ll be easy targets,” Broc noted over comms.

“Tie in your lateral thrusters and use them to translate from side to side,” Talisha suggested. “There’s no restriction on how fast you can jink laterally.”

“Good idea,” Chaim agreed.

“Let your AIs do the shooting,” Talisha added. “You just worry about avoiding incoming fire. And don’t feel like you have to linger long enough to take out the entire shield array. There are plenty of us to do the job.”

“Don’t worry,” Broc replied. “I don’t stay where I’m not wanted.”

“Even with lateral thrusters at full power, the odds of avoiding fire from all four anti-aircraft batteries inside the shield perimeter are...”

“I’m not interested in the odds, Leta,” Talisha stated, cutting off her AI.

“You should be,” Leta insisted. “At such close range, our shields can only withstand five, possibly six impacts before failing. At the fire rate of those batteries...”

“Yes, I know it’s a long shot, Leta.”

“Then why attempt it?”

“Because it’s not impossible,” Talisha argued.

“But it is highly improbable.”

"Which means we'll be big, damn heroes if we succeed."

"More likely we will be dead," Leta corrected.

"Did I ever tell you how encouraging you can be at times?" Talisha replied.

"They're trying to bracket us," Lieutenant Yuati warned from the Aurora's tactical station.

"They're going to need more than two ships to do so," Cameron commented.

"Yes," the lieutenant agreed as the ship rocked from incoming weapons fire. "But they can deliver considerable firepower on the same shield section while splitting our own weapons."

"Comms, direct the Gunyoki to harass those two destroyers," Cameron instructed. "Helm, prepare to jump directly between them, our midship just before their bows. Lieutenant Yuati, be ready on the broadsides."

"At our current closure rate, our broadsides will not get enough shots in to significantly weaken their shields."

"I'm just trying to make them nervous, Lieutenant," Cameron explained.

"Broadsides are charged and ready," the lieutenant assured her as the ship rocked again.

"Jump is ready," Ensign Dorsay reported from the helm.

"Let's hit them with rail guns as well," Cameron decided.

"Swinging all rail guns outward," the lieutenant replied. "I'll rake them up and down ten degrees as we pass," he added, "just to make them nervous."

Cameron was beginning to like the young Rakuen officer. "Mister Dorsay, execute the jump," she instructed as more weapons fire rocked the Aurora.

"Jumping to broadside attack position in three...... two......one......jumping."

The blue-white jump flash once again swept through the Aurora's bridge as the ship jumped ahead twelve kilometers.

"Fire at will, Lieutenant," Cameron ordered.

"Firing all broadsides and rail guns," Lieutenant Yuati replied, activating the Aurora's broadside plasma cannons and midship rail guns.

"Nagoya is jumping," Kaylah announced from the sensor station. "Tanna is veering to port, away from us. She is also targeting us with missiles."

"I guess the Tanna's captain doesn't scare as easily," Cameron stated.

"Tanna has a missile lock," Kaylah warned.

"Comms, prepare a new strike order for the Orochi, using the Tanna's current position and track. Wide spread, full area saturation. Launch the comm-drone as soon as we come out of the next jump."

"Missile launch!" Kaylah alerted. "Ten seconds!"

"Escape jump, five light minutes," Cameron instructed. "Execute!"

"Jumping five light minutes," her navigator replied, executing the escape jump.

"An odd move," Lieutenant Yuati remarked as the jump flash washed over them. "It would have been more effective to put all of his guns on us and pound our aft shields once we'd passed him by."

"Launch comm-drone," Cameron instructed.

"Comm-drone away."

"He knew damn well that we wouldn't have

enough time for our point-defenses to intercept them," Cameron continued. "He wanted us to jump."

The lieutenant's brow furrowed. "Then his intention was to test our response?"

"No, he was just trying to appear to be attacking us but doing so in a way that he knew we could escape. He doesn't want this fight any more than we do."

Talisha glanced at her tactical display as she brought her fighter around hard to engage a pair of EDF Super Eagles that had just jumped in nearby. Just as she did, two green icons representing Broc and Chaim appeared near the capitol complex.

Talisha locked her missiles on the approaching Super Eagles and launched, but both targets jumped away before her weapons reached them. "Damn it!" she exclaimed.

"They are trying to cause you to deplete your supply of air-to-air missiles," Leta warned. "Their shields hold up to our plasma cannons much better than our missiles."

"I know!" Talisha exclaimed. "That's why I'm pissed! I should have known better!"

"Broc is hit!" Chaim reported over comms. "I'm taking heavy..."

Talisha glanced at her tactical display again as the second green icon near the capitol complex disappeared. "Damn it!" she repeated. "Glen! Form up on me! We're next!"

"I'll be on your starboard side in ten seconds," Glen replied.

"Negative," Coburn called over comms. "I'm

already on the right vector. I just need to shave off some altitude."

"I can take your wing, Cobby!"

"Copy that, Davs," Coburn replied. "Meet me over One Five Alpha at two hundred meters."

"I'll be there in eight seconds," Davy replied.

"Giv'em hell, Cobby," Talisha encouraged.

"Erv and I can follow," Clivon suggested over comms.

"Copy that," Talisha replied. "Glen and I will hit them after you."

"You're assuming we'll leave anything for you to hit!" Coburn bragged.

"One-eighty, complete," Ensign Tala announced from the Aurora's helm.

"Put us behind those destroyers," Cameron ordered. "Five clicks, slightly below."

"Calculating jump," Ensign Dorsay reported.

"Gunyoki engaged with EDF fighters at grid Four Five One report EDF are no longer firing on them but are continuing intercept and tracking," the comms officer reported.

"Sounds like some of them are having second thoughts," Lieutenant Yuati commented. "Perhaps your plea was effective after all."

"It won't last," Cameron insisted. "Not unless Fleet Command changes their mind as well."

"Jump loaded and ready," the navigator reported.

"Execute."

"Jumping in three..."

"Tactical, be ready," Cameron stated.

"Two..."

"But do not fire without my orders."

"One..."

"Understood," Lieutenant Yuati assured her.

"Jumping."

"We at least have to give them a chance to stand down," Cameron explained as the jump flash washed over them.

"Single destroyer," Kaylah reported. "It's the Tanna. The Nagoya is not in the area."

"The Tanna may be the bait," Lieutenant Yuati warned.

"Negative," Kaylah insisted. "Tanna has lost all shields."

"Is she targeting us?" Cameron asked.

"Affirmative," Lieutenant Yuati replied. "Missiles and guns."

"Comms, get me Captain Nash on the Ancot."

"Tanna Actual, Ancot Actual, Nash," Robert called over comms as his XK circled the Moscow net-hub, dodging EDF Super Eagles and surface-based anti-aircraft batteries. "Come on, Jas, I know you can hear me."

"I suppose this was your classified mission?" Commander Boynton replied over comms.

"Trust me, Jas, if I had time to explain, you'd agree with what we are doing," Robert insisted as his ship rocked from incoming weapons fire.

"You're asking me to bet my career on it."

"I'm betting my life on it," Robert replied. "Besides, it's the right thing to do."

"And if you fail?" the commander asked.

"Then you're fucked anyway," Robert told him. "In fact, we are your only hope."

After a pause, the commander spoke again. "I don't know, Robert."

"Well, you'd better decide fast, Jasper. The next volley will take out your jump drive."

The Voss's command deck lit up momentarily as they jumped to a new position. For the first time in the last ten minutes, their ship was not being rocked by incoming fire.

"Ten clicks from the capitol complex," Loki reported.

"What's the status of that shield?" Nathan asked Jessica.

"It's still up," Jessica replied. "The second pair of Nighthawks weren't able to reach it. The anti-aircraft batteries inside the shield are picking them off the moment they jump in."

"The Tanna's missiles and guns are locked onto us," Lieutenant Yuati reported from the Aurora's tactical station. "If they unload with everything, we'll lose our forward shields."

"Be ready on that jump button, Mister Dorsay," Cameron urged.

"Always," the navigator assured her.

"Tanna is powering her jump drive," Kaylah announced.

"Incoming message," Ensign Keller reported from the comm-station. "It's the Tanna."

"Message?" Cameron asked.

"Good luck."

"Tanna is jumping," Kaylah reported.

"Well that's a start," Cameron stated.

"Talisha," Nathan called over comms from the Voss's command deck. "We'll jump in one click south of the complex about thirty meters above the surface."

"Thirty meters?" Dylan exclaimed in disbelief.

"Sweet!" Josh exclaimed.

Loki just rolled his eyes.

"We'll approach and come to a hover just outside the shield and draw their fire for you."

"They'll light you up, Captain," Talisha warned.

"Our shields are stronger than yours," Nathan insisted. "We can take a few hits."

"I think you're being overly optimistic," Dylan insisted.

"Is he?" Miri asked Jessica.

"Always," Jessica replied.

"Get ready," Nathan instructed.

"Give me twenty seconds to get into position," Talisha requested.

"Captain," Dylan objected.

"Josh?" Nathan asked.

"Piece of cake," Josh replied confidently.

"New contacts," Kaylah reported from the Aurora's sensor station. "Four more destroyers coming out from behind the moon."

"They're trying to ambush us," Cameron realized.

"Perhaps Captain Boynton was not being entirely honest in his actions," Lieutenant Yuati suggested.

"Missiles!" Kaylah added. "Four from each destroyer. Sixteen inbound. First will reach jump trajectory in ten seconds!"

"Point-defenses have activated," the lieutenant announced from the tactical station.

"Get us out of here, Mister Dorsay," Cameron ordered.

"New contact!" Kaylah interrupted. "Dead ahead! It's the Nagoya!"

"Belay last," Cameron instructed. "Helm, keep our nose on the Nagoya. Tactical, two busters, jump them as they exit the tubes."

"First wave!" Kaylah warned, bracing herself.

Four flashes of blue-white light appeared only a few hundred meters to the Aurora's starboard, impacting her shields seconds after they came out of their jumps.

The Aurora's bridge rocked as the incoming jump missiles detonated against her starboard shields.

"Missiles away!" Lieutenant Yuati reported.

"Helm, hard to starboard! Full power!" Cameron instructed. "Jump as soon as you get a clear line!"

"Second wave!" Kaylah warned.

Four more missiles came out of their jumps, again to the Aurora's starboard side. Luckily, the ship's sudden acceleration caused the two missiles on the right to pass aft of them.

The Aurora's bridge rocked as two more missiles impacted their starboard shields and detonated.

"Clear jump line!" Ensign Dorsay reported. "Jumping!"

"Starboard shields down to twenty percent," Lieutenant Yuati reported as the blue-white flash from their escape jump washed over the bridge.

"Status of the Nagoya?" Cameron asked Kaylah.

"Both busters got through her forward shields," Kaylah reported, "but we jumped as they detonated."

"Launch a recon drone," Cameron instructed. "In and out, quickly. Recover at grid Three Two Seven."

"Launching recon drone," Kaylah acknowledged.

"Helm, take us to grid Three Two Seven."

"Grid Three Two Seven, aye," the helmsman acknowledged as he started his turn.

"Recon drone away," Kaylah reported.

"We will need to protect our starboard shields," Lieutenant Yuati suggested. "Six missiles brought them from full power down to twenty percent. It will only take two more impacts to bring them down."

"If those idiots would stop blindly following a criminal, this would be over," Cameron commented.

"Jumping to grid Three Two Seven," the navigator announced.

"Technically, Captain, until properly adjudicated, you would be considered just as much a criminal as Admiral Galiardi."

"Perhaps," Cameron agreed as the jump flash

washed over them. “But my crimes are against EDF regs, not the Earth’s constitution.”

“Point taken.”

“Recon drone has returned,” Kaylah announced. “It has taken fire. Its shields are down to forty percent. Receiving telemetry now.”

“Show me what we’ve got,” Cameron stated.

A display window appeared in the middle of the Aurora’s semi-spherical view screen, showing a tactical map of the Earth-Moon system. Red icons were all over the place, all of them moving toward the Earth.

“Christ,” Cameron exclaimed. “I guess he called in everyone within jump range.”

“Eight destroyers, seventy-eight gunships, and of course, the Cape Town,” Lieutenant Yuati detailed. “They appear to be setting up a blockade of the planet.”

“They’re going to need more ships,” Cameron stated.

“The Nagoya has lost all forward shields and the forward section of her port shields,” Kaylah reported. “She appears to be moving into position to protect the Cape Town.”

“They appear to be ignoring all the other ships in our fleet,” Lieutenant Yuati surmised, studying the display on the main view screen more closely.

“More ships will arrive soon,” Cameron stated. “When they do, that’s when they’ll start attacking our fleet.”

“Any idea how long we have until that happens?” Lieutenant Yuati wondered.

“Minutes at the most.” Cameron replied. “But most of them will be Cobras. There are only twelve destroyers total, and last time I checked, they were patrolling the Jung-Sol border. I doubt Galiardi will pull them in, and even if he did, it would take them a few hours to get here."

"What do we do next?" the lieutenant wondered.

Cameron took a deep breath, letting it out in a long sigh. "We're going to have to make a show of force," she decided. "The captains of those ships need to realize that we'll take them out if we have to." Cameron touched the control pad on the side of her command chair, zooming the tactical display on the main view screen in on the icon representing the Nagoya. "We'll go in twenty clicks behind the Cape Town, slightly above her. Her mass will hide us from the Nagoya. We'll launch four missiles. Two standard jump missiles at the Cape Town, and the other two at the Nagoya. The second two will be standard multi-point jump missiles on a trajectory over the Cape Town, and set them to do a one-eighty and jump back to engage the Nagoya head on."

"They don't even know we have multi-jump missiles," Kaylah stated. "They'll never see it coming."

"They'll think all four were targeting the Cape Town," Cameron explained.

"Won't that be, how do you say it, tipping our hand?" Lieutenant Yuati wondered.

"Maybe," Cameron admitted. "But for all they know, the missiles came from somewhere else. We've already taken out the Cape Town's shields and jump drive, all without apparently firing a single missile at them."

"Jumps to engage the Cape Town are ready, Captain," Ensign Dorsay reported.

"We're two light minutes out at the moment," Ensign Keller reminded his captain.

"Good point," Cameron admitted. "If you pick up

a stand-down order when we jump back in, don't be shy."

"Aye, Captain," her comms officer replied.

"If Keller reports a stand-down, don't wait for me to give the order to abort the missiles, Lieutenant."

"Understood," Lieutenant Yuati acknowledged.

Cameron took another breath, sighing. She was about to launch an attack that could result in the loss of Terran lives; lives she had sworn to protect. She was beginning to understand what it was about command that Nathan had always disliked so much. "Jump us to the come-about waypoint," she instructed.

The Voss's command deck lit up as she jumped into position one kilometer south of the UEA capitol complex.

"Holy crap!" Dylan exclaimed, peering out the forward windows from beside Nathan as they skimmed the rooftops. He glanced to his right as the tops of taller trees passed by. "I can't watch this," he decided, averting his eyes and heading aft.

"Take the port auxiliary station," Nathan told Dylan. "We may need you."

"We're being targeted," Jessica warned from the starboard auxiliary station.

"What a surprise," Dylan commented as he took his seat at the port side station.

"All four anti-aircraft batteries," Jessica added. "They're firing."

A moment later, the ship started shaking as her shields lit up from incoming weapons fire impacts.

"Slow us down," Nathan instructed. "Let's give them a good target."

"We're barely moving now," Josh stated, firing up the deceleration drives at the front of the Voss's nacelles.

"Diverting all power to forward shields," Jessica reported.

"Super Eagles are jumping in," Loki announced.

"They followed us," Nathan decided.

"I'm assuming that's bad?" Miri said.

"It isn't good," Nathan confirmed.

"More contacts," Loki added. "Gunyoki, about thirty of them. They're engaging the Super Eagles."

"That should buy us a few seconds," Nathan surmised.

"Seconds?" Miri said, not feeling terribly confident.

"I'm trying not to be too optimistic," Nathan replied, trying to sound calm for her sake.

"Five hundred meters and closing," Loki reported.

"All four batteries are on us," Jessica warned. "Forward shields are down to sixty percent and falling fast."

"Four hundred meters," Loki updated.

"Josh, yaw forty-five to port and slide in," Nathan instructed. "Nose gunner, target the near battery to the west. Ventral gunner, the near battery to the east. Be ready to open fire as soon as that shield comes down."

"Three hundred meters," Loki updated as the ship shook violently from incoming fire.

"We'll be far enough out that I can target the far battery to the east," the Ghatazhak in the dorsal gun turret reported over the intercom.

"Good idea," Nathan agreed.

Josh's focus jumped between his flight dynamics

display and the starboard windows as he swung the Voss's nose to port and flew sideways at a forty-five-degree angle to their course track. "I bet the AI can't do this."

"Starboard gunner, you get the far battery to the west," Nathan added.

"Copy that," the Ghatazhak in the starboard gun turret replied.

"It could," Dylan insisted. "It just wouldn't be dumb enough to do it."

"Two hundred meters," Loki updated, the ship bouncing and lurching from even more intensive fire than before.

Josh smiled.

"Any time now, Talisha," Nathan muttered to himself.

Talisha jumped her Nighthawk to a position one hundred kilometers north of Winnipeg, far from the capitol complex, immediately pitching up. She brought her nose all the way up and over and then rolled over, completing a one-hundred-and-eighty-degree course change in seconds. "I'm counting on you to take out that shield, Leta," she reminded her AI.

"Understood," her AI replied.

"You still with me, Glen?" she asked her wingman.

"Pulling up onto your port side now," her wingman replied.

She glanced to her left, spotting him as he pulled his fighter in alongside her, about fifteen meters off her wing. "I'll target all the emitters to the right; you take the left. And don't forget to restrict your AI's auto-eject mode, or she'll punch you out the moment you pass through their shields."

"Understood," Glen replied.

"Leta, disable auto-eject," Talisha instructed her AI.

"Confirm auto-eject disable," Leta replied.

"Auto-eject disable, confirmed," Talisha replied.

"Auto-eject disabled," Leta acknowledged.

"You are cleared to engage all targets to starboard. Prioritize their shield emitters."

"Understood," Leta replied.

"Slowing to near hover."

"Slowing," Glen replied.

"Setting grav-lift descent profile," Talisha added. After dialing in a descent rate that would put her on the perfect approach angle, she took a deep breath. "Drop shields, Leta. Jumping in three......two...... one......jump!"

Talisha pressed her jump button, instantly transitioning to only fifty meters from the north side of the capitol complex shield dome, flying toward it at a slight downward angle at what seemed like a near-dead stop. Thankfully, the diversion tactic had worked, and all four air defense turrets inside the shield were currently targeting the Voss on the south side.

"Shield penetration in five seconds," Leta reported.

"Here we go!" Talisha called out over comms.

"Three......two......one..."

The shield wall glowed brightly as the two Nighthawk fighters impacted it at slow speed. Talisha's fighter bucked sharply as it passed through the shield, settling down a second later after the penetration was complete. "Raise shields and fire!" she barked at her AI.

"Shields up," Leta replied. "Firing all turrets."

The two Sugali fighters coasted along at slow speed a mere ten meters above the surface, firing in all directions as they slowly moved over the complex grounds. Shield emitters began exploding, spraying sparks all around them as both ships' AIs fired their respective fighters' point-defense turrets more precisely than any pilot could, especially while trying to avoid incoming fire at such a slow speed.

Talisha's eyes widened as she spotted the nearest anti-aircraft battery to her right rotating around toward her. "Watch for fire, Glen!" she warned over comms. She quickly increased her grav-lift power, causing her ship to jump upward as the battery to her right opened fire. The first salvo passed under her, striking her wingman's shields and causing his fighter to roll slightly from the kinetic energy. "Yawing to starboard!" Talisha barked as she swung her nose around to bring her main cannons onto the nearby battery. A bright flash appeared to her left, causing her to turn her head instinctively just as her wingman's fighter blew apart. "Glen!"

Talisha turned back, determined to seek retribution on the battery before her, but she was too late. The battery opened fire. The first two salvos struck her forward shields dead on, lighting them up so brightly that she was temporarily blinded.

"Forward shields have failed," Leta warned.

Regaining her senses, Talisha pressed and held the firing button on her flight control stick, sending repetitive bolts of plasma energy from her own cannons into the air-defense battery assaulting her. The energy charges from the two opposing weapons met in the middle, creating explosions of energy in mid-air between them, but not for long.

Talisha jinked to starboard, hoping to avoid the incoming fire, but was too late. One bolt of energy seared her port side, the other struck her starboard nose, blowing it apart. Her ship lurched, starting to roll to starboard, the result of losing the grav-lift emitters in that part of her ship.

"Increasing inertial dampeners to full," Leta announced as the ship rolled over and fell toward the ground.

"Eject!" Talisha barked.

"Unable to comply," Leta replied, the ship now upside down and falling to the surface.

"Both fighters are down!" Jessica reported urgently from the Voss's starboard auxiliary station. "The shield is damaged, but not down! It's at maybe twenty percent integrity!"

"Did the pilots eject?" Nathan asked.

"Negative," Jessica replied. "But one did crash inverted in the middle of the complex grounds. It's Talisha's fighter! UEA Security is heading toward her position."

Josh instinctively adjusted his flight controls, causing the Voss to continue moving toward the capitol's weakened shield.

"What are you doing?" Loki asked, fearing he already knew the answer.

"We've got the same grav-lift systems, right?" Josh explained. "Maybe we can make it through?"

"It's more complicated than that," Loki insisted.

"No!" Dylan barked. "He's right! But you have to go nose first! The spacing on our bow emitters is almost the same as on the Sugali fighters," he added as he rapidly began entering commands into his console.

"What are you doing?" Loki wondered, noticing changes in the grav-lift fields on their bow developing.

"I'm adjusting our grav-lift fields to better match those of the Nighthawks!" Dylan explained.

"Captain?" Loki asked, unsure if they should proceed.

"What the hell," Nathan replied. "Do it! Gunners, be ready!"

"You'll have to drop our shields," Dylan warned.

"Great!" Nathan exclaimed, turning and nodding to Jessica.

"Hang on, everyone!" Jessica exclaimed. "Dropping all shields!"

"Here goes nothing!" Josh exclaimed as he brought the nose of the ship back around to face forward again.

The Voss rocked violently as incoming weapons fire slammed into her unprotected hull. The crew flinched as bolts of energy streaked past their nose on either side, slamming into their port and starboard forward-facing cargo bays, ripping them open.

The ship lurched, suddenly slowing and bucking as its bow penetrated the UEA capitol's shield dome.

"I'm through!" the Ghatazhak soldier in their nose gun reported. "Firing!"

The Voss's nose gun, now peering through the shield dome, opened fire, spraying the area with energy bolts which blew apart everything they touched. The rain of energy found several emitters, exploding them in showers of sparks. Finally, it found the nearest anti-aircraft battery that had been pounding the Voss. The nose gun's bolts of energy tore the battery open, sending parts flying in all directions.

With the nearest battery down, the Voss's nose gun shifted to the battery on the opposite side, tearing it apart as easily as the first. The explosion of the battery also caused several nearby shield emitters to explode, collapsing the southern portion of the shield dome.

"It's partly down!" Jessica barked. "We've got a clear path in!"

"Raise shields!" Nathan ordered.

"Already on it!" Jessica assured him.

Josh struggled with the controls, barely able to keep the Voss level with the bow grav-lift emitters out of their normal synchronization with the rest of the ship's grav-lift systems. "How about you restore normal function to the bow emitters!" he barked over his shoulder at Dylan.

"I'm trying!" Dylan assured him.

"Firing!" the dorsal gunner reported.

"Shields are up, but our forward shields are fried!" Jessica reported.

"Firing!" the ventral gunner reported.

"Josh, swing us around so that our bow is pointed

away from the main complex and those last two fucking batteries!"

Josh said nothing as he struggled to keep their nose from dipping and plowing into the surface, initiating a slow yaw to port.

"You might want to move more quickly, Josh!" Nathan urged as the ship rocked from incoming fire.

"I'm trying!" Josh insisted. "I can barely keep our fucking nose up!"

"Bow grav-lift emitters are screwy!" Dylan reported. "I can't get them to normalize!"

"Got that fucker!" the ventral gunner exclaimed over the intercom.

"Firing," the starboard gunner reported.

Nathan glanced out the forward windows as the ship passed over Talisha's inverted fighter.

"I gotta set her down, Cap'n!" Josh exclaimed.

"Not yet!" Nathan barked. "Get us closer to the main complex!"

"I don't know that I can!"

The ship suddenly stopped shaking, the incoming fire ceasing.

"What happened?" Nathan wondered. "Did they stop firing!"

"Negative, sir!" the Ghatazhak in the starboard gun turret reported over the intercom. "I stopped it!"

"Picking up ground fire," Jessica reported. "Those idiots."

"Ventral, drive them back!" Nathan instructed.

"Understood!" the ventral gunner replied.

"All guns, target the remaining shield emitters!" Nathan ordered. "I want that fucking shield gone!"

The jump flash washed over the Aurora's bridge, momentarily filling it with blue-white light. The starry blackness of space was partially replaced by the Earth rotating below them.

"Cape Town directly ahead, twenty clicks and one kilometer lower in altitude," Kaylah reported.

"First two missiles are locked onto the Cape Town," Lieutenant Yuati reported from the tactical station.

"Launch two," Cameron ordered.

"Launching two," the lieutenant replied, pressing the launch button. "Missiles away, loading second round. First missiles jumping."

"Missiles have transited," Kaylah reported. "Cape Town is engaging missile defenses."

"Second two missiles are ready."

"Launch second round," Cameron ordered.

"Launching two more," the lieutenant acknowledged.

Two flashes of light appeared in the lower right and left corners of the main view screen as the two missiles jumped away just after clearing the tubes. "Second round of missiles have jumped.

"Helm, jump us forward, ten clicks past the Cape Town," Cameron instructed. "As soon as we transition, yaw us ninety to port."

"Jumping forward twenty and yawing ninety to port," the helmsman acknowledged.

"Lieutenant Yuati, port broadsides on the Cape Town, starboard on the Nagoya. But keep the port cannons at half power. I want to bloody their nose, not blow off their face."

"Jumping in three..." Ensign Dorsay began.

"Understood," the lieutenant replied.

"Two..."

"Comms, order both ships to stand down all weapons or be destroyed," Cameron instructed.

"One..."

"Aye, sir."

"Jumping."

The blue-white flash washed over the bridge again, although nothing appeared to change on the main view screen.

"Cape Town is behind us, Nagoya ahead of us," Kaylah reported.

"Yawing,"

"Assigning targets to broadsides," Lieutenant Yuati reported. "Port broadsides at half intensity."

"Fire when ready," Cameron instructed.

"New contacts," Kaylah reported. "Nagoya is attempting to intercept. One down... HIT! Direct hit on her bow!"

"I have firing solutions on both vessels," Lieutenant Yuati reported. "Firing port and starboard broadsides."

"I'm detecting multiple hull breaches on the Nagoya," Kaylah warned. "Her power levels are fluctuating wildly."

"What the hell?" Cameron started.

"Secondaries!" Kaylah added. "The Nagoya's ZPEDs are becoming unstable! They'll go critical in less than a minute!"

"Cease fire to starboard!" Cameron ordered.

"Cape Town is launching missiles," Kaylah warned.

"They're firing the big guns at us as well," the lieutenant added.

"Twelve jump flashes!"

"Ten-light-second escape jump!" Cameron ordered. "Execute!"

The ship rocked hard as two missiles impacted their port shields, multiple explosive rail gun rounds joining them.

"Failure in primary jump array," Ensign Dorsay reported urgently. "Switching to secondary array!"

"Get us out of here, Ensign!" Cameron barked as two more missiles rocked the ship.

"Port shields down to twenty percent!" Lieutenant Yuati reported.

"Jumping!" the navigator announced as the jump flash washed over them.

"Hard to port, twenty degrees!" Cameron barked. "Jump us another five light seconds as soon as you complete your turn!

"Twenty to port, aye!"

"Five light seconds, aye!"

"Engineering, Captain!" she called over her comm-set. "Get the primary array back online!"

"I'm working on it," Vladimir assured her.

"New contacts!" Kaylah reported. "Four Cobra gunships to starboard, two clicks and closing fast. They're firing!"

"Plasma turrets, Lieutenant!" Cameron instructed.

"More contacts!" Kaylah added. "Eight Gunyoki! They're attacking the gunships. The gunships are breaking off."

"Turn complete," the helmsman reported.

"Hold jump," Cameron ordered. "Wait for my call."

"Holding jump," the navigator confirmed.

"Cobras are jumping clear!" Kaylah reported. "Gunyoki are jumping after them!"

"Now, Mister Dorsay!" Cameron ordered.

"Jumping!"

"Kaylah, get me a status update on the Nagoya!"

Cameron instructed as the jump flash washed over the bridge.

"I'm getting a Mayday call from the Nagoya!" Ensign Keller reported from the comm-station. "They're abandoning ship!"

"They're going to want our blood, now," Cameron surmised.

"I'm detecting eight escape pods from the Nagoya."

"She has twelve," Cameron commented.

"They've managed to eject one of their ZPEDs," Kaylah added. "The other one is still unstable."

"How long do they have?" Cameron asked.

"I'm surprised it hasn't gone yet."

"Shouldn't they eject it as well?" Lieutenant Yuati wondered.

"The ejection system must have failed," Cameron commented. "That's why they're abandoning ship."

"Two more escape pods have ejected," Kaylah reported. "Last ZPED is going critical...she's coming apart!" Kaylah turned and looked at Cameron. "We just killed the Nagoya, sir."

"How many made it out?" Cameron asked.

"No idea, sir," Kaylah admitted. "The ZPED blast is screwing up my sensors.

"If ten pods made it out, and each of them was full, that's eighty survivors," the helmsman commented.

"Out of one hundred and twelve," Cameron stated, staring straight ahead.

This is not what I signed up for, she thought.

Two Reapers appeared behind blue-white flashes of light, settling into a hover ten meters above the Voss as she settled down onto the UEA capitol complex grounds. The Reapers shifted slightly, moving to the forward end of the Voss, to either side of Talisha's inverted crashed fighter. The Reapers descended a few more meters as their side doors opened, and six Ghatazhak jumped to the surface from each.

As they hit the ground, the Ghatazhak opened fire, sending a barrage of stunner blasts at the advancing UEA security forces, dropping them with ease. The UEA security forces, however, were not firing stunners, and their heavy fire was quickly draining the Ghatazhak's shields.

While eight of the Ghatazhak formed a barrier wall and continued firing, four others fell back to Talisha's inverted fighter. One of them dropped to his knees at the front of the ship, between the damaged and undamaged nose cones, accessing the emergency cockpit access panel. Within seconds, he had the panel open and had managed to disengage the canopy locks. The upper and lower halves of the Sugali fighter's clamshell canopy were no longer geared to move together, but two of the Ghatazhak were able to pry the upper ventral canopy shell open.

"Finally!" Talisha exclaimed as she slid out of the inverted fighter. She looked at the stunned Ghatazhak. "What?"

"We didn't think you'd still be alive," one of the Ghatazhak admitted, gesturing toward the heavily damaged fighter.

"The kill shot flipped me over, and I couldn't eject, so my AI cranked up the inertial dampeners to..." Several energy bolts zipped over their heads, cutting her off mid-sentence. "We'll talk later," she said, ducking.

"Good idea. Voss! We've got her! She's alive and

well! Drop your forward shields so we can get inside your defense perimeter!"

"We don't have any forward shields," Jessica replied. "Come on in, but watch your six and our twelve!"

"Let's move!" the soldier barked, leading Talisha along as he advanced behind his line of comrades.

The Voss's aft cargo ramp deployed, and the Ghatazhak charged out, jumping off the sides of the ramp and spreading out, all of them in their mark two combat armor. As they deployed, they fired with both wrist cannons, stunning UEA security forces with ease from inside the Voss's shields.

"Why don't you just go out there with her?" Dylan asked Nathan as he tapped commands into Jessica's station in her absence.

"I think the Earth has had enough surprises for one day," Nathan explained.

"Right," Dylan replied. "I've tied General Telles's helmet camera into your overhead display."

Nathan reached up and flipped down the small view screen in the overhead panel, turning it on. As promised, the view from the general's helmet camera appeared as Miri and her protection detail prepared to disembark. "Protect my sister, General," Nathan called over comms.

"I protect everyone," the general replied.

Miri and the others assembled at the top of the

ramp. General Telles, Jessica, Corporal Vasya, and several other Ghatazhak had formed a protective ring around her, preparing to move out.

"As the rightful president of Earth, you have ultimate authority on this world," the general told Miri. "However, I would strongly advise you to do exactly as we say, when we say it. It is the only way that we have any hope of protecting you."

"Don't worry," Miri assured him, her eyes wide with fear. She looked at the general, his face amazingly calm and confident. "I'm doing the right thing, aren't I?"

"In my experience, the Scotts always do," the general replied, his comment followed by a rare smile. "Shall we make history?" he added, gesturing toward the ramp.

Miri took a deep breath, summoning up all her courage. After a moment, she turned toward the ramp. "Let's do this," she stated.

"Move out, gentlemen," the general ordered.

In unison, the circle of Ghatazhak, with Miri and General Telles at the center, headed down the ramp. Miri flinched repeatedly as incoming weapons fire from the very men who should be swearing their allegiance to her slammed into the Voss's shields, causing them to flash brilliantly at each point of impact. All around her, Ghatazhak soldiers were firing their wrist cannons, showering the charging UEA security forces with stunner energy. Despite the strength of the Ghatazhak position, the security forces continued to defend theirs with fervent dedication.

The circle stopped midway down the ramp.

"Now," General Telles told her.

Miri reached up, fumbling for her comm-set

control just above her left ear. She tapped it, then cleared her throat, her cough echoing through the Voss's external loudspeakers. "I am Miranda Scott-Thornton, daughter of the late President Dayton Scott, and I am here to claim my legal right of heir-to-office! I hereby order you to cease fire and stand down! If you do not, my forces will subdue you, with deadly force if necessary! I beg of you to obey my command! All I wish to do is to present a DNA sample to prove my identity to all! Please! Cease fire!"

In the distance, she could see Admiral Galiardi as he came out of the main building, EDF spec-ops on either side of him.

"Destroy them!" the admiral ordered his men.

Miri wasn't the only one who spotted the admiral. "Nathan, we have a problem," General Telles warned over comms.

"This is insane!" Lieutenant Commander Perrin exclaimed, watching the events outside from the capitol complex control center. He stepped up to the comms officer's console. "Get me local spec-ops command," he instructed.

"Aye, sir," the comms officer acknowledged. "Commander Tetz on the line."

"Commander Tetz, this is Lieutenant Commander Perrin in command. I need you to order your men protecting Admiral Galiardi to place him under arrest and detain him for multiple violations of EDF regulations and acts of treason against the United Earth Alliance constitution."

"Perrin," the commander replied. "Do you realize

what you're asking? Do you know what's going on out there?"

"I do!" the lieutenant commander replied. "And if you don't do as I'm requesting immediately, my next call will be to UEA security to do the same. Then your men will be fighting two sets of enemies. Do you really want to be the man who started a war between the civilian authority and the military that is supposed to serve it?"

"Two destroyers off our port beam," Kaylah warned from the Aurora's sensor station. "Five clicks and closing fast. They're locking their main batteries on us."

"Helm, hard to starboard. Show them our aft shields," Cameron instructed. "They're the only ones that are still at full power."

"The Chennai is launching missiles!" Kaylah warned. "Twenty seconds."

"Helm, prepare to jump us ahead five hundred clicks," Cameron instructed.

"Aye, sir."

"That will put us in range of Port Terra's defense batteries."

"Can't be helped," Cameron stated. "Besides, if they wanted to be in this fight, they could have launched jump missiles at us long ago."

"Ten seconds to missile impacts," Kaylah warned as the ship rocked from weapons fire striking their aft shields.

"Any time, Mister Dorsay," Cameron urged.

"Jumping in three..."

"Four gunships just jumped in dead ahead!"

Kaylah warned. "Line abreast! Blocking our jump line!"

"Two..."

"Thread the needle, Mister Tala," Cameron instructed, fighting to remain calm.

"Threading," the helmsman replied, changing their course ever so slightly.

"Hold jump," Cameron added. "Your call, Mister Tala.

"Holding jump."

"My call," the helmsman acknowledged.

"Five seconds," Kaylah warned.

The helmsman watched his tactical display out of the corner of his eye as he steered the massive warship in between the approaching gunships. Suddenly, their jump line on the display switched from red to green, and he took his hands off the flight controls as he said, "Jump!"

"Jumping!" the navigator announced as the blue-white flash washed over the bridge.

There was a thud and a violent shake, followed by quiet.

"What happened?" Cameron wondered, looking to Kaylah.

"Our shields brushed theirs," Kaylah reported.

"Comms, contact the Voss," Cameron ordered. "Find out what's taking Miri so damned long! Things are getting ugly up here!"

"What is that?" Josh wondered, watching the same camera feed as Nathan.

"I'm not sure," Nathan admitted, "but it doesn't look good."

A second later, whatever it was fired, lighting up the Voss's aft shields.

"Holy crap!" Loki exclaimed. "That thing just sucked about twenty percent of our aft shield strength!"

Jessica sprang into action, breaking from formation and moving across the line of Ghatazhak to get a better angle on the cannon that the EDF spec-ops were firing. She fired with both wrist cannons as she ran, but the spec-ops cannon had a shield of its own, and she wasn't getting through it anytime soon.

"Shields are down to forty percent!" Nathan warned over comms. "Two more hits, and we lose aft shields!"

Another blast slammed into the Voss's aft shields, causing them to flash brightly.

"All Ghatazhak!" General Telles called over comms. "Target that cannon! Shoot to kill!"

"Aft shields at twenty percent!" Nathan warned. "Get Miri back inside!"

"Spec-ops at the bow!" another Ghatazhak warned over comms. "Deploy the front ramp so we can get Sane inside!"

"I'll give you covering fire!" the Voss's nose gunner announced over comms.

Another cannon blast struck their aft shields, causing the emitters across the back of the Voss to explode in showers of sparks.

"Aft shield is down!" Nathan reported.

His warning was unnecessary, as the incoming fire from the UEA security forces that had been bouncing off the Voss's shields was now slamming into the shields of the Ghatazhak lined up just inside the shield perimeter.

"Maximum force!" General Telles barked, stepping out of the circle of Ghatazhak protecting Miri as they started backing up the ramp to get her back inside and out of harm's way.

With the shield now down, Jessica wasted no time. She charged forth, firing both wrist cannons of her mark two combat armor at full power. "Capsi!" she barked as incoming fire bounced off her personal shields. "Micro-jump! Just behind the enemy lines! On my mark!" she instructed as she charged toward the enemy line just outside the main building.

"Incoming fire is rapidly draining our power," her suit AI warned. "We may not have..."

Jessica took a running leap into the air. "NOW!" she commanded. In an instant, she disappeared in a flash of blue-white light, reappearing two meters off the ground behind the spec-ops cannon position. She landed in a tuck and roll, coming back up with most of her momentum still intact. Two more steps and she was at the wall behind the cannon position. The spec-ops operating the cannon turned, pulling their sidearms to take her out, but she was too fast.

Jessica leaned back slightly as she took two steps up the wall, flipping over and firing both wrist cannons at the spec-ops officers as she landed, killing them both. She immediately turned to open fire on the rest of the UEA forces when an officer came running out of the building, yelling.

"HOLD FIRE!" Lieutenant Commander Perrin yelled as he came out. "HOLD FIRE!"

UEA security forces, as well as the remaining EDF spec-ops who had recently joined them, began receiving new orders over their helmet comms, which seemed to match the orders being shouted by the newly arrived EDF officer. As instructed, their fire began to trail off.

"Cease fire!" General Telles yelled over comms.

The Ghatazhak were far better trained, and their fire stopped instantly; yet each of them stood their ground, crouched in combat positions with wrist cannons still trained on their targets, their weakened personal shields still glowing faintly.

Jessica froze, down on her knees with both wrist cannons trained on the nearest spec-ops soldiers. "Don't make me kill you, boys," she stated confidently.

Admiral Galiardi couldn't believe what he was seeing. "What the hell are you doing?" he exclaimed. "Their shield is down!"

"Admiral Galiardi," Lieutenant Commander Perrin stated as he walked up to the admiral. "I'm placing you under arrest..."

The admiral couldn't believe what was happening. He glanced at the Voss, seeing that Miranda Scott-Thornton, the cause of all his problems, was headed back inside.

"Admiral!" Lieutenant Commander Perrin shouted. "Hand over your sidearm!"

"You fool," the admiral replied, pulling his sidearm and taking aim at Miri.

Her eyes still locked with those of the spec-ops soldiers before her, Jessica moved her right arm a hair to her right and fired a single shot.

A single bolt of energy streaked past the spec-ops soldiers, passing behind the other UEA security forces, and finally finding Admiral Galiardi, striking him in the side of the head and knocking him over.

The spec-ops soldiers tensed up, raising their weapons to take aim on Jessica.

"Nobody else has to die today," Jessica urged, bringing her right wrist cannon back to bear on them.

Lieutenant Commander Perrin ran over to the admiral's body, kneeling beside him and rolling him over. At first, he was taken aback. The entire side of the admiral's head was missing, the other half scorched and nearly unrecognizable.

"Sir?" one of the UEA security officers asked, stepping up beside the body. "What do we do?"

Lieutenant Commander Perrin slowly rose to his feet. He looked around briefly. Before him were nearly one hundred UEA and EDF troops, weapons at the ready. Fifteen meters away was a small contingent of Ghatazhak, clad in the most frightening-looking, black, high-tech combat armor he had ever seen.

"Sir?" the UEA officer repeated.

Lieutenant Commander Perrin looked at Miranda Scott-Thornton standing at the top of the Voss's cargo ramp, still surrounded by loyal Ghatazhak. "We welcome the true leader of Earth."

"Twelve gunships just jumped in to port," Kaylah warned. "They're on attack vectors."

"Twenty-three Super Eagles are coming up from the surface," Lieutenant Yuati reported. "They also appear to be on an intercept course."

Cameron felt as if the situation was rapidly spinning out of her control. Her actions had already caused the loss of at least thirty-two lives on the Nagoya, likely more.

"Gunships are firing," Kaylah reported.

"Port shields at thirty-eight percent," Lieutenant Yuati warned. "Shall I engage the gunships?"

"Where are the Gunyoki?" Cameron asked.

"Grid Two Seven Five, engaging Super Eagles and more gunships," Kaylah reported.

"Captain!" Ensign Keller called out. "I'm picking up encrypted flash traffic from Fleet Command. It's going out to all ships!"

"Can you break the encryption?" Cameron asked.

"It will take time," the comms officer warned.

"Gunships are breaking off," Kaylah announced.

"Every EDF ship on my tactical display has stopped targeting us," Lieutenant Yuati added. "This may be a cease-fire, Captain."

"God let's hope so," Cameron exclaimed with relief.

"Flash traffic from the Voss," Ensign Keller announced. "We're being ordered to cease fire but maintain combat status for now."

"Then it is a cease-fire," Cameron surmised.

"There's more," the comms officer added. "Miss Scott-Thornton has assumed the office of president!"

Cameron slumped back in her chair in complete disbelief. Seven months ago, when she made the decision to defy orders and take her ship to the Pentaurus sector to help Nathan, she was certain she would never see Earth again. Now it loomed large on her main view screen, and there was a pretty good chance she wouldn't be facing a court-martial.

CHAPTER FIFTEEN

Dom Mogan stood proudly on the command platform in the middle of the Ton-Mogan's central command center. All around him were nearly one hundred officers and technicians sitting in concentric circles, monitoring the countless systems and weapons of the massive battle platform. This was the heart of the beast, the most potent weapons platform ever devised, and it was under his control, as were the other two that flew alongside it.

Pentaralom Jung-Mogan rarely showed his face in the command center. As the leader of his caste, his place was not to command the Ton-Mogan or any other ship. Admirals commanded battle platforms, not doms. However, this was an auspicious occasion.

"We will arrive at the attack point momentarily," Admiral Korahk reported.

"There were no signs of detection?" Dom Mogan asked, already knowing the answer.

"None," the admiral assured him. "They are completely unaware of our presence."

"But we cannot be certain," Dom Mogan commented.

"Our cloaking fields obscure our sensors as well," Admiral Korahk confirmed.

"Then they could be waiting for us, ready to pounce."

"We have been in their system for several hours," the admiral stated. "Were they aware of our approach, I suspect we would have been fired upon by now."

Dom Mogan sighed. He had been waiting for this moment for more than seven years. Millions had died on Nor-Patri and Zhu-Anok. Many of them he had known. Some he had even cared about. But more importantly, the honor of his empire had been damaged. Patrian blood had been spilled, and the code of the warrior castes demanded vengeance.

The code of the warrior castes. It had ruled Dom Mogan his entire life. It had dictated his every move, every decision. Honoring it meant honoring his people, his world. Yet everything he had fought to protect all these decades was about to be lost. Trillions would die in the next few hours; trillions upon trillions more in the coming days and weeks. Those who were left would live out their lives in horror, as witnesses of an apocalypse surpassing the bio-digital plague itself. Just as the plague had once done, the Tonba-Hon-Venar would excise both sectors of space of all the ills that had brought them to this point. It all made perfect sense. Sometimes the only solution was to tear everything down and start again.

The logic had always seemed flawless. Harsh, yes, but reality often was. But that logic was predicated on the belief that the worlds of the Sol and Jung sectors were all that existed, or at least were all that mattered. What few worlds existed beyond were of little consequence. Hunter-gatherers barely surviving. Agrarians toiling away in the fields with oxen and plows. Such worlds had little hope of continued existence.

But the jump drive had revealed the truth: that there were more human-inhabited worlds out there than anyone had imagined, and that many of them were quite advanced. The mere fact that these advanced civilizations did exist had caused him to question his own beliefs. They had even caused him to question the logic of the Tonba-Hon-Venar.

Dom Mogan forced himself to set aside all of this. He was the leader of the most powerful warrior caste in all the empire. If he did not complete the Tonba-Hon-Venar, the Kirton or Zorakh castes would, and his failure would be remembered as vividly as their success. If all was to fall, better it was the Jung-Mogan caste who returned honor to the empire.

"Are we prepared for the attack?" Dom Mogan asked the admiral.

"All platforms reported full combat readiness," the admiral assured him. "All fighters, gunships, and frigates are manned and ready for deployment, and all missile tubes are loaded and ready for launch."

"Very well," Dom Mogan replied. "We will target Port Terra first," he instructed. "Once her defenses are disabled, we will send in our assault teams to capture a jump shuttle. Once that has been accomplished, we will destroy the entire asteroid, along with the Earth itself."

"What if they have warships in the system?" Admiral Korahk wondered.

"Their destroyers and gunships are of secondary concern," Dom Mogan replied. "They are of no threat. Only the Aurora and the Cape Town are capable of stopping us. If either of them is present, target them in the first wave."

"Understood," Admiral Korahk acknowledged. "However, the Aurora has not been spotted by any of our recon drones for months."

"In my experience, the Aurora has a nasty habit of surprising us," Dom Mogan explained. "If she surprises us today, make certain it is the last time she does so."

"She is but one ship, my lord."

"As long as the Aurora exists, the future of the

empire is at risk. If she is here, we destroy her. If she is not, we must find her."

"Or course, my lord."

"Then let it begin," Dom Mogan instructed.

* * *

"New contacts!" Kaylah reported urgently from the Aurora's sensor station. "Oh my God!"

That feeling of relief Cameron had experienced a minute ago suddenly vanished. "What is it?"

Kaylah turned to look at Cameron. "Jung battle platforms. Three of them."

"How the hell did they get past our FTL detection nets?" Cameron wondered in disbelief. "Did they just come out of FTL?"

"Negative," Kaylah replied. "They just...appeared. No FTL trail, no mass-reduction field signatures, nothing. Just one second, there was nothing, and the next second, they were there."

"And no old light?"

"None."

"Position?" Cameron asked.

"One four seven degrees, up twenty-five, system relative, at just over a million kilometers out."

"Lieutenant Yuati," Cameron called. "Tactical assessment?"

"The battle platforms are on an intercept course with Earth," the lieutenant replied. "They raised their shields seconds after they appeared."

"New contacts!" Kaylah added. "Missile launches! From all three of them! I count seventy-two total!"

"Comms, contact the Mystic. Tell them to get Borrol here, pronto."

"Aye, sir!"

"And patch me into all EDF frequencies, in the clear," Cameron ordered.

"Tied in," Ensign Keller replied.

"All EDF ships, this is Captain Taylor of the Aurora. Despite the fact that we were ready to destroy one another minutes ago, we now have a common purpose: to defend Earth. Cobras and Gunyoki, concentrate on missile intercepts. Destroyers and gunships, stand ready to engage any frigates that come out of those platforms. Eagles and Nighthawks will intercept any fighters they send into Earth's atmosphere to target surface assets."

"Incoming vid-message from the Cape Town," Ensign Keller announced.

Cameron signaled for the message to be put on the main view screen, and a moment later, Captain Stettner appeared on the screen, looking quite angry.

"Odd coincidence that the Jung showed up at the same time as you did," Captain Stettner accused. "I'm betting you knew they were coming."

"Yes, but we expected them in a few days, not now," Cameron assured him.

"Yet you took out our shields and jump drive."

"I'll answer your baseless accusations later, Stettner. For now, I suggest you spin up your missile defenses."

"We'll hit the lead platform with our big guns," Captain Stettner stated. "It would help if you would take out their shields the same way you took out ours."

"Do not go offensive," Cameron insisted. "Not yet."

"Are you mad?"

"If you go offensive now, you'll fuck everything up, trust me!" Cameron barked. "Aurora out." Cameron gestured for her comms officer to kill the connection. "Connect me with Fleet Command," she instructed.

* * *

Although well defended, the Mystic was far from a warship. Commander Kaplan had enjoyed the challenge of making the converted luxury cruise ship more efficient in her new role as the Karuzari Alliance's hospital ship. It had been a rewarding challenge, but it was times like these, when everyone else was risking their lives in combat, that she missed her job as the Aurora's XO.

But being the XO of the Mystic Empress was about as close to being captain as you could get without actually being the ship's commanding officer. Captain Rainey had been ready for retirement for years and spent much of his time in his quarters, only walking the decks on occasion to keep up appearances. She was the one running the ship day in and day out, and because of that, the ship's operation had dramatically improved.

"Incoming flash traffic from the Aurora," the Mystic's comms officer reported.

The officer of the watch stepped over to the comm-station, picked up the data pad containing the message, and delivered it to Commander Kaplan, who was a few meters away.

The commander studied the data pad, her brow furrowing. "Where is Kor-Dom Borrol?" she asked the officer of the watch.

"Observation deck, upper level, starboard side, table twenty-seven. I believe he is having lunch."

"Lunch is over," the commander stated. "Get his ass up here pronto."

"Yes, sir," the officer of the watch replied.

"General quarters," the commander added. "Helm, prepare to jump us to the Sol system. We'll insert halfway between the orbits of Earth and Venus."

"General quarters, aye!" the comms officer

acknowledged as the alarm klaxons sounded from the corridor.

She might not be going into battle, but they were definitely about to go into harm's way.

* * *

Miri stepped up to Lieutenant Commander Perrin, who, along with the other officers and men around him, stood at attention. She glanced at his name tag. "Lieutenant Commander Perrin," she greeted. "Thank you."

"I was just doing my job, Madam President."

"Nevertheless, it took a lot of courage to do so, considering the circumstances."

"The admiral crossed the line," the lieutenant commander explained. "Medical presented your DNA transmission, and he ignored it. He even put the chief medical officer in the brig. I should have acted then. Had I done so, some of these men would still be alive. For that, I will never forgive myself."

"Leadership carries heavy burdens," Miri stated, putting her hand on the lieutenant commander's shoulder.

"Madam President?" the lieutenant commander asked.

"Something my father told my younger brother when he had the responsibilities of command thrust upon his shoulders without asking for it."

"Must be why I voted for him."

Miri smiled.

"New problem, Miri," Nathan's voice squawked over her comm-set. "Get inside and into shelter, ASAP."

Miri tapped her comm-set. "What's going on?" she asked.

"Just move," Nathan urged. "General Telles will fill you in."

"Lieutenant Commander," General Telles interrupted, having overheard Nathan's recommendations. "We need to move inside, preferably into your command center."

"Of course," the lieutenant commander agreed. "Madam President?" he added, gesturing for her to follow him.

"Ghatazhak!" the general called. "Secure the perimeter and seal off the building. Team Alpha stays with the president."

"We can handle her security," the lieutenant commander assured the general.

"No offense, Lieutenant Commander, but the Ghatazhak will see to Miss Scott-Thornton's safety until further notice."

The lieutenant commander looked to his new president.

"All forces on these grounds will take orders from General Telles and his designated subordinates until further notice," Miri confirmed. "Is that understood?"

"Yes, ma'am," the lieutenant commander agreed. "Right this way, Madam President."

"Nash, return to the Voss," General Telles ordered Jessica over comms. "I suspect Nathan is going to need you."

"On my way."

Corporal Vasya and Specialist Brill turned to the general.

"We should go with Nash," Kit told the general.

"Not today," General Telles replied. "Our job is to protect the president. You four form a barrier around her at all times, until we're certain this is over and the facility is secure."

"We're on it," Kit assured him.

General Telles exchanged a glance with Miri. "They will protect you," he informed her. "Do as they say."

"Where are you going?" Miri asked.

"I will see to perimeter security and join you later," the general explained.

"Aurora is reporting a second wave of seventy-two missiles," Loki announced from the Voss's copilot seat.

"Do they have any idea what the first wave targets are?" Nathan wondered.

"If they do, they haven't said anything," Loki replied.

"So the Jung double-crossed us, huh?" Jessica exclaimed as she entered the command deck through the aft hatch, tossing her mark two helmet aside and pulling off her gloves as she quickly moved forward.

"Borrol warned us that the battle platforms would attack the moment they appeared," Nathan reminded her.

"Yeah, two days from now," Jessica pointed out as she took her seat at the starboard auxiliary station.

"Marcus reports that we're all buttoned up," Loki announced.

"Get us back in space, Josh," Nathan instructed.

"My pleasure," Josh replied, pushing his grav-lift throttles forward. "Nothing worse than being shot at while sitting on the ground."

"What can we do?" Dylan questioned. "Aren't Jung battle platforms huge? I'm talking seriously huge!"

"Winnipeg will be one of their primary targets," Jessica pointed out.

"But aren't there already, like, a hundred ships out there to intercept those missiles?"

"Would you prefer to sit here and wait to see if they're successful?" Jessica asked.

"I guess not," Dylan admitted.

"Someone remind me what the departure jump altitude restrictions are on this world?" Loki asked.

"Screw it," Nathan insisted. "Jump us out of here."

"Destination?" Josh asked as they began accelerating forward as they climbed.

"Just get us back into space," Nathan replied.

Josh glanced over his shoulder at Nathan, surprised. "Why? So they can shoot us down?"

"Hopefully not," Nathan replied, not sounding too sure himself.

Dom Mogan stared at the large holographic tactical display hovering before him over the heads of the circles of technicians surrounding the command platform. Something was wrong.

"First wave is on course for primary target," Admiral Korahk reported confidently.

"Something is wrong," Dom Mogan stated. "Why are there so many warships and in such odd formations?"

"We've identified both the Cape Town and the Aurora!" one of the senior officers in the nearest ring reported. "The Cape Town is unshielded!"

"Retarget the first wave onto the Cape Town,"

Admiral Korahk instructed. "Target the next five waves onto her as well! She must be destroyed!"

"Yes, Admiral!"

"Their positions and course tracks do not make sense," Dom Mogan insisted, still studying the tactical display.

"An exercise, perhaps?" Admiral Korahk suggested.

"And what kind of ships are those?" Dom Mogan wondered, pointing at a grouping of unidentified ships of varying sizes. "That one appears to be as large as one of our battleships."

"Commander!" the admiral barked toward a junior officer in the first ring of workstations. "I need IDs on all ships!"

"Right away, sir!"

"Something is just not right," Dom Mogan repeated.

"Second wave is away!" one of the weapons officers announced. "First wave confirms retargeting!"

"Confirm all platforms are launching," the admiral barked.

"Ton-Orso and Ton-Joja both show simultaneous launch status," one of the comms officers acknowledged. "We are attacking as one!"

Admiral Korahk turned to his dom. "My lord, I recommend we postpone any attack against the planet and concentrate all missiles on the Cape Town and the Aurora."

"Agreed," Dom Mogan confirmed.

Miri and her entourage of Ghatazhak and UEA

security personnel marched out of the elevator and across the security foyer toward the command center.

"You," Sergeant Viano called, pointing at the senior officer at the security desk. "Are you in charge of security down here?"

"Uh, yes," the officer replied, unsure what was going on.

"This is Sergeant Viano of the Ghatazhak," Lieutenant Commander Perrin explained to the officer. "He is currently in charge of the president's security."

"The pres..." The officer looked at Miri. "Madam President," he greeted respectfully.

"I'll need to review your security measures, Lieutenant," Sergeant Viano stated.

"Of course."

Sergeant Viano looked to Corporal Vasya, who immediately began barking orders to the rest of the Ghatazhak present.

"Lieutenant," Miri greeted as she turned and continued into the command center, with Lieutenant Commander Perrin in tow. "First order of business is a change in EDF command authority."

"With the admiral dead, command would automatically pass to Commander Macklay at Fleet Command in Port Terra," the lieutenant commander explained.

"What about the other admirals?" Miri asked.

"There are no other admirals, Madam President."

"What about Seifert and MacDonald?"

"Seifert retired when his wife died, and MacDonald died in a car crash a couple of weeks ago."

"Well at least there won't be any rank issues to deal with," Miri commented.

"Madam President?" the lieutenant commander wondered, uncertain of her meaning.

"You might want to sit down, Lieutenant Commander," Miri told him. "What I'm about to tell you is going to be hard to believe."

Commander Macklay watched the Fleet Command Center at Port Terra in the asteroid once known as Karuzara, orbiting high above the Earth. Despite the sudden shift in their situation, all of his operators seemed to be adjusting to their new reality without missing a beat.

"I've got Captain Taylor of the Aurora on vid-comm!" the comms officer reported.

"Put her on my screen," the commander ordered, stepping up to his standing workstation. A moment later, Cameron Taylor appeared on his view screen. "You've got a hell of a lot of nerve, Taylor."

"You can call me all the names you want later, Macklay. For now, just shut up and listen. I trust you heard my wide broadcast?"

"Like I said, a hell of a lot of nerve."

"Then confirm my instructions to your forces, and for God's sake, order them to refrain from going on the offensive!"

"I'm not about to take orders from..."

"We know things that you don't!" Cameron snapped, cutting him off. "And we have technology that you don't know about, Commander. Without it, you don't stand a chance in hell of warding off those battle platforms, let alone the ships that will follow if our plan fails."

"Your plan?" the commander questioned.

"And be ready to receive instructions from your new fleet commander," Cameron added.

"And whom might that be?" Commander Macklay questioned.

"Admiral Nathan Scott, commander of the Karuzari Alliance."

The commander's eyes widened. "Then the rumors are true."

"Yes."

"How is that even possible?"

"Long story; no time," Cameron replied.

"You're not getting off that easy, Taylor. I'm going to want explanations. We all are."

"You'll get them," she promised. "Assuming we're all still alive an hour from now. Aurora out."

"Flash traffic from UEA command," the comms officer updated. "Admiral Galiardi is dead, and Miranda Scott-Thornton's identity has been confirmed by live DNA testing. She has assumed the office of president, and her first order confirms what Captain Taylor just told us. Admiral Scott is now the commander of all Sol Alliance forces."

Commander Macklay sighed. "A hell of a fucking day, isn't it."

"Third wave!" Kaylah reported from the Aurora's sensor station. "Another seventy-two."

"Cobras and Gunyoki are attempting to intercept the first wave," Lieutenant Yuati announced from tactical.

"Please tell me those battle platforms are keeping a steady track," Cameron asked Kaylah.

"Affirmative," Kaylah confirmed.

"I need strike coordinates based on course and speed, ASAP," Cameron instructed.

"On it."

"Comms," Cameron called. "Prepare another comm-drone for the Orochi."

"Aye, sir," Ensign Keller acknowledged.

"Another wave has launched," Kaylah reported.

"Jesus," Cameron exclaimed. "That's two hundred and eighty-eight missiles."

"I have targeting data for the first and second waves," Lieutenant Yuati announced. "Both appear to be targeting the Cape Town, and unless the third and fourth waves change course in the next twenty seconds, it's a safe bet they're targeting the Cape Town as well."

"Time to first impacts?"

"Two minutes," the lieutenant replied.

"Aurora?" Cameron called. "Can the Cape Town handle that many missiles?"

"Without shields, negative," the Aurora's AI replied. "If all of her missile defense weapons could be brought to bear, she might have a chance, but..."

"What about with us running intercept?" Cameron asked.

"Assuming a fifty-percent intercept rate on all two hundred and eighty-eight missiles, the Cape Town will have a survival probability of seventy-eight percent. However, the Aurora will be destroyed."

It took less than a second for Cameron to make her decision. "Helm, new course. Prepare to jump us in front of those missiles."

"Jump to Sol plotted and ready," the Mystic's helmsman reported.

"Jump when ready," Commander Kaplan instructed.

"Jumping in three..."

"Why was my meal interrupted?" Kor-Dom Borrol demanded as he was escorted onto the bridge.

"Two..."

"Your forces have arrived," Commander Kaplan stated with disdain, not even looking back at the Jung leader.

"One..."

"That's impossible," the kor-dom insisted.

"Jumping."

"They aren't due for..." Kor-Dom Borrol's words trailed off as icons began appearing all over the forward windows of the Mystic's bridge, three of which were quite large and identified as Jung battle platforms.

"Time for you to make good on your end of the deal, Kor-Dom," Commander Kaplan stated.

"Gunyoki are intercepting the first wave now!" Lieutenant Yuati reported from the Aurora's tactical station.

"New contact!" Kaylah announced. "It's the Mystic."

"Comms, tell them to have the kor-dom call off the attack!" Cameron barked.

"Ready to jump," Ensign Dorsay reported.

"Fifty-eight of the first wave are still inbound," the lieutenant warned.

"Damn it," Cameron cursed. "How long until the other Gunyoki reach intercept position?"

"Two more squadrons will be in intercept position in thirty seconds," Lieutenant Yuati replied.

"Time to first wave?" Cameron asked.

"One minute," the lieutenant replied.

"That leaves thirty seconds for intercept," Cameron said, more to herself than the others. She had no choice. "Execute the jump," she ordered. "Put us in front of the first wave."

"Another missile launch!" Kaylah reported. "Another full wave!"

"Jumping in three..." Ensign Dorsay began.

"Channel all available power to our starboard shields," Cameron continued.

"Two..."

"Comms, drop the comm-drone with the strike order, and pass its control codes to the Voss, just in case."

"One..."

"Dropping comm-drone and passing codes to the Voss."

"Jumping."

"Comm-drone away!" Ensign Keller announced.

"Slip us into the missile path and match the Cape Town's course and speed," Cameron ordered.

"Aye, sir," the helmsman replied, exchanging a worried glance with the navigator next to him.

"Mystic is starting their transmission," the comms officer reported.

Nathan, Jessica, and the rest of the Voss's flight deck crew listened to the communications speaker as Kor-Dom Borrol barked orders in Jung to the commanders of the battle platform.

"Doesn't sound very convincing if you ask me," Jessica commented.

"You speak Jung?" Nathan asked, surprised.

"Naralena taught me," Jessica replied. "Our mission to Kohara?"

"Ah, yes," Nathan remembered. "Are they standing down?"

"Negative," Jessica replied. "And there are still over three hundred missiles inbound."

"Targets?"

"It looks like they're all headed for the Cape Town."

"All of them?" Nathan asked in disbelief.

"Captain," Loki called. "The Aurora has just pulled in next to the Cape Town." He turned to look at Nathan. "They're trying to protect her."

Nathan reached up to the comm-controls on his overhead panel. "Aurora Actual, Voss Actual!" he called over comms. "What the hell are you doing, Cam?"

"The same thing you would do," Cameron insisted.

"She's got you there," Jessica stated.

"You can't take that many hits, Cam!" Nathan warned.

"She doesn't expect to," Jessica realized. "They just passed a comm-drone's control codes to us. It's carrying strike instructions for an Orochi missile strike against the Jung."

"Son of a bitch," Nathan cursed as he changed channels on the comm-panel. "Mystic, Voss Actual. Come in!"

"Their shields are already weakened," Jessica

warned. "They can't stop more than a handful of missiles."

"How long?" Nathan asked.

"Twenty seconds to the first wave," Jessica replied. "One minute to the second."

"Voss Actual, Mystic, Commander Kaplan," the overhead speaker squawked.

"Put Borrol on!" Nathan barked.

"Wait one," the commander replied.

"Six squadrons are now working on intercepts," Jessica reported. "First wave is down to twenty-seven inbounds and falling."

"This is Kor-Dom Borrol."

"Borrol, this is Scott. I'm only going to say this once. If those inbounds don't start disappearing in the next few seconds, I've got a fleet of sixteen missile gunships that have orders to shoot-and-scoot until all three of those battle platforms are dust! Do you understand me?"

"Twenty-two inbound," Jessica updated.

"I will do all that I can, Captain."

"Twenty."

"You'd better!"

"Eighteen."

"Fuck," Nathan cursed. "Get us closer!"

"I'm on it!" Josh assured him.

"All point-defenses are firing," Lieutenant Yuati reported from the Aurora's tactical station, his voice tense.

"Five seconds!" Kaylah warned. "Eighteen still inbound!"

Cameron pressed her all-call button. "All hands!

Brace, brace, brace!" Both her hands grabbed the arms of her command chair as she herself prepared for the pending detonations.

Two more missiles were struck by the Aurora's point-defenses a split second before impact, blowing them apart but still detonating their warheads. The sixteen remaining missiles found their target, detonating on impact in a series of near-simultaneous flashes of bright, yellow-white light.

The Aurora's bridge shook violently despite her inertial dampeners' best efforts to reduce the effects of the detonations on the crew inside. Sparks flew from various consoles, the result of energy spikes overcoming protected circuits, while energy from the detonations overloaded shield emitters and eventually found their way to the Aurora's hull and her exposed external conduits.

The sound of tearing metal caused Cameron to instinctively cover her head as an overhead ventilation duct broke free of its suspension, crashing to the deck below.

Cameron's instincts were correct, and a moment later, overhead plating broke loose, missing her by inches.

"Medic!" someone shouted from behind.

Cameron spun around as her comms officer called for a medical team to the bridge. The officer from the starboard auxiliary station was already on her feet and attempting to pull a large section of ducting off of Lieutenant Yuati's body, which was draped unceremoniously across the tactical console.

Cameron jumped up, rushing to the lieutenant's aid as well. She immediately reached for his neck, feeling for a pulse. "He's still alive!"

"Medical team is on their way!" Ensign Keller reported from the comm-station less than a meter away.

"Help us get this off him!" Cameron ordered the comms officer. "I need access to the tactical console!"

Ensign Keller also jumped out of his seat, coming out and around his station to help.

"Kaylah!" Cameron barked. "Shield status!"

"Starboard midship shields are gone!" Kaylah replied. "They must have taken most of the hits!"

"Captain," the Aurora's AI called over the overhead speakers. "All starboard shields forward of frame twelve and aft of frame twenty-six are still intact but are down to twenty percent or less. They will not take another hit."

"Time to next impact!" Cameron barked.

"Forty seconds!" Kaylah reported. "Sixty-eight still inbound in the second wave!"

"Helm! Roll us over! Show them our port side!"

"Rolling over, aye!"

"Channel all power to port shields!" Cameron added as she and the other two officers hefted the fallen ducting from atop the unconscious lieutenant. "Get him down, but carefully," Cameron instructed as a team of med-techs arrived.

"Gunyoki are intercepting!" Kaylah announced. "Their numbers are up to two hundred and five!"

"Just count the inbounds per wave!" Cameron instructed as she watched the med-techs move the lieutenant off the tactical console and down to the deck.

"Sixty inbound!"

Cameron stepped up to the tactical console, finding that the touchscreen console had been too badly damaged to be usable. "Damn," she cursed to herself. "Aurora," she called to the air. "Can you assume tactical control? The console is shot."

"I can assume control of all defensive weapons, but I will require direct orders from you or your designated subordinate to fire offensively."

"Assume control of all defensive systems," Cameron instructed the AI. "Authorization Taylor, Alpha Seven Five Two Tango Four Two Four."

"Fifty-two inbound!"

"Authorization confirmed," Aurora acknowledged. "I have assumed control of all defensive systems. Based on current second wave trajectory, I can deduce which shield sections will take the greatest detonation energy and channel additional energy to those sections."

"Sounds like a good idea," Cameron agreed as she stepped over the fallen debris and made her way back to the command chair.

"Forty-seven inbound!" Kaylah updated.

"Roll maneuver complete," Ensign Tala announced from the helm.

"Recommend taking inertial dampening systems down to minimum safe levels," Aurora added.

"Do it," Cameron ordered as she took her seat again. "Comms, set condition blue."

"Aye, sir!" Ensign Keller replied as he moved back to his station.

"Forty-two!"

"Attention all hands!" Ensign Keller's voice blared

over the loudspeakers. “Set condition blue. Repeat, set condition blue. All personnel in outer areas go to full pressure suits. Lock down all main lateral bulkheads.”

“Incoming transmission from Cape Town Actual,” the comms officer announced.

Cameron signaled for the ensign to patch her comm-set in.

“Thirty-five inbound!” Kaylah reported. “Twenty seconds to next wave of impacts.”

“Drop back three hundred meters and climb ten relative to us, and we can get some of our missile defenses in play,” Captain Stettner suggested over her comm-set.

“That will increase your exposure,” Cameron warned.

“We can take a few hits. More importantly, we can take out more of those inbounds so that you don’t die any sooner than you have to.”

“Thanks, Stettner, but I have no intention of dying today,” Cameron insisted.

“Don’t be an idiot, Taylor,” the captain replied, ending the call.

“Twenty-nine inbound!”

Cameron looked at her helmsman. “Do it.”

“Aurora has twenty-nine inbound!” Jessica reported from the Voss’s starboard auxiliary station. “Make that twenty-four!”

“Cam!” Nathan called over comms. “You can’t stand toe-to-toe with three battle platforms!”

“The Cape Town is far more valuable to Earth than the Aurora, and you know it,” Cameron insisted. “I’m not going to let her go down because I took out her shields!"

"Multiple contacts!" Jessica warned.

"Where?"

"All over the damned place! Dozens of them! They're coming out of FTL everywhere!"

"More missiles?" Nathan surmised.

"Negative!" Jessica rose from her seat. "Jung fighters! Looks like about a hundred of them!"

"He is broadcasting again, Admiral," the Ton-Mogan's senior communications officer reported.

Dom Mogan looked uncertain.

"It is a ruse, my lord," Admiral Korahk insisted. "A clever trick by the Sol Alliance to confuse us, to weaken our resolve. They know they cannot prevent their own destruction."

"Then why do they not defend themselves?" Dom Mogan asked of his admiral.

"He is asking for Dom Mogan," the senior communications officer informed the admiral.

"We must stand fast to the Tonba-Hon-Venar," the admiral insisted. "To do otherwise would bring dishonor to our entire caste."

"And if it is Kor-Dom Borrol?" Dom Mogan asked.

"It has taken us years to get here," Admiral Korahk reminded his caste leader. "It took you months just to get back to us from Nor-Patri, and you have the fastest shuttle in the empire. It is not physically possible for the kor-dom to be here now."

"Ask for authentication codes," Dom Mogan instructed.

"My lord," Admiral Korahk begged. "Do not do this..."

Dom Mogan cast a stern look at his subordinate. "If it is a trick as we suspect, they will be unable to authenticate."

"What if they somehow got the codes?" the admiral asked.

"Then there are other questions I can ask," Dom Mogan assured the admiral. "Request authentication."

Admiral Korahk sighed, looking to the senior communications officer and nodding.

"Voss Actual to all ships! The Jung fighters are going to try to interfere with the intercept of their missiles!" Nathan warned over comms. "Concentrate on the missiles and ignore the fighters as best you can!"

"Four fighters approaching to port!" Loki warned.

"I've got them!" Marcus called from the port gun.

Marcus swung his gun around to face aft, opening fire at the incoming Jung fighters streaking toward them from their aft port quarter. Within seconds, the bolts from his plasma cannons found the nearest fighter, cutting it open and sending pieces flying, the debris bouncing harmlessly off the ship's shields.

Marcus looked over his right shoulder as he brought his weapon forward, but the next fighter was too close for him to get his gun around in time. "NOSE DOWN, KID!" he yelled over his intercom.

Josh rarely listened to his old man, except when he got a certain tone in his voice. Instinctively, he did as Marcus had instructed, pushing his flight control stick forward, causing the ship's nose to dip suddenly. He glanced up, just as the fighter slammed into the shields over the cockpit, causing them to flash brightly.

Josh shared a look of terror with Loki. "These fuckers are suicidal!"

"Gunners, you have got to communicate," Nathan urged, uneasy with how close they had just come.

"If enough of those fighters ram us, we'll lose our shields," Jessica warned.

Nathan reached up for his overhead comm-console, switching channels. "EDF Fleet Command, Voss Actual," he called.

"What makes you think they're going to answer you?" Dylan wondered.

"Because my sister, the president, told them to," Nathan smiled.

The Cape Town pulled slightly ahead of the Aurora, giving her a clear line of fire at the incoming missiles with her forward missile defenses. The turrets opened fire, all four barrels blazing, panning slightly back and forth as well as up and down, in order to lay down an intercept field of explosive rail gun rounds.

The wave of intercept rounds streaked past the bow of the Aurora, heading toward the incoming missiles, breaking apart into clusters of several dozen tiny, explosive charges detonating as they reached the wave of inbound missiles.

Hundreds of explosions lit up in the path of the missiles, tearing more than a dozen of the inbound weapons apart.

"Eight still inbound!" Kaylah warned. "Five seconds!"

Cameron tapped her all-call button again. "Brace for incoming!"

Again, the bridge rocked violently as Jung missiles blasted their way through their failing shields, finding the ship's hull.

"Shields are..."

More explosions rocked the ship as the warheads penetrated the hull and then detonated. Kaylah's panel blew up in her face, knocking her backward and showering her with sparks. Overhead bulkheads buckled, some of them breaking free and falling to the deck. The navigator was the first to die, both an overhead panel and another section of ventilation ducting landing on top of him and destroying his console in the process. The helmsman was knocked from his station, flailing as he fell forward over his console, landing on the forward side on his back, rendered unconscious.

Cameron held on with both hands, barely able to keep from being knocked from her command chair as secondary explosions shuddered through the Aurora's main longitudinal truss with a sickening groan.

"Multiple hull breaches!" Ensign Keller reported from the comm-station, wiping the blood from his open head wound from his eyes.

"We have lost all weapons except for some of our point-defense cannons," the ship's AI reported.

"Midship propellant storage has been hit!" the comms officer added, clutching the sides of his console to maintain his balance as the ship continued to rock from the detonations. "We've lost the starboard flight deck!"

"Captain, Cheng!" Vladimir called over Cameron's comm-set.

"Go!" Cameron replied.

"Main propulsion and maneuvering are down! Jump drive is down! Only one ZPED is working! Structural integrity is down to fifteen percent! Her back is broken, Cam!"

Cameron glanced around the bridge. Half her bridge staff were either unconscious or dead, and half the stations were inoperable if not completely destroyed. The remaining working panels were covered with flashing red and orange lights, warning of failures or impending failures of critical systems all over the ship.

Still she couldn't admit defeat.

"Aurora!" she called. "Are you still with us?"

"Affirmative," the ship's AI replied over the one working overhead speaker.

"Status and recommendations?"

"The ship is no longer combat capable," the Aurora replied.

"Any chance she can be saved?"

"Insufficient data," the AI replied. "Too many of my sensors and systems connections have been damaged to make an accurate assessment. However, the impacts have caused our speed to decrease, resulting in a rapidly decaying orbit. Estimate atmospheric interface in sixty-seven minutes, and there are still three more waves of missiles inbound."

"Time to next wave?" Cameron asked, certain that she would not like the answer.

"Eighty-seven seconds," the Aurora replied. "Currently, forty-six missiles are still inbound in the third wave."

Cameron took a deep breath. "Ensign Keller, sound the alarm. We're abandoning ship."

Ensign Keller peered over the top of his console at the back of his captain's head in the distance, pausing a moment in disbelief. "Abandon ship, aye."

"Sir," the senior communications officer of the fleet command center deep inside Port Terra barked. "I've got the captain of a ship called the Voss on comms. He's asking for you."

"Did he identify himself?" Commander Macklay wondered.

"Uh, yes, but..."

The commander's brow furrowed. "But what?"

The officer moved closer, keeping his voice low. "He claims to be Nathan Scott, sir."

Commander Macklay sighed. "Patch him to my comm-set."

"Yes, sir."

The commander took a breath, bracing himself. "This is Commander Macklay, acting commander of the Earth Defense Force," he replied over his comm-set.

"This is Admiral Scott," Nathan replied over comms. "I take it the president has spoken with you?"

"She has," the commander confirmed reluctantly.

"Good. Then tell your forces to fall back and to stop engaging the Jung."

"With all due respect, sir, the Jung are attacking us."

"Give me three minutes," Nathan insisted. "If the Jung haven't stopped their attack by then, you can throw everything you have at them and at Nor-Patri."

Commander Macklay paused a moment, unsure. Finally, he responded. "You are asking a lot."

"I have a plan, Commander," Nathan insisted.

"It better be a damned good one," Commander Macklay insisted.

"I said I have a plan." Nathan replied. "I didn't say it was a good one. Scott out."

Commander Macklay pulled off his comm-set, tossing it aside in frustration.

"Something wrong, sir?" the comms officer asked, noting the worried look on his commander's face.

The commander looked at the junior officer. "Our CO is dead, and we're being led by the supposedly dead daughter of a dead president and taking tactical orders from the dead president's long-dead son. Oh, and we're under attack by three battle platforms. What could be wrong?"

The officer of the watch, despite his own reluctance, had no choice but to ask. "Our orders, Commander?"

The commander paused one last time. "Order all fighters to fall back to Earth orbit and order all forces to go purely defensive until further notice."

"Sir?"

The commander shrugged. "That kid saved us once. Perhaps he'll save us again."

"Nathan!" Jessica called from the Voss's starboard auxiliary station. "I'm picking up a distress signal from the Aurora!" She turned to look at Nathan. "They're abandoning ship."

Nathan could feel the eyes of everyone on the Voss's command deck staring at him, but he had nothing to say.

Kor-Dom Borrol stood next to the communications station on the bridge of the Mystic Empress, with Commander Kaplan and Captain Rainey standing nearby.

"You have to convince him," Commander Kaplan urged the kor-dom.

"He is not responding," Kor-Dom Borrol replied. "He is following protocol. To do otherwise invites dissent amongst his officers and opens him to challenges from the overly ambitious."

"If he continues his attack, our Orochi will send shield penetrators followed by conventionals, and all three battle platforms will be destroyed," Command Kaplan warned. "Earth may be damaged, but she will not be destroyed. But Nor-Patri will. Then we will be the ones with the technological advantage. By the time your empire recovers, we will already control the galaxy, and you'll be stuck where you are with nowhere to expand. Your only hope of expansion will be to return to your traditions of conquest. You'll have gone full circle and gotten nowhere. Trillions of lives and centuries of work lost, and all for nothing."

Kor-Dom Borrol glared at Commander Kaplan. "You believe I do not realize this?" He pointed at the speaker in the communications panel, from which they awaited a response. "You believe Dom Mogan does not realize this as well?"

"Then convince him to take the high road, for the sake of your people, his people, all people."

Kor-Dom Borrol stared at the commander a moment, then tapped the side of his comm-set again. "Penta, it is Mogi," Kor-Dom Borrol began, speaking in Jung. "I am speaking to you now, not as your kor-dom, but as your old friend." Kor-Dom Borrol paused a moment, thinking. "You once told me that the Tonba-Hon-Venar was not about saving a world, but about saving an empire. I know that you believe it is about snatching honor from the jaws of defeat, but you are mistaken. It is about finding a way to save the empire while still maintaining our honor. To that, I ask you: which action is the most honorable? To lash out in vengeance, dooming trillions and risking the complete destruction of all that our people have created, or putting down one's sword in order to protect it?"

Commander Kaplan exchanged a look with the kor-dom, having no idea what he said.

"A moving speech," Captain Rainey commented. "Do you think it will work?"

Commander Kaplan looked at the captain, surprised.

"What do you think I do in my cabin all day?" Captain Rainey said.

"The young warrior sees only killing as a path to honor," Kor-Dom Borrol continued in Jung. "The old warrior has seen enough to force his views to widen, to see beyond the simple act of killing."

"Where are you, Mogi?" Dom Mogan's voice

crackled over the console speaker, surprising everyone. "How did you get here?"

"The details are unimportant, Penta," Kor-Dom Borrol replied. "All that is important is that we end the Tonba-Hon-Venar, here and now. You must trust me, or all will be lost."

"It is too late."

"It is never too late, my friend. If we abort our attack, the Terrans will share their jump drive technology with us. The entire galaxy will then be within our reach. Imagine it, Penta. New worlds to conquer. Not with weapons, but with explorers, and builders, and scholars. Unlimited resources to support Nor-Patri, without the cost in military hardware and lives."

"And what of us?" Dom Mogan wondered. "What of the warrior?"

"The empire will always need protection," Kor-Dom Borrol replied. "If not from outside, then from within. The time has come for our people to redefine the meaning of honor. Let it start with this moment... let it start with you and me."

Silence.

Kor-Dom Borrol looked at Commander Kaplan and Captain Rainey.

"Forty seconds to third wave impact," the sensor officer reported.

"I'll expect another glass of your five-hundred-year-old coran the next time we meet," Dom Mogan finally replied.

Kor-Dom Borrol smiled. "You shall have it, my friend."

"Thirty seconds," the AI warned.

"All escape pods are away," Ensign Keller reported.

"Aurora," Cameron called to her AI. "Do you still have control of the docking thrusters?"

"Affirmative," the ship's AI confirmed. "Twelve missiles still inbound."

"Dump all available energy into the roll thrusters and put our belly toward the inbounds."

"Ten inbound, twenty seconds," Aurora warned. "Rerouting all available energy into roll thrusters; however, doing so will cause detonations in the thrust acceleration modules."

"Eight!" the lieutenant updated from the battered tactical station.

"I'm counting on it," Cameron replied.

Several small explosions rocked the bridge again.

"I take it those were the acceleration modules exploding?"

"Affirmative," Aurora answered. "The ship is rolling."

"Five inbound! They're past the intercept line!"

"Get to the escape pod, gentlemen," Cameron instructed.

Neither officer left their station.

"Four inbound!" the lieutenant updated. "Five seconds."

Cameron instinctively reached for her all-call button again, then remembered that the three of them were the only ones left aboard. "Brace," she stated.

The ship rocked again as four missiles detonated on impact with the Aurora's hull. More pieces of the bridge's overhead structures came crashing down, along with more sparks and smoke, all adding to the chaos and cacophony of audible and visual warnings all over the ship's barely operating consoles.

"Damage report?" Cameron demanded as the shaking subsided.

"The roll maneuver was effective," Aurora replied. "Damage was reduced. However, we now have several more hull breaches along the ventral side..."

The lights suddenly went out, leaving them with only emergency battery lighting.

"Main power is down," Aurora reported. "Auxiliary power is functioning, but only at ten percent. Bridge systems are operating on emergency batteries only."

"How are you still working?" Cameron wondered.

"Her mainframe has its own batteries," Vladimir explained as he entered the bridge, stepping over a fallen structural member. "Bozhe moi," he gasped, witnessing the damage to the bridge.

"What are you doing here?" Cameron snapped. "What part of abandon ship did you not understand?"

"Please," Vladimir replied as he moved toward her. "Who do you think kept the power working long enough for all the escape pods to get away, or for you to execute that insane roll maneuver? Nathan would be proud of that one by the way."

"Don't you dare tell him," Cameron laughed.

"Tactical sensors are offline," Aurora reported. "All weapons are nonoperational."

"Time to go, gentlemen," Cameron decided.

"The next wave of missiles will arrive in forty seconds," Aurora warned. "Access to the command deck escape pod is blocked."

"She's right," Vladimir confirmed. "The entire corridor collapsed behind me. It'll take us ten minutes to cut our way through."

"Aurora, what's our chance of surviving another impact?"

"There are currently twenty-three missiles inbound," Aurora reported. "We are still rolling, so the impacts will not be in the same location; however, there is an eighty percent chance that a single impact will break the ship in half, causing a fracture along the main longitudinal truss which will open this compartment to space."

"Great," Cameron said.

"I should have stayed in power gen," Vladimir commented.

"Or abandoned ship when you were ordered to," Cameron pointed out.

"Seriously?" Vladimir questioned. "I told you so now?"

"It may be my last opportunity," Cameron replied with a wry smile.

"Captain?" Aurora called.

"Yes, Aurora?"

"The incoming missiles have detonated prematurely."

"How many of them?" Cameron asked, surprised.

"All of them," Aurora replied. "All inbound missiles in all waves have detonated."

"Holy crap," Cameron exclaimed, shocked.

"What? No dramatic countdown? No touching final words?" Vladimir laughed.

"All inbounds have detonated," Jessica reported urgently from the Voss's starboard auxiliary station. "The battle platforms are changing course."

"Are they standing down?" Nathan wondered.

"Negative," Jessica replied. "Shields and weapons are still active, but they're turning off their intercept course. More importantly, they're not launching missiles."

"What about the Aurora?" Nathan asked.

"She's still intact, but barely."

Nathan reached for his overhead comm-panel. "Aurora, Voss! You still with us, Cam?"

After what seemed like an eternity, his comm-set crackled. "We're still here," Cameron replied.

"The missiles have detonated," Nathan told her. "The battle platforms are changing course. It looks like they're breaking off. What's your status?"

"We're dead in the water, and our orbit is decaying rapidly," Cameron replied. "Oh, and we could use a rescue party. We're cut off from the command deck escape pod."

"Hold tight, we'll be there shortly," Nathan assured her.

"Uh...Nathan?" Jessica called, uncertain of what she was seeing.

"What is it?"

"The battle platforms just disappeared."

"You mean they went to FTL?"

"No, I mean they just disappeared," Jessica insisted. "No energy surge from their mass-reduction fields, no nothing. One second they were there, and the next they weren't."

"Fleet Command reports all inbound missiles have detonated, and the Jung battle platforms have disappeared!" the senior communications officer at the capitol complex command center reported urgently.

"What about their fighters?" Lieutenant Commander Perrin inquired.

"They are breaking off as well. They're headed out into deep space, in roughly the same direction as the battle platforms prior to their disappearance."

"Madam President," Lieutenant Commander Perrin said, turning toward Miri. "I recommend we maintain full alert status for the time being, at least until we are certain that the Jung are not attempting to deceive us."

"Agreed," Miri confirmed, wishing to avoid having to explain the entire plan at the moment.

The lieutenant commander turned and signaled the communications officer.

"Lieutenant Commander," Miri said. "I need to ask a favor of you."

"Anything, Madam President," the lieutenant commander assured her.

CHAPTER SIXTEEN

Malcolm Fortune sat staring out the window at the ocean, just as he usually did while drinking his morning coffee. He had long ago discerned that the view outside his window was a simulation, having spent so much time gazing at the waves lapping against the shore, eventually noticing the patterns.

His life had become completely routine since being cooped up in the one-bedroom apartment for the last few weeks. His mornings were spent staring out the window, his days playing with his child and trying to keep him entertained, and his evenings wondering what had happened to his wife.

Thankfully, the relentless questioning that had begun his captivity had eased. For the last week, the daily interrogations seemed more like a conversation between business associates. Common pleasantries, discussions about the weather, movies on the net, current events. But it was still an interrogation. He had seen enough spy vids to know there was a reason for 'Mister Smith' to be asking the same questions every few days or so. His interrogator believed that Malcolm was not aware of the repetitive lines of conversation. But he was. Yet Malcolm's answers were always the same, without any variation, which was easy, since his responses were truthful.

Still, in all their time in captivity, no one had ever told them why they were being held nor where his wife was. He didn't even know if she was alive. He was certain that it was his own government holding him, although he had no real evidence. It was a gut feeling mostly.

And so another day had begun. Another day of not

knowing where he was, why he was there, or what had become of his wife. Another day of not knowing what was to become of him and his child.

The door opened, much to Malcolm's surprise, as no one ever came to speak with him until much later in the day. Even more of a surprise was the man who entered. A soldier, clad in black combat armor the likes of which Malcolm had never seen except in sci-fi vids on the nets. The soldier was older, perhaps in his mid-forties, with rugged facial features and sharp, cold, calculating eyes. The strange man had a confidence that Malcolm had never witnessed, both calming and frightening at the same time.

The soldier entered the room, followed by two more wearing the same futuristic armor. After looking around, he asked, "Are you Malcolm Fortune?"

"Uh, yes."

"What is your wife's name?"

Malcolm's eyes widened. Partly in hope and partly in terror. "You know of my wife? Where is she? Is she alive?"

"What is her name?" the man asked again.

"Lynne," Malcolm replied. "Her name is Lynne. Please, no one has told me what happened to her. I have to know."

"My name is General Lucius Telles of the Ghatazhak. Your wife is well. My men and I are here to bring you and your child to her."

Malcolm felt as if he would cry. "Are you serious?"

"He's always serious," one of the other soldiers assured Malcolm.

"When?"

"Now, if you'd like," General Telles replied.

"Just let me get my son," Malcolm said, rising from his chair and heading toward the bedroom.

* * *

"This is not good," Josh commented as he looked out of the side windows. Outside, the battered Aurora, still and dark, orbited the Earth at a cockeyed angle.

"How does she look?" Captain Stettner asked over comms.

"Like she was beaten within an inch of her life," Nathan replied solemnly.

"She saved our asses," Stettner admitted.

"That was likely her last act," Nathan said.

"She was a damn good ship," Captain Stettner stated respectfully. "With a damn good captain."

"And a good crew," Nathan added. "Are they being rescued?"

"Most of them made landfall safely. They're scattered across South America. Recovery has good locator beacons on all of them, so they should be picked up shortly."

"How is your ship doing?" Nathan asked.

"We'll have partial shields up within the hour, and our jump drive later today. Everything else is cosmetic, thanks to Taylor."

"Sorry it had to happen this way," Nathan told him.

"Once this is all over, I'd like to buy you a drink," Captain Stettner offered. "I'd sure like to hear how it is you're still alive and how all of this came to be."

"I may take you up on that," Nathan told him. "But we've still got some unfinished business back in the Pentaurus sector."

"Well, if you need any help with that, you know where to find us," Captain Stettner said. "Cape Town, out."

Nathan reached up and killed the transmission,

still staring out the windows as his battered ship drifted by to starboard.

"Bridge rescue trunk hatch looks to be intact," Jessica reported from the starboard auxiliary station.

"Will our docking collar mate up with it?" Nathan wondered.

"We installed a universal adapter back on SilTek," Marcus assured him. "It'll mate up with any hatch that will fit inside its docking ring."

"Josh, think you can dock us up?" Nathan asked.

"Of course I can," Josh insisted.

"Cam?" Nathan called over comms.

"I'm here."

"The only way we can get to you is by docking to the bridge rescue hatch on your topside. Can you get to the trunk?"

"The ready room is clear, and the rescue trunk is heavily reinforced, so it should be intact," Cameron replied. "Just don't scratch the paint."

"Seriously?" Josh snickered. "At this point, I'm pretty sure no one would notice."

"That bad?" Cameron wondered, hearing Josh's commented in the background over comms.

"Yup," Nathan replied. "See you in a few."

"I've got an incoming vid-call from the Mystic," Jessica reported. "It's the kor-dom."

"Tell him to stand by," Nathan told her. "I'll take it in my quarters," he added, heading around the ladder rail.

* * *

Nathan entered his cramped quarters on the Voss, going directly to the small desk along the outboard bulkhead. Similar to the simulated window in his original quarters on the Aurora, the window in this compartment served both as a view screen for communications and as the room's computer interface. The only difference was that, when not activated, this window really was a window.

Nathan took his seat, pausing for a moment to let the events of the past thirty minutes settle. Coming down from the combat-induced adrenalin high was one of the worst things for him since it always resulted in considerable fatigue. He wondered how the Ghatazhak managed to mitigate the effect. Someday, he would need to learn their secret.

Nathan switched on the window, activating it as a vid-screen. Kor-Dom Borrol immediately appeared.

"Congratulations, Captain," the kor-dom began. "I must admit, I did not believe you would be successful."

"I suppose that's why you didn't bother to tell us about your cloaking technology?"

"I honestly did not know that it was operational until today," the kor-dom insisted.

"But you did know of its development."

"Our military operates differently than yours," Kor-Dom Borrol explained. "They rarely share details of their weapons research and development with other castes, especially the leadership castes."

"Yet you did know about it," Nathan asserted.

"I have my spies, yes," the kor-dom admitted. "I would offer my apologies for the deception, but they would be insincere, and I believe you understand why I did so."

"In case we failed to remove Galiardi from power," Nathan surmised. "The caste in charge of those battle platforms would have sent cloaked ships down to Earth to steal jump drive technology."

"And they would have kept it for themselves," Kor-Dom Borrol stated. "Giving them the leverage they would need to control whatever rose from the ashes of Nor-Patri."

Nathan didn't entirely believe Kor-Dom Borrol but decided that chastising him further on the matter served no purpose. "How did you convince them?"

"I simply pointed out that there was just as much honor in laying down one's sword to save others as there was to die with it in hand."

"I'll have to remember that one," Nathan replied. "Where did the battle platforms go?"

"To a predetermined staging point, where they will remain hidden for the time being."

"You still don't trust me," Nathan surmised.

"You expected otherwise?"

"I suppose not," Nathan admitted with a sigh. "You know, we're going to want you to share your cloaking technology with us."

"That may prove difficult," Kor-Dom Borrol stated. "As I said, our military is quite different from yours. Besides, now that you know it exists, I am certain you will figure out a way to defeat it. Your people are quite clever."

"Still, it's going to be a point of contention."

"Are you prepared to share your shield-penetrating missile technology with us?" Kor-Dom Borrol challenged.

"In time."

"Precisely," the kor-dom replied. "How is the Aurora?" he asked, hoping to change the subject. "I trust she can be repaired?"

"It's too early to tell, but it's not looking very promising," Nathan admitted.

"Will that put a kink in your plans to deal with the Dusahn?"

"It's not ideal, but we have other ships."

The intercom in his quarters beeped.

"One moment," Nathan told Kor-Dom Borrol, muting the vid-call. "Yes?"

"We've got hard dock with the Aurora," Jessica reported over the intercom.

"I didn't even feel it."

"Yeah, I guess Josh can have a light touch when he wants to. I'm headed for the airlock."

"I'll be there shortly," Nathan replied, ending the call and unmuting the vid-call. "I'm going to have to cut this conversation short, Kor-Dom. We'll send a shuttle to pick you up later."

* * *

"How are we doing?" Nathan asked as he joined the others in the corridor between the Voss's command deck and her common room.

"Hard seal is verified. Skirt pressure is holding," Marcus replied.

"How many people are still on board?"

"Cam only knows of the four of them on the bridge, and the Aurora's AI has lost half of her sensors, so she can't get an accurate count," Jessica explained. "I did a full sweep of her interior and didn't find any other vital signs but those on the bridge. I put in a request with Fleet Command for a head count from all her escape pods. I'd ask for search and rescue teams, but she's losing altitude as we speak."

"How long?" Nathan asked.

"About an hour until she starts to heat up."

"Then we'd better get moving," Nathan stated, stepping through the hatch into the topside airlock trunk.

Jessica entered the airlock as well.

"You want me to go with you?" Marcus asked.

"Stay here for now," Nathan instructed. "We

still don't know for sure if the rescue trunk is fully operational. We may need some gear to get through."

"I'll be here if you need me."

Nathan pressed the button, causing the inner hatch to close.

"We're upside down in relation to the Aurora," Jessica reminded Nathan. "But her rescue trunk doesn't have any gravity, and it's wide enough for us to flip over inside."

"I'm well acquainted with the rescue trunk," Nathan assured her as he opened the hatch above them.

"You are?"

"During my first tour, I used to go there when I couldn't sleep. Zero-G is the best sleep ever."

"How come I didn't know that?" Jessica wondered.

"I never told anyone," Nathan replied as he headed up the ladder.

"What about the night watch?"

"They probably just thought I was sleeping on my couch," Nathan told her as he punched in the code on the exterior hatch controls. After a moment, the red light on the small panel turned green, and the hatch retracted into the hull slightly, then slid to the right, disappearing.

The long tunnel leading to the airlock above the captain's ready room loomed above them, dark and foreboding.

"Shouldn't the emergency lights be on?" Jessica wondered.

"You'd think so," Nathan agreed. "Hand me a light."

Jessica opened up the gear locker, pulling out a small lantern and passing it up to him.

Nathan turned the lantern on, then gave it a

gentle push upward, sending it floating up the rescue tunnel. "It looks to be intact," he decided, following the floating lantern into the tunnel. As soon as his upper torso crossed the exterior hatch, he began to feel himself becoming lighter as he climbed out of the Voss's artificial gravity fields. Once he was all the way through, he pulled himself along, floating up the tunnel in pursuit of the ascending lantern.

A minute later, the narrow tunnel widened, and he found himself inside the inner rescue trunk airlock, just above the captain's ready room. "I'm inside the inner airlock," he reported, catching the lantern after it bounced off the deck of the compartment.

"I'm coming up," Jessica called as she climbed up the ladder and launched herself into the tunnel above.

Nathan moved to the side, looking up at the tunnel exit as Jessica crested the threshold. In a smooth motion, she grasped the handrail around the tunnel edge, tucking into a ball to reverse her body orientation. As she came out of her flip, she stuck her legs straight out and let go of the rail, touching down gently with her feet and grabbing the side rail to hold herself in position.

"Nice," Nathan commented, impressed by her zero-G prowess.

"I've had seven years' more training than you."

"Apparently," Nathan replied, tapping the airlock controls. The hatch above their heads slid closed, and a moment later the hatch in the deck under them opened. Nathan leaned over the open hatch, spotting Cameron below. "Need a lift?"

Nathan positioned himself over the opening, then pushed himself downward, letting the gravity fields inside the Aurora pull him through until he was hanging from the opening in the ceiling of the ready room. He let go, dropping to the deck. "Looks like someone had a wild party in here," he commented, looking around the disheveled compartment. He looked at Cameron, who looked as shaken up as the ready room. "How are you doing?"

"I've had better days," Cameron admitted.

Jessica was next, again transferring far more gracefully than Nathan. "Busted up another ship huh, Cam?"

"Funny," Cameron replied, leading them out of the ready room.

Nathan's eyes widened, and his mouth fell open when he saw the bridge. "Damn, you're lucky to be alive."

"Not all of us made it," Cameron corrected, looking toward several bodies lined up neatly in what little uncluttered area there was of the deck.

Nathan looked at the bodies of the bridge crew. "Where's Kaylah?"

"The wounded were evacuated to medical before the corridor collapsed and cut us off," she told him.

Vladimir appeared from the equipment room door in the starboard foyer, carrying a large data module.

"What's the verdict?" Nathan asked his chief engineer.

"I'm sure I could fix her if I had more time," Vladimir assured him.

"Any chance we can tow her to a higher orbit?" Nathan asked.

"You'd need at least four tugs pushing and pulling, and even then, she might break apart from the tow," Vladimir insisted.

"Could we deploy the jump nets?" Jessica asked. "Use the jump tugs?"

"It would take too long to deploy and synchronize the nets," Cameron told her. "I've already had her run the numbers."

"Her?" Jessica wondered.

"Our AI," Cameron explained.

"Oh yeah."

"I'm afraid there's no way to save her," Cameron stated.

Nathan looked around the battered bridge. "It's strange to be in here without the entire view screen dome working. The last time that happened was..."

"The day you became captain," Jessica said, finishing his sentence.

"I feel guilty," Cameron admitted. "It's the second ship I've lost. I just couldn't let the Cape Town get destroyed. Not because of us."

"You made the right call, Cam," Nathan insisted. "Besides, she died protecting Earth. That's why she was built."

"She was built to explore, to make contact with the core worlds of Earth," Cameron corrected. "To establish diplomatic relations with the Jung, in the hopes of achieving a lasting peace. That's why I wanted to be assigned to her."

"Well, I'd say she accomplished her mission," Nathan decided. "And she did so with you in her command chair."

"Thanks," Cameron replied, appreciating his kind words.

"Besides, I doubt she'll be the last ship to bear the name Aurora," Nathan added.

"Still, I feel like I barely got to know her," Cameron insisted.

"You were her CO for seven years," Jessica reminded her.

"I meant her AI."

"Don't worry," Vladimir told them, holding up the data module. "I backed her up."

"Captain?" Loki called over Nathan's comm-set.

"Yes, Loki?"

"The Cape Town called. They've analyzed the Aurora's descent trajectory and structural condition. They say there's a sixty percent chance she'll come down in one piece, but she'll do so in the middle of Bogata. They recommend she be destroyed in orbit within the next twenty minutes. That way, what's left should burn up on the way down."

"Great," Nathan stated, shaking his head and sighing. "We're on our way," he assured Loki. Nathan looked around one last time. "Aurora?"

"Yes, Captain?" his ship's AI responded.

"Thank you."

"I did very little," the AI replied. "Perhaps on the next Aurora, I will be able to do more."

"Well thank you anyway," Nathan insisted.

"You are welcome."

Jessica looked around at their forlorn expressions. "It's a computer program, people."

* * *

Nathan, Jessica, Cameron, and Vladimir entered the Voss's aft cargo bay, followed by Lieutenant Yuati and Ensign Keller. Along either side of the bay, the majority of the Voss's crew stood at parade rest.

"The Orochi have confirmed readiness," Loki reported over the intercom.

"How much time do we have left?" Nathan asked.

"Eleven minutes."

"Send the strike order," Nathan instructed.

"Aye, sir," Loki replied solemnly.

"Attention on deck!" Marcus barked from the bay door controls on the port side.

All those aboard snapped to attention, their eyes on the large cargo ramp hatch on the aft wall of the bay as it began opening.

Nathan watched as the door slowly opened, the pressure shield emitters around the opening's edge glowing pale blue.

"Two minutes to impact," Loki updated.

Nathan waited until the door had cycled completely open, giving them all a clear view of the Aurora as she began to glow from the upper atmosphere which was now flowing over her battered hull. "The Aurora was a legendary ship," he began. "Not because of her design or her purpose, but because she brought us home every time she sailed. But she was only a ship. It was her crew that made her special. And it will be the crew of the next ship to bear her name that will make that Aurora equally special."

The Voss and the Cape Town flew side by side, orbiting the Earth less than a kilometer apart. Below them was the Aurora, glowing more brightly with each passing second as the air rushing over her hull thickened.

All around them, Gunyoki fighters began appearing behind flashes of blue-white light. Within seconds, there were more than a hundred of them, as well as EDF Super Eagles and Cobra gunships. In less than a minute, the orbit above the Aurora was filled with her comrades, standing at attention in their own way, as a show of respect at her passing.

Eight more flashes of light appeared far ahead

of the Aurora's orbital path, revealing eight jump missiles, the final nails in the mighty ship's coffin.

Nathan, Jessica, Cameron, and Vladimir stood at attention just inside the Voss's cargo bay pressure shield, watching as the eight tiny, glowing dots streaked toward the Aurora. The dots diverged, fanning out to strike from all sides of the vessel as it fell toward its end.

As expected, all eight dots converged on their various targeting points along the Aurora's battered hull, detonating simultaneously in a brilliant flash of yellow-white light. A split second later, the flash faded, replaced by multiple orange and red explosions from within the mighty ship's hull, breaking her apart completely.

Seconds later, eight more missiles appeared, each steering toward the larger pieces of the legendary ship. Moments later, there were more detonations, followed by additional secondary explosions.

All that was left of the Aurora was a field of millions of glowing particles burning up in the Earth's atmosphere, putting on an incredible show for those she had protected, who were watching from below.

"Company! Salute!" Nathan barked, raising his hand in salute to his lost ship as she sparkled in a million tiny fireballs in the distance.

All raised their hands in salute as well, holding it until their leader lowered his hand.

"Goodbye, Aurora," Nathan said to himself softly.

CHAPTER SEVENTEEN

Lord Dusahn stormed into the palace command center, furious at the sudden turn of fortune. For more than a week, he had been able to pour every resource into upgrading the few warships they had left. They had even begun fabrication of self-powered weapons to slap onto the hulls of cargo ships in the hope of defending against attacks on their shipping routes. They had not seen the Karuzari or the Aurora the entire time and were taking advantage of the lull as best they could.

But it hadn't been enough. Resources were low, civilian support was waning, and there were rumors of discontent among his own forces. Every day, he caught a glance from one of his officers or rank and file that struck him wrong. He had even killed a few on the spot. He could feel his dreams slipping from his grasp, and he was determined to pull glory from what everyone around him seemed to feel was defeat.

Now, his struggling empire was under attack yet again, and no one was doing anything about it.

"Why have you not launched a counterattack!" Lord Dusahn demanded as he approached Commander Jexx.

"No one has attacked us, my lord," the commander explained.

"How many ships?" the Dusahn leader inquired, barely able to control his anger from turning into murder.

"Four hundred and eighteen, my lord."

Lord Dusahn suddenly went silent, staring at the commander.

"Three hundred of their Gunyoki heavy fighters,

sixteen of their Orochi missile gunships, one hundred Sol Alliance Cobra gunships, and the Cape Town."

"Their capital ship?" Lord Dusahn asked with surprise.

"That is correct. And one other ship," Commander Jexx added.

"The Aurora?" Lord Dusahn assumed.

"No, my lord. The Jar-Benakh."

Lord Dusahn thought for a moment. "The Jung battleship the Sol Alliance captured years ago," Lord Dusahn remembered. "Either the Sol Alliance has destroyed the Jung Empire, or..."

"The Jar-Benakh has hailed us," Commander Jexx stated, interrupting his leader. "She claims to be a ship of the empire."

Lord Dusahn's expression changed to one of concern. "How is that possible?" Before his subordinate could answer, he added, "Put all forces on alert. Prepare to defend."

"My lord, we cannot possibly hope to defend against so many ships," Commander Jexx insisted. "Attacking the Cape Town alone would be suicide for us."

Lord Dusahn glared at the commander, ready to rip his heart from his chest for defying him.

"My lord, we simply cannot defend against such an armada."

"We will not have to," Lord Dusahn insisted.

"My lord..."

"You forget about Chekta."

"My lord..."

"You have received my orders, Commander," Lord Dusahn snapped. "Execute them!"

"At least answer their hail, my lord," Commander

Jexx pleaded. "That will give us time to deploy our defenses."

Lord Dusahn again glared at the commander. "You test my patience, Commander," he snarled. "Do so again, and it will be the last time you do."

* * *

"Still nothing," the Jar-Benakh's comms officer reported.

"He will respond," Kor-Dom Borrol assured Nathan. "He has no choice."

"He is stalling," General Telles commented. "Using the time to deploy his own forces."

"No matter how he deploys them, he can't beat us," Jessica insisted. "Not unless he blows up the entire planet."

"I'm betting he won't," Nathan stated.

"That is an awfully big gamble," Cameron warned. "You're talking about nearly a billion lives."

"I'm aware of the stakes," Nathan assured her.

"If you doubt Griogair Dusahn's ability to execute the Chekta protocol, you are sadly mistaken."

"I have no doubts about his ability," Nathan replied.

"Admiral," the Jar-Benakh's comms officer called. "The Cape Town reports a positive lock on all Dusahn targets."

"Tactical?" Nathan asked.

"We have locks as well."

"As do the Orochi," Cameron pointed out.

"Instruct the Cobra gunships to jump to blockade positions," Nathan instructed. "No one jumps their way out of this."

"Aye, sir," the comms officer acknowledged.

"You are wasting your time," Kor-Dom Borrol insisted. "He has no choice but to fight, regardless of the tactical situation. Your own operatives on Takara report a general loss of confidence in Lord Dusahn's leadership. If he rejects the challenge, he risks mass defections. Worse yet, challenges from within his own ranks, which he definitely cannot refuse."

"And if he ignores us and attacks?" Jessica wondered.

"You destroy his fleet and any remaining surface defenses," Kor-Dom Borrol explained. "It is one thing to fight and lose, but executing the Chekta without accepting the challenge would bring the ultimate dishonor to the Dusahn caste. At that point, one of his officers would surely execute him on the spot or challenge him themselves."

"And this has worked for your people for a thousand years?" Cameron asked sarcastically.

"I did not say it was not without its flaws," Kor-Dom Borrol admitted.

"I'm getting a reply," the comms officer reported. "It's Lord Dusahn."

* * *

"This is Kor-Dom Borrol, leader of the Jung Empire," the loudspeaker crackled.

"This is Griogair Dusahn, Kor-Dom of the Dusahn Empire," Lord Dusahn responded confidently. "You have intruded upon Dusahn space and are targeting Dusahn ships. Withdraw, and we will spare your lives."

"Let us not waste one another's time, Lord Dusahn," Kor-Dom Borrol suggested. "We have come to adjudicate a challenge for leadership of the Dusahn Empire."

"The Jung Empire has no legal power over the Dusahn," Lord Dusahn argued. "You lost it when you expelled my forefathers from your empire. No Jung caste has the right to challenge me."

"I beg to differ. The challenge comes from the people of Takara. They have joined the Jung Empire and have chosen a leader. That leader now challenges you to personal combat. Accept the challenge, and you may win. Refuse, and you will be destroyed."

"If this world falls, I will implement the Chekta protocol. You will gain nothing," Lord Dusahn warned.

"The Jung Empire cares nothing about Takara," Kor-Dom Borrol stated plainly.

"I suspect the people of Takara might care a great deal."

"Are you refusing a challenge?" Kor-Dom Borrol asked.

"I do not recognize your authority nor the right of any citizen of Takara to issue such a challenge," Lord Dusahn insisted.

"Then you leave us no alternative," Kor-Dom Borrol replied.

"My lord," Commander Jexx urged sternly. "If you refuse the challenge, you will lose the respect of those you lead. As your second-in-command, I cannot allow that. I will not allow that." Commander Jexx removed the safety latch from his sidearm holster, causing the weapon to begin its charging cycle. "Besides, who could possibly defeat you?"

Lord Dusahn looked his subordinate in the eyes, surprised that the young man had the nerve to challenge his own leader, but at the same time respecting him for doing so.

"If by chance you should lose, you will still be able to snatch victory from defeat, and the Chekta may even take out their entire fleet."

Lord Dusahn thought for a moment. "Safe your weapon, Commander. I have no intention of refusing the challenge."

Commander Jexx moved his hand away from his sidearm but did not safe the weapon. He had crossed a line and had no intention of going back, lest the punishment be even more severe. His only hope now was that his leader might lose the battle.

* * *

Cameron and Vladimir followed Nathan and Jessica down the central corridor that passed between the Jar-Benakh's massive hangar bays.

"The Jung crew is secure?" Nathan asked as they walked.

"All fifty are secured on deck five, section A-4."

"And there's no way they can override the lockout?"

"None," Vladimir insisted. "I checked it myself."

Nathan cast a doubtful eye his friend's way.

"Okay, I had Dylan check it over as well," Vladimir admitted. "Trust me, the only way they can take control of this ship is if we give them the control codes, and you're the only one who knows them."

"I still don't like the idea of handing them the Jar-Benakh," Jessica said. "You're talking about a fully armed battleship."

"They're not getting the control codes until they sign the charter," Nathan reminded her.

"I have to admit, the idea of the Jung having jump drive technology is frightening," Cameron admitted as the four of them entered the massive port hangar bay.

"They'd acquire the technology sooner or later," Nathan reminded her. "This way, they get it on our terms."

"Assuming they live up to those terms," Jessica commented.

"They can't earn our trust if we don't give them the opportunity to do so," Nathan stated as they headed across the open bay toward the Voss.

"But they did break the cease-fire agreement," Cameron reminded him.

"And they'll have to work hard to earn that back."

"Captain," Kor-Dom Borrol greeted as they approached. "Or is it Admiral?"

"Let's stick with captain for now," Nathan insisted. "I have about zero interest in being an admiral at the moment."

"Technically, your sister did make you an admiral," Cameron pointed out.

"Only temporarily," Nathan corrected, pointing at her for emphasis.

"Captain," General Telles greeted from the foot of the Voss's cargo ramp.

"Are all your men aboard?" Nathan asked.

"Eighteen in total, as instructed," the general replied.

"You sure you don't want us to go with you?" Marcus asked.

"Not this time, guys," Nathan said to Marcus, Josh, Loki, and Dylan. "If the Dusahn honor the challenge, there's nothing for you to do. And if they don't, there's nothing you could do. No need to risk any more lives than necessary."

"Don't feel right, not goin' with you," Marcus insisted.

"Neli ordered me to get you back in one piece."

"Since when does anyone listen to Neli?" Josh smirked.

"I programmed the ship to fly you down to the coordinates they sent," Dylan assured Nathan.

"Thank you." Nathan turned to Kor-Dom Borrol and his bodyguard. "Gentlemen, are you certain about this?"

"I am the kor-dom. Lord Dusahn would not risk the ire of the entire Jung Empire. In fact, I am your best bet of surviving this encounter, regardless of the outcome of the battle."

"Then by all means," Nathan said, gesturing for them to board.

Kor-Dom Borrol and his bodyguard headed up the ramp, with Jessica and General Telles following behind.

Nathan turned back toward Cameron and Vladimir, sighing. "Well this is it."

"Are you sure you're ready for this?" Cameron wondered.

"Not in the slightest," Nathan admitted. "Remember, if you receive an abort signal, everyone jumps the hell out of here as quickly as possible."

"I understand," Cameron replied. "Good luck."

"Thank you," Nathan replied.

"I'm coming with you," Vladimir decided.

"No you're not," Nathan insisted. "If this goes south, Cam's going to need you. She's going to need all of you."

"Nathan," Vladimir argued.

"That's an order, Commander."

Vladimir did not look happy.

"I'll be back," Nathan insisted, turning and heading up the ramp.

"You'd better be," Vladimir muttered to himself as he watched his friend ascend the ramp and disappear into the back of the XK.

* * *

Nathan sat patiently in the Voss's pilot seat as the ship's AI piloted the ship toward the Dusahn palace in Takara's capital city of Answari.

Jessica glanced at the tactical display in the center of the console. "We've got escorts," she reported from the copilot's seat.

Nathan scanned the skies outside, finally spotting several small dots moving left to right, far ahead of them.

"They're turning to intercept," Jessica warned. "We're being targeted."

"Raise shields but do not engage the intercepts," Nathan instructed.

"Shields coming up," Jessica replied. "Can I at least power up our point-defenses?"

"Go ahead, but lock out the AI's auto-defense capabilities," Nathan replied.

Jessica shook her head as she followed her instructions. "If he shoots us down..."

"Then the Cape Town and the Jar-Benakh will open fire and decimate them," Nathan replied.

"They will not fire," Kor-Dom Borrol insisted, standing behind Nathan's seat.

"You seem to have a lot of faith in Lord Dusahn's ability to contain his emotions," General Telles commented.

"On the contrary, it is his emotions that dictate his actions," the kor-dom insisted. "His ultimate desire is to create an empire."

"Then why the Chekta protocol?" the general inquired.

"He is using it as a means to an end. A way to cause his enemy to take actions which create opportunities for the advancement of his goals."

"He wanted us to challenge him," General Telles surmised.

"Precisely," the kor-dom confirmed.

"And the meeting between General Hesson and Captain Scott?"

"I suspect he manipulated the general to initiate the meeting in order to put the idea of the challenge into Captain Scott's mind."

"But he killed the general," Nathan reminded them.

"Which made the general's intent less suspect," Kor-Dom Borrol replied.

"Fighters are taking up positions on all sides," Jessica reported. "Six in total."

"They likely have orders to destroy us the moment you charge your weapons," Kor-Dom Borrol stated.

"They are afraid we're using the challenge as a ruse to take out Lord Dusahn himself on our way down?" Jessica wondered.

"Precisely."

"That doesn't even make sense," Jessica argued. "We could've done that from orbit."

"His palace is shielded, is it not?" General Telles reminded her.

"Yes, but we have shield busters."

"It is logical for him to send escorts," General Telles observed. "He is simply trying to protect himself against all possible attack scenarios. Fortunately for us, due to his ego, there is one scenario he is unlikely to anticipate," the general said as he turned to head aft.

Jessica turned to look at the general, a puzzled look on her face. "Where are you going?"

"I must prepare for the next phase of this

operation," the general explained as he left the compartment.

Jessica turned to Nathan next. "What is he talking about?"

"Karuzari vessel," a voice called over comms. "If you deviate from your course or charge any weapons, you will be destroyed. This is your only warning."

"I guess that's our landing clearance," Nathan commented.

"Into the serpent's lair we go," Jessica mused.

* * *

Jessica, Nathan, Kor-Dom Borrol, and his bodyguard all entered the Voss's aft cargo bay, joining the eighteen Ghatazhak lined up on either side.

"Where's Telles?" Jessica wondered, not spotting him in the bay.

"I am here," the general called from behind them, having come up from the lower deck.

Jessica's brow furrowed as the general slipped past her, surprised that he had changed into his duty uniform. "Why aren't you wearing your armor?"

"Armor is not required for my role in this plan," General Telles replied. "Why are you not in yours?"

Jessica shrugged. "Same reason, I guess. What if this is a trap?"

"Given the circumstances, that is highly doubtful," General Telles insisted. "However, should this be the case, two more of us in combat armor will not make a difference."

"I suppose not," Jessica agreed, heading toward the ramp control panel on the port side of the aft bulkhead.

"I suppose this is where I wish you luck, Captain," Kor-Dom Borrol told Nathan.

"I suppose so," Nathan agreed.

As the kor-dom stepped up to his position at the head of the ramp, Preto Soray stepped up to Nathan. "This is suicide," he stated, looking Nathan in the eyes. "You know this."

"Do you know why the Ghatazhak are so formidable?" Nathan asked Trever. "It's not their training or their education. It's the fact that they never commit to a fight that they cannot win."

Trever did not look convinced. "I do hope your confidence is not misplaced," he said, turning to follow his leader.

Nathan looked to General Telles. "Are you ready for this?"

"I am always ready," General Telles assured him. "I am Ghatazhak."

Nathan smiled, then gestured for Jessica to activate the ramp.

The motors sounded, and the top edge of the ramp separated from its sealing collar, light spilling in from outside as it began its journey downward.

"Lord Dusahn and his seconds will march out to confront us, as if on the battlefield," Kor-Dom Borrol explained. "It is ceremonial and not to be misinterpreted as an act of aggression. In addition to his eighteen guards, he will be accompanied by four others. Two seconds, his second-in-command, and his magistrate."

"What are the seconds for?" Nathan wondered.

"If both primaries are injured to the point of imminent death, their seconds will fight as teams."

"I see."

"You should be the one first down the ramp," Kor-Dom Borrol told Nathan.

"Why me?"

"The challenger leads his forces, just as the challenged will do."

"Understood," Nathan replied as the ramp touched the ground outside. He turned to General Telles. "After you, General."

Kor-Dom Borrol looked at Nathan, a puzzled look on his face as General Telles headed for the ramp.

"Takara is his world."

"This is most unusual," Kor-Dom Borrol protested as he, Nathan, and Preto Soray followed the general out. "I am not certain how Lord Dusahn will react."

"I guess we'll find out momentarily," Nathan said as they headed down the ramp.

Jessica jumped off the edge of the deck, landing on the ramp one step behind Nathan. "What the hell is going on, Nathan?"

"All part of the plan," Nathan assured her.

General Telles strode confidently down the Voss's cargo ramp, followed by his entourage, who in turn were followed by eighteen Ghatazhak wearing full mark two combat armor. In the distance ahead, a similar entourage came out of the building, led by Lord Dusahn and Commander Jexx, marching confidently toward them.

"Continue forward until he stops," Kor-Dom Borrol advised as they marched toward them.

"Perhaps it would have been better had you informed us of the protocols involved," General Telles commented.

"I could not be certain that the Dusahn continued to honor them," Kor-Dom Borrol replied. "If they do, they will stop at twenty meters distance."

Nathan said nothing, his eyes on Lord Dusahn. The man was older but carried himself well and was obviously in excellent physical condition.

"We are so in the open here," Jessica commented as their entourage continued forward. "There are at least a dozen rooftop sniper positions they could mow us down from."

"Have a little faith," General Telles said.

"Faith?" Jessica laughed. "That's funny coming from a Ghatazhak, especially from you."

As the kor-dom anticipated, Lord Dusahn stopped his advance at approximately twenty meters.

General Telles stopped in his tracks, holding up his left hand in a fist to signal his men to stop as well. After a moment, Lord Dusahn resumed walking toward them, followed only by Commander Jexx, his two seconds, and the magistrate, while his soldiers stayed behind.

General Telles did the same, with Nathan, Jessica, Kor-Dom Borrol, and Preto Soray following.

Lord Dusahn's left eyebrow rose as he neared, realizing that it was not Nathan in the challenge position. "I had assumed it was you who wished to challenge me," he said to Nathan as both parties came to a stop a few meters apart. "And who are you?" he asked the general.

"I am Lucius Telles, son of Isiah, leader of the Ghatazhak, the true protectors of Takara." General Telles stared his opponent in the eye. "I challenge you for control of the Dusahn caste."

Lord Dusahn smiled. "A Ghatazhak? You have no right to challenge me for control of my caste."

"I am afraid you are mistaken, Dom Dusahn," Kor-Dom Borrol stated. "The Ghatazhak have been made a caste of the Jung Empire, same as the Dusahn."

"You cast us out, old man," Lord Dusahn retorted. "We are no longer bound by your laws."

"Perhaps not," Kor-Dom Borrol admitted.

"However, your magistrate might have a differing opinion on the matter."

"The Dusahn were exiled from the empire," the Dusahn magistrate stated. "However, our caste was never formally disbanded."

Lord Dusahn turned, glaring at his magistrate. "This is preposterous," he exclaimed.

"I understand if you do not wish to fight me, Dom Dusahn," General Telles interjected. "I would not want to fight me either."

"I would kill you where you stand," Lord Dusahn snapped, his anger growing.

"I wonder what your men will think, should you refuse a rightful challenge?" Kor-Dom Borrol commented, taking a step to one side, as if to address the line of soldiers standing twelve meters behind Lord Dusahn and his entourage. "Shall we ask them?"

"My lord," Commander Jexx said under his breath. "You are a Chankarti master. You are even better than the masters who trained you. Surely you have no fear of him or any other man."

Lord Dusahn looked at the commander. "I fear no man," he scowled.

"You have no options," General Telles stated. "Fight me here and now, or our forces will wipe your forces from this world."

"And doom a billion of your brethren?" Lord Dusahn chuckled. "I think not."

General Telles took a step forward, a deadly serious look on his face. "Better they die in an instant than in a lifetime of servitude to an arrogant ass such as yourself."

Lord Dusahn kept his eyes locked on his challenger for what seemed an eternity. "Very well," he finally said. "I will fight you, Lucius, son of Isiah...but on one condition. If I kill you, I get to kill him as well," he added, pointing at Nathan.

"Deal!" Nathan exclaimed.

"What the fuck?" Jessica commented under her breath.

General Telles cocked his head slightly right, his gaze still locked on his opponent. "It seems that your terms have been accepted, Dom Dusahn. Shall we begin?"

A smile slowly crept across Lord Dusahn's face, his eyes taking on a maniacal quality. "I'm going to enjoy this day." He raised his hand with a snap.

"Form the circle!" Commander Jexx barked to his men.

"What do we do?" Nathan whispered to the kor-dom.

"Have your men form half the circle," Kor-Dom Borrol instructed. "Eighteen men per side, thirty-six points on the circle."

"Form a circle!" Jessica barked. "One man every ten degrees on our side of the circle!"

The Ghatazhak immediately reacted, following both Jessica's command and the movements of the Dusahn Zen-Anor soldiers.

Lord Dusahn turned his back on them and began undressing in preparation for the bout. General Telles took off his jacket, handing it to Jessica. "Do not let this touch the ground," he instructed. "I just got it back from the laundry this morning."

Jessica smiled, taking the general's clothing as each piece was handed to her. "You've got this, boss."

After removing the clothing from his upper body, the general removed his boots and socks, and then turned to Nathan.

"You can take him, right?" Nathan asked.

"This is what I was born to do, Nathan," he assured him.

"Then go kick his ass, Lucius," Nathan replied with a smile.

The general cocked his neck right and left, making a cracking sound. "This will only take a moment," he said before turning back to face his opponent.

Preto Soray stepped forward. "General, if I may?"

General Telles nodded, and Preto Soray leaned in and whispered something in the general's ear. General Telles looked at him, a curious look on his face. "Interesting," he commented, nodding at the preto.

General Telles took several steps toward the center of the circle, assuming a relaxed yet confident stance, hands clasped comfortably behind his back, eyes locked on his opponent.

Nathan watched from their position just inside their side of the ring of soldiers. "I have to admit, I'm more nervous than I thought I'd be."

"Nothing to be nervous about," Jessica insisted. "It's only the fate of billions resting on the outcome."

"Oh thanks," Nathan replied.

"Captain," Kit called from his position in the ring directly behind them. "You have nothing to worry about. Telles isn't a general because he's the oldest or most experienced of us all, but because he is the toughest, smartest... to use Terran vernacular, the general is a straight-up badass."

"Badass?" Nathan wondered, surprised by Kit's use of the expression.

"Josh and his old vid-flicks," Jessica stated.

"Of course."

"The man trains for four hours a day, then

participates in combat drills for another four," Kit explained. "No one can size up an opponent and find their weaknesses like Telles can."

Nathan turned and looked at Kit. "Didn't I see you getting the best of him in training the other day?"

"You left before it was over," Kit insisted. "He misled me into believing I was winning to identify changes in my combat technique brought on by overconfidence. It is a training tool that we use to improve control of our emotions during combat."

"So getting your ass kicked makes you better?" Nathan wondered.

"Yes, and that could be the general's only weakness. He never gets his ass kicked."

"I certainly hope this doesn't become the first time."

"You know, you could have told me about your little plan," Jessica complained.

"We needed everyone's reactions and concerns to everything to be natural," Nathan explained.

"You believe we have a spy among us?" Jessica wondered.

"No, but we couldn't rule that out, so we decided to act as if there were," Nathan replied.

"I was equally deceived," Kor-Dom Borrol commented, not sounding very pleased.

"Well now we're even," Nathan told him.

"Fair enough."

Lord Dusahn strode out into the center of the circle, coming to stand face-to-face with General Telles, his gaze locked on the general, a menacing smile on the Dusahn leader's face. "I'm going to enjoy taking you apart almost as much as I will enjoy killing your boy-captain."

"If you are attempting to use intimidation as a

method to weaken my confidence, you are wasting your time," General Telles replied, all without the slightest hint of emotion. "But I did find the attempt entertaining, and for that I thank you."

"You Ghatazhak really think you're invincible, don't you?"

"Not invincible, just more capable than the likes of most, yourself and your Zen-Anor included."

"We shall see."

"Yes we shall."

"Gentlemen," the Dusahn magistrate stated as he stepped up to them. "The rules are simple. There are no armaments, and the fight is to the death. Both contestants must stay within the circle. If you breach the circle, the two closest circle keepers must execute you, or their lives will be forfeit as well. The one left alive will rule the Dusahn caste and all of its resources. Do both contestants understand and agree to the rules?"

"Of course," Lord Dusahn replied, his tone dripping with hatred toward his opponent.

"I understand," General Telles acknowledged calmly.

The magistrate then turned toward the circle of soldiers surrounding them. "Do the circle keepers understand and agree?" he asked, turning to the Dusahn side of the circle.

"The Zen-Anor agree," the senior officer of the assembled Dusahn soldiers confirmed.

The magistrate turned to the challenger's side of the circle. "Do the Ghatazhak understand and agree?"

Lieutenant Rezhik stepped forward to reply. "The Ghatazhak understand and agree."

"Are you kidding me?" Kit whispered as the

lieutenant stepped back into position to the corporal's left.

"We have our orders," the lieutenant replied.

"In the event that both contestants die, their seconds will complete the challenge, as will the seconds' seconds."

"And if those seconds die?" Jessica asked.

"Then each side will offer a circle keeper to continue the ritual, until such time as a victor is clear."

"And..."

"Jess..." Nathan interrupted. "I think we get it."

The magistrate turned his attention back to General Telles and Lord Dusahn. "Gentlemen, you may begin," he instructed, turning and walking back to the Dusahn side of the circle.

"I'll try to make your death as quick and as painless as possible," General Telles told the Dusahn leader.

"I shall not," Lord Dusahn snarled, assuming the basic Chankarti fighting position.

The general remained in the same position, his feet shoulder width apart and hands clasped comfortably behind his back, both eyes locked on his opponent.

Nathan and the others watched from the challenger side of the circle as the two men squared off.

"I didn't realize Griogair was so big," Jessica commented.

"The Dusahn were renowned for their size and physical condition," Kor-Dom Borrol explained.

"They went as far as to manipulate their genetics to ensure their males would tower over those of the other castes."

Jessica looked around at the Zen-Anor lined up on the far side of the circle, noting that they were all equally as tall. "I don't remember their regular ground-pounders being that tall."

"Their genetic purity has likely been compromised over the centuries," the kor-dom stated. "Undoubtedly the result of being forced to breed with females from other worlds and accept their male children into their ranks. The Zen-Anor are likely made up of only those of pure lineage."

Lord Dusahn flexed as he bounced slightly on his toes, preparing to face his opponent. After a moment, he settled into a relaxed fighting stance, his right leg back and his arms held slightly away from his body at approximately chest height.

General Telles remained in his previous stance, feet still shoulder width apart, hands still clasped comfortably behind his back, looking more like he was standing at parade rest than preparing for a fight to the death against a master of Chankarti.

Lord Dusahn took two steps to his left, then two back to his right, sizing up the smaller, younger man. His opponent moved nothing but his eyes, which followed the Dusahn leader. "You are either overly confident or incredibly foolish," he stated, assuming his fight stance again.

General Telles said nothing.

Lord Dusahn shifted his weight, bringing his right shoulder quickly forward, feigning an attack to test his opponent's reflexes, but the general did not flinch, continuing to stand still and relaxed. After another moment of staring at his opponent, the Dusahn leader quickly raised his right knee as he pivoted on his left foot, kicking out at the general's midsection, quickly withdrawing his right foot and following with a quick kick toward the general's face. In response, the general moved his right foot back slightly, distancing himself from his attacker just enough so that both kicks, as well as the right backhand blow that followed, fell short by a few centimeters.

Lord Dusahn immediately returned to his previous fighting position, right foot back and left hand forward. Next, he jabbed outward with his left hand as he shuffle-stepped slightly forward, aiming for the general's face.

General Telles easily batted his opponent's fist away, just in time to prevent it from connecting with his face. Lord Dusahn followed by bringing his same hand back across, which the general avoided by bending slightly backward.

Lord Dusahn withdrew a step, satisfied with his first attempt to assess his opponent's skill. "You are not as quick as I expected," he stated, settling back into his combat stance. "I suppose the responsibilities of leadership tend to get in the way of your continued training."

General Telles moved his right foot back to center, his hands dropping back behind his back.

Lord Dusahn stared into his opponent's eyes, seeing no emotion. "I had heard the Ghatazhak learn to control their emotions during combat." Mid-sentence, the Dusahn leader again jabbed out with a left to the general's face, which again the general blocked, this time without stepping back. Another jab with the same hand was blocked by the Ghatazhak leader's right hand, leaving the general's right torso undefended. Lord Dusahn did not hesitate, sending his left hand into his opponent's side, the force of his body's rotation adding to the impact.

General Telles bent his body slightly, absorbing the force of the blow with ease. A split second later, Lord Dusahn's same hand found the right side of the general's jaw, causing it to whip to the left from the blow. The general quickly stepped back again, avoiding the next two punches and the rising knee headed for his abdomen.

Lord Dusahn withdrew a step, settling back down into his ready position, a smile on his face. The Ghatazhak was not unbeatable, as rumored by many of his own infantry. Without hesitation, he charged again, swinging. Left, right, left again, all at his opponent's face.

General Telles backpedaled, keeping his hands at his side. After his opponent's third swing, the general jumped upward, kicking with his right foot into the Dusahn leader's chest, then immediately with his left, both blows pushing his attacker back two steps, forcing him to the center of the ring.

Lord Dusahn immediately charged again, bringing his left knee up toward the general's chest but finding his opponent's right elbow coming down on the Dusahn leader's knee as a counter, followed by the Ghatazhak's left hand, which he swept away before it reached him. It was the first offensive move the general had made, and Lord Dusahn found it rather weak.

Again the Dusahn leader stepped back, returning to his combat stance, smiling.

General Telles also returned to his original, non-threatening stance, but with no smile that might reveal his own satisfaction at the assessment he had just completed of his opponent. The difference was that he had not experienced any satisfaction from what he had learned. Lord Dusahn was obviously well trained and likely a true master at the art of Chankarti. Unfortunately, like with so many others who studied the art of personal combat, he had obviously been more concerned with the ability to kill while not being killed than with the lessons that most disciplines sought to endow upon their students. In the general's mind, it was a shame to waste such skill, and it explained much about the Dusahn caste, as well as the Jung Empire.

Lord Dusahn's next attack involved more kicks than punches, shifting from single front and side kicks to lunging and spinning kicks, all the while mixing in a few strikes with hands and knees. But none of them made contact with his opponent, who deftly countered each attack with smooth movements designed to either evade or redirect the energy contained in each strike attempt.

Lord Dusahn fell back into his combat stance again, pulling at his upper trousers to ensure freedom of movement. "You do not disappoint," he congratulated his opponent. "You will be far more worthy of killing than my previous opponent."

Again the general remained silent, simply standing there, waiting for the next attack.

Another flurry of punches and kicks, mixed in with leg sweeps, all while attempting to drive the general back toward the edge of the circle. Again the general blocked or redirected the blows, changing direction to stay nearer the center of the circle, finally ducking under Lord Dusahn's high kick and reversing their positions at the center of the ring.

"If your intention is to let me wear myself down and thus provide you an opening, you are wasting your time. I could do this all day."

"I am simply observing your style and assessing your capabilities," General Telles replied, finally speaking. "Just as you are doing with me."

Lord Dusahn's grin grew. "I was wondering when you would speak," settling back into his combat stance. "It is apparent that you are quite adept at avoiding or redirecting the energy of my attacks. I wonder if you are equally able to absorb that energy."

General Telles nodded, inviting the Dusahn leader to attack him again.

Lord Dusahn needed no invitation, immediately turning on his left foot as he raised his right one to kick the general in the abdomen, chest, and then face, all in a quick and fluid motion. He then came down on his now-forward left foot and jumped up, spinning around to bring his right foot into the side of his opponent's face.

Surprisingly, the general made no effort to deflect or evade the blows, instead allowing their full force to be delivered to his body. "Satisfied?" the general wondered.

Lord Dusahn smiled. "Yes; a worthy opponent."

"What the hell is he doing?" Nathan wondered. "He didn't even try to block his attack."

"Trust in the Telles," Jessica told him.

Nathan looked at her in dismay. "What?"

"It's what they always told me in the beginning,

whenever I questioned the logic behind whatever training method they threw at me back on Burgess."

"But..."

"I'm just saying."

Again Lord Dusahn attacked, launching another combination of punches and kicks, ending with a knee to the general's left side, causing him to double over from the force of the blow. The Dusahn leader saw his opportunity and raised his right arm straight up to bring his elbow down into the back of the general's head. Instead, he found the general dropping to his left hand and sweeping the Dusahn leader's dominant leg out from under him, sending him onto his back.

The general stepped back, not choosing to press his advantage further, knowing full well that his opponent would not be on the ground for more than a second.

As expected, the Dusahn leader raised his feet and then arched his back as his feet came down hard, launching himself into a crouch, expecting another attack at any moment. When the follow-up attack did not come, he stepped back, again smiling. "Nicely done," he congratulated.

"One does not deserve to lead unless he maintains the very skills he requires of those he commands," the general stated, settling back into his relaxed stance, hands behind his back.

"Quite true," Lord Dusahn agreed. "I suspect that you and I have many similar beliefs. Had we met under different circumstances, we might have enjoyed one another's company."

"Doubtful," General Telles replied. "I don't enjoy the company of egomaniacal, narcissistic dictators."

Surprisingly, this too brought a smile to the Dusahn leader's face. "Nice try, Ghatazhak," he replied, after which he launched into another flurry of attacks.

This time, the general chose to move, bend, and duck the onslaught, rather than attempting to block his attacker's blows. With each strike, he allowed his opponent increasing levels of contact, feeding into the man's overconfidence.

This time, Lord Dusahn did not return to his fighting position and engage in idle conversation designed to taunt his opponent. Instead, he moved smoothly into a new style of attack which appeared fluid and almost choreographed with every new blow flowing into the next with minimal expenditure of energy.

As the general parried the attacks, the words whispered to him by Preto Soray rose to mind. Finally, he decided this was the moment to test their validity. As Lord Dusahn launched into his next combination of blows, the general circled his right hand out wide, bringing it back toward his opponent's left temple. The move happened so quickly that the Dusahn leader only noticed the approaching attack at the very last moment, barely managing to bat the general's hand away.

Lord Dusahn's expression changed, suddenly showing the first sign of concern.

The next series of attacks ended with General Telles in a partial headlock that encompassed his head and right shoulder. Lord Dusahn took immediate advantage of the lock, squeezing with everything he had. The pressure would not kill the general; in fact, it wouldn't diminish him in the slightest. It was merely an attempt by the Dusahn leader to demonstrate his strength over the general.

It failed.

General Telles sent his elbow up into the side of Lord Dusahn's face with all his might, breaking his hold in the process. He dropped to one knee as he twisted his body, freeing himself. The general then shot his leg out, kicking his opponent in the knee, likely causing him to overextend at least one of his tendons.

General Telles stepped back, again assuming his relaxed stance as the Dusahn leader regained his composure, trying not to reveal the pain he was experiencing. "Well done," he said, his confidence still unshaken, despite the expertise his opponent had just displayed. "However, you should have pressed your attack further. You might have been able to deliver a more crippling blow."

"I have not yet delivered my message," General Telles stated calmly.

"And what message would that be?" Lord Dusahn asked, resuming his combat stance.

"You are about to find out," the general stated, a menacing look in his eyes.

Lord Dusahn refused to be intimidated, choosing to attack again before the general could go back on the offensive. Again he unleashed three quick jabs to the face and neck, followed by crosses, backhands, and upper cuts, finally sending his knee toward the general's side and then twisting about while bringing his foot into the general's same side. Again, General Telles managed to block, evade, or redirect every blow, only having to absorb the knee to his side, which he did with ease. When the Dusahn leader continued his attack, the general simply pushed him back by his shoulders. The surprise of that simple act created an opening, and Telles leapt up, kicking out with his left foot into Lord Dusahn's chest, then dropping to sweep his feet out from under him.

Lord Dusahn hit the ground, then leapt up again, expecting to continue his attack. Instead, he found the general standing, firing jabs at him with such speed and precision that the Dusahn leader was unable to block half of them. Blows landed on his face, neck, and chest, blows that were harder than any he had ever felt.

Then it came.

General Telles delivered two lightning-fast punches from both left and right, striking his opponent's left and right ears with incredible force.

Lord Dusahn stumbled backward, dazed and gasping for breath, realizing for the first time since the battle had begun that he might not come out the victor.

"Did you receive the first part of my message?" General Telles asked, pacing leisurely about while his opponent struggled to regain his breath.

"You should......have......struck......while you could," Lord Dusahn panted, still struggling to regain his normal breathing. "I will not make...... that mistake......again."

"You made no mistake," General Telles stated as he settled into his own combat stance for the first time since the fight had begun. "You were bested, as you are about to be again."

Telles shifted his body weight, moving his left foot forward as he dipped his shoulder. The move was a feint, and Lord Dusahn fell for it. The Dusahn leader spun around, bringing his free foot up to chest height, intending to deliver his full weight behind a blow to the general's side. But the general ducked, allowing Lord Dusahn to come down overly rotated and out of balance.

General Telles sprang up, delivering a crushing upper cut to Lord Dusahn's chin, stunning him again. Taking advantage of his opponent's temporary lapse of focus, the general quickly raised his right foot and placed it atop his opponent's left shoulder, then jumped up and twisted around as he dropped his other foot on the opposite side of the Dusahn leader's head. As he began his face-first fall, the general tucked at the waist, sending his head and chest between Lord Dusahn's legs, his hold on the man's head pulling the Dusahn leader downward and forward.

Lord Dusahn went down headfirst, flipped over onto his back, only to find his opponent straddling him with a hold on the Dusahn leader's right knee. There was a cracking sound, followed by pain that made Lord Dusahn's head spin.

The rest of the message had been delivered.

General Telles released his opponent's disabled right leg, then shifted, bringing his left leg out and around before falling backward and driving his left elbow hard into the Dusahn leader's mouth.

Lord Dusahn felt his front teeth break, his mouth suddenly filling with blood. His right leg was throbbing with mind-numbing pain, his knee completely dislocated. He rolled onto his side to spit the blood and loose teeth from his mouth, mentally preparing himself for the next blow. But it did not come.

Lord Dusahn fought through the pain-induced fog, trying to spot his opponent. For the first time that he could remember, he feared for his life. Calling upon all of his resolve, he managed to get back up onto his hands and one good knee. Shaking, he rose, forcing himself upright despite the intense pain. Balancing on one foot, he concentrated, squinting as he attempted to regain his senses.

A voice.

"Did you get the message?"

At first, the voice seemed distant, as if from down a long corridor. The effect quickly passed, and both his hearing and vision returned to normal.

"Do you understand that you are facing your death?" the general asked.

Lord Dusahn did his best to assume a combat stance, one that he could maintain while balancing on his left foot. His dangling right leg sent waves of pain up his body, but he managed to ignore it. There was still work to be done, and if he was to die this day, he would not go down without a fight. Even better, he would take his enemies with him.

Lord Dusahn spat out more blood. "You have not beaten me yet, Ghatazhak."

As the words left the Dusahn leader's mouth, another series of blows which seemed to come out of nowhere landed on his head, chest, and abdomen, and he found himself on the ground again, lying on his back in absolute agony. A moment later, his opponent knelt behind his head and dragged him up enough to be placed into a headlock.

"I tire of this silly ritual of yours," General Telles stated, his words dripping with contempt. "It is time to show your mighty Zen-Anor that their glorious leader was easily bested by a mere Takaran."

General Telles tightened his muscles, preparing to snap his opponent's neck.

"WAIT!" Nathan yelled from the side of the circle. He slowly strode over to the general and his soon-to-be victim on the far side of the circle, only two meters from the Zen-Anor.

General Telles did not release the Dusahn leader, instead holding him firmly, ready to snap his neck at a moment's notice.

"Ease up, General," Nathan ordered.

General Telles did as instructed, easing his hold on his opponent.

Nathan squatted down in front of Lord Dusahn, looking the battered man in the eyes. "I am about to offer you something that you denied the people of Ybara, Burgess, and Ancot." After a moment, Nathan added, "A chance to live."

Lord Dusahn studied Nathan, squinting through the pain as he wondered what the young man's angle was. After a moment, he spat out some more blood, then said, "I am listening."

"You, and all those who wish to follow you, will be allowed to settle an uninhabited, hospitable world, where you may build your empire however you desire. We will even provide you the supplies and equipment needed."

"In exchange for what?" Lord Dusahn snarled.

"You turn control of Takara over to this man," Nathan said, pointing to the general, "and you join our alliance, vowing never to attack another human civilization."

"What assurances do I have that you will keep your word?" Lord Dusahn wondered, his mind still spinning from the pain.

"You have none," Nathan replied. "But your only other option is death."

A grin formed on Lord Dusahn's face. "Wrong

again, young captain," he snarled. "CHEKTA!" he yelled, bracing himself for complete chaos and destruction.

But nothing happened. All he heard was a clicking sound to his left. Lord Dusahn turned his head, spotting Commander Jexx walking toward them, holding the Chekta detonator in his hand, pressing it repeatedly as he approached.

Lord Dusahn's eyes widened in horror.

"I warned you that we did not have enough antimatter to waste on the SilTek attack," Commander Jexx told his leader. "But as usual, you did not listen." The commander tossed the detonator on the ground next to his leader, then turned and walked back to the magistrate and the seconds standing along the Dusahn side of the circle.

"I guess you were right," Nathan told General Telles.

"I often am," the general replied.

"So what's it going to be, Griogair?" Nathan asked.

Griogair Dusahn smiled maniacally, then spat blood into Nathan's face.

"I'll take that as a no," Nathan stated, standing as he wiped the blood and spittle from his face. "General, you may proceed," he stated, turning to walk back to the Karuzari's side of the circle, where he spotted Jessica, Kit, and Lieutenant Rezhik all smiling at him.

By the time Nathan reached the edge of the circle and turned back around, General Telles had dragged Lord Dusahn by his hair to the edge of the circle, leaving him in a sitting position, the Dusahn leader's back to his own Zen-Anor.

General Telles walked around in front of Lord Dusahn, turning back to look at him. "I have decided to let your own people deliver the final portion of the message," he stated. He placed his foot against Lord Dusahn's chest and pushed hard, sending the Dusahn leader falling backward between two Zen-Anor soldiers, the upper half of his body landing outside of the challenge circle. The Zen-Anor on either side of Lord Dusahn drew their sidearms and took aim.

As the general walked back over to Nathan, two shots rang out.

"The contest is decided!" the Dusahn magistrate barked. "Lucius Telles is now the leader of the Dusahn caste!"

"Nice work," Nathan told the general.

"I especially like that last little touch," Jessica congratulated. "Inspired."

"Thank you," the general replied. He turned around, noting the smoldering corpse of Griogair Dusahn. "Zen-Anor! You now serve me! Your new responsibility will be the protection of the interim president of Takara, Deliza Ta'Akar! Assemble your forces and take station at the palace landing pad. She will arrive shortly."

The Zen-Anor said nothing, turning to march away to their new assignment.

"This wasn't part of the plan," Nathan commented.

"It seemed appropriate," General Telles stated, moving past them and heading back to the Voss. "Ghatazhak!" he barked, commanding his men to follow.

"Like I said," Jessica commented, "trust in the Telles."

CHAPTER EIGHTEEN

The building in Answari that had once been the meeting place of Takaran nobility now served as the birthplace of the very first galactic alliance of human-inhabited worlds. Hundreds of dignitaries and their entourages watched from the galleries as leaders from the first twenty-seven worlds each took their turn at the signing table. One by one, each was announced as they stepped up to the table and added their name to the official charter of the new Systems Alliance. After saying a few words to the audience, each leader moved to their assigned position around the platform. Once the last of them had signed, Caitlin Bindi added her name, followed by the legendary Nathan Scott.

After adding his name to the bottom of the document, Nathan turned to face the crowd, posing with the rest of the signatories for the multitude of pictures and vids that would be distributed across the human-inhabited galaxy.

Nathan stood there, painfully smiling and waving to the applauding crowds, thinking about all the times he had been forced to do the same thing during his father's campaigns. His initial attempts to escape his family's political dynasty and forge his own path had led him to virtually the same place, perhaps worse.

But he wouldn't have had it any other way.

* * *

After nearly two hours of mingling with dignitaries and their subordinates, not to mention countless guests, Nathan finally managed to slip out onto a balcony unnoticed.

With drink in hand, Nathan stepped up to the edge of the balcony, looking out over the twinkling lights of the Takaran capital. Although quite different from Earth, the world had a beauty all its own. He especially enjoyed the multi-colored shadows cast by the world's three moons. On nights like this, when all three moons occupied the same part of the sky and were at their closest points in their orbits around Takara, the landscape took on a surreal quality that could not be described.

Nathan took a sip of his drink, breathing in the cool night air. Many had died to make this day possible, and to them, he held up his drink in salute.

"Checking the contents of your glass?" General Telles asked as he stepped out onto the balcony behind him.

"I was just toasting all those who died to make this day possible," Nathan explained.

"A worthy gesture," the general agreed, raising his glass to join him. "To our fallen comrades-in-arms," he stated, holding up his glass. "We will never forget their sacrifice."

The two of them held their glasses up, taking a drink.

"I was surprised to learn that you changed the name of the alliance," the general commented.

"Systems Alliance was too vague," Nathan explained. "Confederated Systems Alliance more accurately portrays its core intent. It was Caitlin's idea. She thinks it will make it easier to sign up more worlds."

"She is a wise lady."

Nathan took another drink, his eyes drifting out to the city skyline once more. "I can see why your people love their world so much."

"You should visit the hot springs before the tri-moon passes," the general recommended. "The steam rising from the water changes colors as it swirls about. My parents used to take us there every tri-moon. It is truly mesmerizing."

"I'll try to see it before I depart."

"When are you leaving?" the general inquired.

"In a few days," Nathan replied. "I still have a few meetings to attend."

"How wonderful for you," the general mused, taking another sip of his drink.

"Ah, there's that Ghatazhak humor again."

"I was surprised that Miranda did not attend the reception."

"She needed to return to Earth. A lot to do, as you might expect."

"How are her children?"

"Quite well. They joined her a few days ago. I'm going back to visit for a few days before I go back to work."

General Telles cast a disapproving look Nathan's way.

"What?"

"Perhaps you should take some time off? You have been through a lot these last few months."

"We've all been through a lot," Nathan argued. "You fought a man to the death for crying out loud."

"I am Ghatazhak," the general smiled. "That is what we do."

"That reminds me," Nathan remembered. "I've been meaning to ask you something. How the hell did you know that you could beat that guy?"

"I did not," the general admitted. "Not until a few minutes into the bout."

"Yet you stood there, as calm as you are right now, facing what could have been your death."

"There were two reasons for that," the general explained. "First, the arrogant are rarely the best fighters, and second, I had an unfair advantage."

"An unfair advantage?" Nathan asked, confused.

"Lord Dusahn feared not only losing, but dying."

"As did you."

"Actually, I only feared losing," the general admitted.

"Because you're Ghatazhak," Nathan surmised.

"Yes, but also because I was scanned by Doctor Chen and Doctor Symyri a few weeks prior. Had I died, I would have eventually been resurrected, same as you."

"Of course," Nathan replied, smiling.

"You have not been back to Earth, other than on dangerous covert missions, since... well, since you died," General Telles pointed out, returning to the previous topic. "You might want to reconsider extending your stay."

"A few days will be enough," Nathan insisted.

"Are you certain?" the general wondered. "It is your home after all."

Nathan sighed, taking another sip. If there is one thing I've learned from all of this, it's that I belong in space, in command of a ship, with my crew as my family."

"It is good to know one's purpose," General Telles stated.

Nathan thought for a moment, taking another sip. "Yes it is. It truly is."

The two of them stood there, staring at the multi-colored shadows cast across the palace grounds.

"It was worth it," Nathan said.

"Yes it was," the general agreed.

"What was worth it?" Jessica wondered, coming out onto the balcony to join them, taking Nathan's drink from his hand.

"That's mine," Nathan objected.

"Not anymore," she said, downing the last of it.

"Finally," Vladimir exclaimed as he stepped through the doors onto the balcony, a drink in each hand.

"Oh perfect," Jessica said, taking one of Vladimir's drinks as well.

"These people do not know how to throw a party," Vladimir complained. "There isn't even any music or dancing."

"It's a diplomatic reception," Nathan reminded his friend.

"That doesn't mean it has to be boring."

"I agree with Vlad," Cameron stated, joining him. "We should blow this place."

"I'm with her," Jessica agreed.

"You're going to be attending a lot of these functions," Nathan warned Cameron.

"Why me?"

"As the commandant of the first Alliance Academy, you're going to have to figure out how to train people from all different cultures," Nathan pointed out.

"How did I get stuck with that assignment again?" Cameron wondered.

"You volunteered for it," Vladimir laughed.

"Oh yeah."

"Why the hell did you do that?" Jessica wondered.

"I just don't see myself commanding a puny little XK," Cameron explained. "Not after commanding a ship the size of the Aurora for so long."

"Don't knock it," Nathan insisted. "Smaller ships have their advantages."

"But they're no good for subjecting your crew to countless drills," Vladimir chuckled.

"They weren't countless," Cameron objected, slapping Vladimir's shoulder.

"To your crew they were."

"And where will you be going?" General Telles asked Vladimir.

"SilTek," Vladimir replied. "I'm leading the team designing the new Expedition-class ships. I have some very interesting ideas."

"Have fun working with all those robots," Jessica chuckled.

"They're called droids, Jess," Vladimir corrected. "Besides, most of the engineers will be human. In fact, many of them will be from Subvert."

"I'm sure you will produce a fine vessel," the general stated.

"What about you?" Nathan asked the general. "Are you finally going to retire?"

General Telles smiled. "Ghatazhak do not retire. I will continue to lead the Ghatazhak on their new assignment."

"Which is?" Cameron wondered.

"We are adapting the Dusahn troop shuttles to serve as quick-response jump ships. We hope the Ghatazhak will someday be able to serve the entire Systems Alliance from a base here on Takara."

"That sounds like a tall order," Cameron opined.

"It does have some challenges," the general admitted.

"Like greatly increasing the jump range of those shuttles," Nathan commented.

"Indeed," the general confirmed. "It will also require additional training for the Ghatazhak."

"And we all know how much the Ghatazhak love their training," Jessica commented.

"You're not going back to train with them?" Cameron asked.

"I think I've gone about as far as I can with the Ghatazhak," Jessica admitted. "I don't have the discipline."

"So what are you going to do?" Cameron wondered.

"Are you kidding? I'm going back to the Voss," Jessica replied. "Someone's gotta keep an eye on him," she added, pointing to Nathan, "and you're going to be too busy."

"I have a feeling we're all going to be busy," Nathan said, looking back out at the city.

Jessica, Cameron, and Vladimir stepped up to the balcony rail, joining Nathan and General Telles as they enjoyed the view.

"At least this time nobody will be shooting at us," Vladimir joked.

"Don't jinx it," Jessica scolded.

* * *

Nathan climbed up the Voss's forward stair-ladder up into her command deck where his crew awaited.

"How are the kids?" Neli asked.

"They're good," Nathan replied. "They miss you though."

"I miss them as well," Neli replied.

"Of course now they've got an entire staff taking care of them," Nathan told her.

"How's Miri?" Jessica asked.

"She's great. Telling everyone what to do is her specialty."

"Must run in the family," Jessica teased.

"We ready to go?" Nathan asked his pilots.

"We've got a standing clearance and can depart whenever you're ready," Loki assured him.

Nathan turned to Marcus and Neli. "I assume we have a full crew?"

"We have bodies," Marcus grumbled, "but I'm not sure I'd call them a crew."

"Well there's nothing like a little on-the-job training," Nathan insisted.

"You sure you don't want to take a few days to put them through more sim sessions?" Marcus suggested.

"There are still thirty-five worlds that we know of that still need to be signed up, and only four XKs available to make initial contact. The faster we sign them up, the sooner we can get those Expedition-class ships built. There are still potentially hundreds of inhabited worlds out there, and we need to find every one of them."

"Your call," Marcus grumbled.

Nathan turned to face forward again, a content look on his face. "Josh, get us back into space... where we belong."

Thank you for reading this story.
(*A review would be greatly appreciated!*)

COMING SOON

The Frontiers Saga:
Fall of the Core

Visit us online at
frontierssaga.com
or on Facebook

Want to be notified when
new episodes are published?
Want access to additional scenes and more?
Join our mailing list!

frontierssaga.com/mailinglist/

Made in the USA
Las Vegas, NV
29 May 2021